I'M JACK & I WANT MORE

FRANK ROCCA

[signature]
2013

*** **REVISED EDITOR'S CUT** ***

Copyright © 2011 Frank Rocca
All Rights Reserved

ISBN: 1461034116
ISBN-13: 9781461034117
LCCN: 2011905136
CreateSpace, North Charleston, SC

"We live in a world where all things, good and bad,
are finally destroyed by change."
~ Sam Harris

TABLE OF CONTENTS

Ch I: The Neighborhood	1
Ch II: The Game-Test – Part I	23
Ch III: Childhood Mysteries	33
Ch IV: Welcome to Collinwood High	49
Ch V: Sweet Home Oklahoma	59
Ch VI: The Royal Flush	73
Ch VII: Funerals & Law-Dogs	83
Ch VIII: Drugs: The War on Minds	95
Ch IX: Friendship	109
Ch X: More Party Spots	121
Ch XI: New Neighbors	145
Ch XII: A Spiritual Awakening	157
Ch XIII: I Need More	165
Ch XIV: The Game-Test – Part II	175
Ch XV: Nothing Changes Till It Does	183
Ch XVI: A Spiritual Quest	195
Ch XVII: That Thing Called Love	203
Ch XVIII: Dependence & Freedom	217
Ch XIX: Group Therapy	225
Ch XX: The *Click* & the "Bounce"	239
Ch XXI: The Arc Completes Its Thrust	243
Ch XXII: The Final Chapter	255

CH I:
THE NEIGHBORHOOD

Collinwood in the 1960s and '70s was a place where relatives were inherited but family got chosen, a time when everybody was linked to somebody for one reason or another. Stratified from ridiculous to pathetic, existence felt nearly tolerable. Then the older we got, our demons surfaced as monsters to hide from; collaborators to hide with; sickness to hide within; unadulterated lunacy I counted on just to be.

Morrison buzzed "People Are Strange" through tinny speakers as Benny and I returned to the Neighborhood after a night of boozing. He said, "Let's stop at Royal Castle's to coat the stomachs with some grease, Jackie. I'm feelin' a little queasy."

At 3:00 a.m., we were its sole customers. As we eased down on counter stools the well-groomed, neatly dressed Benny ordered "Two burgers, hold the onions, and some of them nice home fries" from a short, toothless waitress who cooked and made change.

She asked, "What about you, tattoo-man? Do you plan on eating too, or just watching? Because this isn't a spectator sport, you know. So what'll it be?"

"I'll have the same, and we both want frosted mugs of that fresh orange juice."

Benny reminded her, "And no onions on his, either," while fresh patties and sliced potatoes sizzled on the griddle behind the counter. After she halved oranges and started the juicer he said, "Onions make me sick. I don't even want 'em near my food, okay?"

I leaned forward on heavily tattooed arms to recount a story to a childhood friend: "I almost forgot. I saw one of your favorite girls today. She didn't even ask after you."

"I didn't know I had one. Okay, so who was it?"

"What has red hair, a mouth like a Five Points sewer and punk brothers?"

"Shit . . . I'm glad I wasn't there. I might a kidnapped her ass again."

"Yeah man, there she was, queen bitch herself. And even though she didn't recognize me, she still gave us a case of the blues. She's got a poison mouth on her."

"Did that pig mention again about The Mick's her uncle and how *badass* her brothers are . . . for the hundredth fucking time?"

"What do you think? But check it out; you might enjoy this."

"I'll like this story a lot better if she's chained-up in your basement right now."

"Well, it ain't quite that drastic, but listen at this. So me and a *coomba*–"

She returned from her steam table with our food and snapped, "I'll need the money now. You're supposed to pay when I take your order. Separate checks?"

Benny said, "All on mine," snatched a burger and took a bite. He reached for his wallet as I was about to tell Benny what happened when his face morphed into one I'd seen before too many times. He spit the chewed portion into a napkin, held up an index finger and said "Scuze me, *coom*." Then he turned to the *Jane of all trades* and asked, "Hey! What did I just say? Did I tell you no onions, or not?"

"I don't know. Did you?"

"I told you twice; no onions. How many times I gotta say the same thing? What're you, stupid? I can't eat no goddamn onions. They give me the *agida*."

She glared at him: "Whatever that's supposed to mean. Don't eat them if you don't like them. Just brush them off. It's not a big deal unless you make it one."

Benny stood and smiled, dipped his good hand into his pocket and said, "Okay, you're right. Now you made me feel bad. Here you go; I got a little somethin' for ya."

When she approached he smashed her so hard her face broke his cast. As soon as her feet flipped up and the back of her head smacked the register he hopped over the counter, opened it and laughed, "I told you no fuckin' onions." He took the cash, kicked her and said, "Come-on, *coom*. We don't give these fucks any more business. Where to?"

"I gotta be at work a half hour ago. Drop me off. A brother's already there." Brother, bro, coomba, coom, it all meant loyalty to us.

Eggs and I pulled a 16-hour shift. He said, as he gazed through features that appeared to have been carved from granite, "I've been thinkin' about moving to Italy, Jackie, like the southern part. Now that we scored these railroad jobs and we're still makin' money on the side, maybe work a few years and then lay back in some villa. You could visit and bring back a little cutie. Good plan . . . right, little brother?"

"I'm not too sure about that. How you gonna talk to anybody, ya big fuckin' hill-jack. All you know how to say is *pizza*. Maybe you should be thinkin' more along the lines of Ireland or England, or some shit like that."

"Thanks for the advice, Jackie. I should've known better than to ask."

"Okay. You want advice? Smoke weed and read more. That's how most of the great philosophers like Hemingway and Camus started out. How's that sound?"

"Wouldn't that be great if we could get paid for that? So who's *Camoo*?"

"Just some guy. Hey, maybe I could be an herb critic. I might even quit the railroad for that, Eggs. Cool-out on the beach all smoked up with a Sicilian sweetie and maybe write a novel. Meantime, till you get that villa, I'll continue to blaze-up here while we freeze our asses off in those cold-ass yards till something else happens."

"Good idea. But seriously, though. What do you think? Should I go or not?" asked the raw-boned, rugged-looking guy who spoke softly and was careful not to curse.

"Yeah, Eggs, I think you should. And while you're there, check on something for me. I heard that Jesus and Apollo were half brothers on their father's side. You know, the same sire but out of different bitches. I hear the pope's got a book at home to prove it. Maybe you can check on that for me. You ever hear anything about this shit before?"

"No, Jackie. But I heard somewhere you oughta slow down on the chemicals."

"Hey, man, I'm into synthetics. What can I say? Each to his own, right?" I asked as I pulled curly hair as black as his Cadillac's leather interior away from my eyes. "Now let me ask you something, Eggs. You ever notice how sometimes things seem more like a story told by someone else than it being your own life? You know; like an acid peak during a wet-dream, but the kind you don't ever wanna wake up from?"

"No, little brother, can't say I have. So tell me. What's really on your mind?"

"I've been thinkin', and I think it's all about timing. You know?"

"As usual, I got no idea what you're talkin' about. Nobody ever does," Eggs observed as he braked in front of The Inn and switched off his ignition.

Eggs waved to a few of the Moustache Petes dressed in wife-beaters and loose-fitting pants, each either chewing or puffing their Parodi and DeNobili cheroots. They posted their folding chairs around sidewalk card tables outside their favorite hangout, The Inn. Those grizzled *coombas* spit on brick streets as squad cars slithered away from our microcosm while mothers, wives and sisters schooled daughters and nieces to adopt cultural mores of piety and silence as if they were orphaned children.

"Hold-up a quick minute, Eggs. I gotta tell you who me and Gus saw yesterday."

"Sure thing, Jackie. Tell me inside."

"Nah, it's too noisy in there with that shit music they use. All that square-ass *dago* bullshit we're supposed to like – Sinatra this and Frankie Valli that – fuck that noise. All that garbage does is make me wanna puke. I need to burn this roach while you drive around the block again. Meantime, I'll tell you about who we seen."

"No way. It's gonna look like we're casing the school we keep circling it. Besides, since when do two guys sit in a parked car to talk? That's goofy. Let's go in"

"Are you serious with this bullshit, or what?" I asked as I tugged at my beard. "All the sudden we're queer because we're in a car together? We're the Royal Flush, *coom*. Think about what you're sayin', man. Besides, who's gonna rob Collinwood? There ain't nothin' in that school but problems. Our neighbors probably wish we'd burn that motherfucker to the ground so they can get these racist pricks outta the Neighborhood."

Eggs opened the driver's door while he nodded in agreement, "Yeah, maybe you're right. That's why all these shines are around here now . . . all this busing. But we're already here, so hold-off on the story. This way you can tell Fingers, too. Then you ain't gotta say it twice, right?" He stretched over his seat to grab his leather jacket. From it he handed me a yellow envelope and added, "Besides, it's getting late. Let's go in."

I'M JACK & I WANT MORE

I eased back in the bucket seat and crossed my arms. "You need to relax, *coom*. That's your whole problem. Look . . . All's I'm sayin' is timing is everything, even for stories. Remember when I wrote that one for that fat bitch in English class, Miss What's-Her-Face? You remember. Then she tried to get me to read it in class, remember now?"

"I ain't too sure, Jackie. Why?" he asked, still seated but wearing his jacket.

"You know. She was that younger chick with the huge tits. Remember how she'd lean over our papers and mash them torpedoes on our arms? She told us how important timing is, that even writers need to be aware of timing and shit like that. Remember?"

"You mean that chunky broad with those tight sweaters all the time?"

"Yeah, that's the one. She had those thick lips like some Jew broad."

"Big girl with nice buns, right? Nah, I didn't have her. Why? What's so special about her class?" he asked just as a carload of black youths slowly rolled up in a full-sized Mercury with its stereo blaring James Brown's "It's a Man's World." They got stopped at the red light by The Inn, and then backed up close to where we parked.

Eggs closed his door as I said, "Just forget I mentioned anything about any class, okay? But check-out these *melanzana* and the light's green. See? Timing... Am I right? Now we're supposed to hate each other, even though we all know this racial stuff's a crock of shit. But somehow we get caught-up in it, anyways. You know why? It's because of the time we're in. It always comes right back to timing. Right or wrong?"

Eggs reached under his seat as one of the old *coomba*s on the corner pulled a pistol from a folded newspaper till the intruders were beyond accurate shooting range.

"So why'd you write a story for a teacher about the Collinwood race riots?"

"Please, Eggs, just do me a simple favor and forget about that goddamn English class for one second, okay? School's got nothin' to do with any of this."

"Then why do you keep bringin' it up? You make things confusing like this."

A semi-trucker honked his horn at a muscle car stopped in front of him. Someone in a GTO sat at the light and revved his motor after the light had changed.

I shook my head, "Fuck-it. See? Now I can't finish. Go on; you tell one."

Eggs slumped in his seat: "I got nothin' to say. It seems like you're the one with the story. So go ahead. Now I'd like to hear where all this crazy stuff of yours is headed."

"You gotta remember the class with that big-titted teacher. Her ass stuck out like a shine broad, nice and firm. She had the hots for you, Eggs. Did you fuck that bitch?"

"No way . . . I never even talked to her. Why? Did you do her?"

"Fuck that. I don't go for chicks bigger than me. Anyways, I read an article about that George Carlin guy. He's a comedian. He said you can be a great story teller, but if you say even your funniest one at the wrong time it comes out just average at best. So my thinking is: even a 7-Ha story can flop with bad timing. Follow me?"

"Where do you come up with this stuff, little brother? First we're talking about wet dreams, then some big-breasted teacher I never even had, and now its comedians. I'm confused, but I know a little bit about timing and can tell you this much: If those spooks come back it's gonna be bad timing for them. Why are we still sittin' here, anyway? Come-on. Let's just go inside. Then you can tell us what a 7-Ha story's all about."

"No way . . . too late. Now it's no good. The timing's all fucked-off now."

"Alright, suit yourself. Let's just go in then."

I paused and lit a cigarette. "Okay . . . I'll explain. If your laugh comes out in seven syllables that means it's some funny shit. Now if it's a 5-Ha story, then it's kind of funny but not good enough to repeat. If you only laugh 3-Ha's, that means it's probably stupid but you don't wanna insult the person tellin' it. Then there's the story where you say *Ha* – but just once. Now if that HA is loud, it's probably some twisted shit you're not supposed to be laughin' at anyways – like maybe it's ironic or some shit like that. But if you mumble *ha* under your breath, that could mean you just heard somethin' deep or intense. Once you understand this stuff, then you know exactly what's goin' on. It's about subtleties . . . instinct. It's gotta unfold just right or it bombs. It's all timing."

"I didn't know you were high at work today, Jackie. You tripping right now?"

"Nah. But I told you, I've been thinkin' about some stuff lately. Like the vibe I been gettin' from our other *coomba*s. You sense anything weird with them lately?"

I'M JACK & I WANT MORE

"Weird? Like what?" Eggs asked as he sat up tall behind the steering wheel.

"For example, you notice how lately when Fingers gets around the older guys he acts like a big-shot?" I asked as I slipped into my leather and shook my hair from the collar: "I don't know . . . Skip it. Maybe it's me. Maybe I'm reading too much into this."

"You're wound too tight, little brother. You stay buzzed too much lately and then make yourself nuts with all that wacky stuff. You think too much."

"First off, that's not possible. Go ahead. Try not to think. See? You can't do it. Maybe I'm thinkin' too much about dumb shit. Or maybe that *Click* in my head is real and you should pay more attention. Anyways, you really think I get high too much?"

As I opened the passenger door, that loud GTO returned and sped head-on at us. Its brakes locked-up and the car swerved into a parking lot just before it reached us.

"It's not so much the drugs, Jackie. But all of us think you drink way too much."

"Oh, it's all of us and then me. Is that it? Fuck this. Anyways; I can quit anytime."

"Maybe so. But now you got me thinkin'. Before we go inside, explain one thing. What happens if a story gets more than 7-Ha's but it's just average funny? You know. You hear it all the time, right? Like when a person says something that's stupid and then the other person listening cracks-up, clapping his hands with his head, all tilted back and then doubles over. I never understood that and don't like it. I get nervous when I'm around that stuff and feel like smashing somebody. What's all that supposed to mean?"

I shut my door again: "It means you're schizo and should be takin' psych meds."

"See? That's what I get for even askin' about this goofy stuff. I don't know why I get caught up in these crazy stories of yours. Just forget I asked."

A squad car approached with sirens blaring. Its flashers reflected off parked cars and storefront windows. I grabbed a bag of weed from my jacket, slid my hand outside of the passenger door and flipped it between the curb and the rear wheel as I explained, "Okay. The way I see it is this: Unless you're rollin' around almost pissin' yourself, 7-Ha's is enough. Any more is bullshit. Nothin's that funny. If you use my method, you can detect if some phony motherfucker's tryin' to set you up – if you know what to look for. See? It's all timing. You get it yet?"

"Ha . . . Maybe so. It means the story you wanted to say is this one. Right?"

I released the door handle and eased back to smoke: "Look, Eggs, if while you're talkin' some guy's on the edge of his seat, smiling like he's hearing the one true meaning of life – it's a con-job. Or if some chick's cackling like some fuckin' hyena at every other thing you say, either she's a moron or she thinks you are. All that shit's a red flag for some other bipolar action goin' on. You gotta be careful with these manic bitches."

"So how come you know all these medical terms, Jackie? You read a lot, huh?"

"Yeah, *coom*, I read a lot. And guess what? The more I learn, the more I realize I don't know shit. Now let's get back to that other thing. Sometimes a story can be so goddamn funny you don't laugh at all – like laughing's almost an insult. You know? Like when it's a 'Holy shit!' or a 'No fucking way!' story? Funny, but in a different way."

"Hmmm, I'm not sure. I don't have the time to think about stuff like that."

That same kelly green GTO roared past from behind and again locked-up the brakes. When the light changed the driver torqued his brakes till he sizzled his tires into black smoke that clouded the chilly air with stench.

Eggs rolled up his window: "Now we got a minute. You might as well say your story and get it over with."

"The one from English class or about fake laughs?" I asked as I flicked a Lucky Strike and watched it spin tracers and then explode into a spray on the sidewalk.

"No, the first one. The one about you and Gus. Remember? Funny, right?"

"Fuck-it. I barely remember it now. Let's just go inside. Fingers is waitin'."

"Okay. One thing, though. I can't stay. I promised my ol' lady I'd be home early. So if you wanna hang-out, you can leave with him. You know how she is, Jackie."

"No, *coom*. I don't know how she is, but I know how you're gettin' to be."

"Oh, is that right, Dr. Lorocco? Okay, I gotta hear this one."

"You don't have to admit it, Eggs. You got pussy fever. You're cunt-struck."

"Whatever. Stay here and huff cigarettes and tire smoke all night. I'm goin' in."

I'M JACK & I WANT MORE

We exited his car to meet one of our brothers at our main hangout for a few drinks and to discuss whatever it was Fingers had on his mind.

As usual, one turned into one too many. Doc answered his payphone as I told Fingers, "I gotta story for youse guys. You'll appreciate this. Me and Gus were standin' in line yesterday, waitin' for that Mr. Magoo druggist to fill my script. You know him – a big fuckin' deal to count 60 Quaalude's and drop 'em in a bottle, right? Meantime, some hot chick slides backwards, steps on my boot, presses her ass against my cock and then stays there like she owns it, pretending like she's fiddling around in her purse."

Eggs yawned, "Was it that big-butted teacher? Is that what this is all about?"

Fingers' *Leonardo Strassi* sweater and pressed *Sansabelt* slacks draped an athletic frame masking the dark glare of a sociopath. He yelled, "Hey, doll. Bring us three tequila and cokes and three Buds. But we're gonna need extra shots. Make it happen this year."

"Can I finish?" I asked as I adjusted my shades. "Anyways, some old hag finally wheels her cart all the way past, but this broad's still against the ol' *braciole* like she's glued to it. Then she turns her head sideways and says, 'Oops, sorry.' You know, like it was some kind of accident. But guess what? She don't budge. Then she goes right back to rooting around inside her purse while that perfect ass is still mashed against my cock."

Quick and effortless, like the swoop of a bird of prey, the barmaid gracefully lifted our empties, left drinks and then vanished like a forgotten breeze.

Fingers brushed invisible crumbs off his shirt: "So she was rootin' around, huh? I'd a given her somethin' to root on," he said. "You know what she needs?"

"No, I don't. So meantime, I'm about half-juiced so I nudge her hip forward just enough to ease her off my boot when she spins around all quick-like with major attitude."

"What'd I say, Eggs? Did I call it or not?" Fingers asked with a knowing look.

"I'm not sure. You didn't finish what you were gonna say. So, Jackie, what you're sayin' is you felt-up this chick's buns on line at the drugstore, right? Is this your story?"

"Why are you so obsessed with stories, Eggs? Just pay attention for one minute. Timing, remember? So anyways, then she yells loud enough for everybody in the store to hear, 'You better watch-it, man! You don't know who you're messin' with.' That's when I notice it's Maureen Kelly. But she don't recognize me all tattooed and hairy."

"Fuck that uptight cunt and her whole family," Fingers grumbled.

"So Gus started shakin' his head, snorting and chuckling with those bloodshot eyes of his and says, *'Coom*, did you know I'm on the Itty Bitty Titty Committee? Yeah, in fact, we're lookin' for new talent. You see any no-tit bitches lately?' he asks me."

Fingers slurred, "Are you serious? Why waste your time? You know right upfront what a prick teasin' bitch she is. Fuck her and her whole puke family. I'd like to see her chump brothers try to make a move against us now."

"Yeah! Me too," Eggs agreed. "Sooner or later those drop-shots'll get theirs. Bet long money on that one. But we need to be patient for right now."

Fingers said. "Ha! Patience is exactly what I wanted to talk about. But first let's get back to that dyke. I wouldn't fuck her with her brothers' dicks. What she needs is to be horse-fucked. Better yet . . . That whole Five Points crew needs to get ass-slammed."

"So listen at this part, Fingers. Then this psycho bitch says, 'Hey, man, it's 1978 not the Dark Ages. Apologize, asshole.' Here's her actin' all innocent like it's my fault. Still, I can't get my eyes off that heart-shaped ass. You seen her lately, *coom*?"

"That's your problem, Jackie." Fingers said, as he clinked ice cubes in his empty rock glass at the barmaid, "You get one whiff of some hot crease and right away you lose your fuckin' mind. And I gotta tell you this: Me and Benny think you drink too much."

"Oh, right. Get your refill so I can finish my story here."

"Whatever . . . I already know how it ends up. But go ahead . . . finish."

"Hey thanks, Fingers. I'm glad I have your permission," I said dryly. "Okay, so then Gus starts in again with that red-faced grin and says, 'Scuze me, hon, but I know you from somewhere. You ever been there? You know . . . Fuck City?"

"She says, 'Why are you even talking to me?' then turns her back again."

"So Gus says, 'I'm just askin'. You been there or not? Fuck City, right? It was you I fucked, wasn't it?' You should'a seen her face. That carrot-top bitch turned purple."

"That's a pretty good story, Jackie," Eggs nodded with a serious expression.

"Easy does it, Eggs . . . I ain't finished yet, okay? Meantime, by then she's all kinds-a pissed-off and screams, 'What did you just say to me?' right up in his grill. Then Gus goes, 'You remember . . . Fuck City. Yeah, baby, I'd know that ass anywhere. Mmm Hmm.' But now Gus is actin' all serious like he's not breakin' balls."

Fingers drains the beer from his bottle, slams it down and says, "Fuck all that!"

"So meantime, this broad's givin' Gus stink-eye. Then she says, 'Yeah, I recognize you too, you fat fucker. You're that pudgy kid with a big mouth and a little dick. I'll bet the only thing that grew is your stomach. And if I were you, ass-wipe, I'd be worrying about my own ass.' Meantime, that druggist was trippin' right the fuck out on this broad."

"Gus doesn't go for people callin' him fat," Eggs nodded with a furrowed brow.

"So then Gus says to her, again with those little snorting sounds, 'Don't worry about *my* ass, darlin'. Yours serviced more dicks than a rabbi. In fact, you'd better watch out for all four of your asses. That moldy thing you make a living with, and all three of your asshole brothers.' Then he smiles with those yellow teeth of his."

"Good for him," Fingers laughs. "Me and Benny got plans for them micks, too."

"Hold-up. So here's the best part. Just then that googly-eyed druggist asks her—"

"Hey there," Doc's barmaid butted in. "Where's the rest of your little crew tonight? You kids are almost like some notorious gang now, huh? Yeah . . . well... *anyway*, Uno wants to buy you a drink. You fellas want more of the same?"

Fingers said, "Oh you're like a comedian now, right? Real cute. Yeah, go get us tequila doubles and another round a beers, and then go tell Uno thanks."

"Ha-ha. Tell him yourself, hot-shot. He wants you at his table, like pronto."

"What's up? Does he want me and Jackie too, or just Fingers?"

"He said all three. Are you boys in some kind of trouble again?" she asked glancing over her shoulder, wearing a tight, black mini-skirt as she swished away.

"Hmmm . . . Check it out. You gotta admit it, *coom*. Not bad for an older broad. Check out the way she moves that ass. Man, those thighs are still lookin' creamy good. They say that chick was smokin' hot about 10 years ago, and I believe it."

"Yeah, and we were in junior high. So what? She looks like dog shit now. Besides, she's suckin' Doc's cock, not ours. Fuck these older guys, anyway. They're over the hill. And another thing: What's with Uno still treatin' us like we're still kids. I'm sick and tired a these greedy fucks thinkin' they still run the show around here."

"Can you notch it back some?" I asked. "These guys ain't so old they're deaf."

"Not yet. But they need new blood for the Neighborhood to stay strong. It's gotta be us. Then here's youse two limp-dicks sittin' on your asses at home with the ladies."

"What's with all the attitude tonight, man?" I asked. "And why you gotta talk about this crazy shit in here? Everything in its time and place, *coom*. Patience, Fingers, remember? I mean, isn't that what you wanted to talk about?"

"We've been patient *and* generous. Now it's time to wake the fuck up. We've been payin' tax to this fat cocksucker long enough. Me and Benny been talkin' and we got ideas. We need to play it cool for awhile and keep the envelopes comin' in till we can make a move, right? Okay, so here's what we decided. Our crew should—"

"Whoa. No way, Fingers." Eggs cautioned. "Not in here. Never that."

"Why? What's wrong? You sayin' you can't knock this fat fuck out?"

"Sure I can. Then he wakes up and kills everybody. Why you talkin' like this? Especially in here! We all know what happens if he even thinks about this stuff."

"Yeah, lighten up, *coom*." I agreed. "Uno ain't got much of a sense of humor for shit like this. A little joke like this one can get real ugly, real fast."

"Who says I'm jokin', huh? I told you we got plans. If we stick together we can do this. We're the Royal Flush! But if we splinter it's no good. So, youse in or out? Because the way I see it, one way or another, things need to change. Either we join 'em or just take over. But we can't keep gettin' ripped-off by these greedy bastards."

Eggs hissed, "I don't wanna know nothin' about plans. Leave me outta this."

"Oh, I see. Youse two're curring out on us. Is that it?"

"Eggs is right this time. Besides, I got a kid on the way. You see Benny. He's out there actin' like he's bulletproof, runnin' around with his bat like

Joe fuckin' DiMaggio and I'm his partner. Guess who they'll use to make an example when the time comes?"

"Let me handle Benny. Meanwhile, you sure about her this time? Because we got a lot at stake here, *coom*. I say it's time all of us make a move together. Family's everything. Ain't that what our fathers taught us?"

"Family's everything; no doubt. So which family we talkin' about here? Ours?"

"Speakin' of that," Eggs said. "Me and Jackie gotta work tomorrow. So the move I need to make is one outta here so I can get some sleep."

"Yeah, Eggs, I expected that much. How about you, Jackie? What's it you need?"

"I need you to lighten up. What's your problem lately, man? Let's cut the bullshit and get right to it. Just go ahead and say it, *coom*. What's *really* on your mind?"

Fingers missed his mouth and spilled beer on his shirt. He set down the bottle and smirked, "Oh, by the way, Benny misplaced the seed money. But no sweat. I'm sure—"

Uno motioned to us with a thick, hairy forearm, "Come-on, Fingers. Sit, Jackie. You too, Eggs. Let's have a drink," invited the clean-cut, dark complected man who killed people for a living. One of the Young Turks in Cleveland's crime syndicate, after a few doubles the thick-set man confessed, "My *coomba*, Pazzo, says I worry too much. Meanwhile, I'm sittin' here thinkin' about trust. It's one of them things I can't get enough of. But you can't be too careful these days. Things aren't always how they seem, right?"

"Yeah, Uno, I know what you mean, What ever happened to loyalty and balls? I mean, just look around you. Who's left?" Fingers grinned as he glanced at us.

Uno continued, "To me, loyalty's something more valuable than money. Although you gotta have cash, right? And speakin' of that, I've been thinkin' about money, too. Let's take Jackie for example. You and Benny picked-up a few bucks around town from a few degenerates, right? Now look! You replant those dollars and guess what happens? You might be surprised what grows, am I right?"

"We're just small potatoes, Uno. Me and Benny are just keepin' things real low-key. We ain't tryin' to step inside anybody's shoes."

"Yeah, Jackie's that way," Fingers grinned as he held up his glass for a refill.

The waitress brought a tray of fresh longnecks and shots, the darker one Uno's.

"Salute," Uno said and downed his Crown Royal. "*Coomba*, Pazzo, tells me youse kids are straight." Eggs nodded yes for us. "He says your crew has a thumb on the pulse of the Neighborhood. So here's me wonderin' where a guy like me goes for advice; you know, to people I can trust. Then I look up and here youse are. How about that?"

"Whatever you need," Fingers assured him. "You never have to worry about us."

"Worry? I ain't worried . . . But then I remembered some other things. One thing I hear is Fingers and Benny are planning to invest some real money right under our nose."

"You know us," said Fingers. "We pay the tax every month like clockwork."

"Maybe so, but I got questions. One of 'em is about those hoodlums down Five Points. I hear you know those young Irish gangsters, Eggs. Am I wrong about this?"

"Well . . . I grew up down there, and we're about the same age. You know how it is. Everybody knows everybody else. But we ain't friends or anything like that. I don't like them, and they know better than to mess with us. I got nothin' to say to any of 'em."

"Really? Wow . . . Youse kids are all ready with the answers, huh? Another question is about broads. I can't ask my *coomba*, Pazzo. You know him. He's an animal. He's got no couth when it comes to the ladies. Still . . . I know I can trust *him*."

"You know how we are, Uno. We're with you till the wheels fall off," Fingers pledged.

"Oh yeah? What happens after the wheels fall off, Fingers? Then what?"

"It's just an expression. I didn't mean anything by it."

"Okay, then keep quiet and listen for once. Between us, my ol' lady's goin' through the *change* or some shit like that. She acts like that thing between her legs is lined with gold. I can't even get laid in my own house. Can you believe this bullshit?"

Eggs shook his head back and forth with a strained look on his face.

"Meantime, I hear things," Uno continued. "One thing I hear is Jackie's a crease-hound – got all the gash locked-up for himself. Am I wrong here? Because I'm gettin' the feeling youse are tryin' to hold out on me. So tell me all about these Collinwood broads, Eggs."

Usually quiet, Eggs said, "Between us, you'd be surprised who's pullin' trains – little skanks actin' all innocent. Believe me; they ain't what they seem. Know what else? Most a these so-called tough guys are a joke. I'm sick and tired a that fake tough act."

"Okay, Eggs, settle down," Fingers cautioned. "You never been a good drinker. You get like you're on speed behind this shit. Careful, or you're gonna start drooling on yourself again. You're way too excitable. You need to learn about patience. Remember what I was just sayin' back at our table, when we were talkin' about how me and Benny got plans and shit like that? Go ahead. Tell Uno what we all agreed on."

"Oh yeah," I jumped in. "Fingers said we should hang around youse older guys more often. He said we need to be patient so we can learn, because we got the best role-models right here in the Wood. Ain't that right, *coom?*" Eggs nodded affirmative.

Fingers said. "Hey, I know another good plan! Maybe you should try graduatin' high school first. Then maybe you can be my counsel. How's that sound, Jackie?"

"Yeah, maybe so. And maybe you're the one should slow down on the booze."

"How about it, Eggs? Should Jackie be our lawyer? Shit . . . Why'm I askin' you? Here. Use this napkin to wipe that stupid look off your face, ya fuckin' mouth-breather."

"Oh, I almost forgot," Uno added. "Another thing is this. I decided to let youse kids operate under my flag . . . almost like part of the organization. You get protection and I get half of everything. Another thing: Did any of them scumbag bikers ever ask how Eamon got whacked? Word on the street is somebody from inside's talkin' to Mick."

Fingers answered. "We don't even fuck their broads."

"I see . . . Well, my next question's about that biker kid, Ansel. We think he's the one playin' both sides against the middle. We hear Jackie's *coombas* now with these bikers. Am I wrong about this, Jackie? Maybe you can bring your new friend here so we can get to know each other better. He trusts you, right?"

Blonde hair past his shoulders and a long white beard, Ansel resembled the warrior god in blacklight posters. He was the first and only president of a Cleveland MC called the Wong Gongs – a band of contract killers.

"I'm friendly with him. But Ansel don't trust anybody besides his own club brothers. He doesn't even leave their clubhouse without back-up."

"No? Oh, is that how it is? Then maybe I'll have to send Fingers and Benny to take care of this for us. You think you can handle this, Fingers?"

"I'll talk to Benny. But I'm sure Jackie'll back me."

Eggs agreed, "Yeah, and I'll sniff around down there. See what's up."

"Yeah, you do that, Eggs. Sniff around. Meanwhile, any of youse kids hear *anything,* bring it straight to me. I have faith you'll do the right thing."

Eggs gazed into an empty glass with a blank expression while Fingers twirled a hunk of his hair around one of his good digits. I watched Uno stare at a table behind us.

Two drunks broke our uncomfortable silence: "So here's me, cuz, in the kitchen mixin' a nice pitcher of dry martini's the way we like 'em. I can hear my ol' lady sayin' to her whore sister, 'Yeah, I gotta admit it. My husband's a real fuck machine.' So I start pourin' heavy gin. Here's me thinkin' I'll get tag-teamed by these whacked-out bitches. Her sister's one a them *nympho-chondriacs*. So I walk back in like a gentleman with glasses my mom bought in Abruzzo. You know me, nothin' but top shelf."

"Hold up, *coomba*. You made one mistake. Now it's me, I go a different route. Fuck class – that's for guys that don't get laid. That was your cue. Believe me; I know about these cunts. They was givin' you a signal. That's when you should'a dropped your drawers and walked out with a real cocktail. Follow me? The way I see it, it's best to—"

"Hey! Can I finish here, or what? Right away you're like some fuckin' *psycholotrist*. Just do me a favor, cuz, save your comments till I'm done. I'm tryin' to tell a story ova here. Okay? Okay . . . So here's me carryin' a nice tray with a *mopino* folded over my arm like Mr. Fuckin' Diplomat, thinkin' maybe I'll score double *slutoris*. I got the good booze *and* the imported glasses. You'll never guess what happens next."

"Sure. I know exactly what happens. This ain't exactly rocket surgery, ya fuckin' horny prick. You take a shot at your ol' lady's sister. They smack the dog piss outta you for being an asshole. End of story. Now tell me. Am I right, or not?"

"Swear on your eyes you never tell a soul what I'm gonna say next. This is the type a shit can't never get out, cuz. Not word-one to nobody ever! Never this part; or I gotta go kill these cunts. You know me, cuz; I'll go nuts and everybody dies. Don't make me go to jail again. I'll shoot in a crowd, and everybody knows it."

"What the fuck? You know me from when we was kids. I don't say shit to nobody about nothin'. Who you talkin' to like this? You gotta tell me not to say somethin', like all the sudden I'm some fuckin' rat? Now how you wanna make me act ova here? Maybe you should try to remember who it is you're talkin' to, ya ingrate fuck!"

"Okay. Sorry, cuz. Still, I can't believe it. When I heard those words fall outta that whore's mouth my ears don't wanna work. So here's me, walkin' in, smilin' like JFK with his cock in Marilyn's face. I'm buildin' a world-class hard-on till my ol' lady says, 'Oh, it's you. My sister was just askin' me about that bastard ex-husband of mine. I told her I don't even wanna talk about that son-of-a-bitch.' So I asks her, Whoa, doll, wait awhile. You was talkin' about your ex while I was pourin' expensive gin in the imported glasses? Her twat sister squawks, 'Don't sweat it, asshole. He's in jail, remember? Just fuckin' relax.' Can you believe this bullshit, cuz? This no-class, gutter-slut tells *me* to relax in my own front-room. You know me. I'm ready to blow. So I says—"

Doc screamed at the payphone, "You're what? You're outta your fucking skull . . . that's what! Don't even think about this. I say when it's over. You must have me mixed up with your bust-out husband, ya stupid bimbo."

Uno shook his head: "See? This is the kind a shit I'm talkin' about. You let 'em suck your cock, and this is what you get in return – more bullshit."

One of the drunks behind us said, "Piss on both a them cunting whores, *coom*. I'm surprised you didn't wax the two of 'em. That's my ol' lady, I pistol-whip 'em both till they beg me to let 'em lick each other while I take the movies. After I'm done pourin' cock to 'em, I snuff 'em both. Boom – end of story. Next, I send the movie to her ex so he can jerk-off while he's gettin' ass-slammed by spooks in the joint. Those bitches know from the gate not to piss me off. See, *coom*, the difference between me and you is—"

Doc screamed "You fucking traitor!" then broke the wall phone with repeated slams. When he charged behind the bar for his Colt AR-15, everybody dove and crawled under tables except for Uno and Fingers. Doc sprayed bar-length mirrors and three rows of bottles into a million little pieces of colorful glass which moments before had been arranged like a work of art. He turned to the crowd and asked, "Whoever don't like it speak up now. How youse bust-outs gonna act in *my* joint tonight?"

When Eggs and I peeked from under our table Doc asked, "You got somethin' to say, Jackie? What about you, Eggs? You're the big man. You got a problem with any of this? Or maybe you wanna get involved, huh Fingers? You're my nephew, so I gotta believe you're solid for right now. But don't make a liar outta me."

Uno sauntered to the bar with his rock glass in hand, "Hey Doc, I need a refill. You got so hot you melted my ice. Come-on, *coom*, I'm dry ova here! I need a fresh one, ya fuckin' mad-dog. I got your back, Doc. And you know what, *coom*? Somebody don't like it, fuck-'em where they breathe. Meantime, gimme a nice fresh drink on cold ice."

Once satisfied with the results of his rampage Doc announced, "Okay. Everybody get your dead asses off *my* floor and drink, ya fuckin' cowards. Next round's on me."

After his barmaid poured enough fishbowls for customers to sip in subdued tones, she swept glass into small piles and mopped-up booze from behind the bar.

Those yakkers turned out to be Ice-cream Nicky and his cousin, Sally-Boy, running their mouths as usual. I almost didn't recognize Nicky without his ice-cream uniform. Sal performed odd jobs for Uno. During the day he wore *workies* with a name tag of "Vito" on his shirt pocket. When Nicky wasn't driving a freezer truck loaded with explosives, and when Sal was out of his incognito disguise, they dressed like Hollywood mobsters and hung out at The Inn to study racing forms or to watch sports on Doc's TV.

When they finally resurfaced Nicky announced, "Youse all know who I am. Now guess what? Do I gotta go get the fusees and the ball-bats tonight? Don't nobody make me do it, 'cause youse all know I'm capable. I got a jacket with the Feds 'cause I'm a dangerous man. And don't forget . . . I know the Water Judo."

The only water judo Nicky had soaked through his pants as Dean Martin crooned "Memories are Made of This" from Doc's neon jukebox. He insisted through tears, "Tell 'em, cuz, I'll shoot in a crowd. For strength, *coomba*, I got it! Now I'm gonna pretend this didn't happen before there's a *homicide*! Come on, cuz."

He marched out all tough to change pee-peed clothes with Sally-Boy right behind him. After that episode, whenever Ice-cream Nicky said, "Believe all those stories youse kids hear about me 'cause they're all true," kids winked, "We know . . . dangerous, right? You're not like those other bust-outs, Nicky. Now whatcha got for us today, *coom*?"

But in the bar that night Doc let loose with a sincere belly-laugh – doubled over his machine gun – almost breathless, the only time I can ever remember him laughing. He had to dry his eyes with a bar napkin, after shaking glass shards from it.

Pazzo came downstairs from visiting with his sister-in-law and niece, smoothing perfectly groomed razor cut hair and chewing gum as he asked, "Okay, what's so funny? Were youse talking about me?" as he crunched through broken glass in his brother's tavern. Bobbing his head to a smooth Dino ballad he frowned, "I miss something here, or what?" Then he turned from his reflection in Doc's jukebox to us: "Youse kids thought flunking school and getting expelled was cool. How about now? You feel strong on that floor? Oh, look at this. What's this? You ain't scared, Fingers? Is that it?"

"We ain't scared a nothin'. Fuck-it. We're all gonna die anyways. Right, Uncle Doc? Meantime, we stick together and avoid extra bullshit. *Cin don* (a hundred years)."

"Yeah, Pazzo," I agreed, as Eggs and I stood and walked towards the door. "The way we see it: Dead's dead, and then none of it matters. Fuck-it, right?"

I pushed the yellow envelope towards Uno. He didn't reach for it so I laid it on the bar where he stood. "Oh, and by the way. I just wanted to let you know I got a baby on the way, so from now on Benny's handling this. You know how it is, Uno. Family's everything, right? You're a family man too, right Doc?"

When Doc leveled his automatic weapon at me, Pazzo stepped between us. Doc lowered the rifle and said, "First of all, don't ever compare yourself to me. And you got no idea what my life's like. Youse kids better wise-up before you step on your own dick."

"You're right, Doc. I don't know. And I'm sure it's best that way. I didn't mean any disrespect – sorry. I just meant that you have a wife and daughter is all."

"I know when I'm right! And don't you worry about my daughter one way or another. Understand me, Jackie? You stay away from her. You think you're so smart. Don't come cryin' to us when this colored broad makes a fuck outta you again."

Fingers interrupted, "Easy does it, Uncle Doc. We're all on the same team here."

"Shut your fucking mouth! I wasn't talkin' to you, *yet*. Tell me, Fingers, you still smokin' reefers with shines and playin' stoop-tag with them nutty bitches down Five Points? Maybe youse nigger-lovers feel brave enough to make a move against us?"

When Fingers looked at the ground, Doc turned his fury back at us. "You know there ain't no middle ground here. But youse just don't pay attention, do you? Here's the deal, just in case you're too stupid to figure it out on your own. It's all the way in or stay the fuck out. You're grown men now and should know this . . . but youse don't. I'm tired of repeating myself, so I'm done talkin' here. Now youse kids better go home."

Pazzo said, "Yeah, go on home. And youse two bust-outs better be at work tomorrow. I'll speak to you then. Don't make me repeat myself, either."

The three of us moved toward the door when Uno stuffed that yellow envelope inside his suit jacket and patted his chest. Then he called out, "No, not you, Fingers. Not so fast. Sit back down. I ain't done just yet. I still got a few more questions for you."

Pazzo walked outside with us: "When I was your age, Jackie, your dad taught me how one mistake can change the rest of my life. Another thing he said is that in order for me to have a friend I have to be one. He promised me that no matter how tough things get, all I have do is fight and the pain *will* go away. If you kids wanna be men you'd better stay tough. Don't ever punk-down from a beef or talk to cops. And don't ever leave a friend, no matter what. If you got balls dangling between your legs instead of a crease, then man-up. Play by the rules or you're out – simple! We got no room for snitches, punks or *finocchio*. You know what else? We don't tolerate back-stabbing, double-dealers. Choose your friends or get chosen. And remember: everybody can be replaced. Break the rules and you'll be real sad, real quick. Besides, nobody needs problems with Doc or Uno."

"We ain't lookin' for no beef with any of youse guys," Eggs assured him.

"For such a quiet guy you talk way too much, Eggs. Listen-up, Jackie. Don't go marching around blind. You think this life's all fun and posturing? Criminals are like everybody else. They'll just screw you over for different reasons. Don't ever let your guard down, you hear? And stay away from hard drugs. Are youse two hard-heads paying attention? That's it. I'm all talked out for now."

"Thanks, Pazzo. I heard every word and appreciate the talk."

"Yeah, Pazzo," Eggs chimed in. "Don't worry. We know the rules."

"I'm not the one who has to worry. I made my bones. Now go on home."

I remembered something Sally-Boy always told us, "There's nothin' wrong with getting high once in awhile. But one line you don't cross gets cooked in a spoon. As long as youse kids ain't rats and rapists, or junkies and punks, youse're safe. We're okay with killers, thieves, counterfeiters and drug-dealers, as long as business is someplace else. Just remember this part: Don't ever bring drugs or funny-money to The Inn."

"Eggs, you got time to burn one?" I asked on our way to the car.

"Easy, Jackie. What, you ain't high enough?"

"No, Eggs, I ain't high enough. But I'm about to try again."

My father preached to me on countless occasions throughout childhood and adolescence about fighting through pain to neutralize it. And he was emphatic about a few other favorite points, such as: "No matter what you hear or see, no matter what happens, don't *ever* cross Uno. And don't go to him for a favor, either. Keep your eyes open and your mouth shut. Is that clear? If you're in trouble and Pazzo is around, you can ask him. But I'd rather you clean your own messes. Now go upstairs and get to sleep."

But that night when leaving Fingers at the Inn, after I worked a double shift with no sleep for two days, we made our way back to our respective houses. Eggs cleared his throat: "I think you're right, *coom*. Now that you mentioned it, I see it too."

"So you do wanna burn one."

"You know what I mean."

"Yep, I sure do. He's up to somethin', alright. He acts all different as soon as he gets around Uno and Doc. This Fingers is becoming one shrewd character . . . that's for sure. But he's a brother, right?"

"Hey. You know that seed money Benny lost? It's half yours, right Jackie?"

"I ain't worried about that right now. There's somethin' more important missing."

CH II: THE GAME-TEST - PART I

We grew up during a time of chaos and duplicity, in a place where nothing was as it appeared to be. Yet at the time everything seemed nearly perfect.

Sally-Boy preached, "You're safe as long as youse kids follow the Neighborhood code. Forget all that other bullshit. Forget about laws and sins. Ignore cops, judges and politicians. In fact, fuck their whole system. Me put my ass on the line for some greedy cocksuckers while they get fatter? That shit's not for wise guys like us. Fuck-'em. I'd just as soon go to the joint than let them assholes yank my chain. By the way, youse kids got anything to get high on? The coloreds down Five Points got some good shit right now."

Nearing my 13th birthday Pazzo warned, "Don't hang around Five points."

"Those niggers down there don't bother us, Pazzo."

"Hey! Did I say anything about color? Try listening for a change."

"Okay, sorry. I'm listening."

"Do you know why it's dangerous for you to hang around Five Points?"

"Yeah, because those micks down there are worse than niggers, right?

"Can you stop for five minutes with the racial slurs? You're listening to that trash-talking, Sally-Boy, too much. I was locked-down with some solid Irishmen and brothers. Believe me, being stand-up has nothing to do with nationality or color and everything to do with character."

"Are you gonna say a story about when you were in prison?"

"What? Maybe later. Anyway, The Mick's father, Danny, was a real gritty Irishman from New York, from a *schifoso* (disgusting) place called Hells Kitchen. He was a *Westie*. Did you ever hear about them?"

"Yeah, I think it's like a cowboy or something."

"No, not really. But that's not what I'm getting at here. Anyway, the old man, Danny, worked under 'Mad Dog' Coll. Do you know that name?"

"Whoa! There's really a guy named *Mad Dog*? Is that his real name?"

"I said to stay quiet, didn't I? Now pay attention. This guy, Coll, did hits for Al Capone. After Coll got whacked, those micks set up shop in Cleveland, right here in Collinwood. But Danny was too hungry, and that leads to reckless behavior. He tried pushing Scalish out of the vending business. Guess what? Those bust-outs found Danny in a dumpster with a ventilated face. But by then Mick and his brother, Eamon, were already established. Now you see why you need to stay away from Five Points?"

"Because the Irish hate all Italians, right?"

"No . . . not right. It's because *that* Irishman and his partners hate all Italians from Collinwood. It's more about territory than anything else. The Mick has some close allies up in Little Italy. It's Uno and us he doesn't like and it's been festering for a long time."

"But youse guys were all friends in high school, right? So they know better than to mess with you and Uno now. Nobody messes with Uno, right?"

"Just relax a minute, kid. At the beginning we were buddies, but things changed."

"Okay, I'm relaxed. So which part changed? What happened next?"

"I'll tell you what's gonna happen if you don't stop with the questions. Okay, so The Mick got tossed out of Collinwood high school and joined the Marines, then got booted out of the service. When me and Uno were inside, Eamon stole Uno's girl and knocked her up. After we got paroled those two crazy bastards jumped Uno, put him in the hospital and scattered Uno's brother all over the Neighborhood with a car bomb."

"Yeah, Pazzo, this is old news. Everybody in the Neighborhood knows this stuff."

"No, not everybody. Anyway, Eamon's car got wired for a one-way trip, and then Mick walked into a stray bullet. They thought it was us! Can you believe this? So then guys started disappearing: some got blown-up; some went to jail from mysterious tips called in to the cops; and some others just vanished. It's quiet right now and we want it to stay that way for awhile. You getting the picture yet?"

"Yeah, we heard all about that, too. Mick thinks Uno killed his brother, right?"

"You're quick with the answers, Jackie. But you're not listening. Eamon was plugged in with a few syndicate guys from Little Italy and some rich Jews downtown. After Eamon met with his accident, Uno got closer with the crew from Little Italy. But in the meantime, Mick made his own powerful connections. Let's say things are tense now."

"Yeah. But who's more powerful now? Uno's the man!"

"Oh, excuse me. You must have all the answers. Is that it, Jackie? Maybe I should just be quiet and let you tell this story."

"Alright . . . promise . . . I won't say one word."

"This Mick's all paranoid. So now they're enemies and two of the most feared men in Cleveland, who both live right here in Collinwood. That means there's still a lot of bad blood. And there's younger kids coming up about your age that hate us, too. That means you kids better stay away from them. You paying attention, Jackie?"

I did for awhile. Eventually I recognized that the enemy was a lot closer than Five Points. Blackouts hit quick and often till a terminal case of the "Fuck-its" took over. By then, losing time became normal activity and my paranoia increased the drinking.

Our crew, the Royal Flush, became pros at the *fuck-its*: "Oh, this stuff's addictive and it might kill me? Fuck-it. This shit makes you puke and messes with your heartbeat? I like that kind. She's married and looking to spite her ol' man? Fuck-em both. Oh, he's got a weapon and we're outnumbered? Whatever… Let's just toss it all up in the air and see what happens. Meantime, gimme another drink."

The morning of a life-altering wake-up call, liquid pain shot through my head with each pulse. Squinting through the residue of another all-nighter, I felt something coming. A swollen hand from another encounter with the fog shielded bloodshot eyes as I listened for what was about to shred my brain as I limped inside our house with Gracie.

Um hmm, okay, here it comes. I stared at the phone, thumb and index finger pressed against throbbing temples, and waited. *Fuck-it. I just won't answer.*

Shrillness strafed across my head, embedded into my fresh hangover. I lifted the receiver on the second ring to hear a familiar voice, "Listen close." *I fucking knew it.* "Swear to Buddha, this is the last time I say it." *I could smell it.* "Be careful," the voice warned. "Now let's see if you're as smart as you think you are."

I answered, "I do," and I did. Then he just hung up, and that was that.

With a receiver still in hand, a flat dial tone buzzing through our quiet front-room, I yelled upstairs, "Yo, Butter! You ready yet, or what?"

"Relax, Jackie! It's way too early. You want us to be the first ones there?"

"You relax! I promised Eggs we'd be there at nine." *That's what I get.*

Our little pocket-Pit, tore through the house at warp speed as I ground fists against a pounding forehead. *Now how am I supposed to act behind this bullshit?*

"Are Gus and Nino still meeting us with their new sweeties?"

"Something came up," I mumbled as I untangled the phone cord and hung up.

"What? Speak up, Jackie. I can't hear shit up here."

"You wanna talk, come down here. I ain't yelling this all over the place."

"What are you pissed about now?" Butterscotch demanded as she marched down.

"I got stuff on my mind and need to think, okay?" *Ol' dad was right . . . again.*

"But why are you mad at me? What is it this time, Jackie?"

"I already told you, I'm not pissed." *Not this bullshit again.*

"Whatever . . . Be mad if you want to. There's nothing I can do."

"Hey! What the fuck? I'm not mad, alright?" *Here we go…*"Not yet, anyways."

"Oh. It's my fault again, huh? Is that what you're saying to me? I caused this?"

"It's nobody's fault. I'm just an asshole." *After all I did for those Benedict Arnold motherfuckers – all the chances I took.* "It's got nothin' to do with you, okay babe?"

"Then what's with this shitty attitude, Jackie? Why so defensive?"

"Look, can we just get to where we're goin' without another fight – for once?"

"Just explain then. If you're not pissed, what's with the attitude problem?"

"Jesus Fucking Christ, I'm tryin' my best here. Just back the fuck off one time!"

"See . . . As soon as I talk you get defensive. That's what I mean about you."

"Why you gotta fuck with me when you know I got shit on my mind?"

"Well, you don't have to pick it out on me. Just admit it; you're angry."

"You're right. It's me. I'm mad *and* defensive. So please get off my ass or we just stay home and fight all night. It's your call." *I'm nuts for walking into this trap, anyways.*

"Okay, I accept your apology. So how do I look? Is this too much lipstick?"

"Why you so worried about how you look? Who you tryin' to impress?" *Fuck-it. It's better now than later. I guess this is what I want, anyways. But not like this.*

"You didn't say who called. Was it Mom about my cousin?"

"Nobody. Just Benny. I'll drive." *Fucking traitors.* "I'm too wired to just sit." She and I drove to Eggs' house, and from there the four of us were about to carpool to the grand opening of a club financed by Uno.

"So what's your crazy friend, Benny's, problem this time? Agh, never mind! Fuck those *guinea* jerk offs. You know I have your back," she said all nice like she was two different people.

Hmmm. "Cool, thanks, now lemme think awhile." *Those Judas, cocksuckers.*

"So what's with the walls? You don't trust me? Just fucking say it, Jackie."

Shit... "I'm not mad, and it's not you." I dodged the question, too sick to argue.

"Oh yeah? Well exactly what is it then, Mr. Irritable?" she posed all sassy.

"Things are weird right now." *Here we go again.* "And you know what I mean."

"Don't worry; it's the three of us now. It'll all work out. You can count on me."

Really...? I changed the subject, "Hey, you get the morning sickness yet?"

"Nope. So are you going to breed Gracie or not? I already told you I want a pup."

"We can't afford to pay for a stacked pedigree right now. Besides, I'm too busy."

"Fuck the papers. Breed her to Sinbad again. He's one bad-ass Pit."

"We'll see what happens. Dad says he thinks Sinbad already tagged her in the backyard – through the kennel – fucking horny bastard! So my girl just might have a little surprise package. But speaking of breeding ... When do we have to stop having sex?"

"Not till the last month. It's no big deal. I'll just suck you off."

"When? Now?"

"No. Not now . . . fucking pervoid. Just drive."

"Okay. Just show me your titties, babe."

"Easy, psycho-boy. Can you just keep your eyes on the road?"

"Okay, just one then. Real quick – just the pink meat."

"You're a lunatic. You want us to crash? Besides, we're almost there."

"Exactly. That's my point. Do it now before anybody sees."

"Oh just great, thanks a lot. There they are, right by their car, and they both saw everything."

"Tuck that little turnip away for later. No worries, they didn't see shit. They're too busy pretending to be in love. Look at 'em . . . fuckin' pathetic."

Eggs' wife, an exquisite blonde, was a sister to our friend, Yugo. As Eggs approached he said, "Hey, little brother. Hi, Butter. Jump in. Our car's bigger."

The women climbed in back. They talked a bit too loud and laughed more than usual. We were about to visit a nightspot owned by the Royal Flush called "R-Bar." Butter said, "Don't get drunk again, okay? You promised. Stay cool and let's try to have a good time like a regular couple. It's girls' night, so you boys be good for a change."

Eggs and I navigated in silence, pretended not to listen to their incessant chatter.

"They won't dance. They never do," Butter mocked. "They'll just sit there like big-shots. Okay. Fine! We'll dance with each other and make all those chumps drool."

Eggs was duded-up like Panama Jack turned bad-ass. His ruddy complexion set-off a yellow walking suit. Yugo's very blonde sister looked like an alabaster statue dressed in tight, white clothes over perfect curves. Butterscotch filled a plum-colored bodysuit and faded blue jeans as if they had been spray painted over perma-tan muscle. Our girls looked stunning. But cheery demeanors didn't match their eyes.

Once inside that energy-singed atmosphere, perfume and sweat merged with cigarette smoke and booze. A Freddie King record blazed "Have You Ever Loved a Woman" through a new sound system. As Eggs strutted ahead like a celebrity at a boxing match people formed a path. My eyes scanned the room. *I'll wait...see what happens.*

Although spacious, the R-Bar was packed with wall-to-wall customers. We left rosy-cheeked ladies at our table to congratulate *coomba*s at the bar and to send a round to the girls and to an adjacent table occupied by old friends.

"Come on, have a drink," I offered. *"Tu salude* (Here's to you). Swear to Buddha, we went and got cunt-struck while the rest of our team put together a dream. *Cin don.*"

"My little brothers stepped-up to the big-time. Youse ever need me and Jackie for anything just rattle our cages. Maybe the game-wardens'll let us out for good behavior."

I thought: *Yeah, real funny, Egan. Just shut-the-fuck-up and look tough.*

Fingers shook hands with a loose grip. Dusky complexion and blue-black hair accentuated his simmering rage. "Let's go back in the office so we can talk awhile."

I looked at Eggs: *No shit. So it's him. But this doesn't add up.* "I'm sure we can talk through this, right Eggs? You know – sit down and reason things out like brothers."

"Just stay cool," Eggs warned. "Let's find out what they got to say. But look who's here. Why's Fingers been hangin' out with this psycho, Joey Cagootz, lately?"

Anxiety ripped me in half as Led Zeppelin's "You Shook Me" bounced from floor tile to ceiling. I slurred to Eggs, "The slower I sip the higher I get, but different than before. My coordination's all fucked, too. Check out these lights, *coom*. See how they get dim and then flare back up? Somethin's wrong. The whole world's fluttering. Feel it?"

Ol' ladies went to powder each other's noses while *coomba*s escorted us to where "We can talk." I made plenty of racket till we got inside an office where Joey Cagootz posted at the door like a sentry. He leaned on the butt of a rifle like a cane.

My voice resonated a slow roar as if from another: "I know what time it is. You wanna showdown. Is that it?" *Fading fast.* "What? Now's too soon?" *Stay awake.* Jimmy Page electrified Robert Plant's moans as I stripped off my shirt and slurred, "It's slash-and-burn time, right Fingers? Yeah. It's all or nothin', right *coom*? I dreamed about this. Wait . . . Which part am I supposed ta give a fuck about? Oops. No answer . . . nobody's here but me. Okay. Fuck-it." I punched my friend and it was on.

Tile slick with treachery provided another perspective to view cigar smoke crawling across florescent lights. It folded in on itself till there was nothing but a stench.

Pazzo shouted, "Stay down, Jackie. You're bleeding bad. What're you trying to prove with this? You wanna die? You need to get to a hospital right away, kid."

I heard Butterscotch echo from a million miles away: "He's twice the man as any of you fucking cowards," she screamed. "Yeah, I'm right here. And I don't budge without him. Now what? You coming for me, too?"

Once we were safely outside she said, "You're going to the hospital, Jackie. Don't try to argue about this. I'm not giving in to you on this, understand me?"

"I'm glad I didn't let butterscotch skin or a strawberry afro get in our way. I know I'm still a bit scrambled, babe. I'm not sure of a whole lot right now. But I do know this much: There can't ever be another chick as solid as you. Know what else? I'm not good enough to share the same air with a game dog like our little Gracie. Not because I'm a cur. It's because I was stupid enough to take things like gameness for granted and too drunk to notice where the loyalty really is."

"You know what bothers me just as much as the beating you had to take, Jackie? The fucking disrespect of those pricks is just amazing. That's what! You know what else? Those motherfuckers slipped something in your glass. And, of course, they know you won't turn down a drink. Then, on top of that, not even one courtesy question. They all just assume whatever it was has to be your fault. You know what? Fuck them. It's their loss. Better off you find out now before you waste any more time on them."

"There it is . . . There's that word again."

"Which word? *Fault*? You know the rules better than me. There are only a few lines a person can't cross in Collinwood – even for gurus, babe. It has to be one of two things. Either you really fucked-up big-time . . . you know, committed one of the mortal sins, or they'd rather not slice the pie with you and Eggs. It's their fault, not yours."

"No, I didn't mean *fault*. Fuck that. I've been thinkin' a lot lately about *time*."

"We have all the time in the world. Once you bounce from this, and you will – I'm sure of that – you'll know what this is really about. Maybe now's not that time."

"Yeah . . . okay. So what's it all mean then? People say there's a time and place for everything, right? But I don't have anymore time for bullshitters or disloyalty. Now all's I gotta do is remember exactly what I did while I was losing time in blackouts."

"Then wake up. If what just happened bothers you, then you'll stay sober enough to pay attention. You should be proud they couldn't crack you the way they've broken everyone and everything else. I don't know about you, babe, but I'm proud. You got brass balls, buddy. I'm glad we're having a kid together. In fact, I think it's time to celebrate right now. Just think about it, Jackie. You're free!"

"Yeah, how about that? Wow, a free man now, huh? But I guess I've always been free, and that's why I made so many mistakes along the way."

"Whatever . . . The main thing is you made it out alive."

"I read about this French guy named Sartre. He said we're all damned because of freedom. How about that? He said that because we can do whatever the fuck we please, whenever, that freedom ends-up being the one thing people should really be scared of."

"You sure didn't look scared to me, babe. Besides, fuck that guy. The French are cowards. The point is *we're* free, and now it's time to get out of this trap."

"Yeah, I suppose this is as good a time as any. I don't want some crazy shit to come down on you and the baby because of my drunken ass."

"Good! Then don't drink anymore. Besides, this Neighborhood sucks."

"Maybe now it does. But you gotta admit it, Butter. The Neighborhood was tits-up for a long time. And even now, after all this bullshit came down, the truth is there's never been another place as cool as Collinwood – no matter how explosive things can get sometimes. We got the best education there is. It's all right here."

"Maybe so, but the heat's been turned up. And right now it's pretty fucking far from cool. If I were you I wouldn't trust anybody. And I sure as hell wouldn't be out getting juiced. You could do anything in a blackout and not even remember. Or anybody could take advantage of you, and you'd be too blind to see it. You could have a PhD in street-smarts, but if you're drunk none of it matters. If you're half as clever as you think you are, Jackie, you'll straighten up right now and pay closer attention from now on."

"No worries, babe. I got this under control. Just watch and see."

"You're the one who needs to be watching. Things are changing really fast around here so you should learn to be more flexible, more teachable and even more diplomatic."

"Ha! That's a whole lotta *mores* right there. One thing I'm an expert on is *more*. Like for example: I could go for more pain killer. But I'm really not feeling all that much right now, other than a whole lot of numb and dumb."

CH III:
CHILDHOOD MYSTERIES

During the mid-1950s Cleveland dismantled the public streetcar system. Tracks crisscrossed at "Five Points," the same intersection where Collinwood High School is located. My mom and I walked five city blocks to catch a streetcar to ride trolleys and buses Downtown, to browse at giant stores in the main floor of the Terminal Tower located in Cleveland's Public Square, a 52-story scaled-down version of the Empire State Building. It was the tallest building in the world outside of New York City. Trolley cars followed tracks. Conductor rods sparked electricity from contact points on fat electric cables that generated power to wheels grinding rail through main streets of Cleveland. Short segments, pounded together by railroad spikes, made for clickety-clackety rides to lull passengers. Announcements echoed in dark tunnels as lights glared from transit cars in the Tower's basement, a replica of Grand Central Station. Its energy and confusion were almost overwhelming yet somehow satisfying. Those echo-chamber tunnels prepared us for an array of outdoor stimuli. Skinny Saint Nicks leaned next to money coffers by doors of colossal department stores. Their bells mixed with whistles and honked horns to signal the end of a season and an era.

 At home we focused on a procession of strange trucks through the Neighborhood. Seasons dictated which vendors arrived on our red-bricked streets, crawling at a moving idle. Some honked their horns; others called out of open windows. Ice-boxes and wringer-washers from the Sears, Roebuck and Co. gradually got phased out of mid-century technology. Delivery vans discarded refrigerator boxes on tree lawns for another great vehicle – the garbage truck. If the weather stayed dry between delivery and trash day, we had a clubhouse to shelter us from the adult world of questions and orders. One kid on our street kept his neighbor's cardboard crate under a tree, wrapped with a painting tarp. It survived a few rains, but ultimately trash men hauled away our soggy clubhouse and crushed it with the rest of their stinky mess.

Weather and time fixed schedules along with merchandise for street hucksters. Another merchant who disappeared with the ice-man was the coal truck driver, his vehicle one of the most formidable. It was customary to fire coal furnaces located in basements. It was the only vehicle that actually pulled into driveways. Strapped on the back was a soot encrusted shoot that would slide through famished basement windows to coal bins awaiting nourishment. Shiny, iridescent lumps of coal were beautiful to look at but off-limits to play with. Mini-boulders light enough to be hoisted and tossed helped small boys feel strong like Popeye. But coal dust got scrubbed off with washcloths pressed way too hard as a reminder of what not to do.

The chicken-man hollered from the primered cab of his flatbed pickup. It had wooden 1" X 4" slats for sides. He didn't need to yell; we could smell his tiny wooden crates holding a blinking chicken in each cage baking alive in midday heat. Those on the uppermost layer had fresh air and nothing above to crap all over them, other than the mighty sun or rain. Older women, dressed very much like my mom, in print house-dresses under small aprons, inspected and choose prospective meals for their respective pots, and then carried upside-down squawking hens to backyard chopping blocks.

The fish man wheeled the only food truck that compared in edible stench. The driver honked short and repeated beeps and shouted *Tu pesciolle* (your fish). Brittle fish, stacked on sheets of newspaper, stared out of sightless eyes. Slabs of those dehydrated, salted cod called *bacala*, attracted swarms of flies with their tremendous stink. Our mothers, trained during the Great Depression, were able to transform that mess into nutritionally, mouth-watering suppers.

The "paper and rags" man drove a larger truck piled with recyclable refuse from which he yelled his own pronunciation of *"peppa-rrrakes"* because of how he rolled the "R." The Peppa-rakes man carried out stacks of bundled up newspapers, tattered magazines, irreparable clothing and other fire hazards collected from Collinwood basements.

Our streets also hosted visits from the fruit and vegetable man. But his open-air wagon smelled wonderful. A hanging scale with a scoop-shaped tin dangled by thin chains from a crossbar at the back of his pickup. Once weighed, goods found their way from bushel baskets into brown paper sacks, or weaved wooden quarts and peck containers. Each autumn my parents procured at least one bushel of Ohio Red Haven peaches. Those plump, pink peaches, better to us than any candy, left us streaked with meanders from wrist to elbow on dirty arms from their mouth-watering juice ready to be transformed into homemade pies.

We had a fig man who came around in fall in an ancient station wagon with real wooden sides and rounded fenders, bearing fat fruit with green skins and deep purple insides as sweet as honey. Our family must have been his best customers, because he would park right in front of our house and honk. Since they were not dried, fresh figs needed to be devoured before they rotted. But if one overindulged, those luscious fruits promoted a volatile reaction to the bowels.

The strangest truck in the neighborhood, however, was the "meat-wagon." Actually, it was a city pickup dispatched to retrieve dead animals – providing carcasses were not human. The meat-wagon driver claimed road-kill; natural deaths; murder inflicted by claws or teeth, slingshots and bee-bee guns; or death by the wheels of other vehicles. Male children were fascinated by the dreaded meat-wagon. While the driver was busy with his gauntlets, shovel and rake to gather dogs and cats, squirrels, pigeons, and whatever other city critters he was summoned to collect, we hopped up on the running-boards of his open-sided hearse to view Cleveland's recently deceased.

The Johnny's Potato Chip man made his rounds, too. But the factory was located on our corner. It stood next to a bakery where fresh crispy golden crusted bread topped with sesame seeds protected soft insides that melted on the tongue. Glass cases were packed with huge bear claws and French crullers; jelly or Bavarian cream-filled doughnuts cooling next to caramelized pecan rolls and cinnamon glazed types; lady locks and éclairs; various fillings and toppings more than ample for those jumbo-sized, fresh pastry treats.

The chip factory was my first job – at age eight. Crazy Merle and I got paid 75 cents per day to wash and dry 5-pound packing cans, and all the potato chips we could eat. Fresh potatoes were sliced by a machine and dumped into a fry basket the size of a bathtub, and then immersed into an immense vat of boiling oil. Once firm and somewhat cooled, the chips were gently tipped onto a long conveyer belt. At the far end of the belt was a salt-sifter above the eventual drop-off point, where chips lightly tumbled into open tins waiting to be filled. Just like the adjoining bakery, sensory stimuli from those goodie-mills pulled us like automatons toward delicacies which helped make weekends extra special.

Crazy Merle walked past our house every day, to and from the chip factory. One quiet Saturday afternoon he walked up our steps as our family relaxed on our front porch. Even though my father's car was in the driveway and he was seated on the porch, Merle kept coming. With shaky hands reached forward like Frankenstein, he stammered some unintelligible garble. Drool dangling from white stubbles on his chin bounced as he continued his zombie-like advance toward my sister.

My dad stood from his chair and warned, "Back off and go home, boy, before someone *accidentally* gets hurt." But Crazy Merle continued his slow assent, smiling and frothing with his quakes and quivers. "Don't you even look at my daughter. You hear me, boy? Now turn your ass around and step off my porch."

Merle stuttered, "Na, na, na, no . . . It's li-li-lil' Ja-Jackie." My father, caught off guard, stopped cold on that one, trying to translate what was being said on his own porch. Merle stammered, "Ja-Jackie ta-ta-talks to Gaaaa-od, ba-ba-but the Da-Devil annnnnn-swers. Right Ja-Ja-Jackie? Ta-tell daddy about *Him*."

With that my father walked to the top step and planted a foot in Merle's chest. He kicked strands of slobber and craziness ass-over-head down the stoop. Then ol' dad slid his chair to the top step and sat back down with arms crossed: "You don't fool me with that fake crazy-act. Stay away from my kids or I'll show you what crazy looks like."

After that episode, whenever Merle was about to pass our house on those old slate sidewalks, he'd stop to see if my dad's car was in the driveway. If he spotted the old Chevy, he would walk out onto the brick street till he was beyond our tiny yard perimeter. Merle was crazy, but evidently he wasn't stupid.

Besides street vendors, we had a few other Cleveland heroes who weren't tough guys – like stars from local TV shows. Captain Penny aired weekdays. He was as popular on a local level as Soupy Sales was nationwide. The Captain displayed small, untamed animals, a different one each week, for enraptured city dwellers. He also showed episodes of The Little Rascals, featuring "Pete the Pit-bull" with the circle around one eye. I admired that dog and wanted one just like him. Everybody loved Petey.

We also liked cartoons of Popeye the Sailor Man featured on another local show, by some Buster Keaton-looking guy named Barnaby who wore a straw hat and talked to an indiscernible bird on his shoulder. Popeye got his ass stomped every day by the same big guy with two different names, Brutus or Bluto, depending on when that particular episode was created. Their fights always were over one skinny, ugly bitch named Olive Oyl. Eventually, Popeye would gulp some spinach straight out of a can, with no can opener, whoop the bully's behind and then win the admiration of that two-timing skank who dogged him out every afternoon. Popeye was an idiot when it came to a woman; that much was plain, even to a kid. But he was *game* and had tattoos.

Brutus/Bluto and Popeye weren't the only fights kids watched. Black and white sets presented boxing matches for family entertainment in Collinwood households. My sister played in the next room and pretended not to listen, till the announcer shouted in excitement. Then she'd run in to see who was getting his block knocked-off.

My little buddies and I wanted to kick some ass, too. We wanted to be stars, or to have one – maybe even one like our hero, Pete the Pit. At our house, we sat on the thick, bumpy material of our front-room couch to enjoy some kick-ass entertainment, munching popcorn made from loose kernels fried in a large cast iron skillet. We filled our glasses from a sweating metal pitcher full of fresh squeezed lemonade. But that's only if we had been good that week.

One of our vendors proved to be a good motivator for kids to get good grades, not to drive mothers even crazier. Parents used his wares as positive reinforcement or withheld them as punishment. The driver, Ice-cream Nicky, was the one we kids got to know on a personal level. His white, musical van became a permanent fixture, even throughout adolescence.

It seems like vehicles of one type or another made up large portions of memory. We had ambulances and street cars; amusement park rides and railroad cars; huge automobiles, great trucks and fat motorcycles with sidecars; paddy wagons transporting criminals, as well as specialized autos hauling around politicians, cops and other gangsters. Some other vehicles we rode during adolescence got powered by an obsession with *more*. Old people in the neighborhood told us that with any luck we might realize one day how the greatest acquisition of *more* simply meant getting old. But that was back when everyone over the age of 30 seemed as retarded as Crazy Merle, back when we were still impervious to things like illness and death.

After our bizarre parade of street vendors, odd trucks and paddy wagons, drugs later became other modes of transportation to haul us while on choppers to and from alternate worlds of reality.

School became another vehicle for a reticent boy who tried to stay quiet and out of the way. Kindergarten was where I met Tessa. Her jade eyes sparkled under bangs of silver clouds so foreign to a boy surrounded by dusky children like me. Our teacher, the first *colored person* I'd ever spoken with, sent me home with a note written in mysterious cursive about love-stricken children. Tessa was my girlfriend, even though we didn't actually speak till years later.

I looked forward to school till I heard she might be moving away. That's also when the nightmares began. Fevers consumed endless nights with marathon temperatures of 106°. My mother slathered greasy menthol on my narrow chest. I boiled and shivered inside freezing tee-shirts. A dark, orange cloud above my bed illuminated ghoulish strangers crawling through my second story window.

Our family doctor, a German expatriate, administered shots in large glass syringes during house calls. No matter why he was summoned, he gave a standard hearing test. With a cupped hand over his mouth he would lean next to the patient to loudly whisper the number "63." The letter "R" rolled out the number "Three" in his guttural accent. Drawn to my distorted reflection on the convex, mirrored circle affixed by a rubber strap to his thick bald skull, it took all the strength I could muster to say "63" loud enough to our half-deaf physician. But it didn't matter. I could fake all subsequent tests once I had experienced two of Doctor Sixty-Three's tricky exams. With maniacal nods, even if the answer was silently mouthed, the next move was a large needle through a buttock cheek.

Once tonsils and adenoids had been removed by a different physician not obsessed with acoustic perception, I bounced back as would a dry sponge in a rain barrel. But by then eyeglasses got added to the mix, when my right eye drifted from too many whacks on the head. Those thick glasses made school more difficult for a short, scrawny cross-eyed boy who looked at the ground.

Physical illness disappeared after surgery. I gained weight and confidence grew with schoolyard friendships. But not all was right. Specialists were unaware of visions prior to any fevers or how hallucinations persisted long after raging fevers had ceased. In their place other vehicles neatly filled that void.

As a hungry 1ˢᵗ grader who had slept through breakfast, I shook rain off my coat and sat on the floor to kick out of rubber boots with jangling metal clasps as I announced, "The bunny's dead, Ma. I found out about it in school today."

"Someone told you the Easter Bunny died? Okay, now go hang your coat up."

"Nope, not any ol' Easter Bunny. You know what I'm talkin' about."

"You're crazy. I was just in the basement doing laundry. It's in its box. Hurry up! Go eat your lunch or you'll be late again. Don't make me nervous. *Madonna Mia*, why he does this to me I'll never know."

"Not till we check." *Click* We crept downstairs like we had to sneak-up on death. "See, Ma? I told you so."

"No you didn't! I warned you about this. We don't talk like this, remember? People don't understand our ways, Giacomo. They think it's voodoo or *malocchio*. Now get rid of that disgusting thing!"

Still pliable, I slid the rabbit into a paper grocery bag, dropped it into a dented trash can behind our house and then sprinted down a driveway we shared with our next-door neighbors. Friday afternoon classes were half over and I was ready for the weekend.

My sister's First Holy Communion was the next day. Dressed in my Sunday best, I stood at the end of our driveway hoping to get the attention of my secret love. She noticed me and stopped walking. Head down, concealing a shy smile minus front teeth, I unconsciously scraped a new pair of shoes against rough concrete. I thought I saw her waving at me so I looked up. The first words I ever remember Tessa speaking directly to me were when she screamed "No, Jackie! Please!"

The driveway rushed my forehead with purple aerial bombs. I thought I was asleep in bed till I woke to that monster breathing hot fumes across my back.

Inside my head groaned: *I can't get up.*

A deep voice reassured me, "You're safe, boy. You're out now. But you need to stand up so I know you're okay."

He had pulled me out from a shadow-world between fat, rubber-smelling tires where filth blocked fresh air and light for just an instant too long.

The teenage neighbor who had just run over me knelt at my side. I couldn't move, paralyzed with fear. Momentarily deaf, I saw him pleading with my father. My hearing returned when Tessa grabbed two fistfuls of his hair, sobbing and screaming, "No! Get off of him! If you hurt him I'll kill you!"

I pulled myself up by a thick chromed bumper to reassure her, "No sweat," and then passed out. The next time I woke, forehead bandaged and a capped rubber bag of ice against my back, my family stood next to my bed with their heads lowered like strangers.

On another day when family looked like strangers my mother warned, "Your father's been sick lately, Giacomo, and crabby. You be careful when daddy's eyes change, okay?"

Those eyes smoldered from gray to black that day when he yelled, "Get inside and stay there till I get back," as he helped her to their 1952 Chevy with its dull finish.

Mom's favorite record, Mahalia Jackson's "Amazing Grace," amplified bluesy growls as a neighbor who referred to my dad as "Rocco" shouted to a woman hanging laundry, "The wife just called the hospital. The way she tells it, Rocco's ol' lady's okay, but she went and lost that baby. The Mrs. is inside right now makin' a covered dish to bring over for Lucy's kids. She thought you might want to know, is all."

"Oh my dear Lord in Heaven!" she replied. "Lucy must be a nervous wreck. I made sauce today, so I'll put in a nice lasagna for them and go make a novena at the church. God save its lost soul. A crying shame, this is. What else did he say?"

"He said Lucy went and lost that baby. The way the wife tells it, Lucy was lookin' forward to havin' another little Rocco around the house. Too bad she went and lost it."

I thought: *Who is little Rocco, and how did we lose him?* I cried myself dry after learning my brother, or what I had assumed to be a male child, had been lost.

Dad returned home late and alone, his eyes as cool as ash: "The doctor said it was a change-of-life baby and premature. He said it came out dead and that it was more monster than human. But it doesn't matter either way, anymore. It's gone now, so that's that. I'll bring Mommy home tomorrow. She doesn't need to hear anymore about this from you, understand? You're almost eight years old, Jackie. So quit your sniveling or I'll give you something to cry about. Now you and your sister go upstairs and get to sleep right now."

That's also when the training began. Dad bought boxing gloves for me and the teen next-door. When instructed to fight I refused. The young teen hit me till I cried. Protests increased to sobs. The beating got even worse when I begged. Curled in a ball, I whimpered till it became unbearable. I don't recall much other than a deep voice command, "Fight and the pain will go away!"

Flailing, shrieking, I attacked with blind rage. He wrapped his arms around me with an iron grip and said, "You did good, son. Now go inside and clean up. After supper you can get an ice-cream from Nicky." I knew what he meant.

Our favorite vendor, Ice-cream Nicky, ran an all season business. With each transaction he reminded us, "Youse know those stories youse kids hear about me? Well, believe 'em all, 'cause they're all true. I'm a dangerous man. And youse little fuckin' bust-outs better remember I know the water judo," he bragged as he flexed a scrawny arm toward a cooler that hadn't worked since we knew him. If a kid came with money, he left with bombs or a marshmallow cone. "So what's it gonna be today? Youse little pussies want bottle rockets? Youse got enough balls for a pack a firecrackers? Just let Nicky know what youse need, and it's done. 'Cause for strength, *coomba*s, I got it. Even *you-know-who* don't fuck with the Ice-cream Nicky – and everybody knows this."

"Okay, Nicky. Sure thing. We know who you *really* are (wink, wink)."

Neighborhood fathers assured mothers, "No worries. Nicky's harmless."

My father didn't drink or gamble, but he did like Roman Candles, Cherry Bombs and M-80s on holiday weekends till his heart attack. After that near-death experience, he took time off from shop micrometers to work as lifeguard at a resort owned by Uno's boss. I heard him tell my uncle, "I'm okay. It will be less stress than me staying home."

My father announced, "You're going with me every day. No matter what you see or hear, repeat nothing. Understand?" Every morning we rode in his tank-like automobile with its thick cloth seats. He warned, "And that big pond is full of snappers the size of garbage can lids. There's water snakes in there, too. Stay away from there, boy."

Drawn like a magnet, I hid in reeds where heavy bullfrogs squatted on algae-laced banks of that forbidden pond. From there I witnessed a Neighborhood teen walk neck-deep across its silky, sucking bottom to retrieve a toy for an unknown child.

Walking away from the child Uno asked, "Are you outta your skull, or what? Fuck that little bastard and his bitch mother. There's snakes and shit in there, Pazzo."

"Better me cooling off here than in the lake. I ain't much of a swimmer. But speaking of that: did you know it's the exact size as a football field, and those beaches are the same as end zones? You think I'm breaking balls? Ask Jack. He measured it."

The only time I can recall Uno speaking to my father was while I fake-napped on the pier. "Pazzo vouches for you, Jack. He figures he owes you, so I'm okay with that for now. He says you're old-school. That means I shouldn't have to tell you how to train your kid. He's gotta forget everything he sees and everybody he hears. *Capische?*"

My father assured him, "My son idolizes you guys. He won't be a problem."

"You're busy. I'll keep an eye on the kid for you, Jack," Pazzo offered.

That same day, I watched a pretty blonde float, flashing a set of perfect breasts. When she emitted a blood-churning scream, he executed a head-first plunge from his lifeguard stand and power-stroked toward what she frantically splashed away from. He grabbed by the tail what I later learned to be a grown cottonmouth, circled it overhead like a lasso and then repeatedly snapped the length of its body on the lake's mirror-like surface. Then he flung it on the pier, returned her bathing suit top and swam back like nothing had happened. He crushed its skull with a palm strike against the pier.

On sensory overload, I decided to reach a raft the size of a double garage in the lake's center. *I made it!* I rested, exhaled all my air and dove in with hopes of reaching bottom. It was much deeper than I expected. Fear began to overwhelm me. But I couldn't cur-out after what I had witnessed. With starved lungs I kicked-off bottom for the surface. *Thud* My head collided with something immovable. I was trapped beneath the raft's perimeter. Suffocating, I clawed beneath rusty barrels strapped together with marine ropes. *I'm dying.* Blind from fear, deaf with panic, my narrow chest about to burst, a voice provided direction to a light packed full of breathing-air. *Don't stop.*

Trembling, I struggled onto the raft to pass out into a dream where screams fell silent as a spiral of death formed its translucent coil around my throat under water. I watched in horror as death sank its fangs into its own writhing tail. I strained to pry the dream-snake off itself, to get it off me, but my arms were already dead.

A small, dark rain cloud blocked that orange sun long enough to pelt fat droplets across a sunburned child. Startled back to consciousness, I felt something slide across my ankle. I held my breath and froze. On that heat-blistered raft, marooned 50 yards from shore's protection, that serpent inched across my leg and slid back into its mysterious home. Terrified, I plunged in the water for the security of that tiny beach.

We drove home in silence. Upon arrival my mother screeched, "No more lake for you if you can't stay with your father! Now go upstairs and take a bath."

He moaned, "What the hell are you bitching about now? Can't it wait till we at least get something to eat before you start in again?"

"You think I'm stupid? *Dio mio* Lord, give me strength."

Nothing else unusual occurred during the 3rd grade except the day Joey got his nickname in school. I had lifted one boney cheek ever so slightly to pass gas at my little wooden desk before stench crept through our classroom. Thank God Tessa wasn't there. Some kids looked at their neighbors with accusatory glances. A few examined their shoes. Others sat deathly still and looked guilty. I didn't move a muscle, my face aimed at the chalkboard. Peripheral vision tracked like radar, scanning its perimeter for danger.

Her keen nose led her to our rows by the hallway. She ordered, "Stand, two rows at a time. Something is rotten in someone's pants and I plan to get to the bottom of it."

With a trembling hand inside a chipped inkwell, I rocked my boney ass in hopes of flattening the crusty log in my nasty drawers. *She's getting closer.* I braced a sweaty palm underneath, on mosaics of gum, and pushed my butt down as hard as possible while she patted the pants and skirts of classmates with the deft swipe of an expert. By the time she reached our desks the turd had morphed into a concrete, ass-shaped pancake.

Enrico occupied the desk ahead of me. He whispered, "She knows."

When she neared we slid down. She stopped dead in her tracks, then she raised her head and aired like a hound, nostrils flared, and announced, "I'm close. You four rise from those desks right now for inspection."

A fat kid next to me named Joey tensed-up and began weeping. Enrico turned to stare at him like Joey had turned into a leper. She moved for Joey just before the bell rang. As she dismissed class she instructed, "Joey, you leave first. Make sure you bathe and powder before returning to class. Understand me, young man?"

We passed Joey at full throttle as he lumbered all drooped over and bawling. Rico laughed and sang at him, "Shit-Pa-ants Joey, Shit-Pa-ants Joey." Then he confided, "I knew the crybaby, fat kid would get blamed. You'd a done the same for me, Jackie."

Enrico saved my reputation. That sneak-attack fart-bomb nearly forced me to deal with that shit for the rest of my life. Instead, from that day forward, the fat kid nobody had ever bothered talking to was officially nicknamed "Shit-Pants Joey."

My mother waited at the door: "Get in here right now and go take a bath!"

That night, as usual, instead of homework I drew pictures of dogs, wrote little dog stories, and wondered about mediums other than manila paper and no. 2 pencils.

The following day I announced to Enrico, "I want a motorcycle like Marlon Brando, a dog like Petey from Little Rascals and a bunch a tattoos like the Popeye."

My first skin illustration came by way of a ten-cent bag of potato chips. I decided to blow up the bag and pop it with a sharpened pencil. *Quick and easy, Japanesey.* When the strike fell short, the bag deflated to reveal a pencil stuck inside my wrist. I whined out loud, *"Ahhch . . . This is bad! I can't show them this!"*

So I held my breath and eased it out. *Agh* Then picked out the point. Not much blood to speak of, just a dark hole in pale skin next to a blue vein. I gently washed it but it didn't go away. My next move was for the Q-tips. Up to that point they had been one of life's mysteries. I thought: *No way. I'm not about to stick this in there. It'll heal.*

Then it dawned on me: *I'm the only kid in my school with a tattoo!* The first thing I did was to show it to my sister. Her response was, "You'll probably get lead poisoning and die from being stupid. Now go away and leave me alone, idiot."

I picked at the tiny hole with grubby fingernails till it bled and then sucked it.

I shared with Enrico, "I made it bleed like Daniel Boone after he got rattlesnake-bit. Remember how he cut himself, spit the poison out and then he was okay?"

After that, we became obsessed with the thought of getting real homemade tattoos referred to as *jailhouse tats*. Our dilemma: *How can we get into jail to get tattooed?*

Instead of jail, I requested to transfer to the Catholic school across the street where boys wore navy blue pants, white shirts and blue ties. Girls wore plaid skirts, crisp white blouses and saddle shoes. I vaguely knew a fat Irish boy named Ricky, also known as Bee-Bee Balls.

Bee-Bee and I assisted our pastor who mumbled an Italian accent between toothless gums. By grade six I consumed unconsecrated hosts washed down by imported sacristy *vino*. But I wasn't ever too drunk to notice a little saint in her white dress, webbed in ecclesiastic trances of Latin and incense. Tessa knelt beside her mother as we held a golden paten beneath chins of neighbors so a drunk could administer the body and blood of Christ. Once cleansed, they all wafted out on a Eucharistic cloud of absolution.

"Hey, Bee-Bee, you know what I know? These people ain't really sorry. Know why? 'Cause they confess the same ol' sins every week – just like us."

"What?!? You ain't listening to confessions, are you Jackie?"

"Don't worry, fat-boy, I don't remember how many times you jerked-off."

After school Bee-Bee made a peace offering. "Check it out. It's a *Playboy* with pictures of real nude women! You can have it and take this other one too, okay?"

That other one was a *Life Magazine*, an exposé on dogfights staged in a Mexico arena with spectators seated like at a bullfight. One picture showed a fat English Bulldog and the winner which was an odd-looking white dog referred to as a Bullterrier. It fit the description of what almost beat my dad's dog, Rover, when he was a boy about my age. Another photo depicted a different Bullterrier and a brindle winner. That agile-looking, tiger-striped dog was called a "Pit-bull" and reported to be the best of all fighters.

I declared, "I like those kind! And when I get big, I'm gonna get one."

That same week Benny got expelled and transferred to our school. He told us, "I heard Enrico's fightin' Frankie Fazule tonight. Come on. Hurry up or we'll miss it."

Frankie's straight black hair and pale skin made him look like a rabid penguin with gapped teeth. He broke Rico's nose with the first punch. Benny, caught up in a blood-frenzy, blind-sided me. Bee-Bee pulled him off as diligent *penguins* flocked to halt the melee. When it was over Benny suggested, "Come on over my house to play."

He removed plastic mittens and said, "Take a stone. Pack snow around it with your bare-hands. See? Now look! Ice-balls with surprise centers. Okay, follow me."

We packed loaded ice-balls into a cardboard box and slid it a few blocks. The game ended when a semi-driver took one in the face. When he locked-up his airbrakes, Benny revealed Cherry Bombs he had dipped in glue and rolled in bee-bees. We lobbed mini-grenades at the huge man, and then he lit another as an old man slowed to round the corner. Benny tossed the second one and we grabbed onto the back of the neighbor's huge black car and bumper-skied back to the sanctity of Holy Redeemer. We bailed off, rolled on the icy road and watched the old man wave at us through his rearview mirror.

The next day our nun taught us: "Today's lesson is Original Sin. It's *our* fault, children, that our Lord Jesus was tortured and killed. Remember: *He* died for *our* sins."

I whispered to Benny, "How's this our fault? Is she kidding?"

"If Nazis enter this classroom with machine guns," she said, "to kill those who profess allegiance to Christ, we shall line up against the chalkboard to die for Him."

I asked him, "If Jesus can come back from the dead, how's this fair?"

Benny gave me that bored, eye-rolling look and said, "Fuck him. I ain't takin' bullets for no dead guys." He grabbed his crotch and mouthed to her, "Mow this."

When I laughed, she grabbed my wrist and snapped two wooden rulers across the back of my hand. I hid-out at Benny's till the streetlights came on so I didn't have to explain the swollen hand. Like the pencil in the wrist, I knew I couldn't be right.

After school Benny tossed another mini-grenade between a fat kid's legs. That time Joey really did earn the nickname 'Shit-Pants,' so it all worked out.

Nicky warned, "Light each other on fire again, youse're cut-off – period! I know it's fun like that, but any more dumb shit and all youse get's a marshmallow cone!"

During the summer of '62 our parents moved us away from childhood memories. My last day there was my first confrontation with Frankie Fazule. Before that fight on the church steps I folded my eyeglasses and put them in my tee-shirt pocket. He punched me in my pocket and then gave me a beating. That was the last day I wore childhood glasses.

"Okay . . . alright," I begged. "I had enough. Let's be friends, okay? Come on over my house. I'll show you a naked magazine with real women!" He spit at me through gapped front teeth and yelled "Hog-balls" and "Bullfuck" till I unleashed my dog, Toni, on him. She nipped his heels all the way back to Five Points. Instead of asking my parents to have my glasses fixed, I tossed them in one of our old metal trash cans.

They acted like I'd never worn them. My father said, "Go wash your face and change. Your tee-shirt looks like a used Kotex. We're going to see Uncle."

The other comment came from my sister: "You have Jesus to thank for this miracle. It's a God thing, Jackie. Our Lord healed your eyesight."

"Oh, I see. Baby Je-Je's only lookin' out for us? Or are we all created equal? Your God kills our brother and then miraculously fixes my eye? Is that your story?"

Her Christian observation was, "Drop dead, asshole."

While I visited relatives that weekend my sister called the dog pound because Toni allegedly urinated by the door. When Mom asked if she let her outside her reply was, "It's his dog, not mine. Don't think you can stick me with your dirty work, Jackie. God's punishing you. Our Lord works in mysterious ways. There's no such thing as accidents."

"Ha! You're finally right about something. Everything really does happen for a reason. And the reason this happened is because you can't be trusted."

The next business day my dad called the pound and was informed "Oh, that little Pit-bull? It's been adopted." When he asked the man what they tell people when a dog's been put to sleep the voice on the phone responded, "We say it's been adopted."

"There's nothing we can do to change what's already done, boy, and there's no sense to make your sister feel bad. Don't give your demons enough power to beat you."

I went out walking, hoping to find my Toni making her way back to us. Instead I found Tessa moping aimlessly around with her head down, crying. I ran to catch up with her and breathlessly asked, "Did that punk, Frankie, bother you?" as I wrapped Toni's chain leash around my right fist. "I'll hurt that scumbag for this!"

"No, I'm okay. Nobody bothered me. Everybody knows better than to mess with me or to mess around with me. Isn't that right, Jackie? But that's sweet of you to ask."

"We're moving across the tracks this weekend, up by the pool and that shopping center. You know; that area we used to call Collinwood Heights. You still swim there? Because if you do, you could always come to my house to change. My parents like you."

"Oh. . . . Your parents like me, huh? Yeah, well that's real nice to know. Tell them I'll miss all of you. But my dad won't let me visit boys. You know how Doc is. He's old-fashioned and can be real scary sometimes, too, especially when he's drinking."

"Did Doc hurt you, Tessa? Don't bullshit me or I'll know."

"No, Doc doesn't hurt me . . . not physically, anyway. Hey, tell me something, Jackie. What are you most afraid of? Then she looked up and gasped, "Whoa! . . . What happened to your face, bro? Are you alright?" she asked as she touched my bruises.

"Just a fight; no big deal. It's a guy thing. Just don't cry, okay? And don't be scared of whatever it is you're scared of. I'll help you, whatever or whoever it is."

"Did you know you were my first boyfriend? Actually you were my first and last. Isn't that sad?" she forced a smile with wet eyes and a slightly trembling mouth.

"We didn't even talk back then. I just stared at you. I think I was afraid maybe you'd laugh at me, or run away or something," I said to her pink sneakers.

"Remember when you were up there on the altar in that dorky little black and white cape? You looked so funny, Jackie. Do you still believe in the devil?"

"My father says demons are as real as we let them be and only have as much power as we give them. He told me sometimes the scariest ones are in our mirrors. He says devils and religion and stuff are sheep food for cowards – just more politics to herd cattle."

"I don't remember asking what your father said. What do you think?"

"I think I'm sorry we're moving two miles away. I can't call you, can I?"

"No way, bro. We're not even 13. We can't date yet, right?"

"What about when we're older? Could you see me then?"

"I'd like to, but I doubt it. Maybe Doc will change."

"Yeah, maybe. But to answer your question: No, I don't believe in any of that stuff. The only thing I trust in is this."

CH IV: WELCOME TO COLLINWOOD HIGH

During that summer of 1963 we smoked Lucky Strikes and wore black tee-shirts and Levi's, leather wristbands and twisted white hankies around our foreheads. I had become a true PAK (Punk Ass Kid), impressed by movies like "The Wild Ones" and "Blackboard Jungle."

My first day at the new house I met a little, wiry kid with shaggy hair called Nino. He said all wide-eyed, "Check it out. We got a dirt lot for softball and a shopping center. I memorized delivery days and times when trucks unload. And guess what, Bee-Bee? Me and Jackie are gonna snag watermelons with yellow bottoms and then feast. You in?"

Nino and I climbed up and grabbed two. Squatted in dirt, juice streamed down our arms like pink veins. Faces still sticky with juice and pulp, Bee-Bee Balls acted all hangdog: "I didn't really steal anything so it's not really a sin. Still, I feel bad about this."

"You feel bad 'cause you just ate a whole watermelon," Nino reminded him.

"Nah, that's not it. It just ain't right. Come on, Jackie, walk with me to confession." As we stepped on weathered ties alongside shiny rails he said: "I guess it would'a been a sin if I'd a wasted perfectly good food after it was already robbed, right?"

I didn't answer, lost in my own thoughts that had nothing to do with Bee-Bee's guilt-trip. To get my attention he tossed a piece of gravel my way.

"Fuck-it. I'm done with this shit. I'm goin' home. You comin', Nino?"

Scared shitless of hobos, Bee-Bee pleaded, "No, please. Just walk till we get to the road. I won't throw anything else. Honest Injuns. Okay, Jackie?"

"Listen, Mini-Balls, it's got nothin' to do with what you said or did. It's just that I've been thinkin' about some stuff for awhile, and I decided I'm done."

He stopped: "If you're saying what I think you're saying, you're going to Hell!"

I walked over and put an arm around his shoulder: "Fine. Well then if there's a God then let him strike me dead with lightening right now. He's a punk if he don't. See, fat-ass? Fuck Him! No explosions, no nothing. That means he don't exist. Now what?"

Bee-Bee shrieked and took off as fast as a fat kid can move on a gravel-sloped grading alongside railroad tracks. He didn't look back. Neither did we.

"Hey, Nino, Benny's dad says you gotta be a moron to believe there's no such thing as a coincidence. He says if everything happens for a reason and it's all God's will, then why waste time praying; that if God has a Divine Plan, how can *anything* be a sin? Then that got me thinking about these imaginary friends, like saints and angels and shit."

"I don't know. Maybe they're like this Nick guy that sneaks around dark houses with toys, or some fuckin' Fairy creepin' around in kids' rooms at night looking for teeth, or that rabbit that shits chocolate eggs are real."

"Yeah, I've been thinkin' a lot lately, and it all sounds like a crock a shit to me. How about you, man? Because I think the only things we need to worry about are people, because there's no God. If there was, all this crazy shit wouldn't happen. Right?"

"Who knows about any of that stuff, Jackie? I guess it's whatever you want to believe. Nobody can prove any of it, so nobody knows. But I do know this much: Sometimes I tag along with this *beatnik* guy and help him out with his Sunday paper route. This weekend he had to go to his father's funeral in New York. So tomorrow it's on us, and you're gonna be my partner. How's that sound?"

"No thanks. I have a problem fallin' asleep, so I ain't about to get up early for some measly pocket change. Fuck that bust-out, anyways. Is he pressuring you to do this? Because we can kick that hipster's ass any afternoon or even at night."

"Nah, he's a nice guy. And this ain't what you think. Just trust me, okay? The pay's juicy and we'll split right down the middle, 50/50. Tomorrow's Sunday, Jackie. You don't have shit to do. I promise; you'll be glad."

I'M JACK & I WANT MORE

Just as I was dozing off before the break of dawn I heard a tap on my window and peeked out to see two canvas sacks. Outside, I found Nino with two bags of newspapers rolled-up with thick rubber bands.

"You take the big sack, Jackie. Just sling it over your shoulder and follow me."

"Wait awhile. Why I gotta lug this big one? I don't even wanna do this, man."

"Here's why: Because I'm trusting you, okay? So we can't ever talk about any of this unless we both decide to let someone else know. Deal?" He unrolled a newspaper from the small sack: "Check it out. He calls these *lids*. They're for his special customers. But one of these is ours."

That was the first time I ever saw marijuana. Remnants of sleep cleared to make room for a new adventure. We delivered packages at dawn and then smoked till dusk.

Before I retired for the night Nino said, "Hey. You mind if I run something by you? I have to take an English Lit class this year, so I wrote a story just in case I get behind later on in the semester. If you wanna hear it, I'll read it."

"Sure, I'll listen. I'm a writer, too. Me and my friend, Pazzo, write to keep from goin' nuts. Maybe some day I'll let you read some stuff I wrote."

"Alright, Jackie, here goes. But you gotta tell me if it sounds stupid and maybe help me change it. Okay . . . so once upon a time in a place called *It* there was an Invisible *Thing* who was nowhere, even before *It* had any planets, solar systems, galaxies or universes! Basically, *Thing* did it all from nowhere. Then *Thing* made one pure man, because before Him there wasn't any cavemen or anything like that. Then *Thing* made this guy and everything else, all in under one week! By the time the Almighty *Thing* needed to make a friend for the pure man He was a little low on magic. So He needed one of the guy's ribs to make a pure girlfriend. Stop me if you already heard this one."

"Yeah, I heard this in Holy Redeemer, Nino. But go ahead, anyways."

"Alright, now brace yourself. Here comes another part kind of tough to believe. A talking snake appears in this pure world with a devious plan for those two pure people and then things got worse, basically because it's our fault. Anyway, these two pure people started fucking like jackhammers as soon as sex became a sin and had two kids, both boys. Those kids fucked their mom till they gave her some grandkids and great-grandkids for old grandpa to fuck. Well, that was just the beginning of the end for us. You with me so far? Because you're looking a little zoned-out right now," he laughed.

"Yeah, I'm still with you, Nino. I was just thinkin' about some girl I know is all."

"Okay, so later on this Invisible *Thing* sires His own baby with a virgin who's already married to some other homo, and gets this little bastard, Baby Jay, who had to die because of all the bad stuff we did before we were even born. You follow me, Jackie? This might sound a little strange at first, but I have a book at home to prove all this stuff."

"Yeah, I used to have that book too, but I think I might a lost it or some shit."

"Wait. Maybe I'm getting ahead of myself, and I'll tell you why. Because there was this great flood. But before the flood killed everybody, all because we're sinners and stuff, some old guy got picked by the Invisible *Thing* to chop down enough trees in a desert so he could build a ship by hand that was big enough to hold two of everything in the whole world – even stuff on other continents. They got all these animals and bugs and stuff even before his ship ever set sail! There were even dinosaurs! But after they got saved they became extinct because of some other stuff *Thing* couldn't do anything about. Anyway, the only people left after that *It*-wide flood were the old guy, his wife and their kids. Then just like before, new kids got born from them fucking their own kids. Then every person on *It* came from everybody fucking their own sisters and mothers."

"That's some strange shit right there, Nino. What nationality were these people?"

"I think they were a bunch a Jew *finocchio* (homosexuals). Anyway, later on all these inbred perverts formed religious tribes. Then stuff like fear and guilt popped up because that first man and his whore ol' lady ate some goddamn apple. So the Original Sin was being a stupid, greedy motherfucker. All that bullshit because a pure snake convinced pure people to do bad stuff. So then wars waged throughout *It* and we got dumped on. Okay so far, Jackie? Because all that's leading up to an important part."

"Oh, you mean there's a point to all this? Because besides the parts about guys fuckin' their sisters and mothers, this place sounds a lot like the Neighborhood."

"So listen. These fucking Hindus and Heebs showed up thousands of years before Baby Jay. Even those Chink Buddhists came around way before Baby Jay poked his head out of that virgin snatch. Then these Jew rabbis and their

I'M JACK & I WANT MORE

leader, Baby Jay, dared the Italian mob to mess with him. Those *dagos* were so impressed after they snuffed him they all turned Christian, even though Baby Jay was a baby Jew. Then these other rag-head pricks came into the picture way after Baby Jay stepped on his own dick. But *Thing* made these Arab faggots kill everybody that wouldn't join their cult of dress-wearing gangsters. And after all that bloodshed, some peaceniks who call themselves Rastafarians got created by *Thing* right in our own century, smoking weed in church like it's a fucking sacrament! So when you think about it, we're doing *Thing's* holy work right now by toking on this weed. Make sense? What do you think?"

"I like it. It's all about timing, right?"

That same day, still high, I asked my parents, "I think I already learned enough about religion. When summer's over can I start the 7th grade at Collinwood?"

Momma's boy became one of 3,300 students ranging from 12 and 13-year-olds like me to hormonal seniors. Our school's 6th story tower thrust into an industrial skyline like a stone castle from a horror movie. Nino didn't arrive for another year. Benny and Bee-Bee Balls stayed at Holy Redeemer till Grade 9. I knew Enrico, Shit-Pants Joey, and a baby-faced kid called Yugo who hung around with his sister. I felt intimidated in that school till Chilly Willie arrived. I called him Chilly because he kept things cool. There was nothing extraordinary about him other than his loyalty.

By the 9th grade we hung around at The Inn. Doc let us play Italian card games with poker decks minus the eights, nines and tens like *setta mezzo*, *scopa,* and *briscola* with degenerates who boozed during the day. Tessa's mother let her stay with Doc during summers and other school vacations throughout their separation. When her parents got back together Tessa and I were in junior high. By then I was old enough to know better. We had some of the same friends but rarely saw her outside of school.

A bunch of our friends walked to a movie theater a few miles away. We sat: boy – girl, boy – girl to watch some hokey beach film with Frankie Avalon and Annette Funicello while I inhaled cologne of girls next to us. Some kids wearing doo-rags barged into our row, then pretended to fall and pushed themselves off budding chests.

A few of us waged war while Yugo and I sat, my arms around Tessa and Yugo's sister, while Benny, Gus and Eggs sprouted red spots on their arms.

Those doo-rag bangers scattered when a black cop rushed in. He found a piece of dowel rod the width of a fist with a brad nailed through its center and said, "Now you're *niggers* in the wrong neighborhood. How's it feel?"

That insult didn't faze me compared to the disgrace I was feeling. Unconvinced of my worthlessness, Tessa pressed a firm breast against an impotent arm and said, "To me you're a hero. I know you were protecting me. I know you're not scared of anybody. Maybe I'll let Doc know how you stayed close during the fight to keep me safe."

"I'd appreciate it if you didn't mention any of this to Doc."

"You're right. My dad does have a way of turning things around."

During that walk home I realized my father was right when he had said, "No kid hits as hard as the shame you'll feel if you lose face. Don't you ever back down or quit."

Gus wagged his head and smiled as he took off his bloodied shirt: "Hey, Eggs, you look like a real slob. You oughta try wearin' a clean shirt next time, ya bust-out. Hey, Jackie, you knock anybody out, or what?"

"Nope. I guess I was protecting the girls."

Eggs asked, "Hey, Jackie? Did that negro cop call *us* niggers?"

"Not exactly, Eggs. Not right out, anyways."

"Whatever," Benny said. "I can't wait for school so I can kick some black butt."

When Collinwood became the first integrated high school in Cleveland my father decided, "Either transfer to another school or you're going for judo lessons."

"I can't transfer, Pop. Those guys are my friends. I can't leave them."

"Oh, I see. Friends, huh? You'll find out those guys aren't real friends."

I remembered how Pazzo had said, "You and your so-called friends think you're tough with your sharkskin pants, high-boy collars and picking up girls? You'd better pick up your grades. Your English teacher says you're a pretty good writer for a 14-year old, Jackie. Journaling's a skill I learned in the joint. It kept me from killing somebody in there and catching some real time. Now I do it just to inventory my brain. You should try it."

I wrote stories and drew pictures but didn't show them to anybody. Nor did I show my pencil-hole of a bogus tattoo once we met Five Points PAKs who sported real, homemade tattoos fashioned by sewing needles and Indian ink. Mick's nephews, Eamon Jr., Paddy and Doyle Kelly, and their friend, Frankie Fazule, had outlines of shamrocks.

Another kid from Five Points, who sported a squiggly *pachuco* cross on the back of his hand, offered to tattoo one on me for five dollars cash.

I asked, "You know how to make stars, too? They're better for me than crosses or shamrocks. I wanna star just like the Wolfman had."

I'M JACK & I WANT MORE

At the dinner table I announced, "I found some hillbilly at school that'll tattoo a star on me. Don't worry. It ain't the Jew kind."

My mother stopped eating. My sister watched through her devious grin as she said, "Go ahead, Jackie. Tell them what kind of star you *really* want."

"It's the science kind. I looked it up at the library. It's the kind they use for elements and stuff. You know . . . the same one they use in science fiction movies."

Mom screeched, "Do you hear him, Jack? Say something! This kid's trying to kill me. I'm warning you, you little mothering bastard, you get *any* kind of tattoo and that's it! You can go live in the street. No son of *mine* will have a *tattoo*!"

My father didn't miss a chew, nor did he look up from his plate. In a monotone reply with that deep voice he warned, "You get a tattoo before you're 18, boy, I take you to the hospital and have them cut it out. Do what you want. It's up to you."

I glanced at remnants of the accidental pencil hole and figured a scalpel would go much deeper than any cotton swab. I confessed to Benny, "I've been lookin' at this mark on my wrist. It looks stupid. Besides, we ain't got any money for tattoos."

"No sweat, Jackie. Sally-boy's got a way for us to make some money."

Sally-Boy invited us to an antique party. When we arrived at his apartment his coffee table was loaded with stacks of brand-new $20 bills, the biggest jar of Vaseline petroleum jelly I ever saw and four huge glass ashtrays. "Youse boys smoke up these cigarettes. Be careful to keep the ashes, but pick the butts out and throw 'em in that coffee can. I'm gonna teach youse kids how to make money. Pay attention, 'cause I ain't gonna say this more than once. *Capisce?*"

Sal dipped his thumb and index finger into the lubricant, then into his own ashtray full of ashes minus any butts. With his other hand he lifted a crisp counterfeit twenty. He dabbed a thin mixture of grease and ashes over and under the bill at the same time. Next, he used clean fingers on his other hand to work it in. Then he dabbed the bill with a dish towel (referred to as a *mopino*) to remove excess oil. Last, he rolled the bill back and forth in both hands, crinkled in a loose ball, and then straightened it back out.

Sal assured us, "It's not like we're robbin' anybody, right? I say fuck those squares that work all day and stay home nights like cunt-whipped faggots. Just don't shit your own bed. Understand? Now I'm gonna let youse kids launder this paper into real money. Then this stack is your end. If youse get busted it's on you. If we disrespect our kind, we're no better than those *jungle bunnies* that fuck each other up the ass. These hillbillies are just as bad. They deserve to be ripped-off, because they rape their own sisters. And did youse know that those hook-nosed, Christ Killers cut holes in pork roasts and fuck 'em just like they screw us, our God and this country? Youse know those fake *guineas* that are too scared to get real? They ain't much better. But those *square-heads* are off limits to this money. Know why? Because our whole neighborhood is hands-off. *Capisce?*"

Our next stop was The Inn, where Benny and I chowed down and got fucked-up with genuine coin of the realm. The aroma of freshly baked bread wafted down from the kitchen above his bar. Doc shouted upstairs, "Mama, we need four more pepper and egg sandwiches."

When the food came Benny said to the barmaid, "Don't let our glasses get empty and I just might leave a little somethin' for you."

"Oh, listen at big-bad Benny." Doc said. "You're a con man now, huh? Is that it? Maybe you think you give the orders around here now. Is that what you think, con man?"

"Don't take us wrong here, Doc," Eggs chimed in. "It's just that we love the grub your wife cooks. It ain't nigger-meat like these other dumps try to feed us. And we really like your homemade wine. We ain't lookin' for no trouble, Doc – not in here, anyway."

"Well if you are, youse came to the right place," Doc assured us.

We didn't need to look for extra trouble. Racial conflicts of the '60s pitted students of all colors fed-up with forced busing. Our school hired Pazzo and Sally-Boy as bouncers. After a secret meeting at a funeral home, hundreds of kids loitered between The Inn and our school while teachers hid inside. Cops shoved and threatened us, so we walked in circles, smoking cigarettes on school property during class time. A Five Points kid named Webb fed sugar cubes laced with LSD to horses ridden by mounted police till Collinwood's double doors channeled a black tidal wave met with equal force on a wide apron of concrete steps. Frankie Fazule wore a football helmet and brandished a bowling pin like a broadsword. Paddy and Eamon Jr. swung brakemen clubs. Other kids had pool cues and ball bats. Some used chains, ice-picks, table legs or busted-up chairs as clubs, and even umbrellas with long metal points as bayonets. Cops beat anyone within reach.

That weekend the next meeting was held in Collinwood's auditorium where one Afro-American couple attended. When a stooped-over grandmother stood to speak, Joey Cagootz tapped her on the shoulder. He was a brother to a kid we named "Astroboy" because of how he stayed spaced-out. When she turned and smiled, Cagootz punched her face. When her son protested he got knocked down and stomped. The two cops present bludgeoned them out to safety. Nobody saw anything other than a need for change.

The next day Bee-Bee Balls stopped me in the school's basement while I was talking with three younger kids. Bee-Bee whined, "Somebody broke into my locker and robbed my green leather. It's brand new. My parents are gonna kill me. Then a few gritty younger guys appeared."

The gangly-looking Webb said, "That nigger right there's wearin' your jacket."

There was a handful of trouble coming right at us and knew we were talking about them. Of the five, Curtis, a light-skinned mulatto, puffed up and mad-dogged us: "Okay, flukey. Ya'll is about ta get what you axe for. You too, lil' Jack. Come get ya some."

Bee-Bee warned the skinny coat-wearer, "Gimme my stuff or you're dead meat."

Curtis smacked Bee-Bee's face and then spun around: "I'll flukey-doo yo ass in a mah-fucka. Now who else wan some? How 'bout you, Toby-doo? You game?"

Toby dropped the kid wearing Bee-Bee's jacket and I jumped Curtis. When a teacher attempted to intervene he moaned and fell on Bee-Bee. Inky reclaimed the jacket and we scattered. Our team sprinted to The Inn to listen as sirens raced to the school.

Moments later Shit-Pants Joey ran breathless into the bar: "Some prick shop teacher just had a heart attack trying to break up a fight when some shine got stabbed to death in the basement by some white kids. Or was it the other way around? Anyway, the teacher and that spook got hauled away in the same meat wagon. I ain't sure, but they both looked dead to me."

We agreed to meet at the playground and went our own ways. I checked in at home and left back out. Within an hour they rolled up in a hotwired, Buick Riviera.

Webb said "We heard they got warrants and stuff. We better make a move."

Toby suggested, "Okay, we'll pool our money, stock up on Smokies, Blind Robbins and beer, and then head for the Coast to live off the fat of the land."

Inky decided, "We need an official crew so we can be organized, but we ain't got a name yet. What kinda gang's got no name?"

Webb tore out the back seat and with his pocket knife hacked his way into the trunk. "Okay, we can be the No-Names. And today's our lucky day. We got a fishing rod with a tackle box! Somebody look in the glove compartment for a gun or pills."

Inky pushed a button and the trunk popped open. Armed with a fillet knife and a tire iron, we closed the trunk, replaced the seat and headed for The Coast.

"The smart thing is we snag a different car in every state," Toby insisted.

"I like this one," Webb complained. "Let's just steal new plates as we go."

Inky's suggested, "Let's kidnap a driver so we can stay fucked-up."

Too tired to argue I said, "I couldn't care less. Let's just get where we need to go as quick as possible – as soon as we figure out where we're headed."

Webb nodded off at the wheel on some country road and launched us sideways into an ass-deep, water-filled ditch. In pitch dark, we waded through some cold, nasty muck. Rear wheels showered us with ditch sewage while we nudged our borrowed car back into escape mode. With wet clothes and soggy shoes we resumed our journey to paradise in a wrecked car that smelled like a garbage can.

Four weary youngsters idled at a light in midday traffic in some hick town an hour from nowhere. A cop leaned a gun barrel against Webb's temple and commanded in a thick Okie accent, "Who wants to get shot first? Now turn off this car, boy."

Webb asked, "How should we act, fillet special or pedal to the metal?"

The Okie separated the ignition wires and ordered us to stand outside and lean with our hands on the trunk. We heard him run the plates of a smashed Ohio vehicle that held four stinky kids while we waited for another squad car and a tow truck.

"No worries," I told my buddies. "I'll bet Pazzo even has juice out here. These pigs'll feed us a good meal, then give us bus tickets back to the Wood. Anyways, we're all under 18, right? The worst thing that can happen is they stick us in some juvie hall for a day so we can kick some ass and then give us bus tickets home. This'll be fun!"

CH V: SWEET HOME OKLAHOMA

That Oklahoma jail in 1966 consisted of two ranges separated by a metal wall. Both sides were part of what was a giant metal box with metal grates along outer walls facing cinderblock supporting iron steam radiators the length of the jail. There were eight cells in a row in each range with four metal cots affixed to metal walls, two on each side like bunk beds. The four of us lined up outside while a heavy set of keys scraped against a metal faceplate. A few men loitered at the front gate to yell obscenities at him and us.

The fat-ass, redhead with his oversized ring of thick keys said, "You boys get yer asses in that side yonder." I moved to follow when a ruddy, freckled forearm slammed across my chest. He asked, "What're you supposed ta be, boy? Nigra, Injun or Beaner?"

"I'm Sicilian, sir."

"All that shit's the same ta us down heya. Go on now, little *eye-talian* boy. This here's yer new home." With a key to my future, he shoved me toward the *other* range.

I didn't budge, so he wrapped his beefy fist around my arm, pushed me inside and then slammed that cage shut. My stomach gurgled. There were no doors on individual cells. Some men sat on the metal floor. Others paced back and forth or lay on their bunks. I was scared and hated them for making me come to terms with that fear.

A sour stench of body odor lingered due to lack of shower stalls. I needed a shower badly, but it was so nasty in there I could have shit my pants and nobody would have noticed. Each cell was the same, more or less. A low metal receptacle with no seat on a toilet, that wedged between two bottom cots, was more like a stainless steel bucket for piss, puke and shit. That same wall held a sink that resembled a rusty mixing bowl with a corroded faucet in its center. I stood and stared, focused on nothing.

A fidgety Mexican told me, "There's room back with those killers, *vato*. They beat a man to death in a bar fight – a white man. You can go sleep back there with them."

Diarrhea boiled in my guts, my heart palpitated. Drenched with sweat, I rechecked each cell to find men lying on bunks or personal belongings scattered across metal cots. I finally wandered back to the cage of those two alleged murderers. I gave my best attempt to look hard for a 135 pound, 16-year old – all 5' 7" inches of me. I swaggered in on expensive suede and mesh Stetson shoes and introduced myself in a cracked voice, "Hi, I'm Jackie. Is there any room in here?"

One of my cellmates was a silent, brooding man who stood at least 6'8" and was the blackest Negro I've ever seen. His name was Larry. He gave me the once-over and disengaged. To him I didn't exist, which was better than okay with me.

Stan, a light-skinned man of average height and stocky build with an outgoing personality greeted me with a smile, "Grab the top bunk over mine." That football player-looking guy shook hands and introduced himself and his friend and then proceeded to ask intro questions: "What's yer name? What're ya'll here fer? What sorta time ya'll got? Where ya'll from? How old are ya'll, lil' man?"

"I'm Jackie, sir. Pleased to make your acquaintance. I'm mean, glad to meet both youse guys. I'm from Cleveland and I'm 16. We're here because we got caught in a stolen car. We left town because we got in trouble in school."

Stan asked, "You hear those jerk-offs hootin' and hollerin' in the next range over some dumb-ass trucker jokes that ain't even funny? They carry on like that all day. Me and Larry don't care much for rednecks. How about you? You like 'em?"

"Nope, not me. And from what I can see they don't think much of me, either."

"That's 'cause you're about half-*Splib*. That's all ya'll Sicilians are, ain't it? So what cha'll honkies call *us* back in Cleveland?"

"I'm not sure I understand the question."

"You know what the fuck I'm sayin', so answer me!"

"You mean like *hillbillies*, sir?"

"No, lil' man. What's the word for black folks up North?"

I eked-out one careful word, "Negroes?"

"Bullshit. Tell us what the fuck ya'll calls niggers up in Ohio."

"Okay . . . Sometimes we call 'em Niggers, sir. But not usually."

"I already know that ya little fuckin' dumb-ass grease ball! Tell me somethin' I don't know, fool. Damn is this boy stupid. And quit callin' me sir! Hear me?"

"Okay, I'm gonna say it . . . They call 'em Spooks, Jigga-boos, Shines, Burr-heads, Niglets, Spades, Jungle-bunnies, Coons and Moolies. Like that?"

At that point Larry sat up from his bunk and stared as if I were an odd insect he preferred to watch crawl a while longer before he mashed it.

Stan cracked up, "Yeah, man, that's the dumb shit I mean. Ya'll know what these cracka' mutha-fucka's calls us down here, you little fuckin' Yankee asshole?" he yelled although we were a mere few feet apart from one another. "*Splibs*, ya faded piece of dog shit. These punk-ass cracka bitches calls us Splibs! Nah how you like that shit?"

Stan faced the other range and shouted loud enough for all to hear: "Shut the fuck-up over there. These boys are about ta get on our last nerve. Don't you forget in there, we're all locked up together in *this* motherfucker!"

Silently, I crawled up in my bunk and trembled myself to sleep.

In the morning Stan asked, "Don't you sweat nothin' in here, lil' man. I got a brother out there your same age. You just mind your P's and Q's, hear?"

"I'm just tryin' to get back home in one piece. You won't even know I'm here."

"Forget that jive, dude. I need conversation. I likes ta cut-up and have fun."

"Cut up? Hmm. What kind'a fun are we talkin' here?"

"Ease-up, lil' man. It's cool. Be brave and nobody'll mess with you."

"Yeah, I hear you. I'm really not scared. You seem like a good guy. I'm glad I'm on this range, instead of with those fuck-wads on that other side."

"Hear that, Larry? My man here don't go much for red-necks. My man!"

"Wanna know what I think? Youse guys are way cooler on this side."

"Yeah lil' man, we know. So why ya'll talk so funny? Ya'll sound like some stupid WOP just fell off a meatball with all that *youse*, and *wannna*, and *gonna* and all that funky-ass shit. Talk right, man. Ya can't even, can ya? Now take a listen at me. I sound like the movie stars on the TV. But not you. Listen at you, boy. Shee-itt..."

"Yeah, Stan, you sound like these announcers here in Hickville on your bullshit country & western station, 'cause that's all there is down here is hillbillies."

"Hillbillies? Ain't no hills in Oklahoma, ya fuckin' lame-ass WOP."

"Try listenin' to real celebrities. Then youse'll know my voice is normal."

Stan affected a Jersey gangster accent, "Yeah, *coomba*, yooze guys sound real *noi-mal*. Shit . . . Anyway, Jackie's a girl's name. You named after Jackie Kennedy?"

"You're one to crack on names there, Stan. You sure don't look Jewish to me."

Larry rolled over and told us, "Both ya'll need to shut the fuck up, 'cause ya'll sound like a couple fools and I'm tired a hearin' it."

At breakfast I asked, "I gotta eat this garbage again? I can't digest this shit. Ain't they got a menu or somethin'? Do we ever get peppers and eggs sandwiches?"

"What we got's what we get. Same as yesterday and tomorrow. Eat it or don't. This here's tins a cold oatmeal covered by thick-ass crusts of melted sugar. But coffee's comin' hot in those tin cans there. Then for lunch we get the bean sandwiches again."

"Do they ever use Italian bread?"

"What da ya think? We get two slices a stale-ass white bread and six red beans – we count each time – and then more of that thick-ass coffee. Supper we get tins a those same beans in red water that's supposed to be redeye gravy with two more slices a this same shitty bread, only staler, and more cans a that same coffee, only thicker and more bitter. How's that sound for ya'll refined-ass, city-boy taste buds?"

"My mom's the best cook in the world. This is gonna be hard-time for me."

The three of us had little interaction with cellblock mates, save for one isolated afternoon. We lined up books and magazines, newspapers and shoes, anything solid on the side of our range with openings, and used the solid wall for the other side of our track. Stan tried to bet his loafers against my Stetsons. We all joked and laughed. Nobody seemed to mind the cockroach infestation. A scrawny Indian who hadn't spoken till race day wound up with the champ bug. As soon as he collected his swag he let his roach out of the empty matchbox and stomped it on the sheet metal floor. Everyone followed suit.

Later, exterminators sprayed the perimeter with DDT and then sprinkled toxic powder along its edges. Heat and body odor mixed with poison left an overwhelming dizziness similar to huffing lighter fluid. Everyone coughed for awhile and then things quieted again. I had no cigarettes and had wagered away a lousy supper that when that hungry almost smelled like Doc's kitchen above The Inn.

Stan taught me a card game called Thump. "The winner gets to thump the loser's forehead as hard as he can with one finger. Each thump is a point for whatever you're stuck with. The onliest thing you need ta know is how ta sit here and get thumped."

Stan had stubby, thick fingers. When he won a game his thumps were a rapid-fire barrage that would leave his thumpee in a state of disorientation.

When Larry won he issued thumps real slow with digits like baby arms that felt like a slap-jacks. He took pleasure in waiting between thumps, to allow a little swelling to occur and to let us think about the next one before he unleashed it.

One day I actually won a game. By that time my forehead was as knotted as a sack full of marbles. When it was Larry's turn to get thumped I actually wished I had lost. But I knew I had to do it. The big man with shark-like eyes just stared into mine emotionless as I came at him with small, ineffectual child-like hands.

Stan attempted a Mohammad Ali-like face, "Be real careful now, boy, 'cause we float like butterflies and sting like butcher knives."

Come morning, steam radiators down both sides were turned on and set to high. According to some hick radio announcer it was already in the mid-90s and climbing.

Big Larry sat on his bunk and reread a well-worn letter from his estranged girlfriend. He howled in tears and stormed back and forth like a madman.

Stan warned, "When Scary Larry goes in the rage just stay quiet. Get on up in your bunk and keep your dumb-ass there till he wears himself out."

Eyes closed, my back against the wall in a fetal position, I trembled. Everyone slipped back into their cells, on their bunks and out of sight – even Stan.

Larry sobbed and punched those metal walls as he paced like a caged panther glistening from body oil and sweat. Physically and emotionally spent, he staggered back into our cell with a red-eyed, snot-smeared, shiny face. With knuckles swollen like sparring mitts, he curled up on his small bunk and wept himself to sleep.

Before we left Cleveland for our West Coast excursion Chilly warned me, "Where you're going ain't the Neighborhood, bro-ham. Trust these fuckers to the end of driveway – if that."

Curled in a ball, with my back to a steel wall, I woke to haunting echoes of moans and screams emanated from an unknown, unseen inmate in the next cellblock. All night long the same wails and howls came from what sounded like cries of the tortured. After what seemed like hours, I trembled back to sleep to be with the dreams of my brother.

I was startled awake to an inmate yelling: "Shut that fuckin' maniac up or we'll put his sorry ass ta sleep!" That persistent drone of a solitary man weeping and screaming "NO . . . PLEASE, NO!" continued till the onset of a new day of jail. Days blurred into weeks. Time had new meaning.

I thought I was still dreaming when that redheaded, fat-fuck of a Deputy yelled out names of four road warriors, "Ya'll boys from Ohio, step on up to the doors."

Stan informed me, "Ya'll're out, ya little faded piece a bone-shit."

I shook the swollen hand of Larry, "It's been a pleasure to meet you, sir."

He dismissed me with a casual, "Alright now."

When I went to shake hands with Stan he bear-hugged: "Stay cool, lil' brotha." I slipped off the expensive shoes he had admired but he just waved his hand away. Then he advised, "Listen up, lil' brother, you carry a sock in your pocket with about a dozen ball bearings in it. Make a knot in the middle to keep them from falling out. Hear me?"

As Stan laced his fingers through the wire I said, "I know I won't ever see you again, my friend, so I gotta tell you two things: You're as hip and slick as the baddest Italian gangsters I know. Be sure to remember this part, fight and the pain will go away."

Once out I reminded my friends, "It's only been a month and we're headin' back already. I told youse doubters we got juice back home."

Back on the road and re-shackled, we made a bathroom stop so Webb could move his bowels. We begged him not to but he groaned, "I got the stomach cramps really bad. I'll shit myself if I don't go right fuckin' now."

After a stopover in an Illinois jail for a night, the next night we were back in Cleveland. I said to my friends, "I can't wait to see my family and our friends; eat my mom's cooking and take a hot shower. We're almost home, guys."

The driver said, "Don't get too excited, boys. Your next stop is the Juvenile Detention Home in downtown Cleveland. Then, sooner or later, you go to court."

Because I hadn't shaved in about a month I had sprouted a full beard, thick and black, which contrasted with a baby face. In 1966 such a sight was unusual on a high school sophomore.

A supervisor ordered, "Once you're processed and strip-searched you'll wear these white smocks for sleeping; you know, just like all the other girls wear." He laughed and led us to a dormitory. Then he added, "Unit Six is for the most incorrigible and oldest juvenile delinquents from Greater Cleveland. You punks better not be as stupid as you look. Now get your sorry asses in there and be quiet. People are asleep. You make me come back you'll be sorry." Then he yelled, "Now go find empty cots somewhere and get your dumb asses to sleep – quick. And I better not hear any ass-fucking in here tonight."

In a daze, we crept around in hopes of quietly finding our four empty bunks. Adjusting vision to darkness as we stumbled through grumbling inmates, we located bunks, one here and another there, in a room full of anger and testosterone.

Webb bumped into the cot and an argument ensued. The guard ran to the door and shouted, "You assholes better shut the fuck up and get to sleep right now or I'll be kicking some punk ass tonight! But I'll make you strip naked first."

A husky voice grumbled, "You ghost lookin' bitches is about ta have yo asses stomped fo wakin' us up. Get ready ta get punked."

"We ain't here for no problems," Toby said. "But if we can't get along then let's get it on. We're from *Collinwood*. So we're used to loudmouthed niglets."

"You got it, bitch. Ass-whuppin when the sun shine."

Inky grumbled, "You're on. Our *coomba*, Mad Jack, here is the baddest in this shithole. So we'll just see who gets punked tomorrow."

We got transferred at the crack of dawn, once again separated. The central room to my unit had a ceiling-mounted television, two wooden benches and some folding chairs near a glass booth for a supervisor to monitor the unit, although he was seldom available. On the other end were steel picnic tables with metal benches. The main room was surrounded by individual bedrooms. Through a set of double-doors was an enormous bathroom with a line of unsoiled toilets and a large shower room.

That short, stocky prick of a supervisor called Bossman, who was rumored to have a black belt, ordered, "Shave that beard. What are you, some kind of beatnik?

"With a razor blade? I'll need a new one to get through all this."

"Why? That blade's been good enough for everybody else all week. You think you're special? Use some soap and stop your bitching, boy."

That night as everyone watched some stupid TV show I asked a pimple-faced kid seated on the floor, "What's with all those shoes? What kind of scam you runnin' here?"

The meanest looking kid named Henry answered in his driest ghetto tone, "'Cause he a bitch-made faggot, that why. He do like he tol' or face da wrath of da boys. Dig it?"

I asked the shoeshine boy, "You mean you're not gettin' paid for doin' all this? I don't get it, man. Then why you doin' it? Is it like a bet or some shit like that?"

"Ol' flukey get paid alright, with some big black dick up that lily white ass," said Curtis. "Hey, lil' Jack, I'll bet I'm the last mah fucka you thought you'd see in here."

"What's up, Curtis? What're you in here for, man?"

"For awhile, that's what. But not to make friends with you, flukey-doo."

I ignored him and asked Henry, "That kid don't ever fight back? I don't get that."

"I tol' you once. He a fuckin' punk. So he get punked like the bitch he is. You say you don't get it, but he sure do. Dig it?"

Later I heard the shoe-shiner moan in his room. I opened his door to find him bent over his bed, crying. One teen held him face down while another sodomized his behind.

The next morning in the chow hall half of our unit sat at a long cafeteria table lined with chairs. We had glass plates and cups; stainless pitchers of hot cocoa; heaps of toast and a bowl of spicy apple butter. Powdered eggs were served in scrambled mounds.

Curtis sat across for me. He kicked me in my right shin every few seconds, time after time. Not hard kicks, but repetitive irritants in the same spot on my shin bone.

I complained, "Hey, man, easy. That's my leg, not the table."

He grinned, "No fuckin' shit, flukey." Everyone at the table stopped eating.

"Just don't do it again. Okay, Curtis? I'm askin' nice here."

He flashed a toothy grin and kicked me hard in the spot he'd been pecking at.

My stomach cramped so I stood, hoping the gut spasms would cease. With a fork in my hand I heard my voice say, "Do it again and I gouge your fuckin' eyes out."

Everyone jumped up and reached for metal butter knives. The meanest looking kid, Henry, known around the D.H. as "Horrible Hank" spoke: "All ya'll better sit the fuck down and chill the fuck out."

Everyone, including me, sat back down.

Curtis said, "Oh . . . I see. That little *guinea* yo bitch now? Yeah, he sorta cute. Maybe when we get back to the Wood I'll let flukey spit shine my dookey."

"Don't pay attention to that fool. Ease on back before Bossman come."

Another said, "Okay, Henry; we're cool. Let's eat before Bossman pull-up."

Back at the unit I approached Horrible Hank with my hand extended: "I appreciate what you did. I'm Jackie and I owe you one. I don't forget a favor."

With his ghetto accent completely gone Henry said, "Listen-up, Jack, I had your back for two reasons. First off, you showed heart for a white-boy with no backup. Plus, I hear from that fool, Curtis, you're from Collinwood and hang with the bad-ass *guineas*."

"Yeah, I'm from Collinwood. So what? That means shit and nothin' in here."

"Well, when I leave here I get sent to Boy's Industrial School or Boy's Town. If I'm in B.I.S., I'm back in jail and that's my element. But if I go to Boy's Town, then I'm in your school district. *Guineas* on the Upper Eastside don't much care for niggers, even though they seem okay when it comes to hustling up some black pussy."

"Collinwood's got its share of problems, but not everybody's caught up in that racial bullshit. Besides, I'll bet we got as many Splibs in our school as you got in yours."

"Splibs? What the fuck are you talking about, man? Look here, Jack. What I'm saying is I don't need any extra drama in my life right now. You dig?"

"Anybody of any color fucks with you in Collinwood, they need to go through my crew. These guys here with me can handle themselves, and are solid, but they ain't my regular crew. Know this much, Henry: Nobody fucks with the Royal Flush."

He affected a sly look, "Oh, you must be some dangerous dude; huh, little man?"

"No, Henry, I ain't nothin' but a set of brass balls. But my crew is dangerous and respected in our school. But I'm sure that maniac, Curtis, already told you that much."

"He doesn't have to tell me shit, Jack. I know a dude your crew was buying from. He tells me they're all crazy down there and can't be trusted."

During that stint in the Cleveland D.H., I was sent for a psychiatric consultation. In a tiny office filled with books I spoke with a bearded man who played with a loose thread on his sock. He told me I needed to *process* and asked me to share some traumatic experiences from my childhood.

I said, "Well, let's see. During these fever-dreams I kept getting when I was a kid my parent's faces used to morph into masks of strangers."

He asked, "Were you safe as a child?"

"I'm from Collinwood, doc. Nobody messes with us in the Wood."

"I mean your parents . . . your father. Are you safe with him?"

"Yeah, of course. He'd kill somebody if they hurt me or my sister. Why?"

"Did someone sodomize you while incarcerated in that Oklahoma jail?"

"Nah, but I think I might a been Gomorrah-ed one time in Kentucky. How about you, doc? You ever been Gomorrah-ed? It's really biblical. Know what I mean?"

"I see that you are hiding something again, Jack. And I think it is something stemming from early childhood based on your need to create a fantasy world."

"The onliest thing hidin' from me is sleep. I can't seem to find much of that, no matter where I'm at. But other than that, I'm okay. Thanks for askin', though."

The next day Curtis and I stood at a storage locker and examined supplies. He removed a jar and asked, "You know what this is?" When I answered that I didn't he explained, "It's grease. Us blacks use it on our scalps, elbows and lips."

"Bullshit. Why would anybody take clean skin and then rub grease all over it. I ain't buyin' that story, Curtis. You're just tryin' to fuck with me again, right?"

"What planet you been on, man? Black folks ain't got oil glands in our heads. We grease our skin so the scalp don't flake. I'm half white. I ain't gotta use it, but I likes it."

He opened the jar and said, "Smell this, flukey," and shoved the goop in my face.

At that moment I remembered my father's version of the Golden Rule, "Treat others the same way they treat you."

"Yeah, this shit's nice. Try some." I grabbed his tee-shirt and wiped the neon slop. "Oops . . . Sorry about rippin' the shirt, cuz. Maybe grease'll fix that too, huh?"

"You small fo this game. But you even a crazy mah fucka in here, ain't you?"

"As crazy as I need to be. Hey, all bullshit aside, Curtis. Let me ask you something straight-up. Just out of curiosity, do you consider yourself Black or White?"

"You honkies sees a nigger when you looks at me. But brothers thinks I'm some white-boy 'cause I'm so light. Fuck all ya'll. My momma a junkie-ass ho. Pitched me out so she could shack-up with some *cracka* punk givin' up the jing and dope for that *trim*. When that bitch my age she get knocked up by some honky piece a shit like you. I guess that faggot's my daddy. But he ain't never even seen my black ass. Fuck that punk, his bitch, and you too. That ass-kissin' Hank and you can both catch some flukey up the dookey."

After that ordeal I avoided Curtis and hung with Henry and an Irish kid named Curly, a stocky football player with curly blonde hair. Curly was the only white boy in D.H., other than us, who would hold his mud.

Later that night a title fight between Cassius Clay and Zora Folley broadcast live via radio transmission throughout the D.H. Some long armed, flabby kid called Fats, who smiled buckteeth and lumbered around like some big dope, slap-boxed with me during the bout. We tried to choreograph our fake match with the real bout, guided by Howard Cosell's commentary. Other kids formed a circle as if it were a pit-fight and cheered.

We made such racket nobody saw Bossman creep up. He threw kids in all directions and then planted himself between Fats and me with fists braced on hips.

Still laughing Fats said, "It's cool, Boss. We's just playin' is all."

Bossman punched Fats in the stomach and knocked him into a coughing fit.

I said, "It's just a game, Boss. You can see we're just foolin' around, right?"

He caught me in the solar plexus. I went down with a gasp and had trouble catching my breath. I could see Henry and Curly move for him. Bossman whirled a sidekick into Curly's thigh. Curtis clapped his hands and laughed when Bossman faced Henry to say, "Step back or get knocked-out, Hanky. You hang with whitey, you go down with him. Jackie and Curly ain't shit. So what's that make you? Say what? You want some of me? Because right now there ain't nothing but air and opportunity between us, boy."

I could breathe again, so I led them away. "You and Curly throw hands with a guard, youse get flopped instead of probation. Fuck that nigger. He ain't shit."

"Oh yes he is. And I got just the thing to tighten Bossman's shit up," Henry growled. "He better never let me catch his flimsy black ass outside of this place."

The tyrant announced on his microphone, "Fights over, ladies. Kiss each other goodnight and get ready for bed. Anyone has a problem, we'll resume this tomorrow."

When I got back to the unit Curly said, "Your buddy, Curtis, picked a fight with Bossman before he went to court and then punched him. He's already gone, got sentenced to B.I.S. I don't understand that dude. Maybe he's just flat-out nuts."

That weekend was visitation. My visit was from my mother, my Deputy Sheriff Uncle and his wife. Mom and auntie cried and hugged me in front of everyone.

I said, "Whoa. I got a reputation to keep here" and politely squirmed away.

Mom explained. "Daddy's in the hospital with another heart attack. Your father and sister formed a search party to look for bodies." She gave me her look and sighed, "Why he does these things to me, I'll never know. God will punish you for what you've put us through, Giacomo. You almost killed your poor father again. I can't believe something like you came from me. I hope you finally learned your lesson, but I doubt it."

When an announcement was made for visitors to leave they went right back to the hugging and crying, standing up right in plain view of all those thugs.

She insisted, "Tell your uncle right now. Who's bothering you?"

I neglected to mention that I could hardly wait to return to my unit.

That weekend the entire population was in the auditorium in preparation for a talent show. Henry and I sat on the edge of the stage. Some kids pitched-in setting up chairs, while others were backstage doing whatever people do behind the scenes. A special D.H. unit comprised of children up to age 12 played on stage while most others worked. Bigger kids picked on one tiny boy who shivered and whimpered like a pup.

"Is it okay if somebody bigger like *Horrible Hank* picks on you?" I asked.

The tiny kid sat on my lap and whined through missing front teeth, "Those big boys're always pickin' on me and stuff. My name's Artie, and I'm six and a half. Mom don't want me no more. She tol' me get my worthless-ass out and stay out. So I borrowed some money from her man while they was asleep. Then I took a bus to Detroit."

"Detroit? Why Detroit, Artie? You got relatives there?"

"I don't know . . . maybe. But it looks nice there. I seen a picture one time."

Henry inquired, "How do little kids get locked up for running away?"

"I threw a brick through a store window. I didn't steal nothin'. I was real cold and it was raining and stuff. I just needed someplace warm to sleep." Then he vomited on my shoe.

The legendary Horrible Hank sneered in his ghetto jive, "Ya'll punks continue ta bully this child, I'll issue severe whuppins to each and every one a ya'll little freaks."

The next morning I was rescheduled to see that same shrink in his claustrophobic office. He began, "I want you to talk to me about the pain, Jack."

"I'm good. The only thing is I still ain't sleepin' much, but that's normal for me."

"You need to learn to trust more, Jack, and to *process* about early memories."

I answered, "Okay, I'll share. I can trust you, right? Here we go. This is the God's honest truth, okay? You ever see that show Leave it to Beaver? Well, that's my family."

His reply was, "Humor is a common defense mechanism to mask pain. I want you to share how falling asleep presents a problem for you. You can tell me anything and it will never be repeated. Your secrets are safe with me, Jack. You are safe here."

I explained how sleep remained one of life's many mysteries, that as a kid it crept up while I read a Catholic Bible, my volume of Greek mythology with "Cleveland Public Library" stamped on its edge, or a compilation of dog stories from my grandparents. Secure on a wooden crate next to my piss-stained mattress, those pages of gods and heroes offered fabulous inconsistencies and much needed diversion.

When he asked, "Which memory causes you the most anger?" I remembered trying to erase the thought of my dog being crammed into a metal box with other pets, all discarded like broken toys, to be suffocated together during the ultimate act of betrayal. Each night I tried to change one word of what had transpired the night I left her alone.

He asked, "Have you ever been physically abused? I'll know if you're keeping anything from me. This is a time for healing. So you can be open and honest, okay?"

"Nope. That's about it, doc. There's nothing else I can think of."

In the morning we received notice that we were to face the "Hanging Judge." My buddies threw up fists in triumph. I gestured back with a nod and half-hearted grin.

That day crawled till the infamous hangman doled out three year sentences at B.I.S, tapped his gavel and then gathered-up papers. He paused long enough to terrify us and then suspended our sentences for probation, thanks to my Deputy Sheriff Uncle.

Once outside I squinted: "I know I've only been locked up two months, counting the jail and this place, but everything's out of proportion. Regular things look too big or real small, or too bright or fuzzy, or too loud or quiet. Everything seems so strange right now and looks too real to be true. Maybe I need glasses again."

My uncle said, "That doctor in there says he thinks you might have something called a *Delusional Disorder*, but I told him you just needed a good kick in the ass."

Invincible Dad, recovered from his heart attack said, "Your mom was hospitalized with a breakdown while you were pretending to be a tough guy in Oklahoma. Those jailers never even called us – not once! You know that? We thought you were dead, boy. We could sue their asses off. But maybe better off we all learn from this and move on."

My parent's house looked like a phony movie set. I wanted to bolt out the door as soon as I walked inside. Everything looked fake. Instead, I sat on the nine-foot long, Italian provincial sofa with its plastic cover as my father approached, boring holes through me with eyes that resembled those on stone statues. When he extended a hairy fist, I flinched. He opened his hand to expose a small box.

"Go ahead, boy, open it."

Inside the white cardboard box I found a wristwatch. I asked, "What's this for?"

In a cracked voice he answered, "It's because I love you, son."

"I'm sorry for all this trouble, Pop," I said as my voice cracked. "I didn't mean to hurt any of you. I'm really sorry, Mom. I promise that from now on I'll try harder to do things different."

CH VI:
THE ROYAL FLUSH

The very next night, Fingers and I went to a YMCA dance to hear music and hopefully meet new girls. He asked, "See those three punks over there hot-boxin' their smokes? You know them Irish scumbags?"

"Yeah. That's the Kelly boys from Five Points. The oldest one's Eamon Jr. Paddy, that red-head, is a pure maniac. Doyle's the youngest and maybe the meanest of the bunch. They hang with some Italian scumbag named Frankie Fazule. I've had my share of problems with that fat-fuck, but they're all bad news."

"Well the part you don't know is they all jumped me last week."

"Tell you what, Fingers. We'll get a few guys from the Neighborhood and go find these punks tomorrow . . . kick that ass. How's that sound?"

"I know . . . You're worried about probation," he noted as he slipped on brass knuckles. "But I could use a little help here. They already saw me, so if I don't make a move they'll think I'm weak. Alone we're nobody, but together we can call the shots. One day we're gonna run things, Jackie. Then you'll see. I don't ever forget."

"These mick fuckers are tough and got balls. What if it backfires?"

"We can't let that happen. We gotta break 'em. Uncle Doc says, 'Don't let nobody fuck you over unless you like gettin' ass-slammed.' I gotta at least try it, Jackie."

I still carried pent-up rage and a nylon sock tied in the middle with marbles in its toe. As I pulled the slapjack out of my pocket I said, "Sure, okay. Fuck-it. I wanna do it. But if we're gonna do this let's make it worthwhile, just in case we get busted."

Afterwards, as Fingers stripped off a ruined shirt, he vowed, *"Cin don, coom.* This makes us blood brothers for a hundred years. There's no turning back from this. Now we gotta organize. You know Eggs and Gus from Five Points? I already put 'em on stand-by. They're ready to throw-down and sign up anytime. What-da-ya say? You in?"

"I can get Benny and Nino to join, too. Yeah, fuck-it. Let's do it."

"These other assholes got no class. They need to learn about respect."

Pazzo taught us, "Respect is a major piece of street-life. It has to be earned. In the Neighborhood we build invisible walls to keep us safe and everybody else out. When you find new people, keep 'em on a short lead. If you see a hairline crack, get to work. Instead of trying to fix somebody, use crowbars and excavate with sledgehammers."

By age 16 our crew adopted the Collinwood doctrine as a lifestyle: "Always bounce back, because shame hurts worse than any ass-kicking. Never tell on anyone – no excuses or passes. Mothers, daughters, sisters and ol' ladies are off limits – no exceptions, no second chances. Don't ever leave a friend in need. Never quit, no matter what. Don't trust anyone except our own kind. Trust your instincts, because the *Click* doesn't lie. If you fuck-up, deal with it quick and make sure it's over. But nothing's ever over till we say so. You can get high but never shoot dope. You can forgive *certain* things but don't forget anything, because you can bet your sorry ass nobody else will."

My friend, Fingers, born Zeno Scarpetti Jr., was the only child of hard-working immigrants from Naples. They moved to Collinwood to be near his mother's sister who had married a local bad-ass called Doc. Those sisters gave birth in 1950. Fingers and his cousin, Tessa, were raised more like brother and sister than cousins.

At age 15 he already was a butcher in his parents' delicatessen. One day his father walked in and noticed a blood-soaked rag wrapped around his son's hand and asked, "Zeno, why so much blood with this nice meat? What do you hide in that *mopino?*"

"I lost a fingernail, Papa." Don't worry. I wrapped it up real tight so the meat don't get ruined. But I gotta go see the guys. We got plans, okay? I'll be back early."

"Stop talking and unwrap the hand." Secured in a tourniquet like it would mend itself, he found his son's left pinky dangling by a strand of finger meat. "Zeno, how can you do such a foolish thing? Forget the plans. We go to the hospital now."

Fingers took a razor-sharp knife from a butcher-block and severed the piece of skin that had held the fingertip. "What's the big deal? Look, I still got plenty of fingers."

From that moment on everybody called him "Fingers." When teachers refused to use the nickname he stopped attending classes. Our school counselor threatened, "Zeno, you can be arrested for incorrigibility if you keep cutting school."

"I already told you once; my name is Fingers, didn't I? You might be too young to retire, but we could arrange disability. You wanna test me on this, teacher?"

The day Fingers dropped out of school, the same day he turned 16 in the 8th grade, he reminded me, "Remember how Pazzo's always sayin' we gotta be careful who you let in our circle? Remember he said people usually ain't who they seem to be? Then he said how people change, usually for the worse, remember? Well we gotta be careful and make sure we stay the same way we are."

Benny was our first member. Then Gus and Egan got the nod. Gus was a stealthy thief and treacherous. Egan was quiet but maintained a reputation as a ferocious street fighter referred to as "Sir" by classmates. We named him Eggs. He was hardboiled and could really scramble. They wanted to be Italian. We wanted to be big. Our last member was Nino. Friendship like ours looked like forever at an age when everything seemed provisional at best.

Younger kids formed their own crew with our blessing, calling themselves the "No-Names." Their club was comprised of Chink, Dago Red, Inky, Toby; Webb and Slick. Webb stood gangly where Slick was pudgy. Both blue-eyed, blonde-haired kids lived down Five Points. Chink and Dago Red were pure *guinea*. Chink, dark complected with high cheekbones, glared through slanted eyes. Dago Red got his nickname from his red hair. Inky and Toby were hybrid outcrosses from Italian fathers and Irish moms.

Benny's appraisal of the No-Names was, "But what-da-these fucks got to offer us? The book's been closed since Nino, and as far as I'm concerned it stays closed."

I looked for friendship outside of gangs and found a tall, beautiful Hungarian girl named Maggie. She looked Eastern European with soft brown eyes and light brown hair accentuated by high cheekbones and wide, full lips. At 16, I was old enough to drive and to recognize how her family was disgusted because I wasn't white enough for her.

Her parents lectured, "You could do better than this grease-ball. Sicilians are just niggers turned inside out. Other Wops don't even trust those scum-buckets."

My mother told Maggie, "You're a good girl . . . too good for my Jackie. Maybe you should find a nice boy with a future instead of wasting your time with this idiot. And maybe your parents are right, honey. Maybe you should have kids with your own kind."

After a few wasted semesters in the 10th grade I finally passed. Maggie felt safe in one of the toughest interracial schools in America during a turbulent era. I assured her, "I've been thinkin' about shit. I decided I'm gonna graduate, stay out of jail and maybe even go to community college. Then maybe someday we can have a family."

"You in college? You're smart enough, alright. But you lack the discipline."

"You'll see, Maggie. I've wised up. I ain't gonna let the past keep me down."

As we discussed our future together we both felt familiar tremors rumble through the floor. I shouted, "Go find your friends and stay with them."

Then I bee-lined to its epicenter to find Curtis knocking down white kids like cutouts in a shooting gallery. When I found Nino knocked cold, I blind-sided Curtis with a reverse punch to his head. He laughed, "Oh okay, flukey-doo. It's all yours now, son."

A body shot knocked me out on my feet for a moment. I bounced off other brawlers and used the momentum for a spinning roundhouse kick. A jolt of shoe on cheekbone let me know my Stetson connected. I thought he would drop. Instead, he lunged. The Coach put me in a double arm lock while Curtis dug fingernails into my throat. When the principal and Pazzo intervened everybody slammed on the brakes.

As Curtis got dragged away by Coach he warned, "We ain't done yet, flukey. I'll be seein' yo greasy ass real soon. You know me, lil' Jack. I keeps the shit real."

Curtis and I got suspended for one week with a warning, "If this resumes, both of you will be expelled. We don't care who starts it. This is your last chance."

While on suspension, I ran into Frankie Fazule. He offered his hand in truce and said, "Sorry if I was an asshole. Let's bury the hatchet, okay? Come on. I'll show you how to ride my bike and then let you drive it. Hop on, Hog-balls. Let's ride!"

Frankie blasted off full speed and rode us right into the core of a brutal ghetto during the peak of the Hough riots, then called out like a street huckster, "Bull-fuck . . . youse black, nigger cocksuckers!"

There I was, stuck on the back of his rice-burner in the midst of armored vehicles, fire engines and squad cars while mobs burned buildings and looted stores.

I screamed in his ear, "I want off this motherfucker before I stab you!"

His response was to pop a wheelie and dump me in the street. He took off yelling, "Bull-fuck, baby!" Then he hung a U-turn and made a milkman stop so I could hop on. He warned, "Don't you ever fuck with me again, Hogballs, or you're dead."

Frankie crashed red lights and stop signs all the way back to Collinwood. When he dropped me off with another wheelie he smiled to Nicky with his picket-toothed grin.

A couple of older guys present were part of the Collinwood Safety Patrol, armed thugs who cruised the Neighborhood to keep our streets safe from other armed thugs. Doc, Pazzo and Sally-Boy were among the main safety patrollers that afternoon. Ice-cream Nicky was on the corner but had been banned from entering their cruiser.

Sal demanded to know, "Ain't we got enough trouble in the Wood already, Jackie? You know who that bust-out runs errands for? Next you'll be bringin' *tizzuna* (blacks) around here. Take your dick outta your hand and wake up, ya little fuck. How many times we gotta tell ya? Stick with your own kind. The way that hillbilly drives that motorbike he's gonna hurt somebody. Don't make it your fault, kid."

"I didn't bring him here, Sal," I answered defensively. "He's half Italian and has family here. But the fact is I never liked that kid, and after today I hate him more than ever."

Nicky snapped, "You think you're right about this, Jackie? Lemme ask you a question. Do we look like assholes? Huh?" as he hiked-up his white ice-cream pants.

Pazzo sniggered, "Easy, Nicky. He a good kid. Jackie don't hang around those bust-outs. What're we gonna do with these crazy kids, huh Doc? They just wanna be like us, right Sally? Now go right home, Jackie, and think about what just happened here."

That night Pazzo said: "Nicky means well, but he panics like a little girl. You ever hear about his can't-miss score, when he insisted to be the wheel man? I should have my head examined. Him and Sally robbed a car so me and Sally-boy can burglarize a safe in Eamon Kelly's beer joint, The Shamrock Club, right? Nicky swore he knew which night to make our move, when it would be stuffed full of illegal cash . . . meaning no cops."

"Nicky's a good driver, right? I mean, he's a professional ice-cream truck driver."

"Keep quiet and listen, kid. So meanwhile, we're inside the bar and everything's running smooth till idiot, Nicky, runs inside all out of breath."

"I thought he was the wheelman. Why's he inside?"

"Easy, kid. I'm telling a story here. Okay. So this imbecile Nicky says, 'Youse guys know I can handle. I parked that piece a shit like we agreed but cops was givin' me the stink eye. You know me, *coom*. I don't rattle. But they know what's up.' Sal yells, 'Get your dead ass back in that car or we'll tie you up and leave you for Eamon.' Meanwhile, we can't crack the box so we use a dolly from the bar to wheel it outside. I say, 'Better yet, Nicky, pull the car up and help us load this in the trunk. Just don't panic again.' So here comes Nicky about 15 minutes later: 'You know me, *coom*, steady as a rock. But these pigs made me lose concentration. I can't remember exactly where I parked. Maybe Sal can come with me. I don't wanna draw too much attention wanderin' around and have to whack some nosey neighbor. Youse know I'll do it.' So here's me, Jackie, about ready to use Nicky's head to smash open that fucking safe."

"Was there really cops, or was Nicky on drugs? Because he acts like a burnout."

"Settle down. I'll get to that part. Anyway, after another 15 minutes those two show up in a different car because Nicky lost the first one. We used wooden planks and cinderblocks for a ramp and muscled the safe into the trunk of a Chrysler Imperial. Even though they took a good car the trunk wouldn't close. Then the rear bumper scraped the street. So a patrol car rolls up. Turns out they really were watching Nicky."

"It that when you and Sal did time? We heard about this before from Nicky."

"I did a year and Sally-Boy got two years. Your dad pulled some strings and got me out early. While we were inside, Eamon and Mick double-teamed Uno and almost beat him to death with slapjacks. Nicky didn't snitch, but he got shock probation after he had a nervous breakdown. So Uno bought an ice-cream truck and put him to work selling fireworks and policy slips. When Sal got paroled, Uno let him run the book. We figured things would get easier after Mick's brother, Eamon, disappeared."

"They got jobs for being solid. What about you?"

"Never mind about that. But I'll tell you something right now, kid. This life ain't what you think. Being with a crew's like being married, only divorces are against the rules. Fair play means nothing. And once you cross certain lines, there's no going back."

I recalled Pazzo's words the day Benny found me in the teacher's parking lot with a Louisville Slugger. Benny parked: "Hey, I like the bat thing – all nice and legal like. You're an inspiration. I'm thinkin' about gettin' into sports, too. So what's up, *coom?*"

"That fuck of a Math teacher tracked me down at the beginning of the semester and asks me, 'Why were you in class the first day, and not since? You're making me look bad cutting my class if you go to the others.' He says, 'I'll make you a deal. If you come to class every day you won't have to take one test or turn in any homework and I guarantee you'll pass.' I told him morning's way too early for him to be coming at me with all these numbers and shit. All that early math freaks me out, Benny. I warned him right up front that I won't make it to school every day, that sometimes I'll be too high or just regular sick. But l gave my word that if I was there I'd be there. We shook on it."

"Are you serious, Jackie? You actually believed that piece a shit?"

"He promised, 'You can sleep on your desk every day and pass, as long as you don't cut one more of my classes.' If I was in school, I showed up on time for his boring-ass class. So today we get our report cards. Look at this shit. Not only he gave me an "F," but it's in red ink. There's only six weeks left in the semester. Even though I don't really give a shit about passing, the thing is he fucked me over and I ain't lettin' it slide."

Benny hissed. "We'll get that lyin' cocksucker as soon as he gets near his car. That piece a shit teaches the wrong subject, 'cause his ass is history."

Pazzo entered the lot: "What're youse two lunatics up to now? This better be juicy. A teacher spotted you taking practice swings. Now none of them will leave."

I explained and then asked, "A deal's a deal, right? I'm committed to this thing, Pazzo. I ain't backing off unless you tell me I have to. But I'm gonna lose face if I do."

Pazzo snatched the report card out of my hand, spun around all wide-eyed, and marched back into school. Benny shouted, "Go, Pazzo, fuckin' mad-dog *coom*-boom."

When he returned, Mr. K accompanied him. Mr. K had to have his shirts tailor-made to accommodate grapefruit-sized biceps and a torso like a bull gorilla.

In the report card we found the old letter grade had been whited-out and replaced with a beautiful "blue D." Pazzo said, "Now pretend like youse're scared. They're still watching from that window." Then he nodded at the teacher, "Night, Mr. K."

Mr. K said to us, "Wise up, guys, before it's too late." He turned his back and said, "Goodnight, Mr. Russo, and thanks for your help."

Pazzo soundlessly waved his hands in exaggerated gestures until we left.

Benny noted, "Look at this. All's well in the Wood. It's like some Cinder-fucking-Rella story, *coom*. I'm real touched. Now let's go get fucked-up."

My final high school clash occurred right before the semester's end. Curtis notched things up and tried to intimidate me while I was with Maggie. After a sleepless night, I walked in his classroom during a lecture and yanked him up by his Afro.

As I dragged him into the hall he squalled, "They got me by the flukey-doo."

We rolled around till he pinned me to the floor with punches. From underneath I pulled him down, secured a closed guard and applied a guillotine choke till he went limp.

Pazzo picked me up and mumbled, "You fucked-up big this time, Jackie."

While the principal was out, Nino, Eggs and Gus marched into his office: "You get stabbed, *coom*? Is that your blood? Just give us the nod, Jackie. Whatever you need."

The counselor burst in yelling so Gus suggested, "Hey, I got a good idea. Jackie's jammed-up for a ride home. How's about we call Benny and Fingers to come get him?"

Instead he phoned my mother and suggested my father come fetch me. He arrived with a grim expression and said, "Let's go." In the car he asked, "You think those maniacs are your friends? Wake-up, boy," and then remained silent all the way back.

At home I said, "No offense, Pop, but times are different now. You're from another generation. There's no way you can get what's goin' on with my crew."

"And you're so full of shit you can't see straight. You hear yourself?"

My mother and I appeared downtown for a hearing with the President of the Board of Education. He said, "Mrs. Lorocco, your son does not belong in the same building with school children." Her shoulders slumped like they had in juvenile court. "Or you can appeal my decision." She perked up till he added, "Because Giacomo's still on probation it would be a bad idea to involve courts in this. Good day, ma'am."

After I got expelled from every school in the Cleveland Public School System Benny confided, "Me and Fingers decided to waste the nigger for you. How about this punk-ass principle and that Board of Education fuck? Should we get them, too?"

"I'll pass on all that. Fuck school. Let's move on and make some money."

My father's suggestion was, "What you need is a hobby other than beer, fistfights and those miniature hoodlums. There's an ad right here in this newspaper for pups. It says they're Pit-bulls from a game bloodline. Let's take a ride."

We brought Sinbad back to a place that respected gameness. My mother, who professed to hate animals said, "The only way he stays is if he gets weekly baths and is housetrained in two days. Since I'll have to do all the work, he's my dog."

"That's fine, Mom. I can barely take care of myself right now."

Instead of being burdened with anything resembling responsibility, I allowed myself to be absorbed into the pulse of Collinwood's metronome and its relentless beat.

When Sal's wife found out he had been unfaithful with Doc's sister she spewed in a drunken rage about an affair with Doc. Those incidents spurred the newest fiasco which occurred outside of The Inn. Doc and Sally-Boy emptied their guns at one another, then each staggered off in an inebriated victory march in separate directions to reload.

Uno ordered a sit-down: "Listen close. Nobody's right on this. Don't youse dummies know pussy only comes in one flavor? The bullshit ends here and now. Keep your cocks in your ol' ladies or put 'em in your fists – end of story. Violate this treaty and youse'll deal with me. I shoot quicker and straighter than both a you maniacs put together. Don't test me on this. Now shake hands and that's that. We got bigger fish to fry with those goddamn Irish."

A unique thing about a crew is being a part of a thing, while being apart from most everything else. And part of being apart is looking and acting the part. For our part, we became fast learners.

Our crew had been legendary in high school. But school was out, so kids' games were a part of the past. Our newest paradigm shift: we had become adults with legal expectations. One law had to do with consensual sex with a female before her 18th birthday. We could be charged with Carnal Knowledge, or even Statutory Rape. The way priorities broke down for us was this: brothers, sex, drugs and reputations. Fuck laws.

Yet in one day we became too old to have sex with other teenagers, unless we waited to give that same girl the *treatment* on the day of her 18th birthday. In that case, we would be regarded as studs to be admired. Like a Cinderella chastity belt, pussy miraculously transformed from an undeveloped organ to juicy womanhood in just one tick past midnight – truly a miracle.

Another is that we could legally buy 3.2 beer; not that we ever concerned ourselves with trivial things like legalities. The way we had it figured, we had grown old enough to do prison time and slaughter Viet Cong, yet were still too young to vote for those who sent us to jails and wars. Those bully tactics just added to our bitterness. No more detention home, prison was next. So turning 18 proved laws did affect us in some ways, whether we liked it or not – and we didn't.

Our reaction was to buzz and bang harder than ever. *Self-destruction? Sure, I'll take two.* We had reputations to maintain and priorities to fulfill. We strove for Neighborhood Hall of Fame status. Our top three categories were: Baddest Motherfucker; Craziest Son-of-a-Bitch; Coolest Bastard. Being solid wasn't a category because it was a given. Other than the Neighborhood and status, not much else mattered except our crew and immediate family. All else was bullshit. Collinwood became a training camp for organized crime and deviant behavior, and we proved to be honor students.

We bought into selective bullshit because we wanted to. We were self-deluded, not stupid. Repetitive mistakes got added to the tab, paid later with rationalization, justification, minimization and denial. Because we brought reality down through our own filters clogged with psychoactive corrosion, tinted eyes showed what appeared to be growth in the fog. Semi-sobriety or garden-variety addiction? Genetic imbalance or substance-induced psychosis? How does one distinguish maladies from madness and reasons from excuses while spun in a web of surrealism? *Fuck-it.*

CH VII: FUNERALS & LAW-DOGS

Benny and I spotted two cute girls as we cruised through Five Points. With his styled hair, *Ban Lon* shirt and tailor-made pants, Benny explained, "No offense, *coom*, but let me do the talking here'. You look like a caveman. You'll just scare 'em away."

He stepped out on spit-shined shoes, and with a disarming smile held open the door as he offered, "Whoever's game to get fucked-up today, hop on in. It's our treat."

While he drove, one of them said from the back seat, "She's Carly and I'm Maureen Kelly. Maybe you know my brothers. They're badass dudes. My uncle is Mick Kelly. I'm sure you've heard of him. He rules all these Collinwood *dagos*."

Benny said, "Nope. We're from Little Italy. Never heard of 'em. Are you Irish?"

The freckle faced one continued, "She isn't but I am. Why, is there a problem?"

"Nope, no problem. In fact, I like Irish people. I heard Irish girls like to party. Is that straight? How about we go buy some hooch and find a nice parking spot?"

Carly's olive complexion complimented a virginal smile. She answered while she shook long black hair out of her face, "Sure thing, man. Let's get crazy."

I got out and sat on the grass with Maureen and our half gallon of Chianti. Benny crawled in the backseat with the cuter of the two and a six-pack of P.O.C.

Tired of her droning on about The Mick and her brothers, and especially about having my hands moved every time I cupped one of her tits, I wanted to leave but Maureen insisted she wasn't going anywhere till the bottle was empty.

I walked to the car and said, "Fuck this. I'm ready to roll. Let's boogie." Instead of waiting for an answer I opened the car door and asked, "What the fuck is this shit?"

Carly pleaded while Benny tugged her hair and back-handed her face. "Suck my cock you fuckin' slut. Open that pig mouth while you still have some teeth left."

I urged, "Come-on *coom*, it's my turn. You go drink with that other whore."

He laughed: "Yeah, you're right. Fuck this uptight cunt. Where's the jug?"

Carly, with eye make-up smeared over flushed cheeks begged, "I'll stop crying, okay? I'll be quiet; I promise. I'll do anything you want. Just please, don't hit me."

I held her trembling hands and spoke slowly and softly to the beautiful girl, "Listen to me and do exactly what I say. Get dressed right now." I released her hands and instructed, "You wait here. I'll be right back. Don't budge till I say so, okay?"

Benny seemed amused by stories from Paddy's red-headed sister, who sat on the ground next to his feet and blabbed about her gangster brothers and their friends.

"I need to be somewhere," I urged. "Let's drop these bitches where we found 'em so I can tend to a piece of business. There's still enough time if we move now."

Carly wiped her face with tissues from her purse. She sat like stone while Maureen chatted and drank, oblivious to what had just transpired in that same backseat.

We dropped them off where we met. That time they exited behind me. When Carly took my hand and squeezed I got a glimpse into the most fragile soul I'd ever seen. My heart ached as she wept, "I'll never forget you . . . I owe you . . . I love you."

As they walked away Benny spit a loogie on Maureen's back and called out "Hey, Maureen, if you don't like it go tell your bad-ass brothers. And just remember this, Carly, you owe me one. Now I got a case a the blue-balls, ya fuckin' selfish bitch."

That day I wanted to kill Benny. Instead, I rewarded myself with an 18th birthday present. Fingers and I set out for Sandusky, because tattoos were still illegal in Cleveland.

As we drove I complained, "This is pure bullshit, plain and simple! We gotta drive all the way out to this shithole. Can you believe gettin' inked in Cleveland is actually against the law? What the fuck is that all about, anyways?"

"Fuck these rules, *coom*. That just makes me want one even more."

Upon arrival we found rules painted on the wall: "No tattoos given to drunks. No work finished on people who act up. No tattoos above the collarbone, beyond the wrists or below the ankles. All work must be paid for in advance. Cash only. No refunds."

He said, "Read these rules here, pal. If you agree to the terms you have to sign waivers, and then I need to see some folding money. Have you fellas been drinking?"

"Drinking? Forget booze, man. We're into synthetics," I assured him.

"I don't want any trouble, pal. I'm a God-fearing man who abides the law."

"Oh yeah? Well I'm sick of all these goddamn rules for every swingin' dick," Fingers said. "There's rules for being born, for living and even for getting buried. Now there's rules for tattoos? You know what? Mother-fuck rules and rule-makers. Hey! Try to focus at this right here, pal. See? Is this cash green enough to change any rules?"

"Okay pal," he said. "It's your skin. Just don't come back complaining you were drunk and regret your tattoo. Pay me first and I'll get to work."

Blind in one eye with missing appendages on the artist's strong hand, a bucket of water sat next to him colored from various inks mixed with blood of previous clients.

"Hold-up. Is that well water in there?" Fingers asked the illustrated Cyclops.

He stared between us, holding a sponge dripping blue water: "You drunk, pal?"

"Ah, fuck-it. This guy seems crazy enough to be trusted. Lets go for it, Jackie."

I asked, "You got any stars? Let's see 'em. I need a special kind – a pentagram."

"A pentacle is a religious symbol, pal, like a cross," he said. "You don't seem very religious to me, fella. Are you sure about this?"

"No crosses. I need a pentagram on the palm of my hand like the Wolfman had. Don't get me wrong. All that Satanist crap is as much bullshit as all the other lies. I just like that kind 'cause it's a big *Fuck You* to society. So gimme one a them."

Quasimodo with his bucket of blood said, "No can do, pal. I'm not getting involved in any of that stuff. But I'll put a pentagram on your shoulder. It's a sign that shows your spirit is mixed with the four elements. It's spiritual, but not religious."

After he spritzed my raw tattoo with alcohol he asked, "You ready yet, pal?"

"Yeah," Fingers answered. "I wanna heart with a ribbon that says Mom & Dad."

"Smart thinkin', *coom*," I agreed. "They can't get mad about that."

My mother used my fresh ink as a new weapon. "Look at him. I can't believe a thing like him came from me. Say something, Jack!" My father ignored it, even though I sat right across from him with my sleeve rolled up at the dinner table. To him it was invisible ink.

People had warned us, "Don't get a tattoo; you'll be sorry." They were right. We were sorry we hadn't gotten more, but that was easily amended. We returned with a stencil I drew: a hand of six cards, all aces of clubs, inked on our chests with the words *Royal Flush* underneath. For the next piece I planned to get Maggie's name. Two weeks before the wedding we got into another fight over her parents. We were just two scared kids trying to play house, so we looked for an excuse to bail and both did just that.

Newly acquired freedom of adulthood also introduced another run-in with the law. Carly invited me to her junior prom, so I rented a tux. The night before the event I got a call from a drug dealer in Little Italy we named Astroboy. He was the crazy little brother to a lunatic named Joey Cagootz – which was why he was allowed to deal drugs.

"Jackie," Astro slurred. "I'm laid up in this motel with a brick of herb, a jar of downers and two hot, naked mammas. Help a brother out, *coom*. I'm all fucked out."

"Sure thing, Astro. Anything for a friend, right? We're on our way."

Yugo drove Eggs and me to a motel room that smelled like a Haitian funeral. Astro, all thick-tongued and droopy eyed invited, "Help yourselves, my cosmic brothers."

Eggs shook his head: "No thanks. I'm engaged. You go ahead. I'll just watch."

I dipped into Astro's drugs and those two girls to enjoy my first French *sangwitch*. Next, Yugo got double-teamed by them. We left Astro passed-out with two naked girls curled-up together in the other bed. I needed rest for my prom date.

Fingers called early: "Loony Lonnie nabbed Eggs and Astro for statutory rape. They got 'em both locked up. I'm comin' over now. We gotta get the fuck outta town."

"No way. It can't be them, 'cause they were with me last night."

"This ain't a rumor, Jackie. Eggs phoned me from jail. I'll be right there."

I told my father: "Hey, Pop, just a heads-up so Mom don't flip her wig again. Me and Fingers are gettin' dropped off at a hunting cabin for awhile, but there's no phone."

The next day we hitchhiked to town to call home from a payphone. My father said, "The cops know you were there. They're keeping Egan and that lunatic kid, Astroboy, locked up till you turn yourself in. What do you need me to do?"

"Don't do anything yet, Pop. Just make sure Mom don't go berserk again."

I asked Fingers, "Why ain't Yugo caught? What's up with that shit?"

"Let's drop these *Black Beauties* to shake our hangovers. Then we'll hitchhike back to Cleveland to find out why his luck's so goddamn good."

My father drove me to the jail. The cops kept their word but then locked me up. Wired from the speed, I paced in my tiny cell. *Yugo poured the cock to those bitches, too. We all saw it. Why didn't he catch a case? Nobody's that goddamn lucky.*

A detective, and a mad-dog cop we called "Loony Lonnie" (behind his back), brought me to an office and a cup of coffee. Caffeine was one of the last things I needed while cranked up on speed. The dick provided a big, greasy Cheerio he referred to as a doughnut. The deep-fried flour stuck to the roof of my mouth so I asked for more coffee.

"Sure, Jackie, whatever you need," said the detective while Lonnie glared. "We know you're too smart for those guys. Don't kid yourself; they're not your friends." He took a pad of paper from a briefcase: "We have statements implicating you. Now you have a chance to protect yourself. We just want to help, kid." He set the pad facedown on his desk. "Now tell us who else was there and you can get bailed out, too."

"What's the paper say? Who signed? Let's see."

"They both gave verbal statements. Your *friend*, Egan, signed his."

"Eggs? Really? Okay . . . Fine. Let's see a signature. I know what his writing looks like." I reached out and flipped it over to find a blank page. "Fucking cops..."

Lonnie growled, "We ain't showin' you shit, you little cocksucker! A little punk like you'll be real popular in Mansfield Reformatory, because that's your next stop."

"Just like I figured . . . more bullshit. But consider the source. Right, Lonnie?"

The *good* cop said, "Your friends gave you up as soon as you weren't around to defend yourself. How else could we get your name? Why protect those rats?"

"It's not about them. But I don't expect you to understand *Omerta*. It's the Sicilian code of honor. Hey, can I ask youse guys for one simple favor?"

"Sure. Lonnie told us you're okay. Tell us what you need and we'll see."

"I need to go back to my cell. Oh yeah, and next time I'll need chocolate milk, not this shit coffee. And another thing . . . But wait. First, what I really need right now is—"

Lonnie yanked me from my seat: "We're not fuckin' around, anymore! Sign a statement right now or die of old age getting ass-raped. Or maybe your family will luck out and you'll get shanked in the chow line. You're a disgrace to the Italian race."

"Me? What about you, man? Did you believe I was stupid enough to trust you? Hey! I'll bet your kids're real proud of you, huh? Nice fuckin' nickname, Loony Tunes."

He threw me across the room into a water cooler. My head smacked a five-gallon glass jug. The *good* cop offered, "Speaking of names, just *whisper* the name of your friend, Benny. Just say it was him and you're home tonight."

"Fuck that. I'm done talkin'. I got nothin' to say unless it's to my lawyer."

My father retained a gangster attorney who told me, "When the girls left that room they got picked up by a patrol car and were threatened with arrest for prostitution. They got scared and told a story about a drug dealer and claimed they had *sex with men*."

"That figures. It's a great way to get out of trouble and have stories for their friends. I guess they forgot how they asked me to shower with them while they soaped each other's tits. Or how about when they went down on each other in front of everyone? It must have slipped their minds when *they* asked if they could double-team me."

The judge declared, "I'm suspending sentence in lieu of three years probation."

According to my lawyer, "Your Slovenian friend didn't snitch. The cops don't know Yugo's street name because he's a nobody. Those girls were so high they probably confused the name *Yugo* with the term *coom*. Who knows? Regardless, you're free."

Still a teen and single, I pondered injustices of our legal system while I puffed a fatty with my hand on Carly's 17-year old breast. By then she had been set-up by her best friend, Maureen, and raped by Paddy and Doyle Kelly, so she stayed far away from Five Points and under my protection.

She asked, "Why does possession of a safe drug that grows wild, or fondling an inviting woman's body, send peaceful people to violent prisons? How can that possibly solve anything or help anyone? I just don't get it, Jackie. Do you?"

Hanging out with Carly meant less corner time with my club brothers. On a night when they congregated without me, I was told Eggs waved bye as he reached for the cop car's rear door. Lonnie's partner, O'Reilly, told him, "We need to cuff you first. Come on, Egan, work with us. You know, protocol and all that horse-shit. We'll bring you right back." Lonnie and his sycophant hauled our main gorilla off for interrogation.

Nino claimed they went right back to smoking weed, fists up to Eggs who smiled in the back seat and nodded his head. He said they shouted after the cop car, "Don't let your meat loaf, youse fuckin' assholes. We'll smoke one right here for you, Eggs."

Eggs later reported, "They shackled me to a cell and beat me with nightsticks. They told me if I didn't help them set-up Uno they'd snuff me, plant a smoking gun on me and then write on my toe-tag that I'm a fag. Then they made me walk home."

The next night, Yugo and Poochie were arrested for armed robbery. Benny got hauled in for questioning. During another drunk-a-thon, Poochie confessed to Yugo, "I might have slipped when them pigs were beatin' me. But it's cool; I didn't mention a last name. I'd never do any weak shit like that. I should file a lawsuit against those pricks."

Based on that information we told Inky to hold a birthday for himself, even though it wasn't anyone's birthday, and to invite Yugo and Poochie.

Fingers told Yugo, "Make sure your buddy comes. Tell him Benny's outta town."

At the party Inky said, "Go upstairs, Yugo. We got two spic whores paid-up for the night. They're up there doin' *sangwitches* right now."

Inky's hall light was burned out or missing. Seated in a wooden chair in an empty room, Fingers instructed him to enter. We drank beer and smoked cigarettes till Fingers ordered Yugo, "Go back downstairs and ask Poochie who else wants double pussy."

Yugo groaned to the downstairs troops "I'm all fucked out, fellas. Go on up. Or are youse cowards all scared of a little snatch? It ain't got teeth, youse fuckin' babies."

A drunken Poochie announced, "Fuck-it. I'll try both a them sluts on for size."

Benny crept through the back with his trusty neon bat. As Poochie rounded the landing, Gus yanked a burlap sack over his head and flung him down the steps. When he finally stopped screaming Benny turned the bat on Yugo. As we dragged Benny away he yelled, "After you tell those pigs you fucked-up you're gonna give me $1,000.00 cash!"

Benny's explanation was, "Yeah, I smashed your brother-in-law. So what?"

"Don't ever put me in this position with my wife again," Eggs said.

"What? You choosin' that bust-out and his rat friends over us?"

"It's not like that, Benny. That kid's her brother, and I can vouch he didn't rat."

"Okay, Eggs. If you want to be responsible for him, then it's on you now."

"Whatever, just stay out of it, Benny, and leave Yugo alone. I'll handle Poochie."

Poochie's new story became, "I got mixed up. It's a guy kind a looks like Benny but ain't him. Benny's no thief far as I know. It was just me and Yugo pulled that job."

Yugo had legal fees so he entered an ice-cream parlor with a crisp fifty dollar bill. He ordered two hotdogs with everything.

The waitress said, "Sorry, I can't take your order unless you have something smaller. My boss will be super pissed if I give you all our smaller money."

"No problem, doll. I need two male banana splits – the kind with nuts. While you're at it, gimme two large malts and two a them big bags a chips ova there. I'm in a bit of a rush, doll. So make it happen, okay sweetie-pie?" and handed her the fifty.

She sighed, "Okay, I'll do it for you. But I hope I don't get into trouble."

When she opened the register Yugo slid a pistol from under his shirt. "Okay. Real nice now, hon. Hand me all the green money and nobody gets shot today." The girl put his fifty in the register and slammed the drawer. He warned, "There ain't no witnesses in here, sweetheart. Gimme the money so nobody has to die," as he aimed the gun at her.

"Go fuck yourself, you fucking bastard! I was even thinking about giving you my phone number. Now you went and ruined everything. Fuck you!"

He wore his cunning look, "You know what? Me and you'll split this cash right down the middle. Fuck your boss. He pays you shit. This is between us darlin', okay?"

"That's it, you fucking moron. You expect me to rip-off my own family? My manager is my brother. I hate you, you stupid prick!"

"Okay, sorry, darlin'. I didn't know it was family. Charge me for everything and take a nice tip for yourself. Okay? I'm real sorry here."

"No! Not now," she screamed through tears. "You went and fucked everything up! I'm calling the law!" Because he hadn't worn a mask that girl clearly saw his face.

The next night we recognized some other faces as a car sped through Collinwood as if it were on an interstate. A kelly green GTO crashed a stop sign and hit a kid on a shiny bicycle. It went straight up in the air and the boy rolled over the top of the car.

We yelled, "Wait up! This kid needs a hospital and we don't have a ride."

Rather than a remorseful motorist it was Frankie Fazule and the Kelly brothers. Frankie shouted, "Hog-balls, youse fuckin' faggots," fired shots at us and fishtailed away.

The street lights were on, so the boy was late and his new bike was wrecked. Chain guard dragged on the brick street, handlebars twisted like pasta, one pedal reflector glared like a possum's eye from where it had fallen. As we ran after Frankie, a conservatively dressed man slowed next to us in a station wagon with fake wood-paneled sides.

Fingers shouted, "Emergency! Pull over!" The driver braked at the curb.

Once inside Gus explained, "Some smash-and-dash asshole ran into a little kid on his bike. The one we're chasing after did it. Follow that GTO!"

I rode shotgun, with Fingers and Gus at our backs. The driver, whom none of us recognized, mumbled, "I'm sick of these drunken drivers. My kids play not far from here, and they probably ride their bikes in the street, too. This neighborhood used to be safe."

We saw Frankie had turned down an industrial road and slowed. As soon as we were within range I drew a snub-nosed .38 and stretched out the window. When its rear windshield shattered, Frankie zigzagged to a clean escape on a straightaway.

Our driver asked breathlessly, "Now what?" as I tucked away my pistol.

Gus answered, "Fuck-it, let's just go back. We're out of ammo. We can't catch these assholes, anyway. But they won't be back anytime soon. They know better."

Our driver cautioned, "Listen to me, guys. Don't smoke any cigarettes unless there's writing on them, okay?" Then he smiled, gave a wink and puttered away.

Gus laughed, "Oh well, at least we didn't have to kill anybody yet tonight."

Later that night Rico and his little brother found us at The Inn: "We just had a slug-out with Frankie and his *mick* buddies in our front yard. Frankie emptied a pistol at our house, so my dad blasted a shotgun at their car. They promised to be right back."

Gus said, "I guess I spoke too soon." We hopped in his car and followed the boys to where we found their parents munching popcorn, watching television with a 12 gauge leaned against the father's recliner. Rico switched off the TV to give us more details.

Gus overturned the front-room coffee table for a barricade, its top against the picture window facing the street as a shield. He and Fingers positioned themselves on the floor behind it and lit up a joint. I sat on the sofa to further question the parents.

Rico's father left and then returned with a hunting rifle. He asked, "Who wants this?" We drew pistols, which till that moment had been concealed under flannel shirts.

Their mother brought a platter of salami sandwiches for homeland security. "I wish I had something better. The coffee's fresh and the beer's nice and cold. Oh! And no smoking that stuff around Rico's little brother. You kids think you're big shots smoking grass. You don't realize there's marijuana in it. That's something we don't go for around here. They say grass makes people demonic."

"No offense," I tried to explain. "We won't smoke it here to respect your house. But the truth is we usually stay outta trouble with this stuff. It's when we drink that we get crazier. And yeah, we do know what's in this grass. It's called freedom."

"But it's a sin against our God and our country," she insisted. "Don't you kids value anything? I remember when you were an altar boy, Jackie. What happened? All you kids used to be sharp dressers. Now you look like beatniks with that hair and beards."

"We'd be a lot safer off in our country if this weed was legal and booze got outlawed," I said. "And no disrespect, but as far as religion goes: it's just opinions. Nobody's right or wrong when it comes to philosophy. Nobody can prove any of it."

"But *pot* smoking is just wrong, Jackie. That's why it's against the law!"

"Yeah, I agree with Jackie," said Enrico's younger brother. "The only reason this stuff's a problem is because some idiots said it was."

"You better watch it, junior," his mother warned.

"Tell you what," Enrico said. "We won't judge you just because you don't agree with our generation. So why hold it against us because we have different ideas? Come-on, Ma. You've known them since they were kids. You know they aren't demonic."

"Yeah, we're still us," I agreed. "Just a little hairier and with a few skin illustrations, is all. The reason we smoke this stuff is because we like the spiritual place this weed brings to us. It's like a religious experience, only better. It's spiritual, because it anoints us with mind-meld."

"All I know is if God wanted us to smoke grass he'd make it legal," she sighed.

"Okay," I laughed. "You're right. I'm gonna shut up now. Let's just be glad we didn't have to shoot anybody tonight. Then we wouldn't have time to worry about such important things like which religions have more juice with God, and illegal weeds. Anyways, since Pazzo scored us these sweet jobs at the Collinwood Yards, we're hard workers into different things."

Penn Central, later named Conrail, provided a taxable wage. When Neighborhood guys came to work sick, tired, too buzzed, or brought cases of beer into cabooses or shanties, other workers ignored it or used with us. But it all worked out. We covered for them and even signed their time slips when necessary.

Besides all that, and marking off whenever we felt like it, there were other perks. Boxcars sealed with federally protected metal bands offered a challenge for drunken gamblers into bookies and loan sharks, or players on the sly. So when shipping manifests were not available, federal seals and olfactory senses enabled us to shop at the all night rail-mart. Old-timers wanted quantities of razorblades and golf balls. We didn't shave or golf.

Instead, we walked tracks to sniff for boxcars full of new car tires. Eggs kept a van for whenever we hit the jackpot. When one of us scored, we divided profits. Another market was brass ingots, sold to a salvage yard owner who crushed stolen cars from insurance cases. He got paid for not looking in any trunks.

The railroad also could be treacherous. Snow and ice in brutally cold wind made climbing metal ladders on moving cars and throwing frozen switches more creative. During summer we dealt with electrical storms or worse. At times raw animal hides were hauled in gondolas. They attracted swarms of meat eating hornets and flies. Stench from those rotting skins was reminiscent of the dreaded *meat-wagon*.

Worse yet, rats patrolled the yards at night in search of edible cargo. Detected by squeaks and scurrying, black, beady eyes could be seen reflected off moonlight. Corn and soybeans accumulated on sidings from swaying cars or in mounds between rails from loose hatches beneath hoppers. Grains fermented when rain mixed with summer heat. Intoxicated rats grew fearless. The railroad provided lanterns, flares and elastic straps to wrap around cuffs, to prevent rats from crawling up pant legs. When surrounded by rats, we lit a fusee and flicked scalding, liquid sulfur at them. It was an entertaining job for we stoners.

CH VIII: DRUGS: THE WAR ON MINDS

Alcoholics drink to ease psychological pain, to get numb and forget. My friends and I maintained a steady buzz at maximum capacity to hone enough meanness with the correct amount of darkness to stay balanced, but not to forget – never that. I wanted to see and remember between blackouts and fuck-ups – to make sense of it all. Yet for some odd reason the higher I got and the longer I stayed buzzed my luck got even worse.

Uno preached, "Addiction is suicide for cowards too weak to live and too scared to die. That's why our people sell drugs. It's like a public service for gettin' rid of scum that fuck-up the gene pool. You can't trust a junkie, politicians or cops, colored people or women – period. Our kind sticks together or we fall apart." He spoke, we paid attention.

Before Chink's brother got sent to Vietnam he told Chink, "I'll be sending home statues packed full of *China White*. You peddle most of the dope, but far away from the Neighborhood so Uno and them don't clip you and take our shit. Stash the profits and squirrel away whatever you don't sell. You can dabble but be careful. This shit's primo. If I make it back home we'll split everything 50/50. If I don't come back it's all yours."

Chink sold enough heroin to Nerk's junkie crew to buy a Panhead and a game-tested dog. The rest went up our noses. His brother returned from Nam to find the bike wrecked, dog stolen, unsold dope and money gone. He stood in disbelief with a shattered Buddha statue in his hand and asked, "How can something like this happen?"

Chink laughed, "You send me pure heroin every month and tell me not to get addicted? But hey, fuck-it. At least now you got no worries with the law, right? I swear to those fucked-up Buddha's you sent home, I did you a favor. I saved your dumbass from gettin' all strung-out. You should thank me, ya stingy bastard."

"You did me a favor? Is that what you're saying to me right now? I get shot at so I can commit postal felonies every month, and now you're gonna swear to Buddha you saved *my* dumbass? I'm a *stingy bastard*? You aren't even my brother any more. And you forgot something real important, dumbass. I've been killing motherfuckers for the past year. You're gonna pay me back every penny or swear to Buddha I'll snuff you, too."

From that incident the term "Swear to Buddha" was coined and became Collinwood jargon which held more meaning than its predecessor. Contents of those Buddha's, along with local acid, helped change the temperature of our neighborhood.

Enrico, an honors chemistry major with a year of college under his belt, smeared Vitamin-C tablets with brown lysergic acid diethylamide-25. We dubbed his product Brown Smudge. It nudged us through doors that once opened couldn't be closed all the way, as black lights illuminated the pathetic struggle of others.

A version of consequence became tepid, tempers raged even hotter, and impatience with others chilled like hot ice. As with the math teacher in the parking lot ordeal, a yardmaster and I had made a deal at the beginning of my shift. If we got our work done, he agreed we could leave early so I could return a borrowed car. As it turned out, I got fired for choking that yardmaster when he tried to weasel out of our deal. I might not have over-reacted as violently had I not been dope sick and hung-over. Regardless, that time off work provided me an opportunity of a lifetime.

Bee-Bee Balls still lived with his parents and had money saved from his job so I suggested, "Let's get our heads together West Coast style." On the way to California we met genuine redskins who freely roamed the countryside. Well . . . sort of free.

Somewhere out in New Mexico or Arizona on old Route 66, on a hot morning in some desolate patch of nothing, we spotted a biker wearing a shiny white helmet lying facedown in the dirt. A white Honda Dream lay about 30 yards from its rider.

As we sped past Bee-Bee said, "If I was any kind a man I'd stop to see if that guy's okay," as he watched through his rearview mirror in morbid fascination.

"Pull over, fat-ass, and I'll check." Instead, Bee-Bee backed up all the way to the bike but stayed in his car, still watching through his rearview mirror like it was television.

"Hey man, you okay?" I asked the guy. No reply. I nudged a leg with my boot. No response. I grabbed a new jeans jacket. No reaction. I turned him over to find a helmet full of ground meat where his face should have been. He had no features or pulse.

"Let's split. There ain't nothin' out here but sand and heat, yet this guy's coolin' off already. Help me look for some ID so we can make a call in the next town."

"I ain't touchin' that thing, Jackie. Did you see its face? Let's get outta here."

I lifted a wad of hundreds from his wallet. "He won't need this where he's goin'. Hey, I gotta tell you somethin' right here and now, Bee-Bee. You oughta think about growin' some balls. And another thing: You're still a fat, Bee-Bee Balls motherfucker."

"Why you gotta say this for? Besides, I weigh less than you now."

"That's not the point, fat-boy, and you know this. We're talkin' attitude here."

"Well, what exactly is your point then?"

"My point is just this. You can weigh less than Gandi and you'll still be a fat-ass."

"Well you're not perfect. You're crazy, Jackie. How are you gonna fix that?"

"Yeah, I'm crazy for being all the way out here with you, ya fat fuck."

"Why you gotta start? Do I judge you for robbing dead guys? Do I tell you it's a sin when you say you're an atheist? Anyways, fuck-it. It's already done. You hungry?"

That night we rented a room. No pool or restaurant, not even a TV or phone, but it did have a bathroom, a bed and a cute desk clerk who called herself "Flower."

"Hi. They call me Cool Ricky. This here is Mad-Jack. We're from Cleveland."

Once in that shitty room I said, "Cool Ricky and Mad-Jack, huh? You been up too long, and I'm freaked from all that gruesome shit on the road, Cool Ricky. So the bed's mine, and your skinny butt can go in that corner to get familiar with that cot."

While dozing we heard a soft rap at the window. Bee-Bee pretended to be asleep. I flipped out my knife and flung open the door to an empty parking lot behind our clerk who smiled me fully awake. She eased past the blade and locked the door behind her.

The longhaired girl sat on our floor in lotus position and said, "My shift just ended. You dudes ready to party?" I moved close to make sure I had first shot to peel off those tight, faded jeans. Flower wore a low-cut midriff top, so I had a good view of her slender waist and firm tits. She asked, "You hippies about ready for a California dream?"

I responded in the best hipster slang I could muster at that late hour, "Sure, baby, that's what Clevelanders are all about. You wanna get down? Let's get funky."

She slid her hand into her Levi's and pulled out a napkin. In it were three tiny purple pills. By then the fake sleeper was like a cat by an electric can opener.

"Have you dudes ever done real *Purple Haze*? Dr. Leary made this stuff and it's right here in Greater L.A. It's everywhere out here, man. You still want to get down? Have you ever been experienced? Come on, dudes, let's get psychedelicized."

She wet a fingertip and lifted a pill, wrapped her lips around her finger and slid it in ever so slow and swallowed. Then she dipped her tongue on the napkin and came up with another. She pushed it in my mouth and swirled to be sure I'd keep the stuff dreams are made of. Her kiss tasted like grape candy. Next came Bee-Bee's turn. Nourishment got deposited into hungry mouths. We let them dissolve as we prepared for flight.

I passed Bee-Bee's sack of weed to Flower and asked, "Can you roll, sweetie?"

She produced papers and twisted up bombers in strawberry and banana wraps. With candy-flavored drugs, we sat while the fabled acid excited exhausted brains.

"Let's take these over to my room," she offered.

"California's already awesome and we just got here!" Bee-Bee squealed.

Upon arrival I noted, "Your room looks like a Kurosawa movie. So what's with the Buddhist temple and those candles in a half-circle? And what about that platter with the apple on it? It can't be real, right? Check it out, Bee-Bee. It's too perfect enough."

"I'm one with the apple, Jackie. It's the most beautiful thing I've ever seen."

Her brace of candles flickered at sporadic intervals in her otherwise dark room while we communicated in silent language till Ricky said, "Fuckin'-aye right. This Dr. O'Leary sure knows his stuff. We've finally arrived, Jackie. Everything we ever wanted is right here. We can finally be free." *Whoa, what?* "We can be whatever we want out here." *Is this asshole is a closet homo?* "I don't know about you, Jackie, but I'm starvin'. Let's just put a little something on the stomach, just so we can relax."

With legs folded like good stoners, we ignored him and reverted to mad topics only *heads* can appreciate. When someone hit on a deep subject she'd say, "Outta sight, dude," or "Far-fucking-out, man," or "Right-on with the right-on," or "You cats are groovy to the max." Or she would pose a rhetorical question like, "Can you dig it, man?"

I added some Neighborhood lingo: "Cleveland's tits-up, but so far L.A.'s the real deal. These Cali bust-outs got one sweet-ass scene out here, Flower. Swear to Buddha, little Flower, this groove out here's as tight as Collinwood pussy."

Flower flinched when I mentioned Buddha. She flipped on a strobe light that made the entire room pulsate to a Ravi Shankar album. Our entire world became a monochromatic scheme. She walked backwards into the bathroom and then came out topless. Everything in the room was black or white, except that apple and her areolas. Hand still on the doorknob, she backed in and walked out – door closed and reopened – over and over again as the sitar and strobe pounded like a metronome in our shared mind. We became transfixed by iridescent nips glowing hot-pink beacons.

"Check it out, Bee-Bee. That door's the center of this universe. Those glowing titties are the main artery of life. Feel it? I don't ever wanna leave this room, man."

Bee-Bee leaped up, snatched the apple off its platter and took a bite just as she walked out. She screamed and knelt, face on her knees: "Hare mothers – Krishna fuckers – Hare mother fuckers," as that sitar squalled colorful notes across the strobe lit room.

"Look . . . See these heartbeats inside this apple, Jackie? Watch how they're getting bigger and then slower. See 'em? But I promise I won't eat no more of it. Just talk her back down to a safe place before she flips completely out on us."

"Too late, man. She's already there. We ain't gettin' laid now, topless or not. Let's head back to our room so we can pretend to sleep for a few hours."

Eyes closed, I could still see the apple's rabbit hole blink in and out of reality.

At daybreak we continued our voyage into homes that smelled of rawhide, crash pads inhabited by strangely familiar people who made multicolored candles and fast friends. In relationships where last names were inconsequential, we became brothers and sisters for a night. Men were peaceful and considerate. Delicate women wore earthy fragrances and flowers laced through braded hair during journeys taken without leaving a room.

Within days we had been accepted as part of their community, but after a few months of floating around in heaven we went broke. The drive back was a grueling three days of dreading plastic people in fake places. My coming home present was a shake-down. As I cruised in my father's Olds 88, wearing green John Lennon Granny Glasses, I got nudged over by Loony Lonnie and O'Reilly.

"We know you just got back from the West Coast, so don't try anything cute." They slammed me against the car, yanked out the back seat, rifled through the glove box and trunk, then threw my father's seat and belongings on the street. Lonnie added, "You lucked out this time," punched me in the stomach and they zoomed away laughing.

Astroboy pulled up and asked, "Why you campin' out here, cuz? Get your stuff back in your dad's ride and drop it off. We'll go over to my crib. I got some cid."

"Yeah, dig it. Let's go get Chilly."

My longhaired friend always wore dark shades and love beads around his neck, faded Levis and a tie-dyed tee-shirt, and steel toed boots – just in case.

"I found a *collective consciousness* test we can do, Astro."

By then Astro hallucinated even when he wasn't on drugs so Chilly and I decided to use the space-cadet for a psychedelic experiment. In another room I wrote, "Why bother with a kangaroo court? We're all slaughtered like pigs, anyways."

It wasn't anything I'd heard, just some off-the-wall piece of nothing from the collective. I reentered to sit and smoke. The *hookah* hoses drew up brassy resin from stale wine while I tried to think of nothing other than those written words hidden in my pocket.

I said, "Write what I'm thinking." Tuning forks resonated waves of perception.

Chilly's note read, "No trial, no jury, just punishment. Nobody cares anyway."

Astro had scrawled a cartoon of a tattooed long-hair that looked like him. Beneath the childish drawing he scribbled, "Kill . . . Kill . . . Kill. . . . . . Fuckin' pigs, kill 'em all."

I offered up my note, "Why bother with a kangaroo court? We're all slaughtered like pigs, anyway." I asked, "You figure we'll find the *Click* if we ever quit tripping?"

Astro said, "Yeah, man, it's the mind-meld. It's everywhere, cuz. It's normal."

Chilly explained, "I'm not sure yet, bro-ham. Normal for me is LSD, THC. MDA, ESP, FTW or any other initials to experience another plane on some other dimension."

Just then Bee-Bee walked in, already tripping, face frozen with a cheesy grin. He asked, "Anybody hungry? Or is it just me?"

"Don't start, fat-boy," Astro warned. "Sit your lard-ass down. We're doin' mind-meld here."

The next morning we stopped at Royal Castle's in a nearby ghetto called Hough where we feasted on mini-burgers and paprika-coated home fries, washed down with frosted mugs of birch beer and freshly squeezed orange juice. Astro and Bee-Bee sat between us and quibbled like Jew great-grandmothers over a bin of damaged goods.

Bee-Bee Balls complained, "If you'd get a job, Astro, you can buy your own stuff and maybe even treat a friend to something once in awhile. Doesn't that make sense?"

"Why should I when I got bitches like you to buy shit? Now shut the fuck up so I can eat in peace. You're bringin' me down, Mini-Balls. You always gotta ruin my high?"

"Thanks a lot, Astro. That's what I get for taking care of a brother."

"Did I ask you to buy me anything? You know what? Fuck you and this greasy food. And don't ever call me brother again!" He continued to stuff his face and gulped down half-chewed gobs with slurps from a mug of pulpy orange juice. Then he told the waitress, "Squeeze me up another and give the bill to lard-ass here next to me."

While the waitress sliced oranges in half to make another batch, Chilly and I looked through what was visible. The *Click* sounded like an alarm. *Incoming. . .Dive!*

We jumped over the counter just as she spun with knife in hand. She also sensed danger but mistook the real threat for us gnarly looking freaks. She moved closer with the knife overhead, pointed to lunge, during a long, slow-motion instant, till the ground shuttered beneath us. That was when the building imploded.

We hopped back onto a floor shattered with strewn glass to avoid being stabbed. Bee-Bee hid under stools along the counter. Its plate-glass front was everywhere except where it had been. In its place was a beat-up looking car that had skidded to a stop inches from Astro. His fringed leather vest and tattooed chest framed a chromed automatic in his belt. Astro picked shards of glass from his plate as he continued to grind his free brunch.

"Wow, man; now that was far-fucking out. This is why I dig trip so much, bro-ham. This kind a shit never happens when we're straight. Fucking awesome!"

Bee-Bee crawled out panting like a sick dog: "Yeah . . . Dig it, bro-ham."

Astro, as if on cue, threw his plate behind him like a Frisbee and crashed it on the hood of the car inside the eatery. He declared, "I'm sick and tired a this bullshit!"

Bee-Bee gasped, "What the hell are you talking about? Why'd you just do that, Astro? Now I'll probably have to pay for that, too."

"Suck-off, fat-ass. I pay my own way. I just let punks like you come around so you can feel important."

I cracked up – *apple-cheeks* – couldn't stop laughing. We climbed over the car and ran to Bee-Bee's ride, laughing like imbeciles. Later we read in a newspaper that the driver had suffered a fatal heart attack and was dead when his car wrecked the building.

On the return trip back, Astro still needled Bee-Bee as he chauffeured us after buying everybody a meal. Bee-Bee steered with his knee; forearms up and hands forward like a cartoon hypnotist. He howled like a rhesus monkey. In the rearview mirror we saw a mad-clown's Halloween mask as he shrieked, "Hot red wax is squirtin' outta my fingertips. Check it out. It's goin' right through the windshield. Look! That's why I can drive with no hands. See? The red wax is steering my car. But then once it's outside it turns clear. Crazy, huh? How's it just do it like this?" When he noticed the gun he asked, "You see the red wax too, right Astro?"

Psycho-boy rubbed his pistol with a napkin. Its barrel pointed at Bee-Bee's stomach: "One thing I hate is a greedy fuck. Fat people are stink hogs. Hitler was right. Fat-asses should all be starved to death. Don't sweat it. I ain't gonna shoot. But anybody can fuck-up once in a while, right? Like when you was yellin' in my fuckin' ear while I'm tryin' to chill. Or, you drivin' with no hands while I'm holdin' this piece. I might feel bad if I accidentally shot you in that puss-gut 'cause of all your red wax and shit. Then we'd have to dig some big-ass hole to drop your pig body in before you stink even worse than you do now – all because you're a chump can't old his mud. Hey . . . Hold up . . . What's that? Whoa . . . You want me to zip you? 'Cause that's the vibe I'm gettin' here. You really want me to clip you, don't you? Am I right? Should I shoot?"

"You don't need to belittle people who look out for you, Astro-man, just so you can feel better about yourself. Bee-Bee's peaking-out too, so ease off. He's generous because he wants to, not 'cause he has to. He's our friend."

"Oh is that what *we* think, huh? So he's *our* friend? Is that it, guru?"

"Yeah, Astro," I chimed in. "If someone's nice to you then he needs to be fucked-over, right? Maybe we're idiots because we're stupid enough to be cool with a fuckin' psycho like you. But don't play that gun-threat game with us. We ain't playin' threat games today. Can you dig it? In fact . . . You know what? We oughta take that piece and smack the piss outta you with it while fat-ass watches. How's that sound? We're together, remember? We'd do the same for you, Astro. Even Bee-Bee would back your crazy ass – and you know this. You're way too high, man. Cool-out before you step on your own dick again. Why you gotta ruin our buzz? Am I right, bro-ham?"

"Right-on. If you squeeze one off in Bee-Bee, just remember you ain't fast enough to clip all of us. We're trippin' too, Astro-man. So how you gonna make us act back here? Now tuck that shit away before you go and fuck-up again."

Astro mumbled, "Oh, okay . . . I see. Now I'm gonna tell you some—"

Bee-Bee Balls squealed, "Holy fuck" and locked-up the brakes.

Astro crashed into the metal dashboard and dropped his gun. Chilly vaulted over the seat and almost through the windshield. He snatched it up, ejected the clip and dropped the gun where it had been while Astro checked his forehead for blood. Then we saw why Bee-Bee jammed the brakes. A huge, dun-colored canine with a mane like a lion posed in the middle of the street during broad daylight like he was directing traffic.

Bee-Bee asked, "Youse guys just see this shit, too? Or is that like the red wax? Beause that's the craziest dog I ever seen! Is that one of them Rockwilders?"

Astro reclaimed the gun and said, "No, you fuckin' dummy. It's one of them big, goddamn German-Pinschermans. Now just shut the fuck-up or no more weed! I'm vibing-out with the dog. One more word, fat-boy, and you're cut-off."

"Easy does it, Bee-Bee. Somebody's pet got loose is all. It's just a hybrid, right bro-ham? It's nothing as exotic as a Rottweiler, Astro-man."

"Yeah, whatever, wise man . . . I'm not talkin' to you. Hey, whale-ass, how about I stick a lead pill in *El Lobo* and you? If you don't ease off that gas pedal I'll put you both to sleep. Huh? . . . Say what? . . . What'd you think just then? . . . Oh, you think I won't? Okay. Come-on; test me. Both a youse mouthy motherfuckers can test *me*."

Bee-Bee drove slow and kept his mouth shut. Astro's one-sided conversation ended when he flipped us off and tucked away an empty gun.

Back in Collinwood, we ran into Toby. He let us know about a party at Inky's place. Nerk was already there with Enrico, who had pissed away a football scholarship and a 4.0 GPA to pursue hard drugs and card games at The Inn. Rico wasn't chemically dependant but he was addicted to the Neighborhood.

Although Nerk cooked-up in a spoon and drew up that Buddha juice into a new syringe, nobody was willing to let him do the honors with all his nervous tweaks.

I offered, "Seeing how I've given shots to dogs, I'm almost like a vet. I'll go first." At that time I didn't know the first thing about blood borne pathogens. Still, the idea of shared needles creeped me out unless it was for permanent skin desecration. As soon as I pressed the plunger I slurred, "Whoa…Okay, I get it. I understand now what the big deal is. I like this kind. Still tripping, and now this? Okay, *now* I've been experienced. But this shit's too good. I better not fuck with it too much. Yeah . . . I like this real good."

Within moments, each was absorbed in a personal dreamland. That Buddha-bump crept over and through, tingled archaic pleasure centers with glowing mini-orgasms.

The next day a bunch of us drove in Bee-Bee's car to Byron, Georgia for the Second Atlanta International Pop Festival, an extravaganza even bigger than Woodstock. Governor Lester Maddox warned that concert goers would be arrested, but over a half million adolescents showed up anyway. Because Nino began to indulge in a lot of his own product, he actually trusted Astroboy with a fresh batch of Brown Smudge for the concert. As with Chink and his brother, the deal was that profits were to be split 50/50.

The Allman Brothers opened the show while Astro sat on the trunk of a cop car that crept through the masses. Blessing those hungry birds, he dropped tabs into open mouths as the car slithered through hordes of naked worshipers. Nino, Chilly and I were so loaded we missed most of the bands. I remember crawling around on hands and knees with Chilly right next to me, rolling in mud and laughing like kids.

I'M JACK & I WANT MORE

As usual, Astro brought lunacy to another level. After mainlining speed all weekend, with no sleep for days, he took 35 hits of Brown Smudge as a single dose.

Enrico met some well dressed hippie who offered him a job running a nightspot called the Cheshire Club like the one in Cleveland. We smoked-up at Rico's apartment till we ventured out to absorb that club's southern aura. The doorman, Melvin, did security at night and by day was an Atlanta cop. Chilly and I checked IDs with him to verify ages of prospective sweeties. Restless, we ventured to a larger venue to hear a semi-famous band of little interest to us. I was restless till I met an Angel.

"Hi. I'm Jack. How about you?"

"I'm bored and I'm Angel," she slurred. "And this music is vomit. I'm not feeling the groove at all. Let's boogie. You game?"

I remembered our fathers' advice: "When you go somewhere with someone you stay together and leave together." But we made exceptions for cute girls with hot bodies.

"Game? Shit . . . That's exactly my game."

Chilly just shook his head with disgust. My hearing was notched back for how slow and deliberate she spoke. But her words weren't as important as the way she moved her mouth. I blazed-up a fatty pulled from behind an ear as she led me out to a car. I watched her suck dragon hits with pouty, wet lips wrapped around that dube.

Although that chick was blitzed on another level, I insisted she drive. Head on her lap, my hand found what was hidden under her shirt – braless, supple breasts. She drove way too fast for any person that high. The radio blasted a Moody Blues classic from the mid-1960s called "Go Now." Between her warm titty and that cool song, I floated on a cloud with a cherub. Angel swerved into a wild turn, down a side road and then yanked into a driveway. All I could think was: *More bumps . . . We need more bumps.*

She smashed into the front porch of a ranch-style house and spat, "Ah Shit! Oh well. Fuck-it. Come on in. We can worry about this in the morning. Let's get to bed. I need to lose these clothes. My pants are getting too tight. I think maybe I'm knocked-up."

"No expectations or commitment? Oh yeah, let's work it just like this."

We stumbled into a dimly lit house where I spotted a shirtless, skinny kid about my age, leaned against a refrigerator sipping from a gallon jug of milk. Without looking he belched and with a southern twang asked, "Who the fuck's this asshole?"

When I squeezed his neck and pounded his head into the door, milk splashed across floor tiles. "Guess what? You must not a read your horoscope today. Looks like you fucked-up again. Know what else? Now you gotta go stand outside. This shorthaired geek's callin' me an asshole? I got his asshole right here," I said as I grabbed my crotch.

He stumbled out into the dark mumbling, "Fuckin' asshole."

I locked the door like he was never there, then stretched out on a fold-out sofa as she peeled off her clothes. When I began the touchy-feely game she complained, "I'm too high right now." She snuggled up next to me and purred, "Let's wait till morning, okay?"

With Angel's head on my shoulder, thick hair cascaded over my left arm. "You're the type for me, baby," I grinned. "Shady and sultry, no guilt trips, insane father or crazy uncle to deal with. My Tessa's pure. You're pure trouble and on a dead-end street headed for nowhere." I rolled over and crashed hard from a heavy dosing of T&T.

I understood Tessa was too delicate and clean to be with the likes of a kamikaze pilot like me. Yet while I dreamed she urged: *Wake-up if you still want me, Jackie.*

I rolled back into daylight and thought: *Maybe my luck will change. Still curled into me but already dressed? Well, I guess I ain't gettin' fucked today.* "Hey, wake up, Angel." *Uh oh, did that asshole creep in here and waste this hot piece of ass? Nope, you're still warm.* I shook an arm but she didn't budge. *You OD'ed on me? Damn. Now what? But wait. What's that other noise ... So familiar...It's almost like—*

Her waking words were, "Time to boogie, man, like right now!"

Ahh, shit... A wave of nausea washed over me as I remembered her creative attempt to park. "Where's that fuckin' asshole, anyways?"

"Forget him. We don't live here. Come on, man, let's go."

I said, "Shit! I guess I'm the asshole, wide open and backed against a giant dildo."

In the light of morning the front of that expensive-looking home in its new development was caved in and wrapped around the nose of her car, a porch pillar across its crushed hood. We slid in the car through open windows. Somehow its motor cranked-over on the first turn. *Yes! We're alright.* She put the shifter in reverse and gassed it, but the rear wheels just spun and dug themselves deeper into freshly rolled sod.

"Push me out, dude. We need to get the fuck out of here – like pronto!"

I lifted the pillar and shoved it on the ground while she rocked the car forward to reverse. *Sirens . . . My luck's about to get worse – if that's even possible.*

As the car lurched out of its ruts, the porch collapsed just as we spotted flashers on the next road. I took off for woods behind the house. Never much of a runner, on that day I felt I should have been a track star till the barrel of a gun gouged into my back.

Someone roared, "Down in that mud or I'll shoot yer spine, ya fuckin' asshole."

Well, that made it official. I dropped into wet leaves. He cuffed and dragged me out front and shackled me to a tree by the road. Angel sat in his cruiser. After a television crew filmed a chained-up beast, that cop allowed me to join her in the backseat.

With his left arm out the driver's window he leaned back and asked, "Ya'll cool?"

"Sure, man, we're cool. I'm from Collinwood. I'm sure we can work this out."

He gave me a dirty look and rolled up his window. "Don't say nary a word ta her, hear? I'm gonna do some talkin', and ya'll er gonna listen-up real quiet like. Course, ya'll er screwed fer breakin' and enterin' and destruction a property. A stolen car ain't gonna help none. Havin' burglar tools in the trunk don't help yer case much. Oh yeah. We went through yer girlfriend's purse while you was chained up and found a syringe and powder that looks an awful lot like heroin. And we found a billfold that just might belong to you, boy. Is this here yer name, Giacomo Lorocco? What's that, like Mexican or somethin'?"

"My name's Jack. I'm Sicilian. And she's a no-class, gutter slut."

"Right. We ran her name. She's wanted in Florida fer prostitution and drugs and the like. Skipped out on bail, she did. Ya'll picked ya a real winner here. Didn't ya, boy?"

"Hey man, I'm from Cleveland. I never saw this cunt before last night and don't know shit about anything else. As far as I'm concerned, you planted that stuff on her. You almost shot me for no reason. Why would I believe you?"

"I'm about ta haul yer sorry butts down ta stationhouse. No talkin' now. Hear?"

After we were booked and fingerprinted the arresting cop said, "Here's yer wallet back, son. Give 'er a good check-through ta see what's missin'."

"Nothing's missing. I got sick and couldn't find my friends. She offered a ride but we were drunk and got lost. She's just holdin' my wallet 'cause I was pukin' and shit."

Then we heard a clamor of voices just outside the booking room as he said, "Thanks ta ya'll, now I'll have ta stay after shift till we finish this ugly business."

Two cops for next shift entered: "Jackie! What in the world you doin' here, son? Last time I seen you was last night, and you was at the club with me. What's this about?"

I never thought I'd be so happy to see a cop. Melvin listened to my story and said, "I'll call Rico. If he'll verify they left you without a ride, I'm satisfied. Stay cool, son."

I turned to Angel: "Hey, they already got you nailed. Why you wanna drag me into some phony bust? How you gonna act here? Show some fuckin' class."

"This asshole don't know shit," she said. "You think I'd fuck with this loser? Anyhow, he's asshole buddies with that cop. I'm sure he'd skate, anyway."

Melvin made the call and in a few minutes Enrico arrived all sleepy-eyed.

The arresting officer advised, "Don't you never visit Atlanta again. Ya hear?"

I gave Melvin a hug and promised, "I owe you, bro. I'm leaving for Cleveland today. I won't forget you, my friend. You ever quit the cops and need work, look us up."

Enrico found Astro wandering around downtown Atlanta. He said, "I decided I'm staying here to work and to finish my degree. Take this space cowboy back with you."

Bee-Bee drove, stopping only for fill-ups and piss breaks. We made it back in time to check with Pazzo to see if I still had a job at the Collinwood rail yards.

"Jackie, you know I love you like a little brother. I'll do my best to get your job back," Pazzo said. "But from now on you need to be responsible and accountable for your behavior and consequences. My advice is quit drinking and wake-the-fuck-up. Sooner or later you'll step into a pit of snakes where no amount of favors will work. But for now, I think we can fix this mess. Meet me first thing in the morning at The Inn."

"What do you mean by morning? You mean like before noon?"

"Don't start . . . Be there at 8:00 a.m., dress neat and clean, and no hangover!"

CH IX: FRIENDSHIP

A hearing was scheduled at the trainmaster's office for that same day. Pazzo served as my union rep. Before we entered he said, "That old prick hasn't mentioned assault because he's got nothing solid. Now promise me you won't act crazy like those *schifoso* (disgusting) bikers you hang with. You used to be a good dresser, Jackie. What happened to you? By the way . . . Maybe we can get compensated for lost wages. But listen close at this part: you go along with anything and everything I say. *Capisce?*"

"All I want's my job back, Pazzo. If you get lost wages you can keep 'em."

"That's almost half a year's back-pay. If I get it we'll split 50/50 after tax."

The investigation was held first thing in the morning. That bothered me right off. I was drunk the night before and rolled-in with one hell of a hangover. *Why can't they conduct business in the afternoon like civilized people?* I sported clean Levi's and a white tee-shirt to accentuate fully-sleeved arms and my dog-tooth earring. Pazzo stood next to me in his *Ban-Lon* shirt, neatly pressed *Sansabelt* slacks and spit-shined Stetsons.

"My temples are throbbing, my mouth's dry as dog's bone-shit and my stomach's on fire. I'm a little edgy right now and could use a beer to stay on the rails, Pazzo."

"Just stay cool. And remember: I do all the talking. We get one chance here."

We arrived on time to the old trainmaster's office, a Sidney Greenstreet look-alike sloppily dressed in a cheap suit. He was accompanied by a cute stenographer with great legs barely covered by a hint of a mini-skirt. The secretary, with pencils and paper on her lap, was set to transcribe the proceedings of that little kangaroo court. The yardmaster I had choked was absent but provided a deposition from which the trainmaster read.

"It says here you refused to perform duties as a conductor; that you ordered your crew not to work any longer and then deserted the job. Do you dispute any of this, Jack?"

Pazzo stood-up: "I'm Jack's counsel and will answer on his behalf. Now we're not denying he left the job. But . . . well . . . let's just say there's extenuating circumstances of a personal nature."

"I see," replied the trainmaster who looked unimpressed. "And exactly what would such *extenuating* circumstance be, Mr. Russo?"

"How about we drop the formalities? You can call me Pazzo. Now what do we call you?" he asked with his fox in the henhouse grin.

"You may call me *Sir*. Now please continue, Mr. Russo."

Pazzo shot me his *You'd better play along,* look. "Well sir, my client had diarrhea. Jack farted and accidentally shit himself. He didn't want to leave, but he had no choice."

The secretary jerked her head up so fast she dropped papers on the floor. *He could've said anything. Why this?* But I knew the drill. *Fuck that uptight dyke, anyways.*

As she leaned over to gather scattered materials, Pazzo and I noticed those perfect legs that had been pressed tightly together were about a heads-width apart. We stared at those creamy thighs as they showcased Utopia while she fumbled around to regroup her belongings. Pazzo knelt down in front of her to help as she strained to get her things as quickly as possible. He rooted around like a Bloodhound at her crotch. The son-of-a-bitch looked ready to hunch her leg at any moment when lard-ass interrupted.

"All right now, that's quite enough! Let's sit down and gain composure."

Pazzo, all red-faced, posed a lecherous smile and returned scattered papers.

The trainmaster, who must have worn his suit as pajamas asked, "Why didn't Jack merely be truthful? I can't see how any of this is valid. We agree the yardmaster is a reasonable man, don't we? I'm sure he would have permitted Jack to go home for a quick shower and a change of clothes. Why couldn't Jack ask a simple question?"

I thought: *Fat-man, you're the one should consider changing clothes. You make Lt. Columbo look neat.* I grumbled, "Okay, you want a question? How about you go—"

Pazzo jumped up, "Now wait one minute. You're 100% right, Jack. I agree. Yes, how about you go and explain what you would do, sir. Because there's no way I'd say one word if I had a hot load in my drawers. I'd get out quick. Besides, the yardmaster was delinquent by not making proper inquiries. Jack's pants were loaded with liquid shit! What would you do if you had putrid diarrhea running down your legs right now? Would you mention it to the little lady, or would you just discretely walk out?"

Pazzo sat and gave another cheesy grin to the girl who by then looked as if she were ready to heave breakfast instead of papers. Then they looked at me; he doubtful and she appalled. She leaned away as if I might soil myself at any moment. Her nub of a nose wrinkled like I already had. *Fucking Pazzo!*

The slobby trainmaster leaned forward as if to sniff for telltale signs, then addressed me for the first time since Pazzo had taken the lead. "Is this true, Jack?"

By that time I figured: *Fuck-it. This cunt hates me anyways.* "Yes sir. Every word is right on the money. I was embarrassed to mention it. I had *agida* and a bad case of the screamin' skeets, just like Mr. Russo here said. At the time, goin' home to shower seemed like the right thing to do. Next time I get a sick stomach I'll let someone know."

The secretary noted every repulsive word about the alleged mishap in my drawers. I wanted to explode in her sweet little pants, but I could forget that move.

The trainmaster said, "I'll agree to reinstate your seniority but there will be no back-pay. From now on you are to inform the yardmaster on duty of anything pertaining to work. The reason I'm giving you this chance is because you've not been written up before or brought in on any other disciplinary actions. Don't come in front of me again."

My job stayed intact till the "full crew law" became dismantled in 1982 by congressional mandate. Thanks to a squeeze by Reagan, 3/5ths of Conrail employees over 17 states found themselves out of work. Reagan was the same genius who instituted mandatory minimums for drug convictions for personal use. Reagan's trickle-down economics felt more like a dose of the *clap* then it did economic stimulus. By then I was beyond broke and about to lose everything. Pazzo advised us to meet with Uno at The Inn. I contacted my club-brothers. We convened at Benny's and drove in two cars.

Uno grinned: "Well, well. So the Royal Flush wants work, huh? Youse deadbeats ready to grow some balls and take some chances? You're gonna die cryin' or tryin'. Take your pick. Youse're plannin' on runnin' for mayor or some shit? Or maybe Jesus is gonna climb his ass off the cross to save you 'cause your so fuckin' special. Guess what? You're like everybody else, unless you're part of us. We stick together and make our own luck. Don't go waitin' around till somebody moves against you. Then it's too late."

Benny spoke for us: "We're game for whatever and ready for the fast track."

"We'll see about that. For now, I'm gonna let you and Jackie put some money on the streets. Profits get taxed every week. Don't be late. If youse let anybody slide, it's on you. Fingers, you and Nino are gonna sell our weed and pills to the niggers. Youse make the deals. We give you a cut based on your sales. Eggs and Gus and gonna pull some burglaries and robberies for us. We'll need other work now and then – maybe brace somebody or do a little collecting. Anybody here got a problem with that?"

Fingers assured the made-man, "No problem. We're glad to help."

Benny agreed, "Yeah, it's time we get more involved."

As soon as we left Eggs complained, "I should've said no. My ol' lady'll kill me if I'm out doin' gangster stuff once we're married, and I'm gettin' hitched this weekend."

"You can't back out now," Fingers cautioned him.

"Don't worry," Benny grinned. "You just don't see the end-game yet."

Gus assured his childhood friend, "Nothin' bad's gonna happen, *coom*, not when Uno's got our backs." Then he looked at us and said, "See? Eggs ain't even worried."

"Yeah, I ain't worried," Eggs grinned. "I got someone else even meaner than those guys to worry about."

"Uno's got our backs, huh?" I asked sarcastically. "Hmmm, maybe that's the part we should worry about the most. But I don't wanna be the only holdout, so fuck-it."

In preparation of the blessed day Eggs chose Gus to be his best man. Benny, Fingers, Nino and I comprised the remainder of the wedding party. We got paired with girlfriends of the new bride so we could line-up in church wearing formal clothes, hangovers and bad attitudes. Stand, sit, kneel . . . stand, sit, kneel . . . like we were dogs at obedience class.

At the reception Eggs explained, "Uno thinks I'm a hillbilly. That means sooner or later I'll be the fall guy, so I'm out. But I'll always be your brother, no matter what."

He and his bride moved to the bottom floor of a two-family Neighborhood residence. On a brisk autumn evening, nestled in with his pretty wife, the couple above them entertained friends. As the night wore on company became louder. Someone pounded on his door and yelled, "Hey tough guy, wanna come out and play?"

Eggs dialed Chuggers, our other favorite Collinwood bar, and said, "I called 'cause my ol' lady asked me to. I told them punks to keep it down. When Paddy's brother-in-law told me to go "F" myself I went for him and he flipped open a knife. So I shoved my wife inside and now I'm wastin' time on this phone. If youse ain't here in 15 minutes I'll settle this my way."

Fingers and I had been smoking Lebanese hashish all night. Ten minutes later we pulled up at Bee-Bee's house. There was a Kelly green GTO parked in Eggs' driveway. We charged through Eggs' front door to find him pacing like a caged animal.

I advised, *"Coom*, let's have a sit-down. Maybe resolve this bullshit, right? Let's do the smart thing for the little lady."

Eggs jerked his head, "I'm done talkin'. Youse ready or what?"

"How many guys are up there?" I inquired, hoping to hear two or three.

"Not enough. Let's do this right now or I go it alone."

Fingers shrugged, "We're already here, *coom*. Fuck-it. The quicker we kick these punks' asses the faster we get back to the ranch to chill."

I thought: *Man, I'm way too stoned for this shit...* "Okay then, let's roll."

Eggs, a man of few words, left deep impressions when he did speak. He walked to his back door, flung it open, and shouted up the hallway, "Come down here youse stupid motherfuckers." Eggs seldom cursed. That told us we were beyond talking.

Fingers and I walked to the front yard, all Chinese-eyed, to what sounded like a stampede rumbling down those back wooden steps. Fingers found a golf club leaning against the porch and steadied himself in the center of the tiny front lawn. I stood at his back. Eggs planted himself between us and the driveway. When the back door slammed open, glass shattered. They roared down the driveway, straight for us, growling a drunken war chant.

"Tag the first one with that club. Then I'll—" *Ahh, Fuck me...Not again.*

There they were: Frankie Fazule, Paddy and Doyle Kelly and two others, one of them the husband of who turned out to be Paddy's little sister, Maureen. By then Paddy and Frankie were crew members of Collinwood's Irish Mob.

Eggs pinned Paddy's brother-in-law against a car in their driveway. Doyle jumped on Eggs' back. Fingers wacked Paddy with the golf club before Frankie yanked it away and knocked us both down. Paddy was overzealous with his stomps, so Frankie's chopping range had been limited. Fingers, lying next to me, threw up-kicks while I deflected blows. But my left arm had been injured. Numbness almost covered the pain.

Fingers cheered, "It's Gus' shit-wagon!" when car tires screeched at the tree lawn.

Everyone paused. That sky-blue rust-bomb was a beautiful sight. Doors flung open. Gus, Benny, Nino, and even cur-ass, Bee-Bee Balls stormed out. *The team's in formation and lookin' good.* Bee-Bee tried to load a pistol in the driveway but dropped bullets. Gus ran to the passenger side and snatched the piece away from Bee-Bee.

Fingers and I got trampled into the lawn. Nino rolled around with Paddy while Benny kicked him. That crazy fuck, Frankie, decided to leave off us for a moment so he could decapitate Benny. He swung that golf club so hard, it whizzed by and sliced the air…*Whoosh*. But still no sign of Gus or Bee-Bee Balls in the fight.

Frankie flipped open a knife and slashed my shoulder, then lifted the blade like an axe when the first round entered. As he looked down at his chest the second one hit. Blood spots welled up on his white tee-shirt. When the third round found him, Frankie dropped the knife. Paddy snatched-up the golf club, whacked Benny in the arm and then charged swinging at Gus. By then Gus was hitting empty chambers and spent cartridges, because Bee-Bee had dropped half the bullets. Bee-Bee and Nino knocked Paddy down and wrestled back the golf club. When we heard sirens everybody except Benny scattered. He threw his keys and said, "Go on home, youse fuckin' babies. I ain't finished yet."

Flashers glinted off parked cars. Gus lifted Benny, ran with him under his arm and stuffed him into his car. Nino nailed it down a side street with the headlights off and pulled into a random driveway till it was safe to get Benny to a hospital. Eggs went home. Fingers and I hoofed it over to Bee-Bee's. His parents were out. We uncased and loaded his father's shotgun and a .38 Special just as a car skidded to a halt at the curb.

After I taped a Kotex to my shoulder and changed into one of Bee-Bee's shirts, I peaked out the front window and said, "Just as I thought. Check this out, *coom*. Maureen's out there right now pointin' to the house and yackin' away to these pigs. Fuck this snitch bitch and that firm ass. She could be sittin' on a gold mine for all I care."

The ambulance took off with a riddled Frankie. Someone knocked at Bee-Bee's front door and demanded, "We need the little *dago* that ran here after the shooting."

Bee-Bee Balls invited them in. "Hello Officers. Welcome. Now how can I help you fine gentlemen? Would either of you like some fresh coffee, or can I tempt you with something a little stronger?" All that crap squeezed through a shit-eating grin.

O'Reilly sneered, "Cut the bullshit, punk. We already know what happened. Somebody here's in deep shit. Are you Benny Fingers? We know he's here somewhere. Produce that midget *WOP* right now or we toss the place and arrest everybody."

"Well gentlemen, like I already tried to tell you two formidable peace-keepers—"

Fingers and I walked in to make sure those cops didn't find us hiding with guns.

"Who got shot?" I asked.

Fingers chimed in, "Yeah, we heard shootin.' What's goin' on out there?"

O'Reilly laughed, "Where're youse two little faggots been hidin' at?"

"He was sleepin' and I was takin' a dump," I answered. "What's this all about, anyways? Can't a man shit in peace around here? Or is that a crime, too?"

Loony Lonnie asked, "You always take a dump with your coat on? Get over here and strip that pea-coat off. You too, dick-head; nice and slow the both of you. Peel those jackets and drop 'em on the floor. Raise your arms and place your hands on your heads."

Numbness began to fade when pain surged through my arm like battery acid. Fortunately we spent most of the fight on the ground. Our faces and fists were unmarked.

"Now lower one hand and show some ID – nice and slow," O'Reilly commanded. "Keep the other one on your head. That goes for you too, fat boy. Hand over some ID. Which one a youse punks is Benny Fingers?" Then he giggled, "Holy shit! Zeno Scarpetti Jr. and Giacomo Lorocco the 3rd? Are youse assholes kidding me? Is that really your names? These licenses better not be fake. So what-the-fuck kind a spic names are these? Hey Lonnie, look at these addresses. These two little cunts don't even live here. Can't youse jerk-offs invent a better story than this?"

"I know these two losers and so do you," Lonnie said. "Take a good look. They just have longer hair and more tattoos now. You know 'em by their street names. The one with the coat is Jackie and the other one's Benny Fingers . . . both of 'em pieces of shit."

Bee-Bee Balls interrupted, "Hey! What's your problem? They're Italian names and they're my cousins. How's it your business, anyways? This is *my* house."

Lonnie jumped in: "Cousins, huh? How'd an Irish puke like you get Italian cousins? You don't quit running your yap, we run the three of youse in. Now I want answers, and I mean right now! You wanna talk in *your* house or in *our*s? Our house has bars and locked doors. You got exactly three seconds, ya sawed-off mick!"

"Okay. Here's what happened, sirs. Our moms all went to a wedding shower. You know how women are. So the boys are here with me. We heard shooting and sirens. Then you officers pounded on the door and scared the living daylights out of us! Wow. I'm still shaking! Look at my hands. And I promise you, Zeno is not Benny Fingers."

O'Reilly wisecracked, "Whatever. But now we know who youse little faggots are and where you live. You better hope nobody dies. We're goin' across the street to talk to your other girlfriend, Egan. Your stories better match or we'll be right back. Don't take any Girl Scout hikes. Oh yeah, and tell your *coomba*, Benny Fingers, we're on to him."

Their radio summoned them to a wreck just as Benny phoned to update us. "That ambulance carryin' Swiss Cheese Frankie got into a head-on down Five Points. Some drunk ran a red-light. Hey, Jackie, maybe there is a God. Maybe that fuck'll die and it'll be the pigs' fault. Youse guys shoot anybody else? We got shovels and lime ready."

"Check this shit out, Benny," I laughed. "These Laurel and Hardy fucks are on a manhunt for a shooter named Benny Fingers. Fuckin' assholes!"

Nino shouted from the background, "Did that fat fuck die yet?"

Fingers took the phone from me, "If not, we can arrange that. But nobody can say we don't pay our debts, right Benny? In fact, none of 'em better say shit."

Nino got on the phone: "Frankie the psychopath will wanna settle this out of court. I heard The Mick has big plans for him. Even though Gus stays on our side of Five Points now, he won't be far enough away after all this shit came down."

Fingers reassured them, "Guess what, Nino? This ain't over till we decide."

Afterwards Benny and Gus decided to rob a gas station in Little Italy, another area dominated by Cleveland's *La Cosa Nostra*. A drunken Benny stuck a gun to the grease-monkey's face and announced, "This is a mother-stickin' fuck-up."

The attendant chuckled: "Go on home, kid, before you hurt yourself."

Eggs punched the guy through drywall. Benny pulled him out, sat on the guy's chest and leisurely pistol-whipped him while Eggs grabbed the cash drawer.

The next night we were asked to stay and close at Uno's speakeasy. Two drunks ignored last call. Benny approached them with a Billy club in one hand and a butcher knife in the other. He handed me the handle of the club and said, "If they make a wrong move hack 'em up." He slapped the knife into his hand and threatened to beat them to death. When they saw his blood gushing they ran out yowling like banshees.

I needed to clear my head, so after a long sleep I stopped at my parent's house to see what was for supper. I sat at the table while my mom removed sirloin steaks coated with Italian bread crumbs and roasted rosemary potatoes from the oven. She cursed, "I hope you have a mothering bastard just like you, Giacomo! How could a monster like you come from somebody like me? Look at you! Always drunk. You're killing yourself and everyone around you. I want you to know I changed my prayers from St. Jude for protection to baby Jesus so he'll take you in your sleep. God made a mistake and took the wrong son."

With her *malocchio* (evil eye) curse fresh in mind, we went to Chuggers where I encountered a drunken Tessa, a condition as rare for her as it was common for me.

"Hey you! I know you," she giggled. "Aren't you the guy with that cute girlfriend named Tessa? Wow, you're bushy! When did all this happen?"

"Bushy? Is that almost like a compliment?"

"Sort of, but not really. You used to be a cute little boy. You know that, Jackie? But now you look like a beast. Are you an animal, bro?" Then she accidentally spilled some beer on the front of my shirt. "Oops, sorry 'bout that. Hey, I'm only playing around. You don't mind if I play with you, do you?"

"Mind? What makes you think I have a mind?"

"No, no, not that kind. I mean like a gold *mind* or a *mind* field. You know, bro?"

"I know you're drunk. That's what I know. You wanna know what else? I think me and you are about a breath away from stepping into a minefield. Careful..."

"I'm always careful. That's my whole problem. That's why I'm drunk right now," she laughed. "See how careful I am, Jackie? It's because I picked nobody else but you."

"Maybe I better take you home now, okay Tessa? Come on, let's go."

"Are you mad at me? I'm sorry about spilling my beer on you."

"Nope. Actually it feels kind of good. It's gettin' a bit warm in here, anyways."

"Come here and let me clean you up real good," she posed all sassy as she rubbed my chest. "You don't mind if I take care of you, do you, Jackie-boy?"

"You're killin' me, here. What's it you're lookin' for? Just say it so I know. I'm too wasted for head games, babe. And I don't wanna make a mistake with you, okay?"

She answered with lips on my mouth, a deep, hungry kiss. Under her silk shift I felt nothing other than unblemished skin on a lean, firm body. "Is this plain enough, Jackie boy? You sure you're up to this, badass? But you really don't *need* to answer. Or are you too messed-up to walk me to my car? I guess maybe I need to go home alone again?"

"Nah, I'm not *that* wasted. Swear to Buddha, it's good like this for me."

Tessa knew that when somebody from the Neighborhood said those words it meant more than the other overused phrase people mindlessly vowed by rote.

When we raised glasses she smiled, *"Cin don" (For a hundred years)*.

She took my hand and we headed for the door. She pressed heat against hunger as I thought: *Fuck Doc. This ain't about him. That motherfucker can get shot, too.*

She cautioned, "I hear you loud and clear, bro. You need to chill about that or I'm gone. And remember, hot-shot, I'll never be anybody's sweetie. Are you cool with that?"

Nino pulled us from rapture that was about to move to the ranch. "Fingers and Benny got a beef and shit's about to hit the blades. Benny's hand's still all stitched up."

We smashed the place with bottles and chairs. I explained to Nino on the way to the ranch, "Fuck-it. It's better this way. I'm on a collision course and don't wanna drag a nice girl like her down with me – unless she asks real nice-like. But if I get involved with her that would force Pazzo's hand against me, and I don't ever want that."

"You're right, *coom*. Pazzo will take his brother's side every goddamn time. Family first, right? Plus, we know he loves Tessa more than life. It's not like there's a pussy shortage out here or anything. Find something else."

"You're right; and most of 'em ain't got a lunatic father and a gangster uncle to deal with, let alone a maniac like Uno for a godfather. Nah, I'd better pass on that. I'll stick with Maggie and Carly for a minute. Those two keep me plenty busy as it is."

During one of our last weeks together, in that incredible hour when the sky sprays magic onto a dark world, Maggie and I lay in a pile of contented nakedness inside a gorgeous late morning to watch a sunlit halo of Carly slip into a translucent peasant dress. We dropped off Carly, picked up my Airedale, Butch, and headed for Cleveland Metroparks. We waded into the river onto a flat boulder. A fresh handful of Seconal got washed down with greenish-brown river water. They grabbed fast and hard.

I slurred, "I just want ya ta know how I 'preciate you keepin' shit real."

"Is *real* a condition defined by others, Jackie? Or is it whatever we decide?"

All thick-tongued I answered "All's I know is I'm *real* fucked-up, baby."

After my nap she dusted off confusion with a gentle kiss: "Nope, you're not dead. So what happened to the ghosts who weren't born? Are they the same ones that can't die? Remember the ones trying to rip oldness away from that place where all the colors blur?"

"Did I talk in my sleep? What did I say?"

"Plenty. My head on your heart; my eyes closed with yours. But no words, baby-boy, just the stuff of dreams. I kept your soul with me till you came back. Now you have mine. Should we die yet, or maybe just wait for it to find us?"

I should have asked her to marry me right there. Instead, I whistled-in Butch to end that dream in the stream. He splashed his way back and shook river water onto our sun-baked flesh. When Maggie offered to drive. I slurred, "I ain't even that fucked-up. You got anymore drugs?" as I squinted through Ray Charles shades.

"Your nose is on the windshield, Jackie. At least let me steer as far as my house."

I returned the car with a wet dog, crawled up my parent's porch and through the front-room, up their stairs to sleep in my childhood bed. I sensed that I was dying.

A cemetery was the last place Maggie and I tripped. We paid respects to her brother, a good kid who had been gunned down by Astroboy's brother, Cagootz, a maniac who never did time because his family was all mobbed-up. At the grave, we poured a cap-full of electric Sangria on his headstone and shot-gunned it with sweet plumes of herb. At dusk Maggie and I retired in a mausoleum to celebrate life atop a cool marble slab on a windless evening. We slept till sunlight crept beneath the tomb's doorway.

I woke to the sounds of her crying: "Why . . . why . . . why? I fucking miss him so bad I can't stand it. Goddamn-it... How could he go and die on me like this?"

As I hugged her she wept, "Jackie, I can't get used to the idea that I'll never see him again . . . never hear his voice or feel his energy . . . never see that smile or hear his laugh. I feel so empty without him. I worry about you too, man. You're scaring me. You over-do everything and then don't know when to stop. How much is enough?"

"No worries, sweetie. It's just partying. Your brother was a great kid, everybody knows that. And he lived a full life. He did everything he ever wanted to do. He just happened to be in the right place at the wrong time in his life. He pulled a blade in self-defense the same as I would have. He didn't know that motherfucker had a piece."

"Yes, but that doesn't make it any easier to deal with. And now you're slipping away too, aren't you? No matter what happens between us, even if you never want to see me again, promise me you'll back-off the pills before you OD. You don't have to quit, Jackie. Just notch it back a little, okay? I can't lose you, too. I just don't know what I'd do if I lost you," she sobbed with her head pressed tightly against my chest.

"I've been thinkin' about stuff lately, Maggie, and I think it's about time for me to start makin' some serious changes. I want more out of life before it slips away from me like it did your little brother. Don't you want more out of life, too?"

CH X: MORE PARTY SPOTS

While Gus and I trained our sights on our crew being patch-holders for the Wong Gongs, Benny repeated his stance about our own club: "I ain't votin' anybody in till one of us dies or goes to prison for life. Fuck Eggs if he choosin' that Polack broad over us."

En route to inspect and bid on an arsenal the No-Names acquired in a gun store robbery, we considered prospective members. We discussed Toby as a likely candidate for the Royal Flush, because he was the one to put Mick's heir apparent into an early grave.

Fingers prophesized, "Toby's gritty, true enough, but he's a time bomb with a bad fuse and as reckless as you, Benny. We got a fulltime job tryin' to keep you outta trouble."

"Hey, Fingers, I thought babysittin's a girl's job," Benny wise-cracked. "Just worry about yourself. I'll take care of me."

Nino suggested, "We should take Pazzo's advice and keep Toby on a short leash to keep our eye on him. What do you say, Jackie?"

"The only thing I wanna keep my eye on is a set of firm tits," I answered.

"There's more to life than pussy," Fingers philosophized.

After we dropped off Fingers and Benny at The Inn, Nino suggested, "Let's you and me head south for Spring Break. Can you get off work for about a week, Jackie?"

"Work? Fuck work. We'll leave tomorrow afternoon."

Nino and I arrived at Ft. Lauderdale in 24 hours. While I stepped into a bar to leave a piss he purchased a sack of what were said to be shreds of dried psilocybin.

"Look at this stuff, Jackie. This is supposed to be desiccated magic mushrooms, but it looks like dehydrated dog shit to me. What do you think?"

"Nah, it don't stink. Maybe we bought some peat moss."

He tasted some and with a thoughtful expression said, "Nope . . . It's not peat moss or dog shit. That's for sure. Try some," and handed me a wad.

I gagged, "Fuck this! It's tree bark. Let's go take a refund from those chumps."

"Wait awhile. How the fuck do you know what tree bark tastes like?"

We washed half of those pieces of whatever down with beer when I remembered tabs of window-pane in my watch pocket. We dropped two each and maintained our hunt.

With LSD, it doesn't take much, but it takes about a half hour to really feel it. About 20 minutes after we dropped the acid Nino grinned, "I guess it ain't tree bark."

I nodded, "Fasten your seat belts, *coom*. And let's go find those hippies."

With color flashes and light tracers, the acid had yet to take hold. On our hunt Nino talked a smooth line and picked up two ladies. A cute blonde, Lorie, glowed from neon sunburn. Wendi, her brunette girlfriend, wore a dark tan and foreboding expression.

In our lobby stood four giants in basketball jerseys, all with hair like Moe from The Three Stooges. One of them introduced himself, "I'm Jed, team captain. And I'm about ta show ya'll fellers how Kentuckians party. Let's roll, boys."

He called out to his friends, "Ya'll need your rest, son. Don't wait up."

Nino warned, "Be careful, big man. You might get more than you bargained for."

"Don't worry 'bout me none. I'm a big boy."

"Well if you insist, big-boy, then all aboard for a magical mystery tour."

We arrived at the room with two sweeties and Jed. Our two neighborhood buddies sat and smoked with four other guys. Three of them we vaguely knew from Little Italy.

The fourth was Astroboy's crazy brother, Joey Cagootz. He said, "Peace, bros. I know that dude was your friend's brother, Jackie. He had a knife in me, and youse all know this. But we're too stoned to get into this right now. Besides, we're the only *dagos* down here. The smart thing is we truce-up. This ain't the time for drama. We cool?"

"Yeah, man . . . timing. I dig it. Let's just chill," I lazily agreed.

"So who's the giant?" Cagootz asked. "Hey, big-boy, see this chunk a chocolate wrapped in foil? It's opiated hash, and I ain't talkin' corned beef. You game?"

Jed spotted a bottle of tequila laced with invisible Windowpanes: "Yaaah Hooo. Ya'll go on ahead. Just hand that bad mutha-fatha ova here, boys. I ain't never had me no darn *tee-quee-lee* before. But by-gosh, this here's Spring Break. So let's party hearty!"

"Hold up, Jed, that ain't regular tequila," I warned. "There's something in it."

"I don't give a care 'bout no worm, son. To heck with a goll-darn worm."

Nino looked up at Jed's chest, "It's not what you think. You've been warned, okay Jed-o? Now sit your big ass down and I'll grab you a few beers."

Jed reached up, over and beyond him, uncapped the potion and swilled down a healthy dose. He whooped, "YEEE-HAHHH! Get down, get funky – let's get it on!" His smile quickly faded. He looked ready to barf so he passed the jug.

Before the next in line took a sip Nino explained, "This was supposed to be the engine for a batch of Hairy Buffalo Punch we were gonna make. It's potent; go easy."

Cagootz advised, "You better stay here with us, big-boy. That shit's electric. You ain't goin' nowhere for awhile, *capisce?* Sit and learn from experienced men."

Jed proclaimed, "'Lectric, acoustic, it don't matter much to me, son. I'm all about gettin' fried tonight. Alrighty then . . . bring it on!"

Cagootz took a swig and passed it to Wendi. She drank and handed it to Lorie, and so it went till the circle was almost complete. Jed took another chug. Nino and I didn't need any, so I recapped the bottle and held onto it while a metal hash pipe made its rounds. We passed around brews to wash down its lung-wrenching sweetness.

When I attempted to pass Jed the pipe in that smoke-filled room he protested, "Nope, not fer me. Thanks just the same, boys. I'm a drinkin' man. I don't mess with none a that dope stuff. Good ol' alcohol's good enough fer a country boy like me. Ya'll go ahead. Knock yerselves out, son. I'm about ready to get *tee-quee-leed.*"

Nino noted as he held in a plume of hash with little snorts, "Check it out, *coom.* That beer looks like a V-8 can wrapped in that big hick's meat hook."

Lorie sat at the table by the only light. She asked, "Can I cut a piece off this Aloe plant?" She slit the plump, green petal in half and told her friend, "Wendi, my skin's on fire right now. Rub this on my back please, but go easy."

When Lorie slipped out of her tank top I absentmindedly passed the electric bottle to Jed. By then I couldn't care less if anyone drank piss from the toilet or jumped off the balcony. Lorie's small tits were stark white, contrasted by hot-pink skin.

"Now we're talkin' old-school, baby!" Cagootz howled. "Light my fire, doll."

Wendi slowly rubbed the inside of a fat leaf on Lorie's tender skin. Eye movements blazed across the dark room like shooting stars. Wendi's gentle touch might have eased some of Lorie's pain but she was killing us with titillating caresses. Wendi cupped one of Lorie's breasts so she could salve around its perimeter. Nobody breathed; afraid they would notice us and stop. By then the hash pipe was cold.

Jed knelt down with hands raised to the ceiling and spoke in an unrecognizable language: "Kay squeeze-o, kay tits-o. Kay pink-o, kay nips-o. Kay eat-o, kay cunt-o. Kay lick-o, kay crack-o. Kay prick-o, kay tease-o. Kay crease-o, kay wet-o. Kay stank-o, kay pig-o. Kay smash-o, kay *dago*. Kay rape-o, kay no-no. Kay bust-o, kay jail-o."

Lorie asked, "What the hell did he just say?" as she slipped back into her top. This dude's creeping us right out." Pissed-off eyeballs cut into Jed like poison darts.

Wendi huddled up against her friend, arms wrapped around one another.

Jed spewed, "We Southern Pentecostals speak in tongues; so leave me be whilst I do my prayin'. Kay suck-o, kay puss-o. Kay lick-o, kay split-o. Kay munch-o, kay blonde-o. Kay two-o, kay dike-o. Kay drunk-o, kay craze-o. Kay fight-o, kay wop-o. Kay jump-o, kay me-o. Kay leave-o, kay soon-o."

Cagootz yelled, "This hick's one crazy motherfucker! Go on ahead, big-boy; talk more of that nutty shit. You're trippin' us right the fuck out, dude."

Nino added, "Yeah . . . rock-on, big man. You're with friends, right? Just don't come at anyone too fast. Understand?"

Jed: "Ahhh, Leetle Nee-no. Say *Kay*."

Nino: "Say what, motherfucker?"

Jed: "No . . . no . . . No kay swear-o, kay Nee-no. *KAY! . . . SAY KAY!*"

Nino: "Okay, Jed-o. I'll play... *Kay*."

Jed: "Kay nee."

Nino: "Kay nee."
Jed: "Kay nee-no."
Nino: "Kay nee-no."
Jed: "Kay nee-gro."
Nino: Kay nee-gro."

Jed: "Kay nee-gro, kay day-go. Kay craze-o, kay drunk-o. Kay lose-o, kay mind-o. Kay-knife-o, kay slash-o. Kay stab-o, kay sin-o. Kay burn-o, kay hell-o. Kay split-o, kay quick-o. Kay pray-o, kay soul-o. Kay kill-o, kay doom-o."

Wendi said, "This guy's brain is stretched. He's a fucking mutant lunatic and he's weirding us right out. Keep that freak away from us or we're leaving."

Jed to Wendi: *"SAY KAY!"*

Wendi: "No! Fuck off, asshole." She lifted the knife and aimed it at the kneeling pituitary mishap's forehead. On his knees, Jed was as big as the tallest guy in the room.

Lorie encouraged her friend: "Stab that freak! It's his fault my skin aches."

Jed announced, "This here ain't no regular hooch, fellas! Man, I ain't never drinkin' nothin' but *tee-quee-lee* from here on out. Ferget beers! Them ol' Mexicans sure know their stuff, boys, 'cause this here is definitely the one fer me."

"You want another snort, Jed-o?" Cagootz asked. "Say Kay, ya big fuck."

"Naw, I believe I'll pass fer right now. Ya'll go on ahead. I ain't never been drunk like this before. I don't feel much like raisin' heck fer some reason. I reckon I'll just mosey on over ta my room ta pray over it and the like. I just feel sorta like watchin' and listenin' fer awhile. Ya'll know what I mean?"

Joey Cagootz said, "I guess it's time for us to move on down the road, too."

The girls stayed till sunrise. Before they left Wendi asked, "Can we snip off another leaf, and can we keep this knife? That mutant fuck is out there somewhere."

The day portion of our trip, when everything seemed too real, giants sat in our lobby about to return to the hills of Kentucky. Jed's hair was wet and neatly parted to one side. He sat like a totem pole with Stretch Armstrong hands folded in his lap.

His friends related their odd night and even stranger morning: "We'll make darn sure this boy never drinks tequila again. One minute he's kneelin' and squawkin' some language he tells is church talk, callin' us *Kay fag-o* and *Kay shit-o*. Next, he's bouncin' off beds and walls like a big ping-pong ball. We didn't get much shut-eye with him chantin' in tongues all night. Come mornin' we got woke up to one heck of a mess. He smeared peanut butter all around the windows. When we asked him why he'd do such a fool thing he told us, 'to keep out the *demons*.' When we asked who on God's Green Earth are the *demons* he said, 'they're *shadow-people* that comes with the night air.' Do ya'll know a thing about these Florida shadow-people he's so scared of?"

Nino answered, "Yeah, but they're not exclusive to Florida or any other state – unless you're talkin' about a state of mind." He looked at me and said, "Sooner or later we have to do it, *coom*, before it's too late. Maybe when we get back."

The first time I sobered up happened a few months before my birthday. I offered a bet, "I think I'm gonna quit gettin' high for awhile. It's no big deal. You know why? 'Cause I can quit anytime I want to. So who wants a piece a this easy bet?"

Webb said, "I gotcha covered. Let's make it a hundred."

Slick added, "I'll take a hundred on that, too. I just might quit my job."

"Okay, fellas, you're on. I got an even two hundred that I won't use anything except coffee or tobacco till my birthday."

Gus grinned and wagged his greasy long hair, "I think you just stepped on your own dick."

Toby mocked, "You're an alkie and a junkie like the rest of us. Just face the truth and quit shittin' yourself. You'll never quit and you know it."

The plan was for us to meet at Inky's. The day of the party I announced, "I've been as dry as a camel's snatch for three months. So I'm gonna get fucked-up real good, but I'll just hold off till tonight. Oh yeah, and I won't collect the money. Know why? 'Cause it ain't fair to get paid from friends on a sucker bet. Like I said, it's no big deal."

Webb demanded to know, "What the fuck's a sucker's bet supposed to mean?"

Slick sniggered, "How do we know you ain't been partyin' on the side? Just 'cause you say so? You probably blacked out again and can't even remember all the times you been drunk since the bet. Besides . . . You're a bullshitter just like us, Jackie."

"Shut the fuck up, ass-wipe," Gus grumbled. "When Jackie decides to pick-up he'll do it with us. You think everybody's a sneaky, degenerate fuck like you."

Slick, who balded young, was an ace mechanic. His family didn't mind parties at their house and hot scooters stashed in their garage, which increased his popularity.

The lanky blonde, Webb, worked tugboats in the Cuyahoga River, hauling cargo from ships docked in Lake Erie to Downtown Cleveland warehouses. He scored cases of whiskey and boxes of steaks for the cookout. Nino provided weed, cola mix and charcoal.

Chink, and even the innocent looking Dago Red, both were shooters. Inky and Toby were covered with tattoos, all scarred-up like match-dogs. They loved to street fight. All of them, except Slick, were killers.

When Inky fired up his water pipe I said, "I want that sticky bud as much as I wanna put my dick in Barbara Carrera. That bud smells, tastes and feels as good as I'd bet she would. Yeah, pass that bad motherfucker over here," as I watched bizarre things slither in terrariums.

Festivities began with everyone in top spirits till alcohol spirits took over, when Slick referred to Nino as his bitch. Gus punched Slick in his eye and Nino stomped him.

Then Benny pulled a gun and said, "Let's waste everybody to set an example."

But potheads prevailed. Eggs and Nino encouraged Benny to leave with them. Fingers, Gus and I were the only members of our team still there. Chink and Dago Red rode their bikes home. Webb shacked-up in a bedroom with his sweetie.

As Fingers and I spaced out on their tanks he whispered, "See what I mean? This Benny's a ticking bomb." We continued to watch as one aquarium bubbled from an aerator for piranhas. Inky's boa curled up in another. The third held Toby's pet tarantula.

Inky lifted the lid to the arachnid's tank, grabbed the tangerine sized spider in his bare hand and pitched it against a front-room wall. It splattered with a thud. At a snail's pace, the tarantula slid down the drywall and left slug marks behind in a trail of spider-gut slime. Toby marched over to the boa's tank, jerked it out and pinned the writhing snake on the dining room table next to a butcher knife kept there for unwelcome guests.

When he raised the blade over his shoulder Inky warned, "Doncha do it, Tobe. 'Cause if you do it, swear to Buddha I gotta get mad. Do I need to get mad?"

The blade came down like a guillotine. Toby placed his hands on either side of the wildly coiling, headless body and glared, "Go ahead. Get mad.

Like I give a fuck... Now what?" The dead serpent raveled around his feet just as the bodiless head clamped onto Toby's hand. He shook it like he was on fire.

Inky chuckled, "Now what? That's what, ya dumb fuck. See? That's whacha get for bein' a dick. Now who's the chump? Stupid motherfucker."

Webb stumbled out of the bedroom and dropped into a beanbag chair. He tossed a joint to me as he settled in to watch the show. Gus grabbed the snake head by its bloody stump and pried its clamped jaws open with his knife. As soon as Toby had use of both hands he charged. Inky met his advance with equal force. We sipped whiskey and Cokes and smoked as we admired their work. When they got tired Fingers and I separated them.

Inky went to his room where the son of a famous fighting champion awaited his master's return. Toby slammed down more shots, went outside for awhile and reappeared with his dog carried like a fat baby. He walked into the bedroom and tossed it on Inky's dog, then pounced on his snoring friend. After we allowed all four to expend some energy we cleaned-up the dogs, administered antibiotics and put them away for the night.

Toby said, "Okay, I'm cool now. Still, I think you might've over-reacted."

Inky put out his hand to shake. When Toby hissed and turned to strut away in victory, Inky blasted him in the liver and dropped him to his knees. Toby flopped backwards. Wind gone, the top of his head rested against Inky's boots.

Inky said, "Woops, sorry. Looks like I'm over-reacting again."

Inky snatched a spear off his wall, raised it above his head and then yowled a war-hoop. I grabbed the top half of the spear while Fingers road-blocked him into a wall.

Once things settled again Webb gave a pearl of wisdom: "Are youse assholes drunk or retarded? First off: don't ever kill nobody in front of witnesses. That's rule number one. Besides, Toby's a brother. You wanna kill? Let's go someplace and do some killin' right now. Count me in. I'm just in the mood." Webb omitted any other rules.

Toby stood and puffed out his massive chest. He pledged, "I owe you one, Jackie. Swear to Buddha I won't ever forget this, brother."

Through all that, Slick snored. He could have slept through a killing. Years later Dago Red actually did. His front-room rug drenched in blood, he woke next to a gutted and beheaded corpse as he dreamed of a better way just inches from fresh death. The samurai sword taken from his wall naturally was covered with his own prints.

But that night of my birthday party at Inky's, we settled down long enough for the host to remember a new party game — his leg-hold beartrap. Displayed like an urn on a small, high table that looked like a sewing machine cabinet, the trap's metal teeth appeared to be singing Foghat's "Slowride," vibrating speakers as tall as a man.

Inky boasted, "This is a man's game, Jackie, so take notes. I'll show youse boys what real balls look like. Go sit down and watch, Gus. You too, Fingers."

"Deal the cards, Inky-dink," Toby dared. "Let's see what you got, sucker."

He stumbled over to the spring-loaded trap and set it off with a lightening strike. It slammed shut with sickening finality. He reset the trap and plopped down on a beanbag chair. "Like I said ladies, stay in your seats so's youse girls don't get hurt."

"Fuck-it. I'll try if nobody else has enough ass, but you know I'm snake-bit."

Gus grabbed his crotch and said, "Hey, Inky, I got your ladies right here." When I stripped off my riding jacket Gus said, "Fuck that drop-shot, *coomba*. We ain't gotta prove shit to these bust-outs. Let *him* be the asshole. He's used to it."

I staggered towards that mega-mouse trap while Foghat built up steam. The strike on the bait-tray was as fast as Inky's but a tooth hit the nail of my ring finger as "Slow Ride" peaked in crescendo, because I hadn't balled-up my fist on recoil — way too drunk.

Inky snickered, "Quit whining. You sound just like some little girl."

Webb said, "No big deal, right Jackie? You just knocked a little bark off. Think of it like another tattoo, cuz."

On reflex I grabbed my hand and squeezed. There wasn't much blood. But bone was visible. For an upright moment my world reeled. Nerve endings exploded from where a fingertip had just been.

Through clenched teeth I grunted, "We'd better ride before I can't."

We kicked over our bikes and blasted off before my throttle hand no longer worked.

After signing in with some half-asleep elderly nurse, a short Arab doctor came out to tweak my finger and say, "Umm Hmm" and then left me in an otherwise empty waiting room. Gus and Fingers phoned Benny and Nino. Those two arrived in a car so Nino could ride my scooter back to the ranch. I smiled as I listened to my brothers roar out of the parking lot.

Finally settled in a room, a pretty nurse brought me to a fresh shot of Sodium Pentothal. Later, an older nurse entered to wheel me to an operating room. She was shocked to find me awake and presumed the young nurse forgot to give the pre-surgery injection.

I assured her, "That *cute* one did a fine job." She ignored my comment. When I added, "My tolerance's high from years of doin' dope, hon. So I need more." the back of her hand swiped air between us. After deliberating, she gave me a second shot. By then I was crushed yet awake in a dreamy way. Double-dosed on yummy sedative, I was still cocky as a rooster in a drag-pit. I slurred, "Dig it, sweetie. Just gimme one lil' taste more and I'll be all set."

As she wheeled me into a bright roomful of masked strangers I said, "Bunch a sneaky bitches hidin' like some lone-fuckin' rangers. Fuck all a youse towel headed pricks. Where's that know-it-all doctor? I like them assholes about as much as prosecutors and the *clap*."

From behind I heard, "He is talking in his sleep. Ignore him and proceed."

"Oh yeah? How'd you like ta suck my dick? Ya fuckin' pepperoni-smoker."

The surgeon instructed, "Cover his face and he will stop talking." He switched on his bone-saw – truly a disgusting sound. Next he ordered, "Pin back his shoulders."

I was too loaded to muscle away from trained nursing arms. Instead, I informed the pristine doctor, "Touch me with that ...I kick a blade in yer face. Now how you gonna make me act here, doc? Up to you."

One of the nurses gasped, "I don't think he's asleep, Doctor!"

"I've already said to ignore him. Nobody can be awake after two injections of sodium thiopental. I've seen this before. Now please do as I ask."

Again I heard what sounded like a kitchen blender on puree: "Okay, doc, you're holdin' my left forearm. So tell me. Am I asleep, chief?" *Do we kick him in the leg or head?* I felt him release his grip and lightly grasp my bicep. "Okay, now you got my upper arm – same side. Am I out cold, doc? I'm just askin' you 'cause I ain't too sure."

One of the nurses groaned, "Oh my God! He really *is* awake!" At that point the bone saw switched off and the blindfold was removed.

I slurred, "So what's up, doc? Believe me yet, cuz? Or do we pretend you're right. Is that what this shit's about? I tried ta tell your bitch I do lots a downers. But she's like you. She knows more about me than me."

My armpit got shaved so a long needle could be inserted deep a few times till he hit pay-dirt with a brachial nerve block. When my arm felt as if it belonged to somebody else the cloth was returned over my eyes and the bone-saw again made its sickening whirr. I felt nothing when the sound changed to a lower grind, as saw engaged bone.

Then that same elderly nurse with an attitude the size of Compton wheeled me to a different, very cold room. I inquired all thick-tongued, "You blind or stupid? I ain't goddamn sleepin' ova here. See me? Lookee here. I'm wide-ass awake. So tell me this. Why'm I goin' in ta this recovery bullshit for?"

"Because! That's why. And please, don't curse. Just hush and relax."

"Relax? In here? Fuck that. I already told ya I ain't asleep. Get me outta this deepfreeze, big mamma. Don't make me act the fool in here. You don't wanna see that."

The seasoned veteran wheeled me back to my room to avoid further disturbance. But she warned, "No more of your shenanigans."

"Unhook me from all these tubes an' shit. I need ta leave a piss."

"You will use this urinal. I'll hold it for you. You're still in recovery."

"Recovery my left nut. You expect me ta piss in a goddamn bottle while I'm layin' on my back? You wanna *watch*, don't ya? You're one twisted chick, lady."

"I've already asked you not to curse. And don't worry; I've seen a penis before."

"Yeah, I'll bet you seen plenty a schlongs in your time, darlin'. Just not for a while though, huh? Now refresh my memory, gramma, 'cause I'm all fucked-up here. Did I say unhook me now or later? Which one?"

"This is all the nonsense we'll tolerate. Do you hear me, mister? You curb that filthy mouth. This is a hospital, not a saloon!"

I reached under my hospital gown: "Unhook me so's a man can give a proper leak or I piss all over the floor an' watch your sorry ass clean it up. Understand, lil' missy?"

Reluctantly, she complied. I sudsed up toilet water with a flood of urine before being re-hooked to monitors and tubes. She warned, "If you fuss like that again I'll have to disconnect you from the injectable Demerol. It's this button I'm placing in your good hand. If the pain gets bad you can get another dose, but only every 2 hours. Are we clear, young man?"

I smiled, "Yes ma'am. You won't get any trouble outta me. The pain's real bad. Guess I'm shamed ta ask, like it's a weakness or somethin'. But I need help. Thanks."

After tapping that button like Nintendo on speed dial I phoned Benny for a ride home and checked myself out of there.

Back at the ranch Benny noted, "You been floppin' with those junky bikers and faggot-ass hippies too much lately. You're getting' soft, *coom*. But don't worry; I won't judge you for hangin' with a bunch a pussies that can't be trusted."

Pazzo had taught us as kids, "Druggies are looked down on by all addicts, even by drunks, even though they all play in that same schoolyard between now and suicide. Once people cross that pickle-line everything changes. But don't ever believe addicts can't be trusted. They can be trusted to rob family and to roll-over on friends. Everything changes along with appetites, and once that happens nothing's ever the same. You can buy from and sell to addicts, and even party together once in awhile. But stay away from harpoons. If wise-guys mess with needles they're yanked from the loop with a one-way ticket."

Ansel preached to the Wong Gongs, "If 1%ers shoot dope they're out. So remember this: Once a junkie always a scumbag. Fly right or get shot down."

As usual, our scooters lined-up at Chuggers to wet unquenchable thirsts. We heard yelling outside. An already drunken Inky pulled in the lot and smashed into Fingers' Chevelle. We exited to see Inky smack Fingers and knock him inside his car.

Inky shouted, "You wanna make me act crazy? Bring it on, Zeno the queeno."

Fingers pulled from his back seat, of all things, a scythe and laughed, "You fucked-up big this time, punk-boy. Now I gotta act like an animal."

He charged as if he was trimming trees and brought it down like a guillotine. Inky instinctively ducked and weaved sideways as he brought up a hand to block. The blade caught the meaty part between thumb and index finger and filleted it to his wrist. Inky unbuckled his belt and cinched it around his wrist to halt blood that squirted like from a Kool-Aid dispenser. He wrapped his shirt around his hand to keep the drumstick in place. Slick drove while Inky expertly held one end of his belt between his teeth.

Thinking drama was over for the night, we left only to run into a major league problem at the Cheshire Club. Nino was putting moves on some babes while Benny picked on everyone. During a set from a forgettable band, two hoodlums wearing black leather car coats and slicked back hair strutted through the crowd all puffed up. We weren't too high to recognize Frankie Fazule and Paddy Kelly heading straight for us.

When Benny flashed a set brass knucks, Frankie pulled a gun and said, "Uh oh! I guess it's Hog-balls time. Ain't it, Paddy-boy? Looks like these ladies got caught short."

Gus flicked open his knife: "Fuck with somebody your own size, hillbilly-cocksuckers." Gus loved it when he could call someone else a hillbilly.

Frankie grinned through gapped teeth, "Bull-fuck, bitches. I guess it's bad luck night, huh Gus? Say a prayer, Hog-balls." Then he fired three shots in rapid succession.

BANG . . . the first shot knocked Gus few feet back.

BANG . . . the second, also in his torso, left him leaning against the bar.

BANG . . . the third bullet hit. Gus slumped over, slid to the floor like Toby's tarantula as he eased on down. Nino rushed to sit next to him, to assure him he wasn't alone.

I have to admit it, Frankie was a pretty good shot for a drunk. So when he aimed for another I hoisted a chair while Benny climbed on his back and hammered Frankie's face with the knucks. I stood to his side and smashed his legs, but that stubborn bastard wouldn't fall and didn't drop his gun. Paddy put the boots to Benny from behind.

BANG . . . a fourth shot fired toward Gus. Nino jumped on Paddy. Benny kneed Frankie's elbow from behind to redirect his aim.

BANG . . . a fifth shot rang out as Benny dragged him down with a rear-naked choke. Frankie faced the ceiling with Benny underneath strangling him. Nino wrapped himself around Frankie's shooting arm as Paddy stomped Benny's head.

Just as I threw the chair at Paddy, BANG . . . the sixth shot whizzed *zzziiippp* past my ear so close I tasted gun powder. Temporarily deaf, I saw he used a revolver. Once all six rounds were safely spent I moved to his center with a fresh chair. Benny choked him real good as the crowd silently screamed and scattered.

All at once my world distorted. Hearing returned as I struggled for air. My face was on fire. I teed-off on a silhouetted figure and watched it drop from where the pain had been. I had been blinded and desperately needed to breathe.

Someone yelled, "It's not them. The other guy has a gun. Somebody help. Get those big guys with the gun. You cops are assholes!"

Cops? I tossed the chair, moved towards the light along with the current of a fleeing mob, across the street and then dove under a vehicle for cover as my vision gradually returned. I crawled farther back in the lot as searchlights panned the lot for the guy who broke a cop's arm with a chair. I could see to settle under a Jeep. My breathing was better, but my skin still felt like someone had doused me with kerosene, tossed a match in my face and then pissed in my eyes sockets to extinguish the flames.

The driver, in a hurry to get away, fumbled in her purse to unlock the Jeep. She gasped in a panic, "Oh my God! Where's the fucking keys! Shit, shit, shit!"

Her friend yelled, "Hurry! These assholes are all crazy. Cleveland sucks!"

Afraid she was going to run over me, I reached up to get her attention.

She shrieked, "IT'S GOT ME!" Her friend joined in the scream-fest, although she had no idea why they howled and ran away from their open vehicle.

I rolled between rows, crawled underneath vehicles whenever possible, snaked back up to the front to see if Gus was dead. I could see Nino with him. Cops questioned onlookers who walked away or pointed with animated gestures down the road.

Someone shouted, "We keep telling you, it was the other guys! You beat the crap out of the wrong people. No wonder everybody hates cops..."

Gus recovered nicely. No major organs had been damaged. He attributed that miracle to clean living and the healing powers of cocaine. Benny took as long to heal as Gus, because all the stitches had been ripped out of his hand during the scuffle and shredded his palm. After that episode Gus and Benny became more treacherous than ever. Whenever we left the Neighborhood we carried guns or switchblades.

Back at Chuggers a month later, a fully recuperated Gus and I sat at the bar eating bowls of steamed clams while Slick shot pool against himself. Slick was drunker than a man should be while playing any sport as AC/DC pounded "Dirty Deeds Done Dirt Cheap" on the jukebox. We heard a couple of loudmouths roll-in every bit as drunk as Slick.

One of them asked, "Hey, baldie, you wanna play nine-ball or some Hog-balls?"

I whispered, "Are you packed, *coom?*"

Slick lost on the break playing nine-ball against Frankie and then refused to pay.

Someone cracked a cue stick against the pool table. We heard Paddy threaten, "We'll kill you and any other motherless fuck don't like it. You Bull-fuck with us, you're as good as fertilizer. We're killin' machines, me and Frankie is. Wanna test us, baldie?"

Gus mumbled, "How you wanna act, *coom*." *You smell that thick artery blood?*

"Yep, it stinks like a dead whore." *You smell it too, huh?* "Okay. Cool, calm and dry, right Gus? Let's just see how it plays out." *It's real close, and we're not strapped.*

A flimsy steak knife with a round tip was my only weapon. We still faced the bar and kept our heads down. Gus pulled his pig sticker. *Better stay cool for right now.* We felt that *Click* stronger than ever before, so we kept our noses in bowls of steamers.

"One goddamn time I leave the house without my piece. Why didn't that *schifoso* piece a shit just die? How do we waste these guys in front of Slick and a bartender, and then skate away from this mess? Just tell me that, *coom*."

"It can't happen, Gus. Stay cool, unless we have to make a move. Now's not the time. Let's just feel our way through this, okay? Trust our instincts and let's see what happens." *Don't turn around. Not right now... Just keep your head lowered, Gus.*

"Swear to Buddha, Jackie, we can get the drop on 'em. We'll rush 'em from both sides and punch holes in 'em real quick like." *Don't worry. I'm not budging just yet.*

"They know what'll happen if they push this shit too far. Slick ain't hurt, and that hillbilly ain't said word one to us." *Stay cool, Gus.*

"Fuck Slick. Let's just waste both a these cocksuckers right now."

The clam broth tasted metallic like a fat lip. "You feel it yet?"

Frankie's stank breath crawled across the backs of our necks, even though we could hear him on the far side of the pool table. *Shit! They made us.*

Frankie said, "Well I'll be double Bull-fucked. Lookee here, Paddy-boy. Is this what I think it is? Youse two again, huh? I guess we still got unfinished business. So what-da-ya-think, Hog-balls? Do we just kill Gus and let these other pukes slide?"

"Nah . . . Fuck-it. Let's just do all three in a spray."

Static squelched from a radio by the door and in walked O'Reilly. "Oh, it must be ladies night. Oops, sorry fellas, I thought you were women. Uh oh, is that an unregistered gun, Frankie? How's about I tell your boss you're waving a piece at girls? Oh, it's just a couple of grease balls. I should have stayed outside."

Paddy warned, "Don't think we're lettin' this slide, Gus. Youse're just lucky ol' Hog-balls here's friends with my uncle, or we'd spray both a youse pussy motherfuckers all over this bar – long-haired fairies." Then they stormed out.

Gus gritted his teeth and squinted bloodshot eyes. He loosened his ponytail and flipped his hair over his shoulders. I turned up my collar and pushed away my bowl. Eating crow didn't go well with seafood.

Slick yammered, "That punk-ass hillbilly had his piece aimed right at the two a youse clam eatin' motherfuckers. I can't believe youse limp-dicks just sat there and let that fat, *guinea* cocksucker call us fairies. Youse guys are gettin' too old, man. Too bad the No-Names ain't in formation tonight. We'd a butchered those simple bitches."

"Wake up, Slick. The only fairies must've been on our shoulders. You don't get it. You can't feel that crystal wire connecting our brains. The *Click* don't lie."

"Jackie's right. You're too goddamn drunk and stupid to know the difference. Like for example, in about a hot minute we're about to get company." Right after those words fell out of Gus' mouth our crew slammed open the door.

Gus and I played eight-ball against Fingers and Benny. Nino and Eggs talked story with the bar-keep while O'Reilly got drunker and smarted off to everybody.

O'Reilly asked the bartender, "Since when did this become a nigger bar?"

Without looking up from the table Benny said, "Eat shit, Porkie." Then just as smooth as the underside of a tit, he sank the eight ball in a corner pocket as Johnny Winter did a guitar riff of "Highway 61" from the juke box.

When the song ended, O'Reilly said, "You *dago* queers talk plenty of shit, but you know better that to mess with a cop," and then back-handed Eggs across his mouth.

Gus pushed him out the door and onto the hood of a car, held his throat and warned, "You better lighten up, badass. Hear? Or you might not leave."

O'Reilly ranted, "I'm calling Lonnie and the troops. Then we'll see!"

Benny held the cop in a Full Nelson while I confiscated a piece hidden in his belt and a badge from his pocket. We left him thumped-up in a pile of whine across the hood.

Fingers slammed O'Reilly's face into the car and asked, "How you gonna act when your boyfriend ain't here?" as he jerked a fistful of thin hair. "Who's the tough guy now, huh? How you gonna make *us* act, you stupid fuck? We got you right where we want you. Now beg, or we feed you to the Benny."

"I got a shovel in my trunk!" bellowed a pissed-off Benny. "Let's take this pig-fuck for the morbid drive. Payback is one motherless fuck. Ain't it, pig?"

O'Reilly pleaded, "Alright already. Enough is enough. Just give me my issue."

"Gimme the piece, *coom*. Believe me. It's for his own good. And that fuckin' bartender knows better than to make a squeak. Either way, I got a big trunk. Then his expression changed. "But I'm calm now. Look at me. Now hand over the piece and let's clean this mess up. I'll stash his heat till he's sober. Hurry up. We gotta do this fast."

When I handed Benny the pistol Eggs tackled him just as he was firing a round.

"Okay, please," O'Reilly begged. "I had enough. I'm finished with this. Just give me what's mine and I'll go. No grudges. I swear it. It's all my fault, okay?"

We fled to the ranch to make plans and to drink ourselves into a stupor. Benny said, "I better hide somethin' here just in case we get busted tonight."

Benny lifted his shirt. He had a thick manila envelope shoved down his pants marked, "Seed Money." He tossed it on my only good piece of furniture.

"What the fuck you doin' carrying around our life savings? Is that all of it?"

"Naw, just half. I'll stash it at my dad's. The other half's at my mom's house," slurred a drunken Benny who fell on the couch.

I passed him a fresh tequila bottle and answered the phone. It was the proprietor of Chuggers. "O'Reilly said they'll be back to blow you *guinea* bastards off the map. You guys'd better leave town ASAP till things cool down. This is serious."

"Fuck this layin' low bullshit, Jackie. Get your father's shotgun."

Back outside, me with the shotgun and him with O'Reilly's pistol on his hip and the jug in hand, a squad car slowed and then parked.

The passenger said, "If you guys don't have the best alibi we've heard all night you're headed straight for the tank. Okay, who's first? Go ahead, take your best shot."

Best shot? What's he mean? Is that cop code? Why's he stalling?

Benny gave me a strange look so I blurted out, "If youse guys don't wanna do nothin' about these fuckin' niggers, we will. We're sick and tired a this bullshit!"

Benny added, "Yeah, we're fed-up. Who does somethin' about the little girl?"

The driver lowered his head, "What's this about?"

Benny chimed in, "The girl that just got ass-fucked up behind Mickey Dee's, that's what the fuck *we're* talkin' about!" *Phew! He's not black and they're actually buyin' this bullshit.*

"Oh yeah . . . So enlighten us. How is it you know this and we don't?"

"Because she's our cousin. That's how, goddamn-it. Her mother just phoned us."

"Okay, tell you what. You guys go back home and stay there, and we'll go take care of it. Now scram or we haul your lucky asses downtown."

"We don't need any trouble. Youse won't see us for the rest of the night."

Back at the ranch we finished the bottle and dropped some Valium. The next thing I remember is waking with a dry mouth and pounding headache to a ringing phone.

O'Reilly's barber brother called to say, "If the gun and badge aren't returned by today he gets fired. My brother's an asshole, and I'm sure he deserved that ass-kicking, but he's got kids. Bring his things to the barbershop. I'll guarantee your safety."

I stumbled out to the leather couch we'd taken from a guy who owed us money, right to where I last remembered seeing Benny. All I found was an empty tequila bottle.

I phoned him to hear a cracked voice that sounded as lousy as I felt, yet Benny made it back to the ranch within 20 minutes.

"Youse guinea bastards lucked-out big-time. Last night at Mick's bar, The Shamrock Club, Paddy got into it with some longhaired freak. The guy told Frankie to suck his *shillelagh*, so Frankie shot the guy right off his barstool. Then they just sat back down and ordered another drink. Mick's got juice and witnesses who'll say anything for him. My brother says Paddy'll get shock probation and be back on the streets within a few months. But he says Frankie'll catch a life sentence for this stunt."

We left O'Reilly's cop issue and then gathered up a few brothers. The plan was to stop at the No-Names clubhouse to look over some merchandise. After we purchased every gun and rifle they weren't keeping, a bunch of us packed into Nino's car to score some dope. A drunken Toby called out, "Hey, Jackie, you forgot about that thing. I need an appraisal. Come-on back in for a quick minute." He swaggered inside the house.

I'M JACK & I WANT MORE

I walked in to find Toby leaning against a wall by the front door with beefy arms crossed, a toothpick between yellowed teeth. "You wanna make some fast cash?"

"That depends on how much and what I gotta do."

"I'm talkin' five grand – clean money – 2.5 each, and alls you gotta do is pick somethin' up and take a little drive. No big deal. I'll handle the rest."

"Sounds too easy. What's the rest, Toby? Don't bullshit me."

"Benny's been crossin' a few lines and word came down from Little Italy that it's his time. The Mick picked up the contract but he's givin' it to me. I'm trustin' you."

"Have you lost your fucking mind? Benny's my oldest friend."

"If we don't take the money, somebody else will. 2.5 each, Jackie."

"You got some balls. Let me ask you something. What makes you think I won't go outside right now and tell Benny what you just said?"

"Because if you do The Mick will hit you, too. And you know this."

"Hmmm . . . Hold-up. Let me think about it. I can't decide just like that."

"Don't take too long, Jackie. The Mick wants his answer tonight."

We walked back out to the car where everyone stood, smoking and passing around a jug of Canadian Club. Toby, rowdy as usual, demanded to ride shotgun.

On our way to Nerk's house Toby leaned back and asked, "So you wanna buy that thing or not? Or maybe I should sell two a those motherfuckers instead."

"Easy does it, Tobe," I answered from behind. "We're trippin' and you're drunk. And you know this. Let's do this the smart way. Okay, cuz?"

"Yeah, Jackie, let's do that. I'll give the orders and you pay attention."

I reached for my pack of Luckies but found something else.

I sat in between Benny and Chilly. Benny mumbled, "Go ahead. Just squeeze one off and it's done. You want to, right *coom*? It feels good like that."

"There's somethin' wrong with this acid, bro-ham," I said as I shook my head. "The colors are all gone. Everything just feels gray."

Chilly whispered, "Careful, bro-ham. Think it through. Head? Too many witnesses, or maybe not enough shells. Leg? Then it's payback time."

"Say what? You talkin' to me? Lower that radio, Nino, so we can hear what this crazy motherfucker's yackin' about back there."

"I'm just sayin' I got yours right here, Tobe. Check it out."

Toby moaned and slumped onto Slick, who straddled the console like it was his scooter. Toby gurgled, "I'm hit! Swear to Buddha, I'm shot." He reached up to grab the seat, his hand covered with charcoal blood like from boxers on black & white TV sets.

Nino yelled, "What the fuck just happened?" Those in back didn't have to ask.

"Well, I had enough fun for one night," Nino said as he pulled up to the No-Names clubhouse. I'm dropping everyone off. Get out, Slick, and help Toby."

Benny's car was at the ranch. We went in to finish our acid peak, but Benny decided to call it a night. On his way home, he encountered Loony Lonnie and O'Reilly at a stop sign. They approached with guns drawn and ordered, "Give us the envelope!"

Benny's left hand was still bandaged, wrapped thick like a boxing glove. He laughed "Oh, it's just youse two fucks. I was worried for a second. Hey, your ol' ladies were here askin' for some hard dick. I told 'em I don't fuck nigger lovers, so they took turns suckin' me off."

Lonnie shot him through the sewn-up hand that had rested on the top of his door. Benny growled in pain and stepped outside to spit a hocker on Lonnie's uniform. Lonnie shot him again. That time he shattered his forearm.

Benny went down hard. When he stood, O'Reilly kicked him in his stomach, dropped him again and said, "Go ahead, wisecrack on us again, tough-guy."

Benny taunted from the ground, "Kill me now, or I'll be back. Bet on that shit."

Porch lights came on and front doors opened. Neighbors made enough racket to prompt those two back in their patrol car.

Benny screamed, "Youse think you're safe 'cause you're pigs? This ain't over!"

The next day while Fingers and I drove back from the hospital he confided in hushed tones, "Between me and you, we need to look closer at Benny from now on."

"I admit he's goin' through a tough time, but he's still one of us."

"You know Joey Cagootz is a stand-up guy, right Jackie? Listen at this. He told me that before Benny took these bullets he was tryin' to strong-arm some connected guys in Little Italy. He's tryin' to move in on them. Can you believe this? Benny's finally gone over the edge, and if he goes down he takes us with him."

"Benny's always been a lunatic, true enough, but he's never turned on us. Besides, since when did Cagootz get so reputable? Fuck those mama's-boys from Little Italy. They couldn't last one day without those older guys up there leadin' 'em around by the nose. Let Cagootz and his crew try to navigate their way through a thousand black militants every day and then we'll see how fucking stand-up they are."

"Okay, fuck Joey Cagootz and his whole crew. This ain't about them. I'm just sayin' Benny can't be trusted anymore. Look at his track record. He's out of control. He keeps this shit up, he's gonna jackpot everybody and ruin everything we're tryin' to build. Uno's leery of him, and that ain't a good sign for us."

"Look, Fingers, I hear you, but we take care of our own."

"Okay, thank you. That's exactly what I'm talkin' about. Let's take care of him."

"What? Fuck that. I respect Uno as much as anybody. He's the last person in the world I'd ever want mad at me. All I'm sayin' is let's not jump the gun here."

Fingers snorted and spit a wad out his window. With a grim expression he nodded his head and said, "Okay, Jackie, we'll just watch him for now. But I'm tellin' you, one more move like that and it's over."

"Let's just play it by ear and see what Uno has to say."

"While Benny's laid-up I'm gonna hang closer to Uno. If he don't trust him, it makes all of us look bad. I gotta say it again, Jackie, he's been fuckin' up way too much lately. I don't wanna pay for Benny's mistakes. How about you?"

"I gotta think. I'll just walk home from here."

As I strolled though the neighborhood, nursing a residual high lost in conspiracies, Toby pulled up and eased off his scooter. During a long ago birthday party he had watched from the ground while I saved his life from Inky's spear. In another close-call incident, I thought I had squeezed one into his head but my pistol was wedged between the passenger seat and door. On that day of my stroll, however, Toby leaned against his Pan Head with arms folded to make his biceps look even bigger and stared emotionless for a long minute.

Finally he spoke: "Hey, sorry to hear about them pigs doggin' Benny. Forget about that other thing, and thanks for not sayin' anything. That's all been squashed. We've had our ups and downs, Jackie. But fuck-it. As far as I'm concerned, we're even." He extended a knobby hand: "But no more mistakes, Jackie."

I shook his calloused hand and looked directly into his eyes: "Chilly once told me how mistakes turn into monsters that eventually show up in our reflections. He said I'd better figure out which side of the mirror I'm on before it's too late."

Toby shook his head, spit out his toothpick, kicked-started his chopper and was gone.

That shooting incident with Toby had been a bad mistake, even though it was not an accident. But I lucked out with him, able to balance the scales before it was too late. The thing with Neighborhood guys was simple: Slick, Ice-cream Nicky and even Bee-Bee Balls were tough and gutsy. In the suburbs those guys would have been heralded as kings. But in Collinwood everybody was rough and game.

More proof of my own out of control behavior surfaced when I woke covered with dried blood and no memory of where I was or with whom. Blood encrusted hands and swollen knuckles matched bloodied clothes from chest to knees. A bedroom mirror showed my face was unmarked. Stripped naked, it reflected unscathed flesh. After a series of phone calls I realized whomever I had been with was not one of us. I ventured outside to look for a body in my car. I found nothing unusual other than four fenders smashed, each marred with different colored paint. *Oh well, fuck-it.*

Then things notched higher up on the Richter scale when 1%ers planted their flag down Five Points to establish their power base. Bikes were left unattended on the border of The Mick's headquarters of killers; adjacent to Glenville, a ghetto populated with Black Panthers and Black Nationalists. MC members, mostly of German and Yugoslavian descent, parked custom machines next to new Lincoln Continentals and Cadillac de Ville's. It was interesting to watch the lack of interaction between made-men and patch-holders. They affected mutual respect in the form of avoidance. Bottom line: none were cops and all were white.

Our crew formed alliances with hardcore bikers and solidified ties with bosses. We also branched out to suburb watering holes where sweeties craved rough rides with hard-edged boys. Ladies of that era were the first to admit they were intrigued by the eroticism of *sangwitches*, to indulge in that sweet-sharing of sexual desires. If we dated Neighborhood girls their fathers knew what time it was. So if I locked-up one of those high maintenance girls it was goodbye to threesomes. That was just one of many reasons why we didn't date Neighborhood girls, unless the goal was marriage or a bullet in the ass. Even if a girl's father wasn't a gangster, he was related to one, knew some or would revert to primal instincts to protect his brood.

Elders treated us well when we were kids, so in turn we respected their kids — most of the time. Everyone understood the rules and how certain mistakes could never be apologized away. Yet everyone we knew seemed to be crashing through life on the nose of a runaway train holding a lit chainsaw. I was fucking up so hard, apologies for repetitive transgressions became as insulting as saying nothing at all. I cared; I really did, but evidently not enough.

CH XI:
NEW NEIGHBORS

My father used to tell a story about mistakes: "During the Depression my dad partnered-up with an Indian called Big Maneto on a 90-pound Yankee Terrier, a Pit-bull/Airedale mix. Legend had it their dog was half-devil. In his second last match Rover beat a wolf-dog that weighed over 100 pounds in less than 40 minutes. It belonged to some Polish coalminers. It ended when their big, shaggy dog started screaming. Those miners returned the following month with more money and a small white, shorthaired dog. It had a long head with pig-like eyes and stand-up ears. It looked like a giant rat that was tough and game. Grampa said Rover had to kill that little dog to stop it, and that the fight lasted over an hour. The next month those same guys pooled their money and came back with a small, well-made dog with black tiger stripes. When Grampa saw another little dog they bet more money than they had. After two hours, Rover couldn't stand. Their Pit-bull died after the match. Rover found his way home, half blind and almost dead. Our fathers weren't so lucky. Before my friend, Little Maneto, and his family returned to Tennessee he showed me how to draw out infection with a poultice of mud and prickly-pear. That was the last time I ever saw my friend, but his gift stayed with us. Rover protected Gramma and us eleven orphans till he was 13 years old. That was when I found him stiff and cold, dead by our half-eaten nanny goat. Next to them were two bloody coyotes with broken necks. Son, I trusted that old dog more than any person I've ever known."

Each night after supper my father's routine was to sit in his recliner to watch the news with Sinbad at his side, to repeat the same words: "You're a pretty good boy, but you're no Rover." Sinbad didn't mind the left-handed compliment. He melted against the chair, bathed in all that attention, wearing his contented Pit-bull grin.

With Sinbad in a safe place, I farmed-out Butch to Ansel so I could pursue *more* during a time when too much was almost enough.

Gus's mom lived down Five Points. Her neighbor happened to be a gorgeous biracial girl known as Butterscotch whom I had not seen in a couple of years. Born from a mulatto mother and a Caucasian father, her creamy skin complemented a soft, honey-colored afro and fast-lane body. The day we ran into each other as adults, Gus and I were kick-starting our Harleys when she glided by to pose for me in her sassy way.

"Jackie, huh? Mmm, okay. I think I might remember you. Weren't you the boy with the tailor-made pants and those spit shined shoes? Yeah, you were a little cutie back then. Look at you now, all hard with those tattoos and all that hair," she laughed. "But you know what? I still see you, and I see something special in your eyes. Tell me something, Jackie. Do you like black girls?"

"I don't know . . . maybe. I ain't too sure. Why, is there a difference?"

"Well, I suppose if you're interested enough you'll find out for yourself."

"Yeah, I guess you're right. So let's just do that. Let's me and you find out."

When my father saw her on my bike he warned, "Be careful, son. It's not fair to bring mongrel children into this hateful world. People can be cruel, especially children. Stick with your own kind, boy."

"I'm still not sure what my kind is, Pop," I said as I put on my shades.

The next day I brought her back to the ranch. When I shared my father's advice her response was, "He can't help it. Their generation got brainwashed by all that racist dribble from another era. Grandma's the same way. They don't know any better, but you're about to. Show me your bedroom. I have a present just for you. You're the first, and if you play your cards right . . . maybe the only. Let's go, tough guy."

Those strawberry curls stuck tightly to her forehead by a gleam of perspiration as she gyrated beneath me. I couldn't stop watching her. What a sight. She was amazing in every way. Her teeth, skin and hair . . . just perfect. Her mouth and eyes were incredible. That sweet-ass body perfect for me. When she finally looked at me she was crying and smiling at the same time.

Then she said, "I've been saving myself for a very special man. I'm glad I waited for you, Jackie. You need a heads-up, though. Your high school nemesis, Curtis, is my cousin and lives just down the street from Mom. He told me he's sorry about you getting expelled. He says he was young, drunk and acting the fool. He says to let you know he can unload all the weed you need to move if it's good stuff. I trust him. He's solid."

"As a matter of fact, me and Benny just absconded a kilo of Panama Red from some degenerate who's into us for a shit-load of money. Yeah, fuck-it, if you vouch for him we can talk. Hook up a meeting – just me and him. We'll see how solid he is."

"He's says if you're cool with it for me to phone him from Mom's so he can come by and talk. You okay with this?"

"I'm willing to let him talk. I'll see what kind of vibe I get from him."

We showered and then headed back to her mom's to make the call. Curtis arrived within minutes. He nodded, "I feel kinda bad about some shit, flukey. It wasn't right they bounced you and let me skate. I told Gramps I started the shit. He said he'd stomp a mud-hole in my ass if I fessed-up to it. I got no grudges. For me, it's all just some school kid's bullshit. I'm guessin' you be the same on this. The other thing is I'm cool with you and my baby cousin hookin' up. She digs you, man. She thinks you're the real deal."

When he offered his hand I shook it: "What's past is done, Curtis. But what's new is this: I got a kilo of primo weed – the best in Cleveland – and I can get more. Here's a joint from that brick. I'll hook you up with a fat elbow. Check it out, man. Have a taste. You'll be glad."

He torched a twisted end, took a deep inhale, grinned and nodded: "Yeah, flukey got him some primo-ass doo-doo. You got more?" He took another hit and handed it back to me. I hit it and passed it to Butter. "Okay. How 'bout this? I'll be takin' the whole flukey if you makes me a sweet deal." Butter passed it to her cousin. Curtis pulled off another long draw and added, "Figure on me movin' all of it, if the shit taste like this."

"Sounds pretty good so far. Meet me here tonight at 10:00, by yourself and with $700.00 cash money. We ain't kids anymore. You set me up, you can bet I won't be understanding or forgiving. But if you're straight, like Butter says you are, then you just made yourself a new friend."

"I dig. I know you. Flukey's all mobbed-up now with the big-time gangster *dagos* back in da *Wood* and these badass bikers up here at the Five Points. Nah, we cool."

Curtis arrived at 10:00 on the dot, alone and carrying a duffle bag. He walked in without knocking and reached in his pocket. When I went in mine for my piece he tossed Butter a roll of bills: "Do me a favor, cuz. Count that green for yo man while I show him a little some-some. He unfolded a square piece of yellow paper. Inside was a pile of white powder. "This here's some righteous *boy*, Jackie. You dig? This gram's for you. Just go easy. This shit's from the Nam. One a my dudes sent a whole flukey-doo back home before he got his ass fragged. Now it's mine. You like it, I'll get you what you needs."

Butter interrupted, "The count's wrong. There's $750.00 here."

"That lil' fitty's for you, lil' sista," he smiled. "Go on. Lock it up, cuz."

I handed him a trash bag and said, "Take a whiff of this, Curtis. Kinda smells like a slice a heaven, ain't it? Alright man, stay cool and thanks for the taste. I'll let you know on this. But meantime, I gotta be someplace. Come on, Butter, let's get in the wind."

"Alright, flukey. Good doin' business. So I'll be seein' you around then, friend."

I kick-started my HD and we were in that wind with a blast of V-twin. Later that evening, after another torrid night of passion, I confessed to a girl whose skin looked to be made of the same ceramic material as one of Chink's Buddha's, "I gotta admit it. So far I have more in common with you than any white girls I've met. I mostly see these little Appalachian chicks. I don't even get along with those bitchy Italian broads. Let's play it by ear. Maybe we can enjoy each other while it's still fun. How's that?"

"Sure . . . Cool by me, Jackie. I'm not looking for any commitments."

After two weeks of pure bliss I had another heart-to-heart with Gus. As we parked our scooters in the garage and headed inside the ranch I said, "Look, *coom*. I hate to sound all sappy and shit, but I got a situation and don't know where to take it."

"I'm all ears, Jackie. Go ahead; lay it on me. But you better hurry before I pass out, because I'm drunker than any man should be who just operated heavy equipment."

'Well, it's that Butter situation again. But I feel like a bitch even sayin' this shit."

"No sweat. We know you got the fever." he laughed. "So what is it? Let me guess. She wants to do a *sangwitch* but you don't want her to lose respect for you?"

"Real funny, Gus. Look: first off, you know me well. I don't give a cat's ass what any of these jerk-offs in the Neighborhood think about me seein' her or anything else I do. It just ain't my job to impress those old pricks. Fuck them greedy bastards."

"Okay, fuck-'em. I agree. So what's the big deal, then?"

"The big deal is I know my family too well. They say they ain't prejudice and all that, right up until my father sees me with a black girl on my scooter. Then he's tellin' me, *Stick with my own kind* and shit like that. Plus, I know my mother's at home freakin' the fuck out about this. You should see the way she looks at me now."

"Oh well . . . I guess they'll get over it . . . or they won't. It's your life."

"Yeah . . . it's my life and my decision. The thing is I *really* dig this chick. But I ain't about to lose my family over some sweetie I hardly even know. I'm fucked-up behind this one. I don't know, man. No matter which way I go, it looks like a bad call."

"As far as I can tell, either way you take a loss on this. Just remember: no matter how sweet that pussy is now, after awhile you won't even be trimmin' that fine ass. She'll be holdin' out just like the rest of these frigid bitches, unless it's to fuck strangers."

"Maybe I'm making too big of a deal outta this."

Following our talk I approached Butter all hang-dog: "We need to talk, babe. Just hear me out first. Then tell me up-front whatever you need to say. Okay?"

"You're the one who needs to talk. So go ahead; spill it. What's the big deal? Are you pregnant, Jackie? Do you need me to make an honest man out of you? Is that it?"

"I'm serious, alright? I've been thinkin' we should stop while we're still friends. Anyways, love fades quicker than a new pair a Levi's – and you know this. Besides, you think I'm ready to settle down? As soon as you feel secure I'll have some blonde slut on the back of my chopper, pourin' cock to her like there's a pussy famine. So come-on, gimme that sweet Butterscotch kiss and say bye before this situation gets messy."

She radiated a sexy smile though moist eyes bluer than ever and asked, "Oh you're doing this for me, right? Sure. I guess I'll ease back into my house and out of your life because my curls are a bit tighter than yours. Wow . . . thanks for nothing, *friend*."

Another of Gus' neighbors, Black Bart, was vice-president of the Wong Gongs. He stood about 6'6" and weighed over 350 lbs. His frizzy hair and full beard made him look crazier than he was. Ansel, the president, looked like a Viking and was ferocious.

That starless night I rode with Bart and Ansel to The Inn after a hard rain. When Loony Lonnie and O'Reilly spotted us out front they braked.

Ansel passed me a handful of Seconal. I pretended to toss something through a hedge next to us. But before I lifted my arm I dropped the pills in a puddle at my feet and stepped on them as I reached for my fake throw. The cops patted us down and then checked the hedges with flashlights.

That weekend turned out to be a hallmark event. Gus and I had been placed on stand-by for a war at a motorcycle show. Bart told us afterwards, "We decided you shouldn't come. Club-brothers from out of state don't know you from a hat full of shit. I had to go through two cops to get out of there. Ansel and a few brothers are in lock-down right now. Pigs are tryin' to stick premeditated murder cases on 'em, sayin' Ansel was choppin' motherfuckers up with a hatchet. But so far they got no witnesses. Both teams live by the same code. You know the old saying: *Three drunks can keep secrets a lot better if two of 'em can't talk.* We ain't ashamed to weed out our own culls."

Gus and I were riding high. We were trusted by the most notorious motorcycle gang in the world. Ansel and Bart became our new best friends.

My father nodded in disgust: "All you did was trade gangsters with silk suits and Lincolns for thugs with Levi's and Harleys. Wake up before it's too late, boy."

"You don't get it, Pop. Suburban chicks love this, gritty biker scene."

"It's just to hurt their parents. Besides, if you think any of these hoodlums are your friends you're in for a rude awakening – if you're lucky."

"It's a different generation now. You can't understand brotherhood like this. Loyalty is a way of life for bikers. It means everything to these guys."

"Oh yeah? I've heard this same crock of shit before."

The night Bart and I rode to the Cheshire Club it was one of those hot, sticky nights perfect for being in the wind. We wore cutoff vests, but mine bore no patch. Inside the warehouse-sized barroom in Downtown Cleveland, we sipped ice-cold brews. After hours worth of drinking and ball-busting, two pink-cheeked college girls stormed past the bouncers and literally ran into Bart. The short one rested her forehead on his chest.

She looked up and asked through a wide smile, "Oopsy daisy. Oh! You guys aren't leaving, are you?" They had those dancing eyes of the mad or the very intoxicated.

Bart said, "Sure, baby, we'll hang for some drinks. Then the four of us'll split. How's that suit you, darlin'?" I bought double-shot tequilas and more beer.

The taller girl yelled over the music louder than necessary, "Wait. First we have to make a toast. Okay. Here's to inventing a new kind of beer that doesn't make you piss every 15 minutes." They nodded in serious appreciation and sipped.

The short girl said, "Here's to one night stands and stupid boyfriends at home." They fell on one another and giggled at that one, and then chugged their shots.

When they spoke to us they shouted. Hot breath steamed against our sweaty necks. But when they talked to each other they pressed their noses against one another's.

"Hey!" I shouted. "I got a toast for us. Here's one to firm tits and tight asses." The girls just looked at one another with exaggerated surprise and then burst into laughter.

Bart said, "How about this one? Here's to Fuck City. You girls ever been there?"

They thought that one was hilarious and gave high fives all around.

The taller girl said, "Here's to getting shit-faced and going for a hell-ride."

He mopped his brow with a rolled-up bandana that had dangled from a back pocket and answered, "Fuckin'-aye- right, bitch. We'll ride youse little hussies all night."

The girl who had collided with Bart asked, "Hey, man, you look like some real badass. Are you dangerous, man? Should we be scared of you, dude? Do you like ride with some scary motorcycle gang?" They giggled like schoolyard kids.

All of us wore frozen grins of the totally blitzed. He turned away for a moment to expose colors emblazoned on the back of his vest, "I ride with the only real club."

He wiped the bandana across his bare chest, still smiling as he turned to face us. *Fuck me . . . there it is.* Bart didn't flinch when the *Click* thundered, as I glanced at two bouncers to see if their radar had picked up on our fresh madness.

The disgusted-looking girl said: "Oh, I see. So I guess that means you're a couple of scumbags, huh?" She looked at her girlfriend and they cracked-up laughing again.

Yep, there's what I wanted to be wrong about. Still grinning, Bart untied the knot from the rolled up hanky, stretched it like a rope and then wrapped it around her neck.

I used some Ice-cream Nicky double-talk on the bouncers, "How youse bust-outs wanna make *us* act? We'll do somethin' crazy youse come any closer. I'll shoot in a crowd. Believe that shit." I noticed the girl on her knees had a blue face. "Don't make me do it, 'cause youse know I will. It's on your head if we gotta kill our way out."

When Bart yanked his bandana from around the girl's neck she hit the floor like a shit-baby. Like a linebacker with a death's head for a number, he elbowed through those bouncers like lane pins as we ran out the doors. We jogged to the bikes, choking on the type of laughter of short-bus students or the very drunk, and roared back to the ranch.

Back at the clubhouse Bart said, "Me and Ansel been talkin' right along, even before the shit hit the blades, and we decided your Royal Flush should take Toby and his crew in as prospects – all but Slick, that is. You know, keep a close eye on 'em. As soon as you tell us who makes the grade, we're gonna absorb your entire crew as a probate club. You, Gus, Benny and Fingers will be flying colors. We'll make the others prospect for awhile. Talk it over with your people and let them know what we decided."

Gus and I were the only two who had voted to join forces with the Wong Gongs.

Fingers asked, "They wanna make *us* probates? Is that supposed to be a joke?"

"Fuck those hillbillies," Benny snarled. "Maybe they can be *our* prospects."

I'M JACK & I WANT MORE

Gus and I dog-sat for my parents that week, with hopes of Sinbad guarding our bikes. Because game-dogs have been bred for hundreds of years to be tolerant of people in the most stressful situations, our idea was a failure so we kept him inside. On a typical night of too much I took him for his last walk-out just before dawn. A boy delivered papers in pitch dark with his un-tethered poodle. The yapping fuzz-ball ran across the street growling and flew into a wide-open mouth like he was a dentist.

When the boy shrieked and kicked in his ribs, Sinbad hunkered down. I remembered a movie where a guy slapped a hysterical person across the face and commanded, "Snap out of it!" I tried that and it actually worked. "Now go find me a thick stick." Then I pried the flattened poodle out of his mouth and we ran upstairs.

"Gus!" I panted as I shook him. "Flush any drugs we might've missed. Sinbad ate a poodle, so cops are probably on the way." I tried not to stare at his naked sweetie.

"Alright, motherfucker," he snarled. "I'm up!" Just as Blondie turned on a lamp he let out a snort and passed out again. *This must be some biker, brotherhood, coomba loyalty test...right?* She walked to a clock glowing in golden nudity. *Okay, just look but don't touch. Big deal, it's only a fine chick with platinum pubes on ceramic-like flesh.* I attempted to turn away as she walked toward me. I struggled to look at her face when that cotton candy was mere inches from me. *Gus, you lucky bastard.*

Sinbad licked Gus's stink feet to break the spell. Roused back to the world of paranoia, he finally comprehended the word "cops." He growled, "Dirty cocksuckers" as he slipped into greasy, riding boots (no socks) and his riding jacket with its zippers, fringes and chromed conchos. Other then those items Gus was nude. He picked up his shotgun and stumbled to the front-room to lie of the couch and resume his snoring.

"I'm making coffee. Would you like anything?" *This fuckin' bitch is game-testing me, for real.* "Is there anything I can do?" she asked. *I'm dyin' here. How could hair just be that thin and blonde?* "I'll make sure he gets up." *How could nipples be such a light shade of pink on those cup-cake sized tits that defy gravity?* "Don't worry; I can make him stay up." *I feel like I'm gonna pass out. Please stop...*

"Come-on, man! As if a flattened poodle, smacking a little kid around and worrying about the cops ain't enough, now this shit? You gotta wake up. A man can only stand so much. I need some help here. Gus! Do you understand me?"

"Yeah, I fucking understand!" he yelled. "I promise, goddamnit! I'm awake. Now let me sleep!"

On that note, Sinbad and I hopped into my '59 black Cadillac we referred to as the "bad mobile." We stayed the night at my parent's house. Cops didn't show up, but the boy's father did. I can't imagine what ran through his mind when he saw them.

Gracie had been in my parent's backyard pen nursing a litter from Sinbad. The following day I carried a 12-week old runt named Idjit to the paperboy's house, the one I couldn't sell. My knock was answered by a stern looking military man with a chest full of ribbons and medals. After I explained who I was and offered the pup he closed the screen door. When it reopened I extended a handful of fat, squirmy pup toward the ex-paperboy.

"It's to show you I'm sorry. My only request is don't let this one run off-lead."

The Army officer reluctantly said, "Son, if you want the pup you can have it." The boy silently declined with a wag of his head and disappeared back into the house.

I asked, "Hey, officer. Did you have any problems with my friend that night?" He gave a disgusted cop look and closed the door on my question.

Gus and I went to Blondie's house where he found what appeared to be a rusty-looking toothpick in a kitchen drawer. He said, "Pick an ear, or should we do the nose?"

"No way in the nose. Which one is the non-*finocchio* ear? And at least clean that goddamn needle. Run it under the sink and wipe it off with that *mopino*."

Gus shook his head and chuckled, "Go ask Blondie, the bipolar, bisexual dyke out there which one's the non-fag ear."

Unsure of which was the correct ear for men to pierce, we walked into the front-room where she was teaching her five-year old how to snort crank.

"I can't fucking believe this!" I yelled. "There's somethin' wrong with your head, bitch!" then snatched-up the kid – a moment too late.

Gus backhanded her, "You're the dumbest cunt I ever seen. This time it's just a slap in your suck. Next time I'll drop you off down Five Points – naked. But you'd probably like that, right? Meantime, why don't you try being a mother for once?"

The child rode his tricycle through the house at full speed. He smashed into walls and furniture while she cackled laughter through bloody teeth.

Back in the kitchen I cautioned, "Be hygienic, *coom*. Don't be *sfacim* (a no pride, jizz-bag) like Blondie out there." I opted for the left ear because it would be visible when I drove a car. It was good logic for a drunk, and damn lucky.

"Okay, *coom*. When you're right, you're right. We're not *schifoso* like that lunatic cunt." He spat on a needle thick enough to sew dog collars and wiped it on his greasy Levis. He poked it through my left lobe and pulled through its dingy-looking thread back and forth, cut it with his knife and tied it in a knot. "This way the hole don't close-up."

"Sure . . . Sounds good to me." I cleaned my blood off the needle with spit and wiped it on my filthy pants before I pierced his left ear the same way.

Blondie, on the couch from a two-day binge of beer and crank, dozed with blood smeared across her pasty face. We gave the kid warm milk and graham crackers and stayed the night. Eventually he curled next to his lunatic mother and slept. At daybreak we returned to the ranch with bloody strings dangling from our ears like used tampons.

"I gotta admit it, Gus, I miss Butterscotch. Sex with her's like thrash metal on acid morphed into a heroin rush. But besides that, she's just fun to be with. I like her."

"So go for it, Jackie. Since when do you give a flyin' fuck what anybody thinks?"

I climbed the stairs to the ranch when the phone shot a ring straight through my heart. As I reached for the receiver, energy ran up my arm and through my guts. I lifted it anyway: "Don't say a thing till you hear me out, Jackie. I understand your concerns. But we do have fun together, right? We dig the same music, the dogs and your bike. But the main thing is I love you. I'm willing to keep this relationship open – no strings. Call me whenever you feel like having sex – no commitments. You can see other girls if you have to, but I'll give you everything you need. I'll even do that *sangwitch* thing you like so much. And I'll swear to it right now, the only man I'll ever be with is you. I don't need an answer right now. Think it over. But I promise, you'll be glad, baby."

"It's not that I don't want to. And you know this."

"Don't feel pressured-out. I just really like partying with you, Jackie."

"Me too. Just let me sleep on it, okay?"

"Good idea. You should sleep on it. I'll be right over," she said and hung up.

"What do you think, girl?" I asked Idjit. "You like her too, don't you?"

At that time in my life, one of the most solid things I had was that runt of a pup. She was already smarter than a few of the No-Names. But nobody wanted to pay big money for a tiny dog, so I got stuck with that militant midget. She turned out to be the best cure for situational depression, hangovers, dope-sickness and even crank paranoia.

After another night of passion with Butter, I fed and walked my little gyp and then put her on the upstairs porch by her mini-doghouse with some fresh water. Then Bart phoned. We decided it was a good day to get chemically crushed so I could clear my head of indecision, to better think through the Butter situation without distraction.

CH XII: A SPIRITUAL AWAKENING

Day-one: I stopped in at Bart's. He had acquired a stack of "Cleveland Blotter," which were 8 ½ x 11 sheets of manila paper like kids colored on, but his were for big kids engaged in other types of colors. It was manufactured by Enrico, the genius who invented our beloved "Brown Smudge," so we knew it was clean. Each sheet was lined with blots of LSD about the size of pennies. The liquid had been placed in even rows, five across and seven down – 35 hits per sheet.

"Me and Gus already talked to our crew about that other thing you said."

"Oh yeah? So tell me what it was I said? I forgot already."

"Remember the part about checkin' dipsticks on the No-Names? You know; maybe bringing them in with the Royal Flush to merge with the Wong Gongs."

Bart yawned, "Nah, I don't remember any of that. Why you askin' about this?"

"Well, they don't wanna jump into anything without thinking it through."

"Whatever . . . Hey, there ain't shit to do today. You wanna get fucked-up?"

"On Rico's blotter? Sure, gimme one."

"One? One what?"

"Okay, fuck-it. Gimme two."

"Now you're talkin', ya little sawed-off *dago*."

When I ripped off two hits he asked, "What the fuck you doin,' man? You're messin' up a perfectly good strip of cid. Gimme that shit!"

"I'm takin' two like you said. How 'bout you? You want 'em? I'll peel 'em off."

"Not two tabs, man, I mean two rows. Don't be a pussy, Jackie."

Not to be outdone I said, "If you take two rows I'll take two. But you go first."

Bart was a world-class ball-buster, generally engaged in some type of prank like some huge, dangerous kid. I thought: *Okay, I'll play along. I'm not about to tuck my tail.*

Instead of ripping the sheet sideways, he held one long-ways and ripped four strips with seven hits of acid on each row. In retrospect, I can't see how it would have made much difference. 10 or 14, either way that's too much for any human to ingest at one time. He chewed them a bit to get them soft enough to swallow, then swilled them down with a can of beer. He belched and walked to his stereo to look at albums.

*Goddamn my fucking big mouth...*I examined those two entire strips and the two single tabs from the other sheet. He put on Black Sabbath's "Paranoid" album and then plopped into his chair. From there he watched to see if I'd scratch or jump the wall.

I said, "Fuck-it. It's sink or swim time. Where you wanna put these two tabs?"

He set them on a table. "Forget those skimpy-assed hits. That shit's for girls."

"Girls? Are girls really coming over? I'll be way too wasted to talk to girls."

"Easy, Jackie, I'm just fuckin' round. Relax. We'll dose ourselves with Reds every few hours to knock off the edge and watch slow-motion psychedelic flicks all day."

Mellowed somewhat by powerful barbiturates, we fired-up our choppers for a high-speed kaleidoscope where blood taillights and headlights like yellow teeth freckled a night of roaring heat at full throttle. I remember pungent smells from pubs and barflies with faces of melting candle wax.

I'M JACK & I WANT MORE

Day-two: Slick and Gus stopped by. Slick had been up for days cranked-up wrenching on bikes. Bart pulled the same spiel on them when Gus's mom called, so Gus chewed the one strip that remained from what had been a full sheet and left.

Back when our blue Levi's looked like chaps, dark and shiny from imbedded motor oil, Slick. boasted, "I can do anything you can, Jackie. Bring it on!"

I laughed till Bart gobbled down 14 more tabs and then handed me two more strips. "You with me, brother? Don't cur-out now ya fuckin' coward."

"I'm with you till the wheels fall off and then we'll roll across like gamesters," I said. "Hell, 14 or 28, what the difference? Is it possible to get higher? I wanna try it."

As we began to peak for the second time in two days Slick said, "This shit ain't even real. Youse silly fuckers are eatin' spitballs and actin' like it's some big deal."

Slick fell asleep on 14 tabs that had yet to take hold, loaded on the red barbiturate, Seconal, Gus returned while Bart was on the phone. Slick mumbled some incoherent babble about whales and started snoring.

I asked, "Hey, Moby, you dreamin' about the country or the fish?"

When Gus returned we walked outside to trip-out on the sky, smoke a cigarette and piss on a tree. When we reentered the breathing, living-room, Bart was on the phone.

Gus crossed his arms and wagged his head, snorting with his eyes squinted as he noted, "This just might be the craziest shit I've ever seen."

Slick, still fast asleep, had an oil-soaked pant leg blazing from boot to knee. He twitched, jerked and then grumbled, "Alright, goddamn-it! I ain't sleepin', okay?"

Bart slammed down the receiver and yelled, "You're burnin' up my couch, you fuckin' asshole! You wanna burn, go outside ya crazy bastard."

Slick jumped up from the sofa and screamed, "Fire! Run!" He hopped up and down on the leg that burned while he held up and slapped the wrong one.

I hollered between laughing fits, "That's the wrong leg, Slick!"

Bart pointed, "Get outside, ya fuckin' pyro! This kid's a goddamn fire hazard."

Slick stopped jumping for a moment to gaze at us bewildered. Then he looked down and screamed, "Holy shit! . . . My fuckin' leg's on fire!"

Slick used one of Bart's couch pillows to extinguish it. His calf was bubbled out and discolored so Gus drove him to a hospital, since he was the least impaired of us.

I yelled after them, "Get more booze, Gus. And don't forget *Barb* is gone. You remember, *Barb*, that little redhead bitch – my Seconal cousin."

I told Bart, "I hope he finds more downers. I need some kind of buffer. Hell, I need a seatbelt and a crash helmet, and maybe an ambulance with a straight jacket. Pass the fuckin' Thorazine. This is the most acid I've ever even heard of anyone taking except for Astroboy, but that don't count because he was nuts to begin with."

Bart ignored me. He talked club business into his old black phone, in code language, with a prospect called Erby. Meanwhile, Bart's attack trained, red Doberman, Carne, walked to the end-table and licked-up the two hits I'd ripped the previous day. I sat mesmerized: *How crazy is this?*

Gus and I liked Carne, but were all about game-dogs. Ansel still had my old Airedale, Butch, as a housedog. Bart kept Carne for guard duty. They knew game-bred dogs were too friendly to suit their needs. It didn't take long till Carne was off to the dog races. Stretched out in the middle of the front-room floor he reached his own crescendo as Sabbath pounded out a steady drone of "Iron Man."

A deep rumble began in the depths of his chest. At first we weren't sure it was him because he lay stony-still like a statue. Bart turned down the stereo and asked him if he was okay. In a zone of his own, Carne didn't seem to hear his master's voice.

I confessed, "He licked-up those two hits of trip. He hit them walking past the table like a drive-by." Bart stared at his dog but stayed on the phone.

The growls increased in volume and intensity. He curled his lip and snarled. We still laughed when he lunged straight up and attempted to bite the ceiling – over and over.

"Okay, I need to make another important call, Jackie. Put Carne in the basement. I can't hear with that crazy bastard carryin' on. Lock him up till I'm done."

That was well before the invention of cordless phones. By nature, Carne was a pleasant animal once he got to know someone. But that day I didn't want to be anywhere near that maniac dog and asked Bart to put him away before he made his call.

"What kind a dog-man are you, ya little chicken-shit, candy-ass motherfucker?"

"Okay, fuck-it. *I'll* put *your* maniac dog in *your* goddamn basement."

I eased toward his choke collar to lead him into the kitchen while he lunged at nothing visible. I opened the basement door wide enough to shove him in and slammed it.

Carne charged right back in and leaped at the ceiling.

"What the fuck, man? I ask you to do one thing. Maybe I need to have Erby come all the way here for some simple-ass shit like this – fuckin' baby."

"Swear to Buddha, I did put him away. Maybe the latch didn't catch."

Bart spoke into the phone: "I guess I have to go, 'cause this little *dago*'s shittin' his drawers. I'll have to put the dog away myself, so Jackie can go wash his ass."

"Maybe the door handle's broken or some shit like that," I said.

"Yeah right, whatever. Are you gonna do it or not? One simple favor... Motherfuckers can't hold their mud. First Slick with his usual bullshit, and now you."

Just then Gus reappeared through the front door. "What's up, youse fuckin' mad-dogs? Slick's got a room with a view for a few days. The best thing for us is to lay low 'cause he's got cops crawlin' all over that leg askin' questions. What's with Carne?"

Bart, with the phone still pasted to his ear, "Thanks for takin' care of that, Gus. I'll check with Slick in a few days. At least I can count on one of youse *guineas*. This fuckin' pussy's scared to put the dog away. He's even tryin' to lie about it now."

Gus asked with a smirk, "You okay, *coom*? I'll do it if you're scared."

"Alright, I'll do it *again*. I'll put *your* psycho dog back in *your* fuckin' basement. That's it, though. This is the last time."

Bart yawned, "Oh yeah, I see. *Again*, huh? When was the first time? Fuckin' bullshitter... Gus, you're *coomba* gets too high and then acts all psycho and shit."

By that time Carne made gurgling sounds, had foam around his mouth and chattered his teeth as he focused on a spot in the middle of the ceiling. Even more careful, I took his choke collar and led the snarling Doberman back into a wide open basement door. I jiggled the doorknob to make sure its catch was fastened. *Ha, now I gotcha!*

"There's no way he's gettin' out. I double checked everything. He's as safe as a crab in a bush. That cur'll just have to attack imaginary shit in the basement."

No sooner those words fell out of my mouth when Carne, eyes as red as his shiny coat, flew back into the room and up at the ceiling in a rage of froth.

That time it was Gus who asked, "What the fuck, *coom?*"

"No way, man. This is pure bullshit. There's at least two of these dogs in here, 'cause I know I put that last son-of-a-bitch away good-n-tight. I might be trippin' but I know the difference between an open door and a closed one! Okay, Bart. What is this, some fuckin' Hitler test camp for Kraut uber-dogs?"

Gus held a hand over his mouth. Bart had a bizarre expression like he was ready to vomit, the phone still plastered to his head. As if on cue, they burst out laughing. Gus pointed an oil encrusted finger at me, all red-faced and snorting. Bart hooted and hollered while the Dobie pounced off furniture and flipped in mid-air to elevate his attack.

"Okay, who else is here? Who keeps lettin' the dogs out? I ain't stupid. I know exactly what's goin' on here." That deduction made them crack-up even louder.

Bart leaned over on his chair, "You fuckin' asshole." At that, Gus slid to the floor next to Slick's ashes. He held his stomach as they continued to belly-laugh.

Bart hung up the phone without any signoff, "Okay. We'll tell you now, 'cause you done pretty good for a sawed-off *guinea*."

Gus shared the secret: "Jackie, that freak-ass dog knows how to turn the doorknob with his teeth. He's a real fuckin' Harry Houdini."

Carne, doing back-flips and biting at air with spittle flying off fangs, chomped at invisible whatevers. Maybe he was high enough to see shadow-warriors. I know I was.

I asked Bart, "So you weren't really talkin' to Ansel, or Erby or anybody else, right?" You were just fuckin' with my head again. Am I right?"

"You take shit way too serious. You're wound too tight, man. We're trippin', Jackie. Lay back and cool out."

"Yeah, maybe I should relax the way Slick did. But he's not cooled-out just yet."

Gus said: "No shit, *coom*, you should'a seen your face – that look was priceless. As far as Slick goes, fuck him. He pulls this same shit every goddamn time."

I'M JACK & I WANT MORE

Bart added, "Yeah, fuck Slick. He's a goddamn fire hazard. Too bad I just took a leak or I'd a pissed on 'em before he burned up my new couch pillow."

Day-three: The beer was long gone, so we resorted to some rot-gut wine Gus had procured on the hospital run. Bart pretended he liked it so we swilled it like fresh lemonade. It was either that or go back to the store. And there was no way any of us were fit to be out in public, let alone actually operate a moving vehicle.

The third consecutive day felt like where one's nearly asleep but not quite – a floating sensation. Things that don't make sense, somehow do. If stirred from that trance to recall any of those vivid, meaningful thoughts, they quickly evaporated, leaving a trace of *almost*. Gus and I went outside to sit on the lawn to watch citizens go to work, cut lawns, and walk their kids and dogs. We puffed on Mexican dirt-weed. We weren't trying to get high. It was like munching popcorn when movie viewers are already stuffed.

I confessed, "I just want you to know something, *coom*. I'm seeing Butter."

"You mean now, like you're hallucinating again or some shit?" he chuckled.

"You know what I mean. The thing is I'm getting too attached to her."

"I tell you something about that, Jackie. Your friends couldn't care less."

Day-three began to take a heavy toll. As I climbed a narrow wooden staircase to the tiny bathroom I passed shadow-walkers in the unlit hall. The mirror was out of focus. I rubbed it with a towel but it didn't help. My eyes vibrated at warp-speed. I yelled down, "Hey, Bart, I'm usin' the tub! I need to rinse these cobwebs off me."

The only answer came from Sabbath droning metal war-chants. As I drew a steaming hot bath to scrub off blurriness I heard "War Pigs" for the Nth time.

Water's freezing. When they realized I had been upstairs too long they waded through shadow-people to find me submerged. Gus pulled my hair and slapped my face till I heaved up filthy soap. Bart returned with the cooler and dumped ice into the tub.

I sighed, "Hot water's broke. Carne must a finally got it."

Still dripping wet, I pulled on greasy jeans and stumbled downstairs to lay where Slick had caught a new pillow on fire with his greasy leg.

Before I passed out I heard a voice that sounded like mine mumble, "Fuck Disneyworld up a Minnie Mouse ass. This streetcar named LSD is *the* magic bus."

Day-four: I brought Slick a wineskin bulging with *dago-red* under my cut-off vest, and in a bag *Easyriders* and *Playboy* magazines and a bottle of Hot Sauce Williams barbeque sauce. I offered, "Here ya go, buddy, rub some a this shit on that leg."

Slick peeled off gauze to expose cooked flesh. "See this? You think it's funny? What happened, Jackie? Straight up, I need to know if somebody torched me."

"Hey man, I was drunk *and* trippin'. How the fuck do you expect me to know? I'll tell you one thing, goddamn-it; you make one hell of a fire – real colorful, man."

"Hardy fucking har, motherfucker. I'd just like to know how somethin' like this can happen when I'm with *friends*," Slick grumbled as he re-bandaged his charred leg. Then he said, "You know what your whole problem is, Jackie? . . . Ahhh, skip-it."

"No. Go ahead, Slick. Straight business. Tell me what you see."

"Alright, fuck-it. The thing is just this: More ain't enough for you. And it ain't just the drugs. I'm an alcoholic and a junkie too, so I'm nobody to judge. But you're a fuckin' pig with everything. And I'll tell you somethin' else. Your own friends are scared of you. Not because they think you're a rat or anything like that. It's just that you're a walking time bomb. You take everything to the limit and then go way past that. Too much just ain't ever enough for your tastes, man. You're outta control."

"Ha! I'll be goddamned, Slick. When I got a garbage disposal like you tellin' me *I'm* over the top, it's time for me to reevaluate my behavior. Thanks. I'll look at it."

CH XIII:
I WANT MORE

Kindergarten had set a tone for future disappointments. Once cleansed by a Catholic God, I fell under the protection of Collinwood. Primary grades paved a way to that minefield where fear morphed to aggression in a school steeped in tension. Life played out like a movie of the week, though I know personal experiences were rich and many. Adolescence, the most frightening of all life stages – so long ago, yet not far behind – got consumed in a battleground of extremes.

We couldn't feature why anyone would pass on all the crazy-shit going on everywhere. We were the correct age in the midst of a social rebellion that gave birth to recreational violence, spiritual drug abuse and sexual freedom. But as with other things that start out great, our tight knit community helped camouflage demons in an ongoing search for usable truths. Survival mechanisms such as gameness and loyalty, although imperative as well as admirable, brought along with them heavy baggage. Bouts of parasuicidal recklessness and self-induced psychoses disguised themselves as freedom during a time when more was almost enough.

A kaleidoscope of bullshit and drugs had clogged my head for so long; getting crazier seemed like the next right thing – right up until appetites changed along with priorities. That's when friends surfaced as both predator and prey: robbing and getting ripped-off; maiming and being wounded; killing and wasting away. But I figured: *Fuck-it. All that's from back then, and then is long gone.*

As I was leaving the hospital someone yelled, "Hey, little man! Is that you?"

I kept walking till I heard, "Oh, too good for a brother now? Is that it, Jack?"

I shook my head to clear remnants of psychedelic cobwebs spun around my eyes as I turned to see a large black man running at me baring the whitest teeth I'd ever seen. I pulled my knife, then yelled "No fucking way" and then tossed it at his feet.

"What's the matter with you, man? You went ahead and lost your mind?" he asked as he picked it up and closed it. "Here, man. Put this away, you crazy-ass *guinea*,"

"Sorry, Henry, but you just freaked the fuck right outta me. Whoa! I can hardly believe my eyes, man. I'm still comin' down from the most acid anyone ever did without completely wigging out. Okay . . . I can see you now. Horrible Hank! What's up, man? Then with a sideways glance I inquired, "Hey, man. And why are you here?"

"Chill, Jackie. Here's the deal. After I turned 18 they cut me loose from the B.I.S. Then I caught another case and wound up in Mansfield. Fuck that place, Jack. Stand-up guys like us are getting wasted over trivial bullshit. After I got paroled I moved my black ass out of the hood. Those niggers are killing each other just for something to do. I stay down here now, working some loser job, trying to pay off a few bills. But I have to tell you, brotherman, these hillbillies down Five Points are as crazy as ghetto niggers. I've been hoping to run into you. I'm tired of being broke. I'm looking to make a few moves so I can get up out of here. Other than that, everything's great. How about for you, Jack?"

I tucked away the knife and said, "Fucking Horrible Hank in the flesh . . . I'll be goddamned. I thought you were a hallucination. Gimme a hug so I know you're real."

While we embraced he said, "One thing I am, my brother, is real. Bet on that."

"Follow me to my place, Henry. We got lots a things to discuss."

"I can't do that, Jack. I don't have wheels just yet. I've been taking the bus."

"Alright then, hop in. I'll take you to my place so we can talk in private. Then I'll drive you where you need to be. Man! . . . It's sure good to see a friendly face."

That week Curtis got busted selling to a narc from his house. Curtis phoned from the 6th District and told Butter, "Tell flukey-doo the bulls put the dookey to the flukey."

She asked me, "Does that mean what I think it does?"

"It means I need a new partner. Let's clean this place up just in case."

Enough evidence got turned in to make it possession for distribution. The rest of that imported heroin and red bud disappeared. Word on the streets was Doyle Kelly was peddling some dynamite skag and smoke.

Butter had been right about her cousin. Nobody else got in trouble. We sent Curtis packages and commissary money, and she visited him monthly at Mansfield.

Restless, I stopped at Henry's apartment and asked, "You still lookin' for work?"

"Yeah, brother-man. My wallet's slim. What you got for us?"

"You still have any connections back in the hood? You know, people you trust?"

"There's a brother got out I did time with at the Field. He's straight. Why?"

"I'm gonna sign my old car over to you. It's a chunk of shit but it runs okay."

"Sounds cool so far. So now I got wheels. Okay, now what?"

"Next I front you a shit-load of the sweetest weed ever. I took it on trade from some degenerate who was way behind on vig and couldn't pay. I settled his loan so he could pull-up stakes. Meantime, I'm sittin' on some heavy product, waitin' for a clever guy like you to turn all that green into gold. Can you handle some weight?"

"What about your crew? They got their finger in this pie?"

"Nope. This is my deal and got nothin' to do with anybody else. You interested?"

"Well, first let's talk particulars . . . like prices and turnaround times."

Up all night with Henry, we discussed old times, recent events and made plans. In the morning I headed for Pazzo's. He and I sipped espresso laced with anisette in his kitchen. I told him, "I've been thinkin' and I think it's time I cash out of the shylock."

"What's the matter, Jackie? You cunt struck again? Who's it now, that colored girl? I gotta admit it. She's a foxy little thing. What's your dad think about this?"

"I got bigger things to worry about. Lately, Benny's reckless even for our tastes. I'm thinkin' about retiring, Pazzo, before that crazy fuck gets me blown away. I got a bad feeling. Did you hear he almost killed some women while I'm with him because she put onions on his burger? Now he's bull-dogging old-timers in Little Italy. He's scaring a lot of scary people. Having money on the streets ain't as important as family – not to me, anyways."

"Having money on the streets is the easiest crime to get away with, kid. But it's also one a guy's most likely to get whacked for. Maybe you see something I missed. Tell me more about it."

"I get this sick feeling that a dark cloud's settling over, pressing down and suffocating me. I even dream about it sometimes. It's to the point where when I'm out and about I'm actually lookin' up for it."

"That's not good. Maybe it really is time for you to move on. You need to trust your instincts, kid. The *Click* don't lie, and you already know this."

That morning I stopped by to see Benny. "I've been thinkin' lately. Me and you bulldogged lots of guys, *coom*, some of 'em juiced up with connected people. We're wading through a snake pit right now, and some of 'em are runnin' blind-scared. That's a dangerous situation. Your family's all mobbed-up, so you're safe. But mine are nobodies as far as these greedy cocksuckers are concerned. I got a bad feeling, is all."

"Man, I'm disappointed, Jackie. I didn't think you'd lose your balls."

"You know better than that, *coom*. It's just that I want more outta life then this."

"Come on, man. Is that all of it? What else is there? Is that nigger you're hangin' around with tryin' to get you to partner up with him in some shady business deal?"

"No, it ain't nothin' like that. Henry's just an old friend."

"Well what is it then? Because there's a piece a the puzzle missin' here?"

"Besides that we've been shovin' around some of The Mick's people, now we're holdin' out on Uno. That just ain't a safe bet. When he finds out, and he will, he'll have to teach us a lesson – so they'll whack *me* to straighten *you* out. If the Mick thinks we're bull-doggin' him for Uno, that game's just as dangerous. He'll off both of us to get back at Uno. Fuck-it. All I want is my investment. You keep the nest-egg."

"Nah, there's gotta be more. I've known you for too long to believe all the sudden you lost your nuts and now you're all worried about these simple fucks. What is it?"

"Things are changing, Benny, and I don't care much for where it's going. I've been losin' sleep over this. I don't wanna be part of Uno's crew. That ain't my dream. And I'm done fuckin' him over. I think it's time for me to settle down."

"Wake up, man! Nobody knows we're skimming but me and you. It's safe."

"Maybe so, Benny, and maybe not. But the thing is: I'm done."

"Really? Hey, what can I say? We're still *coombas*. Nothin' personal, right? But I just ain't holdin' that kind a cash. Why, you need it now?"

"No, *coom*, not now. There's no hurry. Whenever's clever."

As I walked through the Neighborhood, head down while contemplating how much money I would need to move to Sicily, Benny stopped his car at the curb. With a frozen grin he nodded his head up and down, so I nodded back.

"You know I didn't steal half that seed money, right Jackie?"

"I never thought you did, *coom*. Why? What's on your mind?"

"Didn't you and Fingers talk about half the seed bag's missing?"

"I think you might-a mentioned it. But I ain't worried. It'll surface."

Still smiling he said, "Okay. It's cool. But I just wanna let you know I saw you back there last night. No problem – really. I can trust you, right?"

"What? Yeah, of course. Ace *coom*-booms till the end. Why? What's up, Benny?"

"No worries. I just wanna give you a heads-up this time – that's all."

"What's this? Wait awhile . . . You think you saw me back *where* last night?"

Still with the frozen grin Benny nodded, "You know, in the backyard. We're still brothers though, right? I just wanna let *you* know that *I* know what's goin' on."

"Hold-up, man. Have you finally snapped the fuck out? That prison time really zapped your head, huh? You're delusional, man. Take some fuckin' pills, *coom*."

"Why'd you do it, Jackie? Tell the truth."

"Tell the *truth*? Is that what you just said to me? Tell the fucking *truth*?"

"Why'd you really shoot him, Jackie?"

"Who? Toby?"

"Just tell me why, Jackie, because I heard a different story."

"*Why*? I saved your ass, you crazy fuck! Mick wanted Toby to set you up. I couldn't say anything to you or he'd whack the both of us. You know the game."

"Oh, yeah? Well, that's not the way I heard it."

"Okay, Benny, so what's up? Who's puttin' that shit in your head?"

"You know better than that. You made a choice to turn your back on us."

"Whatever. Then just details. What did you hear . . . minus any names."

"I heard the whole thing was a cover-up. I heard you got paid in advance to hit me, and then you shot Toby to cover your tracks. That's what I heard, Jackie."

"I'll be a motherless fuck! Are you for real with this? I'll be a goddamned, son-of-a-bitch. That's what I get for puttin' my ass on the line for a crazy bastard like you."

"I hope you're as clever as I think you are, Jackie. Because if I really believed that shit, I'd never say one word to you. You'd already be gone. And you know this."

"Benny! You're my oldest brother. As nutty as you are, you're the last person I'd ever figure would turn on me. I would have stepped in front of a bullet for you, *coom*. I'd've gone to prison for you rather than whisper your name. I was in your wedding, man. I was even gonna ask you to be my best man. I gotta tell you somethin' right now; I can't even believe the shit I just heard fall outta your mouth. Read my lips, Benny. I saved your life that night I shot Toby. But now, as far as I'm concerned, you're the Invisible Man."

Still with the nodding head and the maniacal smile he replied, "Whatever, Jackie. We both know what time it is, right? So now I'm just watchin' you, that's all."

"I got nothin' else to say till you apologize, Benny. Go see a shrink, *coom*. Take a fuckin' vacation or some shit, man. You've completely lost it."

His car inched away with him grinning and nodding: "We ain't partners anymore. Your choice, remember? But don't worry, Jackie, you'll get what we owe you."

Lines blurred even more. The Wong Gongs absorbed Gus into their club. Then a snake named Erby became a prospect. I passed on the offer to take the pledge with him, too paranoid to trust that many people. The No-Names became official "hang-arounds," except for Slick who wasn't even allowed at their clubhouse. Eggs and Nino shacked-up with ol' ladies. Fingers and Benny pulled even closer to Uno and Doc. They operated out of The Inn, partnered-up with Joey Cagootz and his three cronies from Little Italy.

Even more mistrustful, I crawled deeper inside myself till I decided to place all faith in a person I barely knew. I found her behind my door, hands on hips and head cocked to accentuate her smile. Then she brushed past me and proceeded to take my breath away with one question: "Guess who's pregnant, you lucky boy?"

When Butter met my parents I read my mother's expression. I thought: *No. You're not right. I know what this is really about.*

I'M JACK & I WANT MORE

My mother turned away in disgust. Later she snapped "Wake up and admit what you already know. I don't blame that girl. It's you who started all this, Giacomo, you filthy pig. Nothing matters to you except being with your *schifoso* friends, those stupid dogs and these *putana*. How can you raise a baby when you act like a child!"

"A tree grows from its roots," my father warned. "But we're past all that now. Mom's right this time. You've crossed a line and need to face the facts, boy. Either take care of this baby when it's born, or pay for her to get rid of it before it's too late."

"She won't abort. I already asked her. Oh well, I guess I gotta get married sooner or later. And you don't want your grandbaby living down Five Points, do you?"

My mother hissed, my father sighed, but the stage was set for the next chapter of my life. Henry camped on one side of that tiny hall with Butter's colored family. My *guinea* relatives partitioned themselves on the other. Burned-out No-Names played in their midst of forced pleasantries while a few inebriated Wong Gongs sat and watched. Food average, booze plentiful, other drugs were outside away from the old folks and kids.

After that hazy reception Butter and I staggered outdoors where she slurred, "Whoa, I'm way too fucked-up for the sun to still be this bright. Turn it off, Jackie."

"Are you supposed to be this loaded in your condition?" I asked the bride.

"Talk about a condition. Check out Slick's dumb ass stretched out on the sidewalk. Look at his feet! They're moving like he's walking. That boy's ugly enough. Somebody better hoist his drunken ass up before he scrapes off his face."

Yanked up by Toby and Inky, stride uninterrupted as though he'd been on his feet the whole time, he continued with his secret mission only alcoholics understood.

The party moved on to my parent's house where Butter found me in the driveway smoking weed with Chink's sweetie. Butter yanked her out of the car by her Up-Do. They rolled on the pavement like Bulldogs, dresses above their asses and tits half out.

Chink lit another joint and passed it to Henry as he leaned against his car and yawned, "Let 'em get tired, Jackie. They'll be easier to handle that way." Wedding gown shredded, his sweetie stripped half-naked, Chink dropped Henry off down Five Points while Butter stormed off to our rented house down the block.

That night I dreamed I was on a runaway train, its engine coupled to its own caboose. I woke drenched in sweat, still clothed in a tux but next to a naked woman. I kissed her and offered her a cold one.

Instead of taking the Caffe Corretta cure for the hangover blues, or a morning kiss to officially begin our honeymoon, she slapped my face: "I should have known better than to get hooked up to a one-way motherfucker like you. I'm not forgetting this, Jack-off."

"You're mad because I smoked a joint with friends? Chink was right there. Let's just move past this bullshit, okay?"

"I'm too sick to argue and too hung-over to drive to The Keys. Let's use our money box to fly to Miami. Stop at your parents' house to drop off Idjit, and have your dad carry us to the airport. We'll discuss that blonde whore and a few other things later."

Butter looked clammy so my dad slammed on the brakes. When she bolted past a laundry custodian and ejected the contents from her stomach into a washing machine my father looked at me and said, "I'm no doctor, and this isn't my business."

Once in Florida I asked, "Remember what you offered me, about a *sangwitch*? I was hoping we could do a threesome while we're here so we'll never forget this night."

"You think I'd play tag-team with these skanky bitches down here? Fuck that. Anyway, I have good news and bad. The good news is I just got my period. Isn't that great? But the bad news is we can't have sex for awhile because I'm bleeding heavy."

"Hold-up. You mean I don't get laid on my wedding night and now you're on the rag for our honeymoon? Well . . . good thing I smuggled some weed on the plane and a bottle of Reds. I'll go get a jug of rum. We'll do this Key West thing Hemingway style."

"You need to back off on the booze, Mr. Hyde. When you drink you get all psychotic. You're crazy enough just being normal, Jackie. Wise up."

"There ain't nothin' wrong with me that a good dose a pussy won't fix. But maybe you're right about the booze. I'll just get some beer."

"Whatever, Jackie. You just don't get it. What you need is real medicine. You know; like psych meds – not more alcohol. A blackout drinker can't be trusted."

"Hey, that's good coming from a solid person like yourself. Pregnant, huh? Real nice. You know what? Being with you is like unwrapping a surprise package every day."

"And you love that about me, don't you? It's not the drugs you're addicted to. It's the chaos. That explains why you're attracted to me and your lifestyle. You like it hot and heavy, and to be right smack-dab in the midst of things, or you're not satisfied."

"The onliest thing I'm in the midst of is this bitch-fest with you. Can we just cool-out and enjoy our trip? Look around you, Butter. We're in Paradise. Try to relax."

"Relax? Look at who your friends are. As if those back-stabbin' *dagos* aren't bad enough, now you're hanging out with these low-life bikers and some jailhouse nigger. What the fuck happened to you? Are you going to let this booze get the best of you, Jackie? Are you becoming a drug addict and an alcoholic? You can tell me."

"Alcoholic? Are you serious? I can drop this quick as a dog's turd."

"Then explain the blackouts. Why do you still drink when you know you spin right into the next one? I think you're getting strung out, Jackie."

"So I fucked-up a few times. No worries. I'm too smart to get hooked."

"You're pretty wise, I'll admit that, but not as clever as you think. You take things too far. You're reckless and now you're getting sloppy. People are wary of you now."

"I can still trust Gus 100%. And those No-Names would do anything for me. Plus now I'm almost brothers with the Wong Gongs, too. You worry too much. Fuck-it."

"No, not *fuck-it*. It can't be fuck everything and everyone, and then you expect everybody to have your back. It doesn't work that way, Jackie. It's bad karma. Sooner or later that attitude will get you in something you won't be able to think your way out of."

"Look at you, Butter. No wonder you can't relax. You're too worried about shit like *might's* and *maybe's*. The onliest stuff we should focus on right now are real things that are up-close and personal. All the rest is bullshit, except for the *Click*."

That same night I crashed with the bitter taste of bile in my throat. But before I woke from another hard night of boozing, usually more tired than when I passed out drunk, I experienced a recurrent dream. It was always the same. It began with a vision of me floating above my bed. At that point I was never quite sure if I was really asleep. Then the dream continued to unfold – the same as always.

Beneath me thrashed a serpent adrift in a liquid, crystal world under my bedroom floor that had transformed into a mirror. A dream-snake spotted me, crashed through the glass and advanced up a soundless attack while I tried to call out for help. But my shadow-screams came out silent as that spiral of death constricted a translucent coil around my neck. I watched in horror as it sank its fangs deep into its writhing flesh, to unleash fury against its own tail. During that alcohol induced coma I strained to pry the dream-serpent off itself. But my hands couldn't close and my arms wouldn't respond. All I could do was watch while being suffocated. As I gradually sank deeper into that broken floor of glass shards pointing up like crystal knives, the creature ripped chunks from its body and was about to swallow its own murderous head. I couldn't breathe.

Feet planted in cement, my head lost in a thick orange fog; finally I was able to fling my left arm out as hard as I could. I heard Butterscotch groan next to me. *SHIT!* Startled awake, I looked over to find that my fist had stopped mere inches from her face. Rhythmic breathing continued uninterrupted. Relieved, I stumbled out to the kitchen to make my usual breakfast. Temples throbbed and stomach boiled. I sat alone at our kitchen table staring at a pizza box and a bottle of clear liqueur while coffee percolated. I contemplated an obvious fact: a need for change had arrived.

I felt like I was losing my grip. I was no longer using the drugs. I was being used. Pain outweighed pleasure. So I considered maybe modifying addictive intake to just garden-variety abuse. *But first things first.* I heard Butter stir, her morning stretch, yawn and groan.

I said, "The coffee's almost done, babe. How about a little eye-opener with me to wash down some nice aspirin?"

"Oh, you're making breakfast again? Another double-header anisette in your espresso and a slice of cold, greasy pizza, right Jackie? Isn't that like every morning now? No thanks. I'd like to have my shit together for when we go out to get loaded. It would be nice if you could do the same."

"I'm cool. But I've been thinkin' about some things. I've been considering semi-sobriety. I'm almost gettin' a little sloppy lately. I might be missing stuff. You know – subtitles...timing"

"Wow! You think, Jackie? Maybe almost a little, huh? Is that it?"

"Hey! I'm being serious here. So maybe we'll both start tomorrow. Cool?"

CH XIV: THE GAME-TEST - PART II

Shrillness strafed across my head, embedded into my fresh hangover. I lifted the receiver on the second ring to hear a familiar voice, "Listen close." *I fucking knew it.* "Swear to Buddha, this is the last time I say it." *I could smell it.* "Be careful," the voice warned. "Now let's see if you're as smart as you think you are."

I mumbled to Gracie, "This Benny's a lunatic. Or maybe Ansel was on to something the whole time. But then I wouldn't be alive enough to be thinking this, right? Shit . . . Check me out. I'm standing in the front-room askin' a dog if Benny's crazy."

Ansel, a man who did contracts hits for a living for the highest bidder, confided in an earlier conversation, "Some *coomba* pulled your ticket but I got it quashed. Don't ask who, 'cause that's all I'm gonna say."

At the R-Bar, Eggs and I left rosy-cheeked ladies at our table to blend with customers. Fingers shook hands with a loose grip. Dusky complexion accentuated simmering rage when he offered, "Come on. We'll go in the office so we can talk."

I mumbled to Eggs, "No fucking shit. So he's the one. Maybe Benny ain't so nuts, after all. But I'm sure we can talk through this bullshit, right? We'll just reason it out."

As we walked and waited for the other boot to stomp Eggs agreed, "Yeah, maybe we'll have a sit-down. Let's see what he has to say so we know how to act. I'll be right back. I just wanna let my ol' lady know what's up so she ain't lookin' for me."

Anxiety ripped me in half as Led Zeppelin's "You Shook Me" bounced from tile to ceiling. I slurred, "It's crazy. The slower I sip the higher I get, but a different kind. Coordination's all fucked-up now. And what's with these lights? Dim, then bright. See? Now look. Flared right back up. See it, Eggs? The whole world's fluttering. Hear the echoes? You feel 'em too, right? Everything's in slow-motion. Feel it?"

Inside, Cagootz and his friends posted at the door like sentries. Joey leaned on the butt of a rifle like a cane. Fingers stood next to Uno who watched through dead eyes.

My voice resonated a slow roar as if from another: "I know what time it is. You wanna showdown. Is that it?" *Fading fast.* "What? Now's too soon?" *Stay awake.* Jimmy Page electrified Robert Plant's moans as I stripped off my shirt and slurred, "It's slash-and-burn time, right Fingers? Yeah. It's all or nothin', right *coom*? I already dreamed about this night. But hold up a minute. Just answer me this. Which part am I supposed ta give a fuck about? Oops. No answer . . . nobody's here but me. Okay. Fuck-it." I punched my friend and it was on.

During that test I felt what a game-dog lived in a pit — the pain of being isolated in a strange crowd of friends. The bridge of my nose went numb when I thumbed an eye socket. In self-defense I ripped an ear half off till my left cheekbone got wrecked by a decanter bottle. My father taught, "Treat others the way they treat you." I did, but that just made matters worse. Nothing made sense except attack and get knocked-out again. Tile slick with treachery offered another perspective to watch cigar smoke crawl across florescent lights, to fold in on itself till there was nothing but a stench.

When Eggs intervened, Joey Cagootz smashed a bottle over his head and jammed the broken end in his forehead. Blood squirted. I couldn't tell mine from his.

When Fingers kicked Eggs in his face I growled through swollen lips "Okay, motherfucker, now it's my turn." Blood sprayed his face when I fishhooked his mouth with a thumb and yanked sideways. In turn, a fractured nose spiked my brain. The pattern was simple: knocked-down, back up, knee and elbow, out again to dream I was home in bed. Knocked out four or six times after I had been assured, "We can talk." Fluorescent bulbs illuminated a ceiling very different from my own each time I regained consciousness.

I'M JACK & I WANT MORE

I woke beneath the maniacal face of Joey Cagootz punching my eyes closed, but not before I saw Pazzo catch him with an elbow to the temple as he feigned an attempt to pull him off me. He shouted, "Hey, Joey! You okay?" In exaggerated gestures Pazzo lifted Cagootz, slipped on that slimy surface, and then fell hard on top of him – more of a push than a fall. That big head of Cagootz smacked the tiles and bounced after a dull thud. "Here. Let me help you up, Joey," Pazzo said as he pulled a dazed Cagootz upright.

A deep, familiar voice echoed inside my head: *Get up, boy. Do it now!* In survival mode, I had little choice but to obey. That's when I heard the scream.

Butterscotch's voice reverberated as if from in a tunnel a million miles away: "You *guineas* are worse than niggers. All he's done for you and this is what he gets? Let him go or kill me, too. I won't leave him with you rice-dick faggots. He's twice the man as any of you cowards. I'm right here, and I don't budge without him. Now what? You gonna kill me, too? Chumps better hope he doesn't come hunting!"

Pazzo shouted, "Stay down, Jackie. You're bleeding bad. What're you trying to prove with this? You wanna die tonight? You need to get to a hospital right away, kid."

Fingers reached for the rifle and said, "See? I told you. This crazy fuck ain't gonna stop! So now guess what happens? Now I guess I gotta stop him."

I got up too fast, slipped and fell. I heard ringing when my skull cracked open.

Uno stepped in front of Butter with a paw-like fist raised and pointed his other meat-hook at Fingers while Pazzo helped me regain footing. Pazzo led us out to a bathroom where he and Uno watched my wife wipe blood off me with wet paper towels.

"What are you, suicidal?" Pazzo asked. "Why didn't you just stay down?"

"Would you or Uno? Would Benny? Would my dad? So why should I?"

"You ain't us, kid," Uno answered. "Now go home. This is over. *Capisce?* If you even think about comin' back, you'll deal with me. And you don't ever want that."

"Come-on, baby," she offered her hand. "Let's get you home," Butter said as she led me out. "From now on you don't need anyone but me."

We found our friends huddled outside, his yellow shirt around his head like a red turban. They drove us to our car in silence.

Once home, she filled a warm tub to scrub off a residue of disgust. When I dunked my head to loosen dried clots, the water looked like a vat of raspberry soda with real berries. Matted hair had concealed an L-shaped flap that exposed the crown of my skull. She insisted, "You're going in for X-rays and stitches right now."

Cops arrived bedside to quiz me: "Fell up the steps, huh? Then how'd you get 66 stitches on the *top* of your head? Is this bite mark on your arm from steps, too? Why would you protect people who did this? Are you really that afraid of them?"

"Afraid of who? Tell me this: Why would I wanna help professional ballbreakers? You guys bully people, rob their stuff and then stick 'em in jail for doin' the same shit you do? Besides, I already told you, I fell up my steps and lunked my head. I was juiced, blacked-out and can't remember shit. Just ask her if youse don't believe me."

When they saw her cold expression they simply shook their heads and exited the room. She carried me home beaten down, sewn up, worn out, bandaged and bruised.

"You've been game-tested to the bone, baby, and passed with flying colors. I saw it! That color was dark red and all yours. You can hold your bloodsoaked head up. So now we're finally done with them. Fuck-it. All you need is me. Now let's go get stoned."

I greeted a new morning with the worst headache of my life, only to find Gracie dead on her chain in our back yard. A terminal case of the "fuck-its" settled in. Death permeated the air and stank like me. *Paesanos* narrowed from a Neighborhood cult to a handful of misfits. Gus was inseparable with Bart. Toby and Chink became strikers. Henry was moving *lids* all over town. Things were strained, but cash was flowing in.

Another money labyrinth weaved through a deal where Chink was fronted an ounce of powder by the Wong Gongs. He didn't sell the first gram of Ansel's unpaid crank. Of what he didn't use, he gave to his ol' lady and crew of burnouts.

When it came time to ante-up Chink assured him, "You know I'd never try to fuck you over, bro. I know better than to ever try any dumb shit like that. I just need a little more weight to get right." He got smacked for referring to a patch-holder as "bro."

Ansel warned, "You're a prospect so I'm gonna front you a second O-Z. Don't make me come lookin' for you or your rocker arm won't be the only thing gets taken."

Like a good addict, Chink partied away the dope. Benny extended Chink enough credit to pay for that second ounce but warned, "You try to fuck me, I'll kidnap you're ol' lady and chain her up in my basement. Now here's the deal. I front you this cash. You give me weekly vig till you pay me all of it back, 6-for-5, in one lump-sum. *Capisce?*"

Chink invested in a match dog, tricked-out his scooter and then pilfered away the rest on gambling and more drugs. Not one cent went to either of them. Ansel vowed to kill him. So did Benny. Chink, stripped of his rocker-arm, acquired a new zip code.

Eggs phoned: "Those No-Names are finished. Ansel and Bart beat-up Toby and yanked his rocker, but he's still living in the Neighborhood. Before Inky moved south with Chink, Bart got into a head-on with a car in the wrong lane the same day Benny's house got riddled with bullets. Those guys need stay down there in the woods."

I received a letter from Chink. It read: "My kid knew his grandma's phone number. He told her, 'Gramma, I'm tryin' ta wake-up mommy. But she don't move 'cause she got a red hole on the head. It's holdin' her on a floor. Can you come and take it off Mommy? I don't like it when Mommy does that. Yes, I'm okay. Daddy's with me.' Anyway, that's what he testified. When the old lady screamed, so did my kid. That's when I came out of my blackout. His tiny hands were smeared with her blood. Those are the sounds and sights I fall asleep to, dream about and wake up with every day. Sometimes I dream she's sprawled on the floor reaching up to me because our son's dead, covered with blood. I can't get that shit out of my head. I wonder: *Just one move the other way, or maybe a different word.* I think maybe I'll wake up and laugh about this crazy dream with my ol' lady. But I open my eyes to these same fucking bars every day."

Then Inky phoned collect: "Thanks for bringin' Gracie and Sinbad here while I was strapped down in restraints, *coom*. They didn't let anybody fuck with me, Jackie."

I didn't explain to Inky both of those dogs had been dead long before he imploded. Why bother?

Before Webb moved to Tennessee he bragged, "After I shot Paddy's mick buddy in his throat I poured tequila in the hole. You should'a seen that fuck drownin' on his own blood. To put him out of his misery I ground that spray hole with the heel of my boot. But I fucked-up. If I had to do it over again I'd a smoked his slut, too. No witnesses. I gotta tell you somethin' though, Jackie. None of it seems real now. It's like I just dreamt it."

As if things weren't crazy enough, Pazzo's house got redecorated by a dynamite blast and then The Shamrock Club exploded with the Mick and his ol' lady inside. Again, that lucky bastard survived. Then while Uno's son sat in their car, pretending to drive his dad's Cadillac, a bomb ripped him to shreds – just like the one that had butchered Uno's brother. The next body to surface was, Eamon Jr., found in a Five Points dumpster. Then Toby's house got torched with him in it.

After Benny got the contract on Paddy Kelly, he ushered him out of The Shamrock Club. He must have let Paddy drive to where Benny's Lincoln had been parked. Paddy probably figured he could con his way out of anything serious, because the bartender saw them leave together – the same one who was found dead behind the bar.

Newspapers reported the following morning that police had found a body along with a hatchet inside Paddy's blood-soaked car. Allegedly, the victim was alive during the hacking. After that episode, everybody realized Benny was not just *acting* crazy.

Because Ice-cream Nicky saw Paddy and Benny exit The Shamrock Club together the same night Paddy was murdered, truck bells silenced. No more policy slips, fireworks or marshmallow cones. Nicky went on the lam, and Sally Boy went with him.

While things grew progressively crazier, Toby pledged his loyalty to our friendship. He suggested a bar where we could have some drinks and look at the future. I didn't trust him. But then I didn't trust anyone. We weren't out deliberately trawling for sweeties that night. Nevertheless there she was, as beautiful as ever. I still felt like a kindergarten kid in her presence.

She purred. "Remember what you said the last time we were together, Jackie? Now it's my turn to say it. *You'll be glad.* So what do you think, bro?"

"I think we should have some drinks. What're you having?"

"Let's do more tequila shots – doubles. Hey, wait a minute! Are you trying to get me drunk again? Because if you are, you don't have too far to go," she giggled.

"Well, for the record, that last time I saw you, you were loaded *before* I got there. You know; kind of like the way you are right now."

"That's no excuse. Just admit it. You really would like for me to loosen up so I could take advantage of you. Don't be afraid to say it, little Jackie-boy. Just be honest."

"You want honesty? Okay here it is. You're spilling booze on me again."

"Big deal. That tee-shirt looks bogus, anyway. Hey, let me ask you a question. If you had one wish right now, of anything at all in the whole world, what would it be?"

"I'd wish my wife and your dad were married. How's that?"

"I wish my dream from last night was real, that we really did spend the night together. I knew you'd be here. That's why I brought this note. See? Your name's already on it."

"I didn't even know I'd be here. Besides, you hardly even know me anymore."

"Really? Are you that drunk again, bro, or have you already forgotten?"

"How could I? Believe me, I know."

"You looked lost in your thoughts just there. Tell me what you were thinking about. I need specifics, bro. I need raw truth. What do you see?"

"That we're all sitting around waiting to die, pretending it's not really gonna happen. Like for some reason we're gonna beat the odds. That's what I was thinking."

"Wow, that's pretty heavy. I need another shot. So does that mean we should be together before it's too late?" she asked as she set a neatly folded slip of paper on the bar that she had been holding. "You know what else I was thinking? I was wondering what would happen *after* you showed up tonight. Well, I guess we'll find out."

"We probably shouldn't be playing this game. It's too dangerous because I've been thinking about you, too. But I have a jealous wife and you have a psycho warden."

"Sorry. I'm just very tipsy right now."

We downed our shots. "Don't be sorry. It's just bad timing for us, that's all."

"Why, because my father's an idiot? Doc has a wife *and* a girlfriend, and I can't even date? But I told Mom I had a dream and had to go out tonight to follow it. So when Doc left for the night she let me off my chain." Then Tessa said, "Uh-oh. Don't look now, but Fingers and that maniac, Cagootz, are heading our way."

I wondered: *Is this a set-up?* So I turned to read Toby's face.

"You see these two fucks? I ain't impressed, Jackie. Let's take 'em outside, gut 'em and feed 'em to Inky's dogs. I'll show these cocksuckers what crazy looks like."

"You say something, hillbilly boy? Say it to my face," Cagootz challenged.

"And look at you, Jackie? Where's your respect? What a fuckin' disappointment. Youse bust-outs really think you can mad-dog us? That booze finally pickled your brain."

"I got your pickle right here," Toby laughed and grabbed his crotch.

Cagootz moved for us so I flipped out my knife. "No more ass-kickings, Joey."

"We'll be waitin' outside," Fingers said. "Make sure you bring your friend."

Cops parked in the lot. I asked Toby to stay back and walked to Fingers' car. With hands clearly visible I asked, "Just tell me why, Fingers. That's all I need to know."

"I'll tell you this much, you crazy fuck: Three strikes and you're out."

With Tessa's phone number still crumpled in my fist I crashed at Toby's place. Waking, eyes still closed, I could almost taste her sweetness and still feel those dream whispers caress my neck. Instead of seeing her, I watched a butterscotch stranger breathe deeply inside our small paneled bedroom.

Trying to remember how I got home, the phone rang: "Pay attention, Jackie. Things are gettin' real sticky and we're not connected anymore." The next call from Eggs came weeks later. That's when I learned Tessa had moved out of state.

CH XV: NOTHING CHANGES TILL IT DOES

When Butter and I had experienced marital problems in 1976 during her first trimester my father saw me putt through the Neighborhood with another sweetie. He visited later for a talk. "You act like you have a license to be an asshole. Are you too selfish for this, son?"

"I'm okay, Pop. I just need to sort through a few things is all."

While still on that merry-go-round of chemically induced reality, familiar mumblings came from within the house, or maybe lived inside my head. I'd smile as shadow-figures darted about periphery. *I need more sleep.* But somewhere around the time the baby was born an integral piece had shifted, and the shadow-music stopped.

Once I embraced that tiny creature I fell in love. We named her Gina. She suckled hands too small to be real. Sightless eyes needed me as she fussed about in a cold, new world. Packaged in folds of translucent flesh, she required strength exactly like mine.

My father said, "We're old, Jackie, not stupid. We know you're still a drunk. But I believe you'll take care of your own baby. Don't make me a liar, boy."

Following that advice, that night my mother watched him as he struggled for just one more breath. Butter and I went to my father's wake loaded on downers to endure a line-up of smiling faces and insincere apologies while we stood next to a box-full of loved one.

"Don't get hateful over this," Butter warned. "People just die – that's all."

"No worries. I don't hate god for this. That'd be like blaming Santa because our chimney broke. People have sex and then we get born. I was wrong for bailing on you when you needed me in the delivery room. I won't insult you with an apology. I'll make it up to you. We have one more solid chance before time runs out for us, too."

"Do we? We'll see. I know how you can show me how sorry you are. Housewives get their hair and nails done, and drink wine to wash away the blues, right? Guys gamble, get loaded and go to titty bars. You and me are getting our names inked on each other."

"You know that's the first rule of tattooing. No names, right?"

"Fuck the rules. She'll always be our daughter, and you'll always be my man."

As Gina grew older she claimed, "I hear voices at night, Daddy, but not yours or Mommies when you're fighting in bed. It's more like whispers. Do you ever hear the soft music, too?"

When Butter found out I got severed from the railroad she asked, "Now what, Jackie?" We're stuck with a mortgage, new Harley payments, maxed-out credit cards, and now this kid. You don't have enough gas to go to work so we can buy gas to make money. We're three months behind on everything with no phone, and now they're about to turn off our electric. I'll find a job. You go make some quick cash anyway you can."

Eggs phoned the next morning and asked, "You okay, little brother?"

"I was till you woke me up. Why you callin' this early?" I asked still groggy.

"It's about Benny. I heard someone phoned him in the middle of the night to say his father got rushed to Cleveland Clinic. When he started his car, a bomb went off."

"Ah . . . that's probably bullshit. If it was true we'd know about it."

"I do know about it. Word on the street is Mick hired that probate, Erby, to zip him. Some other guys down Five Points are saying you and Toby did it. Nobody trusts anybody right now. It's a good thing we're outta the loop, Jackie. Another thing I heard is that Uno knew about this before it even happened. I don't know abut you, *coom*, but I gotta get some money so I can make some quick moves. You got any ideas?"

"Nah, Eggs, I got nothin' right now. I'll sleep on it and get back with you, okay?"

I'M JACK & I WANT MORE

Swacked-out on our last Quaaludes, en route to a friend's house for a sack of hydro, I sideswiped Gina's school bus as it rounded our corner. Shattered glass still lay on my side of the road when a cop arrived. Because I didn't have alcohol on my breath nobody got cited. She and I continued our drive together to fetch her mom from work.

Outside waiting for us, she glared at the caved-in fender and broken headlight. Only five words were spoken till we arrived home: "Move over, asshole! I'm driving."

At home I tried to melt the ice: "I'd a never done that if I hadn't a been high."

While changing clothes Butter said, "Ha-ha. Real fucking funny. Man-oh-man, what a useless piece of shit you've turned into. I can't believe what you just went and did. I'm working my ass off all day and you go fuck-up big-time. I told you not to drop those ludes till I got home, you selfish bastard. Now what am I supposed to get-off on? And where are we supposed to get more? Huh, Jack-off? Just answer me that."

"Lighten up, okay? The baby's already freaked-out enough for one day."

"You're going to tell me how to act, you rotten prick? I pay the bills around here. You're supposed to be cooking and cleaning while I'm out earning the money. Instead, you're laying around on your lazy ass, all nice and high on *my* fucking ludes. Then you go and smash the fuck out of our only car. Now how am I supposed to drive that piece of shit? How I got hooked-up with such a fucking loser I'll never know," she yelled.

"You've already been warned. Drop it till she goes to bed."

"Or what? You're the idiot who made her cry. Besides, what the fuck are you gonna do?" she challenged as she poked a finger against my forehead.

"How about I knock you the fuck out?" When I spotted Gina in the doorway clutching a stuffed animal, Butter threw a roundhouse to my jaw. Just as quick, she kicked me in the groin. Then she snatched a brass lamp off the nightstand and whacked it over my head. It was plugged in with the light still on when the bulb shattered down my back.

Gina doesn't remember any of that. What she does remember is her mother's feet in the air when my fist found her chest. She also remembers her mom on the floor sobbing, and how she left in our smashed van and didn't return before she went to bed.

I have no recollection of where I spent the day and night after she returned. A thing I'll never forget is that last hangover. Projectile vomiting to dry heaves, to passing in and out of consciousness on the bathroom floor, my beard matted with puke.

Gina vividly remembers our last argument, too.

I stumbled in the next day and demanded to know, "Who were you with, bitch? Hey! I just asked you a simple question and I need an answer so I know how to act."

"You don't make my decisions, motherfucker. I'm not your nigger anymore."

"Fine . . . Then we're two strangers in the same house till you split."

That night, after a birthday party we had promised to attend for Eggs' son, Butter and I savored necessary truths. Gina nestled in the van's backseat with Idjit while I drove home blitzed on after-market Quaaludes acquired from a warehouse robbery.

All thick-tongued I slurred, "I know what goin' on. Yep, I sure do."

"Oh really? That's good. What in fuck's sake are you rambling about now?"

"Don't make it worse by lyin'. Just try ta be straight for once."

"Pull over, Jackie. You're way too fucked-up to drive. You can barely talk."

"It's bad enough to be a sneak and a liar. But a cunting whore? Wow..."

"Cut the bullshit, Jack-off. It's boring. Just say what's on your mind."

"Okay. I know you been fuckin' around 'cause I can smell it."

"Oh I see, Mr. Asshole. So who is it I'm *fucking around* with?"

With no reason to suspect a black co-worker old enough to be her father, I called a name and noticed the slightest flinch of her eyebrow.

"Swear to Buddha, you get honest and we divide our stuff – no problems. But if you lie, I kick you out on the freeway goin' 70 MPH. Between the two of us, you know I'm not the liar. That's really the issue here, ain't it? It's a big decision, Butter, so take yer time. I'm in no hurry," I said and kept driving as if nothing important had been discussed.

After a brief deliberation, "Well . . . since you already know . . . I mean . . . I was going to tell you, anyway. Really, Jackie, I was just waiting for the right time."

The day she moved out she said, "Let's set the record straight. You pretend real good. But apologies for the same crap are as stale as your demands. Making me feel like shit with Chink's whore on my wedding day was low rent. Fucking around on me while I was pregnant was dirty. Telling me about it didn't make it any better. Not coming into the labor room was just more weak bullshit. You said a million times you'd cut back the booze. But what do I expect from a blackout alcoholic? Nothing, that's what. You consider yourself solid? HA! You chirp like a scratched record, you fucking traitor."

"Oh yeah, I remember. *All I need is you*, right? Wasn't that what you said? Yeah, sweetie, I'll miss you, too. But hey, maybe we can still be fuck-buddies."

"Probably not, Jackie. Maybe you go stick that pencil dick in your whores again."

When I explained to Ansel what happened he said, "You're like a gardener with sore back. You need to quit messing with nasty little ho's. Tell you what. Take a ride to Tennessee to look over some property for us. Follow me? Have your kid stay with your mom. When you get back, that two-timin' whore and your traitor *coomba* will be nothing more than memories. You'll owe us. Cool?"

"Nah, thanks but I'll pass. I need to face my demons and make changes, so I'll start with this. The simple truth is that whore and my *coombas* did me a favor. It's better now than later, right?"

"Hey, man, whatever ... But you were in blackouts about half the time, so you don't know what she knows about your friends or what she'll do with that information. You okay with that? I hope it don't ever come to her blabbing, Jackie. You dig?"

"I hear what you're sayin', Ansel, but no sweat. She don't know shit."

"We're friends, Jackie. But just know you're responsible if she talks."

Watching my daughter pull away to live with a pair of strangers was more than I had bargained for. From that point on, whenever Gina stayed the night it would be as a visitor. We spent every weekend together except for the year I lived Down South. But I saw her every time I hauled product from Miami to Cleveland.

"Mommy said you're doing that dumb stuff again. Are you, Daddy?"

"I'm okay, baby, Daddy's just doing what he has to do till things get straight. But I promise you I won't drink ever again. Okay?"

"Okay, I believe you. Can I ask you something? Is Santa Claus real?"

"I can't say for sure, honey. I doubt it, though."

"Then how about God? Is he?"

"Who knows? Maybe. But your truth doesn't have to match mine, baby. Why are you asking all these questions? What's really on your mind?"

"Remember that noise you used to call shadow-music? Well, it followed me to the new house. But when I'm home here with you, then it's here, too."

That weekend we shared an experience, or a dream. We clearly remember what seems like a dream. *What else could it be?* Details are hazy after all these years; yet, we both remember the same basic elements. We pulled in the driveway to frantic barking, dogs lunging at their chains for the barn. We spotted a fawn that looked to be dead.

"You went in the house and brought back medicine, Daddy. We cleaned up the little deer and you gave it a shot. Then the barn door opened from the inside by someone so you could carry it into the goat's pen. You remember that part, don't you?"

"Yeah, actually I sort of remember. But I'm pretty sure it's just a dream."

"The next morning while you napped outside, it ate and drank with our goat till it hopped over the fence. It stopped once and looked at me before it disappeared into the woods. How can it be a dream when we both saw it?"

That day something spooked our nanny goat. It escaped too, but instead of the woods it ran straight for Gina and was immediately killed by Sinbad. Within minutes, the old dog stiffened-up and was all and blown-out like road-kill from a gastric torsion. She was crushed. Within a matter of moments she watched her oldest friend defend her from what he perceived as an attack and lost his life doing so. She felt responsible and became withdrawn. At her urging, I dug a deep hole and she presided over his funeral service, crying the entire time as if an immediate family member had passed. She begged me for a puppy.

During the timeframe when she left her mother's house to move back in with me, Gina began a series of intermittent low-grade fevers. A local doctor advised, "It's merely growing pains, a hormonal reaction, compounded by common allergies. Give her multiple vitamins with an iron supplement and make sure she stays away from sugar and all dairy products. I've seen this occurrence many times before. There's really nothing to be overly concerned about. She'll be fine."

"You look weak, honey. Are you sick enough to go to the hospital?" I asked.

"I just need a puppy. Remember the dog Grampy always talked about having when he was a little boy? I want one from Butchie and Idjit. Then it will be all my favorite dogs rolled into one. I'll name him Little Rover after Grampy's dog."

"Butch is old. I doubt he can produce. And Idjit's pretty old, too. Wouldn't be better to wait and breed another dog?"

"Please, Daddy. I know a new puppy will help me feel better. Please?"

"Okay, honey. I'll phone Ansel to check if that old dog's even still alive."

On our way back from breeding Idjit to a freshly groomed Butch, we pulled in our driveway to see a large buck on the side of the barn where the goat pen once stood. His doe and their fawn munched grass in the same spot where the goat used to eat.

Gina asked, "Could it be him, Daddy, with his own family? Who opened the door for us, Dad, when you carried that baby deer into the barn? I feel a little dizzy, Dad."

Her forehead radiated heat before I touched her, so I brought her straight to an ER where they were able to control her fever. They gave us a referral to a specialist. When I phoned for an appointment we were denied help . . . no health insurance. They told me to get public assistance from the state. I waited in line the next day only to find out from Welfare that they wouldn't help because I carried a mortgage.

I told her, "I guess we're not allowed to get sick unless we're rich or on welfare." But she wouldn't listen.

On Friday the 13th Idjit birthed a litter of 13 live pups, an amazing feat for an old bitch. Gina laughed, "Look at those little piggies rooting around. Aw, poor Idjit. All they do is eat, eat, eat all day and night. I never saw such noisy little puppies before."

By Monday morning all the pups were dead except for two. I rushed a limp and cold Idjit into the vet's. She died in the waiting room, in Gina's arms. The doctor said she had eclampsia – a lack of calcium – which meant no milk and explained why the pups were so hungry. Gina was devastated and falsely assumed guilt for everything.

What she also did was save two pups. Before school and when she got off the bus she fed and cleaned them, then again after supper and before bed. When her fevers spiked again Gina spoke to something very odd: "I'm not scared of him. I feel safe with him here. Is he the one who helped us with the baby deer? Is he your brother or mine?"

"Let's not talk about this right now. You're getting sicker. Tomorrow we go."

By morning her temperature had again returned to normal. I had her phone her mother to set up appointments. Butter told our frightened daughter not to worry, that she did have health insurance and she would make the necessary appointments. During a time of crisis, resentments temporarily dissipated and priorities adjusted themselves accordingly, while feelings of mutual betrayal lingered.

As soon as the pups were strong enough to lick gruel, Gina's fevers again ignited to high. She moved back with her mom where she was diagnosed with encephalitis.

Ansel was dealing with other bitch-dog problems. When he discovered his own wife's betrayal, he placed her body in a rubbish drum, busted off petite legs with a sledgehammer and then hauled her remains in a stolen van. His story was graphic and disturbing, a reality more surreal than fiction.

I woke from a sound sleep choking on a dream-stench of kerosene and burning rubber asking myself out loud, "How did things get here? Where does all this end?"

Little Rover housetrained himself in one day and could be trusted in the house. He helped me maintain a semblance of sanity. I kept Miss Rover out in a pen with the intention of giving her to Inky and brought her inside every day for them to play.

During early winter I worked with Bee-Bee Balls remodeling a titty bar. Our shift began when the bar closed. So I slept mornings and lived like a zombie, which was nothing new for me. On a cold morning, just getting home from work, my mother phoned: "Can't you stay the night at Ricky's? Better yet, just stay home tonight. I have one of my bad feelings."

"It's not a motel, Mom, it's a bar. And I'm not a customer, I'm an employee. I'm okay, I promise. If I'm tired I'll pull over. Or I can call Bee-Bee if I need to. But I'm fine – really. Now just go back to sleep. I'll call you later when I'm done."

The next call was from Chilly: "Uno needs some work done, bro-ham. It's big money. He says he wants you in as long as you aren't drinking. I have a plan, but we'll need Dago Red for this one. I'll meet you at his place. Don't say anything to Eggs about this. Hey . . . Speaking of Eggs, you sense anything weird with him lately?"

"I'd rather talk about that and some other things when I see you."

I took a pull off the tequila jug and fired up my bike. When I arrived, Chilly was already there. Without knocking, I walked in, took a seat at his kitchen table, and watched as Dago Red fondled a sack of Curtis' heroin.

"Cut out a gram to use as bait," Chilly said. "The rest is yours. Bring Slick so he can tell Erby it's part of a brick from an inner-city hoist. That greedy fuck will snag the taster sack and then want it all. The best part is Erby can't say shit to his brothers about any of this or he'll get bounced from the club. You know how they feel about junkies."

Erby confiscated the bag: "Chink and Inky are walking dead-men. Toby and Webb are finished. You two are treading water. Here's your chance to get right. I want that brick. Don't say shit to Jackie about this. He's hangin' out with niggers now, so he can't be trusted. And listen, Slick. You know what happens if I have to come lookin' for you, right? I'll be at Chuggers later, and so will you – with all of it. I'll pay you then."

That night, Chilly positioned himself outside in some bushes near a window. He saw Erby passed out next to an ancient-looking, wooly Airedale. That blind dog growled a toothless warning till he caught a familiar scent. An unconscious Erby got injected with a lethal dose of heroin. Three days later Ansel found him with a blood stained rig still in his arm, a bag of dope and that old Airedale dead at Erby's feet.

Chilly said, "Sorry, bro-ham. I didn't recognize Butch all old and shaggy. But as bad as I feel about that, there's something worse. Even though the word's out that Erby's a junkie, nobody else can zip one of them. You think bodies piled up quick at that bike show? This shit will get real ugly, real fast if they find out who's behind this. I put a few bucks together. It's time I go. I gotta tell you something, bro-ham. Things aren't turning out the way I thought they'd be. So far, life adds up to about one dry fuck."

My mother phoned again: "There's a bad storm coming. Stay home! You hear me?"

While traveling along a dark road during an early winter storm a spotlight flashed in my eyes as I heard shots. Upon impact, my car swerved into the path of an oncoming salt truck clouded-over in a mist of powdery snow. As I straddled the edge of a ditch, weeds poked through snow magnified by bouncing headlights. My car made a lazy upside-down slide into a soft snow bank with me on the headliner. Once my ball bat was located I exited the vehicle upside-down. The car wasn't as damaged as much as I had imagined, except all four wheels faced the sky.

I stood in freezing wind with my bat . . . just in case *it* returned. After I called a tow truck from my cell a Deputy Sherriff arrived. He asked, "Isn't this football season?"

"My car got attacked. I'm not sure by what, but an animal ran me off the road."

He produced a breathalyzer, tested me and then brandished a pistol as the wrecker inched my car right-side up. When he discovered a fresh blood trail he said, "You'd better be right about this." Easy to track in snow, we found a carcass about 100 feet away. "It's a coy dog. Somebody's hunting after dark. You must have a guardian angel."

Other than a bit bloodied from what appeared to be a single gunshot through its ribcage, the dun-colored canine looked like it was asleep in the snow.

"Fuckin' aye. I'll take this bad boy home so I can have it stuffed and mounted."

The cop pointed his flashlight in my face, "Get in your car and go home right now before I change my mind and cite you for failure to control."

Later that day, one of the last things I can recall is the blur of a primered ¾ ton pickup as it blew through a stop sign. I squeezed the steering wheel and flattened myself against it as I switched from gas to brakes. My car vaulted into another of those waist-high ditches. That time, a front wheel broke off when it crashed against frozen ground. Totaled beyond recognition, my car had been T-boned by two farm boys full of beer.

When I phoned my mother from the hospital she posed her rhetorical questions, "Why you won't listen to me I'll never know. When are you going to learn?" When I asked her what was wrong she snapped, "You think I'm as stupid as you, Giacomo?"

I returned home to sleep it off. Amber eyes burned into me. I could hear someone call from far away. When the beast closed for its kill a familiar dream-roar devoured everything in its path. I woke up covered in sweat to a panicked sound from the phone.

I picked up to hear Carly sobbing: "His friend said he was tripping his ass off when he left for home, even though he told us he was done with all that. A semi-driver reported he hit a strange animal in a blizzard. He couldn't stop in time, Jackie. Then they found him buried in a snow bank. Man-oh-man, I can't believe our bro-ham's gone."

"Fuck me! You mean dead-dead, like gone forever? Can't be. Are you sure?"

"What the fuck, Jackie. Would I make this up?"

"We'll never see our brother again? Is that what you're saying? Now what?"

"Now nothing, that's what. Now everything is worse than before."

Well, I'll tell you what. You can believe this much, Carly. I'm gone, too. I'm sick and tired of all this death. I need some fresh air. You wanna come with me, sweetie?"

"I can't go anywhere till I get this monkey off my back. And I'm not ready to do that just yet. I'm not about to go volunteer for all that pain right now."

"I can help you, and you know this. There ain't shit for you up here. Just come along and we'll deal with it down there, okay? Or I'll wait for awhile, if you want."

"No. You go ahead, Jackie. Call me as soon as you get back in town."

Minutes later Henry pulled in the driveway with his usual smile. He leaned against the car and said, "Hey, brother-man. Here's the last envelope. This squares-away all the product I had. But there's something else. It's time we had a talk."

"Look, Henry, if you're pregnant don't blame me. You ain't my type."

"Ha! That's kind a funny. But on the real side, you're almost right. I feel like I'm in one of those corny-ass soap operas telling you this. But it's my girl that's pregnant."

"Congratulations, my friend. This baby'll change your life, but in a good way."

"Well there it is, brother-man. My girl says if I don't get out of the life, she gone. She says she won't raise-up a child with a drug-dealin' thug for a father who's in and out of the joint. It's all about timing, right? So the fact of the matter is . . . I'm out."

"That's cool. I'm happy for you, Henry. It's time for me to make some changes, too. The only thing holdin' me back right now is nothing. So I'm about gone, too."

"I told her you'd appreciate our situation. Besides my girl, you're the only real friend I've ever had. Remember, I'm a phone call away. And you're always welcome in our home, Jack. You and me got history, brother-man. We're family now."

"Same goes for me, Henry. But I see the signs, too. I know it's time. My life's got red flags shootin' up all over the place like Roman Candles."

"What about this Butter thing? You okay with this? Don't be ashamed to say it."

"I'm more than okay. The only part that bugs me is not havin' my kid with me, which is why I dig exactly where you're comin' from with what you have to do now."

He grinned, "I guess I'll be getting back to my girl before we stand here sniveling like a couple bitches. But we made it, brother-man. It all worked out, didn't it?"

"Yeah, man. It did and it will. That's the way friends do. I'll be in touch."

Before I left town a healthy Gina said, "I never saw his face, Daddy. You know who I mean, right? But I still dream about him sometimes. You know; the one who opened the door for us that night with the baby deer? I hear his voice sometimes but I can't make out the words. Dreams don't always make sense, right Dad?"

"Dreams are just us thinking while we're asleep, honey. It's just a way of sorting through fears, hopes and recent events, even when they don't seem to make sense. When our subconscious takes over, we're looking for newer truths to mend old fences."

"Mom says you're building more walls. Is that why you're leaving?"

"No, baby. I'm not really leaving. I just leased out our house for a year. Don't worry. I'll visit once a month till I get back, okay? I need to figure out some things. I wish you could come along. I'll phone and write every week . . . promise."

Before I pulled up stakes Eggs phoned to say, "Things are crazier than ever. You still wanna move to Italy, little brother? 'Cause if you do, now's a real good time. I'll go, too. You heard what's goin' on out there, right?"

"Yeah, Eggs, I know. Bombings are lighting up the Neighborhood like it's the 4th of July. Revenge killings are filling-up Five Points dumpsters with more trash. Nobody's safe. It doesn't matter who you are. Everybody's a target now."

"Remember when cops used to look like the bad guys, Jackie? I'm not so sure anymore."

"Fuck all these assholes: our ex-brothers, those two-faced bikers, and especially the cops. I don't know about you, man, but I don't trust anybody. Watch me. I'm gone like yesterday, and I'll be there for a minute."

CH XVI:
A SPIRITUAL QUEST

On the road again, I headed for Tennessee with Little Rover and his sister. A friend promoted the reunion concert of Gregg Allman and Dicky Betts. Our VIP table was front row to where they rocked the house. Inky fired up a joint, took a dragon hit that cherried the ash and then passed it to me. Next to us sat the most beautiful woman I'd ever seen, an amazing, exotic-looking creature. She pretended to not see me watch her.

"You look blue sitting all by yourself. If you're sad, we got the cure. You wanna hit this?" I asked, so I could watch her watch me. "No worries. The promoter's a friend. Besides, I'm not a cop or any stupid shit like that. I'm Giacomo Lorocco, a Yankee *dago* from Cleveland. What's your story, sad lady?"

She accepted my peace offering with the type of look that causes a child to blush and incites palpitations in a man. I got lost in ebony almonds that promised depth and darkness. High cheekbones and a silk veil of waist length ebony hair complimented a smile of pearls surrounded by rose petal lips. I said to Inky, "Scuse me, bro. I need to know this woman." I slid my chair behind hers and asked, "Okay if we talk? I feel outta place here."

"Hi Giacomo. I guess I am out of place here, too. But you see: I'm really not sad at all. Unfortunately, this happens to be the way my face looks most of the time. People usually think I'm angry, gloomy or just being a bitch."

"You're way too pretty to look mean, even when you're all gloomy. By the way, my friends call me Jackie. It's easier to say. So what is it they call you, sad lady?"

"Oh, sorry, I'm Ahawi Starr. Yes, I know. It is very different."

"So do you have the blues, or are you some mysteriously tragic woman?"

"Actually, I'm happy right now. The blues makes me feel good all the way to my soul. That's what good marijuana does too – like a religious experience, only it's grounded in reality."

"I might think about being a priest if we can toke at this instead of *vino*."

"If you do that you can't get married. Then you would be the sad one, Mr. Jack."

"Think so? I've already been on that ride. I believe I'll pass."

"What about children, Jackie? When you are a priest you cannot have them."

"Since when? Maybe you should be tellin' that to the pope and his gang of perverts. Far as I know, they have plenty kids . . . mostly little boys from behind."

"You are sort of funny in a dark, sad way. Do you and your friend always do crazy things like smoke dope in bars?" Then she sipped it a few times and held it inside. "Mmmm . . . Not bad. Is this hydro from up in Ohio, or some designer imported stuff?"

"You sure do ask lots of questions. What are you, some kind of herb critic? Because that's the job I want. Hey, how come you got such a strange name?"

"It's not strange, it's Cherokee. I work on my people's reservation droning away with boring secretarial stuff. But it's almost Indian Moon and time for me to soar."

"My dad's best friend was Cherokee. Maybe we're related. Hey, I know an Indian from Cleveland. He's Souix-cilian: half Sioux, half Sicilian and half civilian. Hmm, bad joke. Sometimes I'm funnier than this, but I'm pretty stoned right now. Anyways, this weed's homegrown in southern sunshine and fed on genuine Tennessee Walker manure. A friend around here owns a stable and recycles compost into this. Primo shit, huh?"

Greg Allman moaned "One Way Out," as she passed the ganja back to me. "Ahawi is the name mother and grandmother heard from the Great Mother Spirit when I was born. Cherokee is a matriarchal society and very spiritual. We listen to Nature's creatures and elements so She can guide us. Sometimes we use Her fruits like marijuana, peyote and mushrooms to call the spirits to us."

"Wow. You make church sound great. I just might become a priest after all. Hey, so you think maybe you can convert me tonight?"

"Are you looking for something inside a church or within a person?"

"Who? Me? Hmmm… On the real side, I'm not into religion at all and don't believe in God. My spirit is right now: the music, this weed, and this thing between us. So tell me, sad Starr, what's this Mother Spirit about? Is she a goddess or some saint?"

"It is difficult to explain, Jackie. But it's not religion and we do not worship in a building. The Mother Spirit is – you know – Nature. We don't idolize a punishing 'God the Father.' The god we know was here before religion. It is the god before God. It always was and always will be. Does any of that make sense?"

"Hey, you mind if I sit with you? I can't hear too good over this loud music."

"Sure, have a seat. But I had better give you fair warning. You might be sorry."

"I highly doubt that." I passed the joint to Inky and slid next to her. "You really are out of place – interesting and beautiful. I think it would be fun to know you." She watched me study her and waited for my next move, like we'd rehearsed our lines. "So, anyways, you like that kind—? You know; a name like Ahawi?"

"It is not a matter of like or dislike. I am not superstitious like mother and grandmother, but I do believe in the Earth Spirit. She is everyone, everything and everywhere. She has no beginning or end. Does this make any sense to you?"

"That's cool that you value your own kind. Respect is huge with my people, too."

"But what?" she asked. "I feel a clarifying *but* coming on."

But with us loyalty is just as important. To us it's a spiritual experience. Family should come first. Don't you agree? We don't go much for betrayal where I come from. In my neighborhood integrity is a must and taught to us by our fathers and neighbors."

"Well that is very admirable, I'm sure. But why do you assume we do not value loyalty? And why is where you come from is so special, Mr. Jackie? And if it is, why are you down here with us and not up there with them? I think maybe you are trying to convince yourself that your people are superior. Maybe you need to feel better about some things from back there, so you paint your people with a wide brush more colorful than they deserve? It's just a guess, but I think you carry a lot of pain. Could I be right?"

"Damn! I don't know about you, Miss Ahawi, but between these tunes, that bud and this conversation, I'm pretty-well zoned. How about we dig out after this set?"

"I can't do that. It is a loyalty issue. You should be able to relate."

"So the plot thickens, sad Starr with the Indian Moon. Now I'm even more interested. Lookin' at you makes me feel something I haven't felt since kindergarten."

"I'm not quite sure what that means. I suppose it is a compliment?"

"Hey, I wasn't trying to offend you about that integrity piece. I guess I just felt an urge to let you know what's important to me. Know what I mean?"

"It's okay. I accept your unspoken apology. So far you do not seem like most white folks I have met. Let me share something else with you about my people. In our culture, a sense of timing is as vital as a link with Nature. You appear to be in sync with your ambiance, Jackie. I sense that maybe you can even see the invisible. Am I right?"

I whirled around to find a thick-set brave breathing down my back with drinks clenched in meaty fists. When I asked what his problem was, he looked straight through me and at her. He chugged his and set hers on their table, then told her to get ready as he gave me another bad look and headed for the washroom.

She laughed, "Don't worry, Jackie. He is my fiancée. He doesn't trust white guys. And since he enrolled in the academy, he has become suspicious of everyone."

"Academy, huh? Fuck me..." *Now I hate cops even more.* "Okay, sad lady, but before your cop boyfriend gets back I wanna tell you about the upcoming Pit-bull conformation show I'd be judging at the fairgrounds in one week from tomorrow. You're invited to come and watch. You can be my guest of honor."

"Your guest of honor? I have a feeling there are strings attached to such an *honor*. And why just watch? We shall bring our boy. Wait till you see him."

I spotted her gorilla moving people out of his way to reach his Ahawi. I moved over to Inky's table and shook my head: "I'll be double-dogged. A woman of my dreams right here in the flesh – but as always, just out of reach. She's gorgeous and educated; a blues fan and Bulldog lover; just trippy enough but not too psycho; and a spiritual pot-head with a job. And she seems bored, too. I like that part. But she's engaged. That part blows. So tell me this, *coom*, how does that racist pig score this primo piece of ass?"

"You want my blade, Jackie? Better yet, we'll just follow that fat cocksucker home, chop him up and then kidnap Pocahontas so you can have a new toy at the farm."

Inky's farm had been inherited by his wife, a great-granddaughter of a legendary American gunsmith. Prototypes lined the walls of his front-room. He kept a trash bag full of bud next to his recliner, with Miss Rover at his side. His pipe-stand was an antique pedestal once used by real cowboys. Their house was built next to a creek and was a second floor residence. Its front-room floor was Plexiglas and overlooked their barn. Mellowed-out, watching horses move beneath out feet, I day-dreamed about what life would be like with that remarkable Indian. I couldn't get her out of my head, like she had cast a spell over me strong enough to temporarily get Tessa out of my mind.

The next day, as I walked Little Rover, a stooped-over neighbor ambled up a winding, one-laner that had been formed by a gigantic slab of rock. A piece of straw poked through his scraggly beard. The old farmer came as far as the gate and waited. With gnarled hands, he leaned wrinkled arms on the top rail and stared at the ground.

As he twirled the straw in his toothless mouth, the old-timer looked up and matter-of-factly asked, "Well, let's see here. I hear them red dogs is good dogs."

"Yeah, he's okay. How you doin,' Pops? What's on your mind today?"

"Well, okay then, where ya'll from then, son?"

"Inky and me are from Cleveland. We grew up together."

Curly hair down past my shoulders and a thick, blue-black beard contrasted his pale skin and remnants of a forgotten hair color. I was muscled and hairy, darkly tanned and pretty much covered with tattoos. It looked as though we hailed from different planets. I'd wager that old hillbilly hadn't been as far North as Southern Kentucky.

He mulled through a wrinkled mouth over gums, "Hmmm..., alright now. Is you one a them *Tally* boys from up yonder?"

"I'm not sure I know what you mean, Pops."

"I said her plain enough! Is ya'll people *Eye-Tally* or ain't they?"

"Oh, yeah, sorry, that's what I thought you meant. Yeah, I'm Italian. Well, at least my grandparents were. But I'm American, and proud of it!"

"Well, okay then. So now why ya'll way down here in this lil' town here, son? You been a hidin' out from the laws, have ya?"

The old man watched and waited for something. "Look, Pops, I ain't here for trouble. I ain't a thief or a liar. You can check with Inky on that one." *Yep. There it is.*

"Okay now. That's good then, son. 'Cause we don't cotton to no thieves 'round these here parts. The way we is up in here is ifin ya'll 'er out somewheres, why I'll go ahead and give yer place a good watchin'. And ifin I goes off fer a piece, then ya'll look after ta mine awhile like it was yourn. 'Cause that's the way we is back up in here."

"It'd be my pleasure to watch your back, Pops. The worst thing I might do is hurt a thief. Because a man that steals from a family . . . Hell, that's no man at all."

He drawled through a sly toothless grin, "Well now, we got nothin' against killin'. That is, ifin a man needs a good killin'. It's thieves we don't cotton none to back up in here. Now let's just see then. Ya'll er busy now, are ya?"

"Naw, just chillin, Pops. So what's on your mind?"

"Okay then. Let's just see now. How's about ya'll walk with me over ta my place an have ya a look-see at somethin' real spacial?"

I picked a stalk of fence weed and put it in my mouth and drawled, "Let's roll."

"Make sure ya'll close that gate behind ya, son. That's our law down in here."

Gate secured, wordlessly we set out to parts unknown. Any slower and I would have been moving sideways. The paint was chipped and cracked on his old farmhouse.

Though it was not quite spring, his grass was past knee high from years of reclamation. I offered, "I'll be glad to cut these weeds down if you got a good mower."

"Now that ain't why I brung ya up in here," he spat. "I guess I'll cut-her when I'm a good-en ready ta cut-her. Now I ain't ready, just yet here. I brung ya up here ta show ya somethin' spacial. Member? Ain't that what I said? Now foller me. Hear?"

I followed him inside that weathered barn to his loft steps. He concentrated ever so slowly, as if each wooden step presented a new set of problems. Once up, he eased his boney frame on a bale and pointed a crooked finger for me to join him. On a straw littered floor was a tarp with two large lumps beneath it.

"Let's see then. Ya'll go on ahead, son. Pull ya off that ol' tarp there and give her a good lookin' over. Let's just see what's up under here then. Okay now?"

It was a small motorcycle in a nest of clean straw. Even though the chain, tires, fenders and handlebars were next to it, the bike looked solid. It was a 1926 Harley-Davidson with a 346cc, 1-cyl engine – original chrome and factory paintjob.

The old man asked, "Hmmm... Now whatca think of 'er, son? Ain't she purty?"

"Yeah, man. She's a sweet sight, alright. You probably shouldn't show too many people this bike, Pops. I'm pretty sure it's worth lots a money."

He gave me the same sly grin. "Well, I'm just old right here. Okay now? I ain't nar stupid, ner plumb crazy just yet then. Okay, son?"

"I'm sure that's true. No disrespect intended." I replied to the ancient man with the antique bike. "I'd like to buy it off you. What's your price?"

"Well now, hmmm . . . okay then. Let's just see here. Well, I believe I'll just hang on ta 'er for a bit now. But I sorta figured ya'll just might like ta give 'er a good lookin' over, just ta have ya a good look-see."

"You don't know me from tomorrow. Why'd you trust some Yankee with this?"

"Hmmm . . . well son, ya'll seem ta talk purty straight fer a dark fella. And ya'll er a lookin' steady inta a man's eyes when yer a talkin'. Further, we both knows I'm not shamed ta shoot a thief dead in his ass ifin a man needs a good shootin'."

I pulled out a joint from behind my ear, "Hey, Pops, how'd you like to smoke some marijuana with me. It's homegrown in genuine Tennessee horseshit."

"I use ta, but she just sorta lost 'er appeal a ways back. If truth be told, alls it does is put an ol' feller ta sleep. I already do too mucha that up in here now. Thank ya just the same fer a offerin' a man a smoke. Ya'll go ahead ifin ya please."

Careful to put the ash in my hand in his dry, dusty barn, I listened as he told stories of "Whiskey stills bigger 'en a fancy car and plants taller 'en a growd man."

"Hey Pops, I'd like to ask a personal question. Is that okay?"

"Okay now. Ask away then, son. Maybe I'll answer 'er. Okay now?"

"What's it like to be old enough to have been a part of so much history? I mean . . . well, I'm not sure what I mean."

"Let's just see now. It's just four things here. Firstly, a man learns so much he plum loses his memory. Next is, a man's eyesight'll go from a lookin' at too much right here. Then a man's ears go bad from all the lies he's a hearin', I reckon. Hmm, okay now. Let's see here. Well then, lastly a man is likely as not ta plum lose his memory. That's all of it, son."

We talked awhile longer, with pieces of straw in our mouths, seated on bales stacked up in his loft. Then I offered to help him down the steps. He thought about it and shook his head: "Hmmm . . . well, hold-up then. Let's see here. I reckon I'll just stay up in here fer a spell. Catch me a cat-nap er two, ifin it's all the same ta ya'll. Okay then? So thank ya kindly fer a offerin' an 'ol feller a hand here. Okay, then. Bye now."

When Inky returned from work I told him, "I already met your neighbor. He seems like a nice old dude. He's pretty interesting, too, for a backwoods type guy."

"Oh, I get it. I lived down the road from that old geezer for years till he showed me. I tried to buy the bike and that old coop behind his barn. He's too old to fix it or ride it and too broke not to sell it, but that stubborn old buzzard won't budge."

After supper we walked to the old man's and followed him out behind the barn to see what allegedly was a primered coupe stashed in a field of chest-high weeds.

The old dude chuckled, "Lookee here then, fellers. Best beware a snakes back in here. Ya'll might get more'n ya bargained fer up in these hills."

"Thanks, Pops. But you might've mentioned snakes before we got halfway here. Now the barn's just as far as your car. Fuck-it now. Let's go check it out."

Later Inky said, "I been thinkin' I need another pup. How about we breed Little Rover to his sister? I knew they're still young, but Miss Rover's in heat right now."

"I don't know, *coom*. Look what happed to Idjit."

"I could use a few extra bucks. I might sell some to these hicks down here to train as hog dogs. Or maybe I'll trade 'em off for some guns and dope."

"If you do that, Inky, they'll just wind-up in the wrong hands. You'll be dealing with a bunch of unscrupulous motherfuckers again. You might wanna rethink that one."

"You're right. Fuck-it. I'll keep 'em all. I got chains. I'll build a few coops."

"I'm dog-poor right now, Inky, but I guess I can always feed another good one."

"I heard that, *coom*. Good ones are where you find 'em. I'll hang onto yours till you're ready. You can have pick of the litter."

"Cool. After they're on hard food I'll snag mine and be in the wind. This way my Gina can replace her Idjit with a pup from the same family. If it's a male I'll call him Little Sinbad. She'd like that. Ha! Now you got me all psyched about this project."

CH XVII:
THAT THING CALLED LOVE

The dog show was scheduled for that weekend. Besides local breeders and handlers, other fanciers gathered from all surrounding eight states, plus Ohio and Florida. A local TV station covered the event. While judging Best Puppy I turned from critiquing an entry to watch a woman's long hair lift in an early spring breeze – and her cop boyfriend was nowhere in sight. I awarded the ribbons so we could get to her class.

Ahawi was spectacular, the type of woman who attracted attention without doing anything deliberate. Her dog's class was comprised of extremely fat yearlings and a few that just didn't conform to the breed standard. Genetically, her dog was solidly structured. Along with a stable temperament, he had been fine-tuned into striated muscle. Standing proudly, they reminded me of a painting I'd seen of a squaw bareback on a white stallion.

When I handed her Best Puppy trophy I said, "Winning this means you gotta hang around for Best of Show. You never know, ma'am. You just might get another one."

"You probably don't even remember inviting me; do you, Mr. Big-Shot Judge?"

"Oh, I'm sorry. Have we met before? I'm Jackie. Is this your first show?"

"HA! Yes, we have. And you really are funnier this time, but not by much."

"I'm sure glad you made it here, sad little Starr. Are you glad?"

"I guess I'm glad, even though my fiancée refused to come along to handle his own dog. Why do you do this? He says these shows are for girls and homosexuals."

"Really... Well my guess is you're not a homo, and I'm definitely not a girl. See that? I keep getting a little funnier, ain't I?"

"Yes, that was kind of funny, and a pretty good way to dodge a question. Now tell me this, Mr. Question Dodger: Why do you put yourself out there to judge? Isn't that painting a target on your back?"

"I'm in it for the breed. These misunderstood dogs are heroes with few friends. Lots of guys think these animals are only good for blood sports. I'd like to see those pussies climb in the box and take what the biggest cur can handle. Then those same cowards cull their dogs if they make one bad move. We need more people who show and weight-pull or this breed will become extinct by *humaniacs* in our *free* country. But I guess I don't need to convince an American Native about double-standards, do I?"

"No. But all we hear about are gay rights, affirmative action, women's lib, amnesty for criminals and religious freedom for terrorists. These white people even want to free the lab rats. Weren't Indians the first Americans to be discriminated against? What about us? When is it our turn?"

"Us? Okay, I'll play. What about us? I mean, is there an *us*?"

"Ha!... Funny. Well, I guess I do have to stay now. But since I do not have an escort, it looks like you are stuck taking care of me. Can you handle this and judging, too? Oh, and sign my blue ribbon. But wait; I have a question. What is the real reason you gave us a trophy? What if my fiancée would have handled our dog? Be honest."

"You don't ever have to ask me again to be honest, okay? Anyways, I pick the dogs not the people – boyfriend or not. Now I have a question: You said you never bothered with the shows before, and your boyfriend wouldn't come to this one. So are you here just to show your dog, or did you come partly to see me? Tell the truth."

"Will you sign my ribbon, please, Mr. Jack?"

Instead, I jotted down a phone number. Her dog entered the ring for Best in Show like he was already a champion. After having each entry walk out and back and then stack, I handed the waist-high trophy to Ahawi and said, "They need you to stay in the ring for pictures. Hey, how about I buy you supper after this so we can discuss politics and religion? Or maybe we'll get back to that *what about us* part. I think I like that part."

"You really are funny. You know what? I thought I might faint when you walked towards us with this trophy. And I suppose maybe I was sort of looking forward to seeing you again. Thank you for these wonderful memories, Jackie. Now I must go."

"The phone number is to my mother's house. No matter where I'm at I can be reached through this number. You ever need a friend, don't hesitate to call. I can use a new Bulldog buddy. I lost mine and hadn't realized till right now how much I miss that. Oh yeah, plus the next time I see you I'll sign whatever you give me."

"We are friends now, Jack, but phoning would just confuse matters. When you need to talk to me just look at the sky. I'll be listening."

"I feel like we've been moving towards one another for a long time, Ahawi. Maybe always. Being with you at that concert and now us having this day together means more than you know."

"Are you sure about that?" she grinned, walked away and didn't look back. We knew the rules. We got the cards and played our hands. It was time for me to move on.

Southern Florida is a 28-hour drive from South Collinwood. Being in Tennessee, I was already half-way there. I still needed to cleanse off residual disgust of loss and failure, so I continued south to a place of fond memories.

Florida is also where I got turned on to "freebase," now known as "crack." Remnants of the No-Names settled in horse country, where we chased *rocks* on long weekends. Deals with automatic weapons and suitcases stuffed with drugs and cash were not rare. Kilos of coke came packaged in thick, brown wax paper scribbled with Spanish writing and secured with waxed twine. What was removed to make room for "cut" got cooked and smoked by us. Those base crystals unlocked hearts of aspiring actresses hoping to meet talent agents with unlimited amounts of coke. They hit pay-dirt with us. Manic runs from the Southern Peninsula to the North Coast were as normal as titty-dancers amped-out on poached coke, licking each other during long weekends of frantic ecstasy.

TV provided a cheap lightshow of images on drug-infested nights. That weekend a local newscaster warned, "We're witnessing the third day of continuous storms with no end in sight. There will be heavy flooding in Broward County from canals overflowing. Keep your pets indoors where it's safe. Remember you snow-birds, this is gator country!"

It was a smothering type of relentless deluge. Slick said, "That weatherman's finally right. Nobody can sneak-up on us now. Plus, this house is banked-up. So we should stay above water. Just don't fuck with that snake over there."

Toby stalked the reptile all stooped-over with curled fists next to a mad smile. "Here snaky-snaky. Good snaky-boy. Hold still so Uncle Toby can mash you."

That snake found its own way out. Within a few hours, daybreak let us know the rain had stopped and snakes were done moving for the night.

Toby jumped, "What's that noise? Listen up. You hear wolves or coyotes?" He went outside to recheck for FBI, CIA or any other initialed agency that might be on patrol at dawn, in the middle of nowhere for a couple of nobodies.

He returned with information he eked out a sentence at a time while he built a peanut butter and jelly sandwich on something that resembled bread. Upon closer examination, the inside was the same texture as the crust – gummy. It was as though some demented artist spray painted raw dough to look like food.

As he chewed his creation with a wide-open mouth, purple jelly mixed with those pasty slices slathered with creamy peanut butter. He mumbled, "You might wanna go out back to check on your pup. Somethin's missing, cuz."

The inside of his mouth looked like an abortion. But similar to when passing a car wreck or road kill, I couldn't stop looking inside his mouth as he spoke.

"What do you mean *something's missing*? Like what, Tobe?"

He used somebody's cold instant coffee that had gone bitter the night prior to try to swallow a mouthful of that muck. He chewed louder once the brown liquid turned his sandwich into a wet, spongy mess. Smiling, with chunks of gunk stuck to his teeth, he added, "Go ahead, see for yourself . . . But I promise, you ain't gonna be too happy."

Little Rover was there, but something really *was* missing. He stood on the surface of the water, as high as plump fruit on their dwarf lime trees. I turned on the spigot and let that hose spill over my muddled head, then checked again. What was missing was his doghouse! The flat roof, almost three feet above ground, was not visible.

Rover howled louder than ever from the back of the property, a pitiful and haunting song for such a bright morning. I went back inside for knee-high barn boots. By then Toby picked his teeth, "I wouldn't wear those. The water's too high. They'll fill up and you won't be able to move fast when somethin' gets near you."

"Don't get all paranoid on me, Tobe. There ain't no Navy SEAL team out there waiting for us in flood water. Try to chill, cuz. It's just us here."

"You know, I'm just sittin' here listenin' to this dick-wad on TV. He says be careful if you live near canals, 'cause gators are snatchin'-up pets. That's one thing about gators and bull sharks, they ain't prejudice. They'll snag a person as quick as a duck."

Wearing cutoffs and a pair of flip-flops I waded through waist-high canal water.

Toby yawned, "Oh yeah, and remember the fire ant nests are flooded-out."

Already in the beginning stage of shock, the young dog trembled as if freezing on that muggy day. I swished him around in water and carried him like an infant as those murderous little bastards had their way with us. Nothing could be done till we reached salvation of the Holy Water from that muddy hose. Wrapped up, his eyelids fluttered to a deep shadow-growl. Head swollen twice its normal size, choking from grand mal seizures, he expired on my bed. Later that day, after floodwaters receded, I found a chewed-up eastern diamondback dead inside Little Rover's doghouse.

"See what happened here, Tobe? This little guy was worried he might wake me. My daughter's dog suffered because I was too busy chasin' ghosts all night. Fuck-it. I'm done with this shit, too. This whole semi-sobriety thing is weak."

My next trip home is when I ran into a freshly divorced Maggie. I asked, "If you're finished with that bust-out you wanna go to Florida with me for awhile? Then when my tenants' lease is up we'll come back and stay here at the farm."

"Why are we standing when we should be driving?" When I asked if her father would pose a problem she explained, "He wrecked his bike, drunk again. Now he rides a wheelchair. We'll have plenty of time to talk about this on the way. Let's go."

After a week's worth of experimenting with crack she said, "I hardly recognize these guys anymore. Old friends back-stabbing one another for more poison? Can we go back home now?"

When I phoned my mother to let her know we were headed north she reminded me, "Today is the anniversary of Daddy's death. Stay there one more day."

"You're way too superstitious, Mom. See you tomorrow."

Maggie and I discussed that odd conversation on a Georgia interstate when I felt an uncontrollable aura stronger than any *rush*. I flash-dreamed of driving with my father seated next to me. His voice echoed through my skull, "Open your eyes, boy. Do it now!"

When I woke on the berm I jerked the wheel back and forth and stomped the brake pedal. My eyes darted from windshield to passenger seat. No father, no Maggie, just an open passenger door and an empty bucket-seat. I wondered: *Did she jump out or is this a dream?* Both were logical notions from a person who just woke-up while driving. My shift lever in park, the engine still on, a couple approached with Maggie.

She was crying and hugged me: "I don't like it when you do that, okay? I know it's got something to do with those fucking pills you're always taking. If you stop now, I will too. Promise me you won't die first. I can't deal with all this alone."

"I'm cool, just a little tired. What's goin' on? And who the fuck's this pervert?"

As I moved toward him she grabbed my shoulder and whispered, "Lighten up. They're only trying to help. Look down, tough guy, you pissed your pants. You had a convulsion or something. Let's get you to a doctor right away."

"Thanks. Good looking out," I said to the frenzied couple.

"Jackie, I watched you pull across two lanes of traffic and then park on an off ramp while you were jerking around in some kind of fit. The whole time your head was all the way back and your eyes were fluttering. I know that's not possible, but I saw it."

At the exit there was a little blue sign with a big white "H." We paid for a motel so I could shower off piss and confusion and then headed for the nearest ER. Once there, a huge southern lady checked me in and took my demographics.

She asked, "You think you can tell me how ya'll was feelin' when you was drivin' that car, honey?"

"Exactly the way I'm feelin' right now." Within moments I found myself on a gurney hooked up to IVs. I closed my eyes, laid back and mumbled, "I'm too young for this bullshit. Don't let Maggie in here." A heart monitor rapidly accelerated beeps. The last sounds I heard came from an ER doctor. "Get me one cc of Atropine. DO IT NOW!"

After three days in ICU a doctor said, "We're not sure why you had seizures, so it could reoccur. When it does it could end your life. Don't drive for the next six months."

I admitted, "That's the type a death I hadn't figured on, Doc. I thought I'd get snuffed in some violent shit or croak from an overdose. I didn't see this coming at all."

That hick doctor concluded, "Your generalized seizures could have been caused by minuscule brain lesions from previous head trauma, or temporal lobe epilepsy. Hallucinations experienced in the car could be indicative of a schizophreniform disorder, but without other problems in your medical history I would have to rule that out."

But there were lifelong symptoms he was unaware of: those ignited by fevers, inflamed by alcohol, stimulants and hallucinogenics; placated with barbiturates, weed and hypnotics; visions and sounds to which I had refrained from admitting.

We stopped in for the night at Inky's to rest and to get my half of his two-pup litter. There was a black & tan male we took and named him Little Sinbad. The next night we picked up Gina for the weekend. She was all over that pup but stand-offish with me. The next morning she began to warm-up. By that night she sat against me and said, "I remember you now, Daddy. You're not mean and crazy." *Hmmm...okay...*

Sunday night, after dropping off Gina but before I left town on business, I told a dope-sick Maggie, "Quit being a weakling like your crippled father. Kick the mattress for a minute and you'll be fine, ya fuckin' whiner. Believe me, you'll bounce back stronger than ever. Just suck it up. I gotta go off this *blow*, but I'll try to get right back."

I returned home to find a receipt taped on our bathroom mirror. My pup watched me read its simple message: "I moved back home to be with the other cripple. Love, me."

Little Sinbad stretched out across my feet whining. I stayed up all night waiting for a call. It was Eggs who phoned in the news.

"I'm sorry to have to be the one to say it, *coom*. Maggie overdosed on Xanax and vodka last night. They found her in bed. You know where I am if you need anything."

The inside of my head screamed a roar nobody could hear except me. "Bullshit! I don't believe you. What the fuck's a matter with you sayin' shit like that? Why would you say this to me, Eggs?"

"I'm real sorry, *coom*. It ain't BS. Carly asked me to call you. It's true, Jackie."

"You better be right about this or you're gonna have to kick my ass."

"You know I'd never make-up something like this. I'm sorry for your pain, little brother. I wish I didn't have to be the one to say it. If there's anything I can do—"

"What the fuck am I supposed to do with this? How am I supposed to act now? Did someone hurt her? Tell me straight. I'll kill somebody over this!"

"Don't go ballistic, Jackie. It's just real bad luck is all."

"I'm fucking speechless. I can't talk right now. Maggie knew I was gonna break-up with her. Everybody did. She fucking knew I didn't love her. I hate myself for this!"

"It's nobody's fault. It's something really bad that happened. Nobody's to blame. She just took too much one time too often and didn't wake up. I'm sure it was an accident. I'm so sorry for you, *coom*. Just don't go out and do something crazy."

"No way . . . This just can't be real. I can't wrap my head around this. This is too fucked-up, man. I don't know whether to scream or start killin' motherfuckers."

"I might as well go ahead and say this, too. There's something else crazy I found out. Toby moved back to Cleveland."

"Toby? Did that motherfucker have something to do with this?"

"He's dead, Jackie."

"Whoa! What's this? Who's dead? What the fuck are you saying to me?"

"I'm saying we need to be real careful right now." You shouldn't ever drink again, *coom*. I can't tell you the rest of it right now."

"What do you mean by that? Was Toby anywhere near Maggie when this happened? Or did he get in a wreck or something? Don't fuck with me, Eggs. Just tell me!"

"No, Jackie. It's not safe to talk about this over the phone. It's just a real bad coincidence. But I can tell you this much right now: Toby's death was definitely no accident. If I were you I'd lay low for awhile."

"Are you saying whet I think you're saying?"

"Yeah, little brother, I think so."

"I'm hanging up now, Eggs. I got a lot of things to think about."

At a dog show I had given my mother's number to a lady met at a concert. Our next conversation occurred after Maggie was buried. Ahawi phoned: "Are we still friends? Because I need one right now. I'm wondering if it might be you. I was four months pregnant the last time I saw you. That's why I had to get married. But my husband got killed in a drug raid the same week our baby was born – just last week. Now I feel lost and scared."

"I'm sorry for your losses. I recently lost a friend, too. We don't *have* to be alone, you know. You two can move up here with me and help me raise my new pup."

Instead of an answer she related a story: "Grandmother married a handsome drunk, a gambler from another tribe. He was a dogfighter with little respect. Their son, my father, betrayed mother and me, just like his own skunk of a father had when he gambled away their farm and then abandoned them. Now my husband left me with this infant because he too played a white man's game. So let me ask you this, Mr. Judge: Why should I trust you? Will I have to find my way back home with a fatherless child like grandmother had to do so long ago? Or should I stay here, safe with my own kind?"

"Italian fathers might be maniacs but they stick close to home, even though that's not always a good thing. As far as a dogfighter goes: let's just say I did what I had to do in the past to survive. Understand? So who is it you do trust, Ahawi? Why is where you come from so special? Is your redskinned tribe better than others? I think you're just trying to convince yourself of something that isn't real. No offense, but could I be right?"

"Mother had a dream that my boy and I got carried away by a spiritdog. In her dream, things went different for us than for her. She told me my ancestors' energy scattered across the sky like stars of forever, for whenever my baby and I need their power. I'm so afraid and confused anymore."

Before I had time to reconsider, Ahawi brightened my colorless existence. What was there to think about, anyway? I had nobody, and she was exactly what I wanted.

"This world is full of stories, Jackie, and at times they permit themselves to be told. Ours starts here with you – a tattooed, Yankee *dago*. I remember when your words mixed with blue notes at the concert, and with all that growling at the show. Was yours just noise like those curs make? You talk about things like respect and loyalty. Are you willing to give those things to a woman and her baby, instead of handing another line to an attractive, childless girl at a nightclub? I wonder what we've come to. My baby's not a puppy, and I don't need another son. Let's make sure this is what we really want."

"I've watched guys try to raise other men's kids and saw bitterness follow like hell-hounds. I don't have to be an asshole, and you don't need to be a bitch, right? Either trust me or don't. If I'm your best friend then don't go against me, okay? If I'm always the odd man out it won't work. I can only give you what I have, and that'll be whatever you share with me. But if we both do this thing right it'll be enough. Can you trust this?"

"My husband took me for granted. What we had in our marriage died long before he did." Then she handed me her infant: "If you are who I choose to believe you are, then I give you our lives. For as long as we are together that is the way it will be. The three of us can be one spirit. I am your woman now, and baby Maneto is our son."

"Maneto, eh? What a coincidence! My dad had a childhood friend with the same exact name! Which kind is that one, Cherokee?"

"No. It's Shawnee. The night I went into labor, grandmother had a vision of a great maneto devouring my husband – the same night he was killed. Even though it's the name of two men she despised, grandfather and father, she insisted the baby be named Maneto for the great snake that came to her in dreams. She told me the maneto took the life force from my husband and put it into this baby, for him to be strong and fearless."

"I thought Giacomo was a fucked-up name. Now Ahawi and Maneto? We sound like a bunch of grape pickers. HA! This is perfect for these redneck, jerk-offs out here."

"When my husband became bitter, anger called him to the bottle. During the last month of pregnancy he hit me when I refused to have sex. I began to hum a death chant so the Mother Spirit could find him. Grandmother's vision paved our escape to you."

"From now on I'm with you. I'll be your best friend and a good father to this boy. Just don't punish me for the sins of other men in your life."

"I hear your words and watch your actions. Now you will show who you are."

My mother grilled me: "I guess you have something against white girls? What kind of woman drags a newborn across country to be with a stranger? What happened to those nice Italian girls like that beautiful Carly? What's with all these *putana*?"

Little Sinbad and Baby Maneto were raised together as brothers and became inseparable. He grew quickly into a smart, strong boy. I loved him as if he were my own son. And Ahawi inspired me like no other. Together we shared the best and worst of times, a bi-polar relationship tugging at anchors from the past.

Mom harped, "If you put the same amount of time and energy towards school and work as you spend with your drunken friends and those stupid dogs you could be happy."

When my bong and I smoked our way to an Associates Degree she said, "Too bad your father had to die before he could see this. It's about time you did something right. Your cousins are all successful businessmen. But it's my son who's the *dogman*."

When Ahawi and I received Bachelor's Degrees, the child my mother could brag about was the same one who had disgraced our family with drugs and gang associations. At commencement she hugged me for the first time since her visit at the detention home. She said, "You had everything going for you as a boy and tried to destroy it all with drugs. Maybe it's not too late for you, but I highly doubt it. Do you even hear me anymore?"

"Sure I do, Mom, loud and clear. We're gonna take you out to dinner, anywhere you'd like to go. We're college graduates now. Can you believe this? Let's go celebrate."

"You kids go out. Have a good time. Take me home now. I don't feel well."

At dinner Ahawi said. "I don't want you and your black friend smoking drugs around my son. He's too old not to know and too young to be around it. I've decided to quit and don't want it in the house. Go smoke at Henry's. If you have to smoke here, you will keep that crap in the barn. That's if you care anything about my son."

"Are you serious? I treat that kid the same as Gina. You do remember Gina, don't you? Hey, in all the years you've lived here have you ever taken a drive to see her without me, maybe take her to lunch or a movie, or just hangout for an afternoon?"

"We're not discussing me or Gina right now; we're talking about what you should and should not do. Can't you see what's happening here, Jack?"

"Of course I can. You want to talk? Good! We both see what's going on, but neither of us is doing anything to make it better. What about the changes you were going to make, huh babe? This *is* a two-way street, right? So what will *you* change, and when?"

"Me change? I've changed plenty. I'm a different person now."

"I'll say. You're self-absorbed, suspicious and secretive. At least I'm up front with my bullshit. So I hit a joint once a day – big fucking deal. What would be the difference if I drank moonshine around *your* son? That's a drug too, and a hell of a lot more dangerous in every way. And you know this. Now all the sudden you're going to get all conservative on me. Are you turning into some white-bread chick now?"

"Alcohol is legal, remember? You've been breaking laws for so long you create your own social paradigms. But you can't drink without behaving like an asshole, can you? So now what? Are you going to sneak around? Can I trust you anymore?"

"You have the balls to ask me that? Try looking at you for once, instead of analyzing me. You're every bit as diluted as I am. And as far as *legal* goes, how about if I take a prescription pain pill every night like you do? Is that better because it's legal? Why are you so fixated on this right now? Lately you're always trying to spin things and then dump them on me. Why don't you show me the same courtesy you give to strangers, and to people you don't even like? Oh, I guess I'm wrong about this too, huh? Is that it?"

"Yes. You are wrong. You don't care about me anymore. Just admit it, Jackie."

"Really? What happened to *our* needs as a family? I hardly even know you anymore. You're on that computer constantly. Who is it you trust? Because everything's a secret with you lately. You don't even sleep with me anymore. Why is that?"

"You really are suspicious! You imagine things and make a big deal out of nothing. Okay. You want honesty? You want perfection, Jackie. You need too much, and that's more than I have. Another thing is I miss my family more than expected. But don't worry. I'll never do what Butter did. Cheating dishonors the person who's unfaithful. I'm not her. I'm here, Jackie. Can't we just enjoy today? Isn't that enough?"

"Probably not. I about half-trust you anymore, about as much as I can trust any stranger. For now I choose to believe you're straight, right till you give me a reason to doubt you. The other thing that really bothers me about us is how we talk to one another. There's no neutral tones. It's all extremes with no middle ground. You're every bit as unforgiving and guarded as I am. I can't live like this for much longer. I don't want this."

"Like you always say, Mr. Philosopher, we get what we ask for. You told me attitude and perspective make up our priority lists, and that choice controls our lives. If you are all that unhappy with the way we get along then make some adjustments."

"It's back on me again, right? You want me to reprioritize so I can change our worlds? What about you? That couch has become your bed and the TV replaced me as a friend. You rarely even answer me when I talk to you — too busy chatting or watching one of your *important* TV shows. I'm fed-up with being your second-string team."

"You don't understand shit! I'm trying to deal with things, okay Jackie?"

"So let's deal with them. We used to process and resolve things together, remember? What's happened? You even flinch lately when I touch you. What's *that*?"

"I have too much stress on me right now, Jack. I can't sleep with anybody . . . not right now. I can't even relax enough to have a conversation, let alone that. My mind never shuts off. I stay on the couch with the TV on because of the racing thoughts. I need to divert, to refocus. I'm really scared right now and feel like I have nobody."

"Ahh, that's real nice. Spit in my eyes and then kick me while I'm blind."

"I'm just being real, Jackie. Isn't that what you want — brutal honesty?"

"Yeah, thanks. Much appreciated. It's strange the way things work out, huh? I've been your one true friend, and look what happens. First my brothers turn on me. Now my own wife doesn't trust me. Yet I treat you right and have always been straight with you."

"It isn't about loyalty or deception. Doesn't a lack of joy count for anything?"

"It sure does in my book. But you're the one creating all this distance."

"I'm not keeping score, Jackie. I just know what I feel."

As students of the Great Mother Spirit, we read Her symptoms and obeyed Her signs. She and her boy simply disappeared one day like a spirit hawk at dusk.

I decided it was time to get lost in a familiar compulsion.. School had not only rekindled a passion for writing, it also paved a way for unexpected rewards.

CH XVIII: DEPENDENCE & FREEDOM

After I had tied on that first beer binge in junior high I didn't care about fitting in or social drinking. My mission was to get shit-faced as often as possible. Fast and hard became my game. Then I fell in love with marijuana, till it no longer worked well enough. The *more* I wanted was an upwelling found in the major leagues with hard booze and other hard drugs that filled us with more emptiness.

Opioids such as heroin and morphine, and synthetic counterparts such as Demerol, Diluadid, Opana and OxyContin give crushing blasts that pins a person down in a sultry, sweaty web of ecstasy. The first time I did Vietnamese heroin in Cleveland I thought: *Okay...I totally get it now...So where have you been all my life?* After that initial encounter with IV heroin's golden glow, archaic pleasure centers drew us to a heavenly dreamland. And I found out how its buzz endures on various levels with surges of mini-orgasms to excite every nerve ending in the body. Opiate abusers are content for longer periods of time than stimulant addicts. But they pay dearly with protracted, painful withdrawals characterized by severe body cramps, weakness and nausea. During detoxification, the urge to relieve dope-sickness becomes even more powerful than cravings for the high, self-respect or even survival. Because injected and inhaled opiates provide a rush more intense than a sexual climax, users want more and addicts need more.

The first time I smoked freebase was the first time I actually enjoyed cocaine. Before that spring, spent in a Florida kitchen full of psychotic chefs, coke had been nothing more than expensive crank. I figured: *I don't need this. I can get nervous for free.* So I rationalized freebase as "experimentation" for a few months, as soon as the first inhale woke-up all receptor sites to surround sound: *Okay now...So this is what the big deal is.* Its swirling, silvery smoke winding up a glass chamber turned me into a believer. Garage doors slammed down over an elongated skull pulled into a roaring tunnel – that vortex of the *rush*. With multi-climaxes nearly as intense as marathon sex, freebase quickly becomes a marriage of best friend, lover and worst enemy. If a person wants to destroy mind and body real fast, crack is one way to go. With inhaled stimulants, the come-down is a mind-fuck of trying to free oneself from psychotic episodes on a runaway rollercoaster. The ride doesn't stop with a hit – it begins. Within moments of that first taste, the search continues till stash, money and sanity are gone.

But as it turned out, the old demon alcohol proved to be as the most dangerous love affair I had ever been entangled with. Blackouts began early-on.

As an adult, finally ridding my system of alcohol was the toughest thing I ever did. Staying away from drugs was easier than I had once thought. But because that deviant lifestyle had defined who I was, in which capacity I had enacted and with whom, after years of addictive usage I eventually found myself in a chemical dependency treatment facility.

My first AA lead wasn't what I expected. The chair-person introduced their speaker: "It's my pleasure to bring you a man all the way from Erie, Pennsylvania. A legend in the rooms of Cleveland, Ohio, I give you Vito R., a recovering alcoholic."

The clinical director said to me, "Oh no, not him again. I hope there aren't children present. I hate to say this, Jack, but that Vito character is clearly over the top."

"Okay, alright, everybody settle down," Vito said. "Take a seat before you have an accident. Yeah, you too, in the back there, cop a squat and relax. Don't worry. The doughnuts ain't goin' nowhere, ya bust-outs. I'm Vito R., a recovered alky, and I'm here to share my strength and hope with youse sick and suffering junkies. Now I got a few things I can tell ya, but I can't call names. Swear to Buddha, it's for your own safety."

It was Ice-cream Nicky's crazy cousin, Sally-Boy, at the podium. When he spotted me he wagged an index finger back and forth like a little windshield wiper. "Alright, real quick like. I'm gonna get right to it. This disease took me places I thought I'd never go. Believe me; I paid high prices for bein' a low-life. Even though my pig of a wife did a bunch a dumb shit in her blackouts I took her back for the sake of the family. Meantime, to save face I had to shoot up my own neighborhood. Guess what?. She keeps on drinkin' and blames me. Why? Because she's one a them *tri-polar* bitches. So what do I do? Same thing. Why? 'Cause I'm an alky, that's why! She tells me I gotta quit the booze or else, so I agree. Not good enough. Meanwhile, she's a *diabetriss,* but still chuggin' booze like a champ. Then she leaves for Tampa with some other degenerate. So here's me with my friends, Jack Daniels and Bud, headed to Florida to take care a business. By the time I hit the state line the bottles're as empty as my wallet. Next thing I know, I'm wakin' up in the hoosegow wearin' the orange uniform and a bad headache, thinkin' my luck can't get no worse."

"So I says to some bust-out next to me, Jesus Frickin' Christ – scuze my French – this is my third DUI. All because I followed this *slutoris* all the way here to Miami, and now I'm gonna lose my house." He paused to stare at a woman in the front row for effect.

"So this drop-shot tells me, 'Hey buddy, this ain't Miami it's Daytona. And you ain't here for no DUI, you ran some guy over on the beach.' *Minchia*! That's the kind a shit it took to wise me up. So I dried out in the state pen. Meantime, I know me. If I drink any hooch in there I kill everybody. Now that I'm sober I understand I'm powerless behind this shit. I admit it; I can get a little wacky sometimes.But what kind a maniac's on a beach at night? Right? Meantime, all this should be a good lesson for my kid. Guess what? He's worse then his lush of a mother. You think he'd learn. But here's him out there qualifyin' for junkie Hall of Fame. He thinks he's a big shot with the fancy drugs and his *cidrule* (turd) friends. He'll be the next loser in this place – if he's lucky."

"Anyways, lemme close with this stuff: You knock on the house of pain, you get admitted to hell. So how youse wanna act? Don't do what I did. Do whatever youse gotta do to stay strong. You work the recovery, then watch it get easier. Just don't cur out, ya frickin' cowards. Tough it out till the miracle happens. And don't go gettin' all cocky. Understand? Oh, youse still wanna get high? Okay. Go out and get laid, ya friggin' queers. What's a better buzz than that? Am I right? Okay then, I'm still Vito R."

Sally-Boy was the last person I expected to see in a treatment center. Evidently he used the name, Vito, as a disguise in the AA meetings, too.

The director glared at Sal with disgust. "Well, Jack, I apologize for that. I hope you're not easily offended. Do you think you are cut out for this type of work? Not everyone is, you know. Counselors get paid in two ways. One way is a bi-weekly check deposited into your bank account." *What's that?* "The other payment comes every time you have a breakthrough with a patient. Are you up for a challenge?" *Challenge? I want that.* "If you're ready, your hands-on education can begin with an internship on Monday. I am impressed by how you had the gumption to earn a degree in middle age. One crucial piece you lack, however, is that you aren't in the program. We are willing to give you a chance if you can adapt to the disease concept of treatment and recovery. Familiarize yourself with how our program works and personalize a 12-Step model. Remember, there is only one way to stay sober. By the way, Jack, have you ever been a team player?"

"Me? Actually I was pretty handy with a bat and played on a winning team for years," I assured him. "I won't let you down. I've learned to think on my feet while growing up in Collinwood. I'm honored to be trusted with such a fragile population. I'll do my best. Thank you for this opportunity. See you Monday, bright and shiny."

Other than odd jobs with Bee-Bee Balls, rehab offered my first legal job since the railroad, and my only health coverage in 20 years – plus, paid vacations and sick time. Already in my 50s, a door of opportunity awaited in front of me. All I needed to do was turn its handle and push. Even Black Bart's Doberman could accomplish that simple feat.

It felt good to be trusted again. That first day taught me about fire drills. I sprinted to clear out rooms and shut doors while a deafening alarm blared. GHEE-ONK! GHEE-ONK! GHEE-ONK! Passing a TV area, I stopped dead in my tracks and walked backwards.

Casually leaning on a wall, a patient held a fingertip in one ear and a phone receiver on the other. I banged on a thick pane of glass to get his attention. He didn't budge.

I opened the door waving my arms. GHEE-ONK! GHEE-ONK! GHEE-ONK! The man unplugged his ear and held up a finger, giving me that *I'll be off in a minute* gesture.

I shouted, "Hey you, hang it up!" to a nodding head.

The patient yelled, "SHUT-UP! I CAN'T HEAR." then re-plugged his ear to the thunderous GHEE-ONK! GHEE-ONK! GHEE-ONK!

As if it were my only phone during my own personal alarm, I felt like punching the receiver into his mouth. GHEE-ONK! GHEE-ONK! GHEE-ONK!

Purple rage flooded my eyes. I screamed, "HANG UP NOW, GOD-DAMNIT!" a moment too late. A startling silence amplified that last word throughout the hospital.

Calmly he said, "I gotta go. Call you later. Some rude prick says I'm not supposed to be on the phone for some reason." He looked at me for the first time: "What's your problem, man? Can't you see I was on the phone? I pay your wages, dude."

Hyperventilating, I attempted a smile: "Okay. I apologize for cursing. But nobody can be on the phone during a fire drill. We're not even supposed to be in the building."

"Fire drill? Why didn't you say so? All I heard was you yelling and swearing. Are you finished abusing me yet? Wow, what a fucking asshole."

The next test came disguised as a pretty girl. Nursing paged me to facilitate a crisis intervention with an 18-year old. Heather, a 4.0 cheerleader, appeared to be a beautiful girl with greasy hair matted against a pasty complexion of her innocent-looking face.

"Speak only if you feel the need to talk. I don't pretend to have all the answers," I tried to assure her, "and I won't deliberately give you bad advice."

She confessed, "I had everything going for me. I was the golden girl. Smart guys and popular jocks wanted to date me, but I pissed it all away. School was easy and I had a full-ride at a good college. I had it made and then went and trashed everything."

I handed her a tissue and sat quiet, waiting for her next move. She rubbed fearful eyes with stem-burned fingers and chipped nail polish, as she blew her nose.

"Booze gets me nauseous. Weed makes me paranoid. So I tried other stuff. You know why? Because you fuckers told us marijuana makes people crazy. When we found out you assholes lied, we figured you were lying about the harder drugs. too. While I was drunk some guy turned me on to crack. He seemed okay at first. Then nights turned into weeks with swats off that glass dick. I became so mentally sick I wanted to die. I begged God to help because I couldn't tell my parents I'm a junkie fucking a drug dealer! It's not like I was a virgin or anything, because I'd already slept with my boyfriend. I thought this guy liked me. But mainly I knew he'd take care of me. That's not prostitution, right?"

Her tone changed. "Then his friend came into the picture. They knew I couldn't keep getting money so they treated me like their whore. He promised to pay for rehab, but it was always *tomorrow*. The last time I partied with them they called me their 'fiend.' One held my arms while the other shoved his thing in my butt. It hurt so bad I screamed. Then they slapped me around and took naked pictures of me – fucking filthy pigs! I wish I could chop their dicks off and watch them bleed to death. Maybe that's why I cut myself. All I know is I was too weak to fight them. When I finally got honest with my parents about the drugs they cried. I never saw Dad cry before. They thought I was just smoking marijuana and were afraid to push the issue. They knew I'd just deny it and then act mad at them for saying such *evil* things to me. I hate myself for what I did to them. I'm such a fucking whore. I can't believe what's happened. My whole life is so fucked."

"When you're actively using, even if you have the best intentions of quitting, you're powerless. Right now you're heavy into withdrawal; plus, you're eaten up with guilt and shame. What you're feeling is both normal *and* temporary."

"No," she whined. "You don't fucking understand. I feel like I'm going to jump right out of my skin. My insides are on fire, and my nerves are totally fucked! My head aches so bad . . . I can't take much more. All you motherfuckers repeat the same stupid lines: 'God this, and the 12- Steps that...' Nobody cares, especially you; you fucking asshole. You just want my parents' money. Fuck you and this place! You jerk-offs stand up and preach these robotic lies to us, but you don't do shit. It's just more talk."

I rolled up my sleeves and leaned forward to expose fully tattooed arms to the girl who felt so misunderstood. Finally she looked into my eyes – once again listening.

"Are you sure I don't understand, Heather? You're not the only one who's fucked-up before. I was high for longer than you've been alive. But I haven't been in slavery since before you were born, so I might know which way is better. If you think we're the enemy then maybe you should go back to your room and cry yourself to sleep."

"Fuck you! Just go away and leave me alone. Call my parents to come get me."

"Okay. But first, let me guess. When the cravings got bad, drugs meant more than health, family and even life. Integrity was a memory. Now you feel lower than worm shit, right? You think you have no chance at a *real* life again. You're afraid your parents will never trust you. You don't believe you can do this. Stop me when I'm wrong."

"Go on; keep going. You don't seem like much of a bull-shitter, anymore. Before you rolled up your sleeves you looked like some addled professor, or a money-grubbing doctor or some other old hypocrite who learned about drugs in books. But I see now that you just might understand. I'm sorry for being such a bitch. I'm listening, okay?"

"You're ashamed of the things you've done, but shame is a waste of time. I should be executed for all the shit I've done. You're not a freak or a whore. You're not bad but you are sick, and that difference is huge. You're not helpless or hopeless, but you are powerless. It's not the same thing. Soon you won't be able to relate to the monster you became. Today you have options. Do you believe in a Higher Power, Heather?"

"I might believe in something, Mr. Jack, but it's not that fairytale they taught us in Sunday School. I'm not sure what I believe. I think something must be stronger and better than me – at least I hope so! God, I'm so fucking scared."

"The word God is a symbol. It can be whatever positive energy gets you through the day, as long as it doesn't hurt you or anyone else. A Higher Power can't be a person because eventually that person will disappoint you. It can't be an object, because a tree will die and a doorknob will break. Some people choose the sober community as a Higher Power. Do you believe in nature and love? If you accept nature as the ultimate force and can still feel love, then you already have a god of your understanding."

"I'm sorry I'm not more with it, but I feel like shit," she complained. "Yes, I feel nature and still believe in love. I love my parents more than anything in the world. When we visited Yellowstone I felt more spiritual than I did in any church. When we stayed on the ocean or in the Rockies they gave the same feeling. But when I'm strung-out, nothing matters except not to feel crazy. So I used more and got crazy enough to rob money and jewelry from my parents, just so I didn't have to fuck those assholes again. Now I'm not sure which was worse. Can I really do this, Mr. Jack? Please be straight with me. So far I don't buy one thing about all this God crap and their AA cult propaganda. I feel like I'm being controlled by some mindless lab techs who just repeat whatever they read and hear from other zombie morons. I feel so lost; I wish I could just disappear."

"I'm telling you right up front, you'll be sick and want to go home. You'll say you don't want to get high, and you'll believe it. But if you leave, you will use. It's not sobriety that's making you sick, it's still the drugs. If you make it through the weekend you'll feel better and want to leave because you'll think you're cured. That's your disease trying to hold you in slavery. But guess what? Your chance is as good as anyone else."

"I have to trust somebody. But I hurt so fucking bad I don't think I can make it. Even today feels too long. This weekend seems impossible. Please help me. I'm dying."

"Okay, little girl, I'll work with you if you promise to allow me to help. I'll bet you've even entertained thoughts that hurting yourself and being dead might be better than this. But there are worse things than death and addiction. A sweet-pants like you doesn't want to detox in jail without meds. What about if dope-sick *friends* do a home invasion because they know your parents have money? You think you feel bad now?"

"If I buy into this disease bullshit how do I get stronger if I surrender? That makes no sense at all. And what does *turning it over* mean? Who am I giving something to?"

"More intelligent questions. That's why I like you. Thanks to mistakes we understand what nobody could teach us. You've heard this before but didn't believe it. Now you know your limits. Thanks to the pain, you'll be smarter than that cheerleader with the 4.0 GPA. And because knowledge and experience are power, that means you'll be stronger than ever. You're rewriting your legacy right now. Are you up for that, or would you rather be that scared little girl who fucks strangers for dope? Oh yeah, and about surrender . . . I surrender my garbage to the trash man every week. Understand?"

She blurted through fresh tears, "Okay, fuck-it, I'll stay. But I can't take anyone else hurting me and I'm done hurting myself. I'll try it. If I feel better I'll hang around till you guys throw me out. How's that sound, old man? But I can't do this alone."

On her discharge day from treatment we embraced. That gorgeous girl held me close and whispered, "I'll never forget you . . . I owe you . . . I love you." Those same words came from another terrified girl long ago, their meaning every bit as powerful.

"And I thank you for reinforcing an important lesson. Back when I was still full of testosterone and booze I had overlooked how a year-old Pit-bull merely looks and acts like a mature dog but in reality is still only a pup."

"Sorry, Mr. Jack, but that one zoomed right over my head."

"You've given me back something I haven't felt in awhile. And for me, it's a feeling more valuable than a garbage bag full of dope."

CH XIX: GROUP THERAPY

Along with my promotion to Primary Counselor in 2013, I found myself in charge. So if things went wrong, there was nobody to blame but me. My first group consisted of men all still in the detoxification unit. I composed a topic of conversation to challenge some conventional rehab ideology, to serve as a diversion for when things got slow.

I phoned Horrible Hank for advice: "Most counselors try to convince them their problem is being too willful. I plan to let them know relapse stems from a *lack* of will, not because of it. They get force-fed a stale diet of Judeo-Christian principles with nothing new to get passionate about. I'll try to offer them a spiritual approach that's secular. I know this type of logic goes against old-school AA philosophy. What do you think?"

"I say fuck-it. Go for it, Jackie. From what I saw in the joint, spiritual advisors and counselors offer cookie-cutter answers for everybody on everything. Bring your thing the way you feel it, brother-man, the way you really believe. Keep it real and it'll work. Not just because it's fresh, but because you shoot from the heart."

"Thanks, my friend. I've been working on a handout just in case my first day in group gets boring. If you have a minute, I'll read it right now. It's only one page."

I read him the page I had been working and reworking for days. I wrote it in hopes of reaching agnostics and atheists who really wanted to get sober but were turned-off by crumbs left over from the 1930s. It was the type of thing I like to read. Although the words made sense to me, I worried its message might be viewed as a problem instead of a solution and expressed those concerns to my friend.

"I dig it, Jackie. It's you, man. This is a new age, my friend. Street people are a different breed now. Bangers and hustlers learn from warrior poets these days, brother-man. They're thinkers with real questions. They'll respect your philosophy, Jackie, because it's straight from the trenches – not just some bullshit puked back from something you swallowed behind guilt and fear."

I took Henry's advice. After cursory glances by some, handouts found their way inside Big Books, on empty seats and the floor. We watched one guy nod off while his head bounced off a wall-mounted hand sanitizer. As we began obligatory introductions the door to that bare room, accommodating not much more than a desk and a circle of folding chairs, burst open. A muscular, middle-aged man with a beard and long hair glared at us as he yanked a seat from our circle. He spun it around and sat backwards in it with his thick, tattooed arms dangling over the back of that cheap plastic chair.

I also handed him a handout that read as follows:

Things I WILL NOT tell you are underlined:

Your best thinking got you here...
Your best thinking got you into treatment and can keep you sober one day at a time if you continue to make sober choices.

Your worst thinking led to poor choices and all this current wreckage.

Do the opposite of everything you think...
Being actively addicted is being sick, not stupid.

Behave, while in treatment and recovery, as though loved ones are watching.

Everything happens for predetermined reasons...
Yes: cause & effect; action & reaction; intention & manifestation; the dialectic & timing. That is about as cosmic as it gets.

Define a problem and develop its solution instead of laboring over why problems exist. If you don't like it, enlist help and change it.

God doesn't give us more than we can handle...
Don't tell that to a person just diagnosed with a lethal disease or the family of a suicide. We all get our share of the best *and* the worst.

Mother Nature and Father Time do not single out anybody for anything – *good* or *bad*.

If *We* indulge in more negative behavior, *We* compile more unmanageable costs. So it's how we opt to deal with situations.

Choice has nothing to do with recovery...
Choice has *everything* to do with recovery. Recovery is a series of daily choices.

You have a choice to resolve problems while sober or mask consequences while using.

You have a choice to engage in a sober support system or reengage chemical slavery.

You have a choice to think you are helpless and hopeless or to know you are powerless.

You have a choice to remain abstinent today so not to wake up dope-sick tomorrow.

You have a choice to maintain sobriety one day at a time – or not. Which do you choose?

I began: "I'm Jack and I'm your counselor. Let's go around the room. We'll begin with you," I said to the man at my left. "Tell us your name and drug of choice."

The clean-cut, middle-aged client said, "I'm James B., a recovering alcoholic."

"Wilson – meth head and ladies man," said a scrawny Latino.

"My name is John and I'm a grateful recovering addict," said the smiling old man with the kind eyes.

We all looked at the next patient in our circle as foam collected on his shoulder. Wilson explained, "Don't mind him. He's nobody, just a dope fiend in withdrawal."

"I'm Dago Red, a drunk and a junkie. Youse guys can call me Red," said the next man in the circle. "Hey, Jackie, is that you? Holy shit! How the fuck did you ever get to be a counselor? You were the worst one."

"Good to see you're still above the lawn, my friend. We'll get to that later."

I looked at the patient who arrived late. With his head down he said, "My name's Rocco *Mad-Dog* Russo. You can call me Roc." He looked up: "Better yet, you don't even need to talk to me at all." Then he looked at me: "And I'm here to tell *you* one thing right now: I ain't sleepin' with no crazy niggers," said the dope-sick, tattooed biker.

Russo, who appeared to be in his late 20s, was one of the potential time-bombs in my care. Thanks to him, we acquired a new topic. This *Mad-Dog* had been admitted over the weekend, higher than a giant sequoia.

Russo's verbal attack got diffused by the old man's smile and wag of his white nappy head. John said, "I shared with Russo here about losing my wife. I told him I gets lonesome, I cry when the sun come up in that big house. There I goes to the jitney station and asks the boy could he fix me up. He sure did, with some rocks. I had me some Grey Goose to knock the edge off. One night I wakes up to the bright light. There sits my late wife, right next to my casket – crying, with this glow around her. But she don't notice me yet, not the real me, only that one layin' up in that pretty box. I saw her just as plain as I can see you. So I scrapes my stem and takes me one last hit when she cursed me out loud. Never in my life did I ever hear that woman curse. Then I goes to my daughter's of a morning to tell her I saw mommy big as life. I'm scared she'll get all over me 'cause I'm scrawny as a sick dog, so I puffs up my cheeks with air – all blowed out real good – so's not to look like an ol' crack-head. I was talkin' about it when she says my vision's a sign from the Good Lord. I'm a religious man with a home-church, so here I still am."

Russo said, "Yeah, that's real touching. But you might be in the wrong hospital."

John still smiled when he said, "God loves you, son, and so do we. I know it's only a vision, that it's the drug talking. But right then it looked as real as the day she passed in that hospital bed. Maybe I just need to believe she's lookin' out for me."

"Yeah, whatever, old man. Just find another place to hallucinate. I ain't here to babysit some old psycho. I got my own problems. My girlfriend dumped me 'cause I caught another case. So now I gotta play this game, but I don't need any extra bullshit."

The other powder-keg in the group, Wilson, was bi-polar and addicted to methamphetamine. The 19-year old, Puerto Rican bounced his heels up and down, powered off the balls of his feet. Wilson had a rap sheet for violence and had been diagnosed with an intermittent explosive disorder. He interrupted, "Hey, *Mad-Dog* Russo, I'm Wilson *Psycho-Loco* De Jesus. Apologize to that gentleman right now."

"This ain't none of your business, Jesus," Russo warned. "Don't say shit to me."

Wilson's knees halted from the crazed bobbling motion as he asked, "Or what?"

I interrupted, "No last names or personal attacks. We'll discuss this one speaker at a time. No threats, accusations or interruptions. And please, direct all comments to me."

Russo glowered through what had morphed from cool ash to pits of hot tar, "Fuck with me and find out, *beaner*. Now how you wanna make me act in here, huh *spic*?"

Wilson jumped up and raised his hands shouting, "How about right here, right now, *guinea* motherfucker? What you waitin' for, huh grease-ball?"

Russo stood, flipped his chair backwards and ripped the tee-shirt off his chest, "Okay, bad-ass. Let's do this thing. Let's go right now . . . *Rican* piece a shit."

When I stood so did Dago Red, puffed out like a cock rooster, right by my side.

I needed them to look at me so I yelled, "Everybody sit the fuck down now! Put your asses back in those chairs or you'll be goin' home a lot sooner than planned. Don't push me. I'm not playin' here. Do it right motherfucking now!"

Then I calmly added, "Let's just consult out handouts for a minute, okay?"

Dago Red sat down and chuckled as the group resumed stares at the floor. I had just broken three major rules during my opening moments as a real counselor: *Don't lose your temper; Don't curse at clients; Don't challenge or threaten patients.*

I said, "Sorry for the outburst. Let's look at some facts. We're all on the same playing field here. I'll share something I learned the hard way. It's not what we have; it's how we use it. It's not what we did; it's who we are right now. Here's more: Arrogance is *thinking* I'm better than others. Confidence is *knowing* nobody's better than me. Confidence comes from giving, accepting and sharing. That's how we get – by giving. Hey, Roc, please apologize. You'll be glad. John is somebody's father just like the loving father you have at home, the one I'm sure you would defend with your own life."

That struck a nerve. Old John saw it too. Russo sighed, lowered his head and mumbled what might have been an apology. The old man walked across to give him a hug, one standoffishly returned with a one-hand pat to a frail shoulder.

John said, "Thank you, son. I won't calls you no *Mad-Dog* 'cause I see good in you. I'm sure your father's a fine man and proud of you, too. Your apology means the world to me. And I'm still your friend, whether you likes it or not."

Wilson took his turn: "Okay, I'll throw my disease under the bus, too. I was laid up in a flophouse on a floor dirtier than outside, railed-out skinny and cold all the time. These *vatos* let me crash at their crib 'cause I'm a chef. You know; I cook meth. These was my people, a bunch of Ricans, you know? No way I could go home like a pin cushion, so me and my girl did what we had to do, you know? So I went shopping at drug stores for ingredients. When I come back she was all beat up and crying. They was calling her *puta negra*. Her story was they raped her, so I pulled my shank. They told me she's a rat, that they took pictures of her with cops. When I looked at his cell I got tagged from behind. Next thing I know I'm outside in a puddle. A guy owed me money walks by and tosses me a bag with enough crumbs for a bump, just enough to get me moving. I fish out my rig, but I'm too sick and beat-up to stand. So I draw-up some of that puddle water, you know? I need a hit so I can go back and waste these sleazy fuckers. But as soon as I take my medicine somebody's whoopin' my ass again. This time it's a cop. That's how I wound up in jail. But it turns out what that fucker gave me wasn't crank. It was like baking soda or some shit like that. Then I make a call and find out my girl's in rehab. Next thing I know I'm in drug court for my spike, and now I'm here. That's my story."

James spoke next: "Thanks, Wilson. "I'm a Toledo policeman with a wife who wants a divorce."

Everyone fidgeted. Russo had managed to unintentionally insult his counselor's daughter with racial slurs and then accidentally degrade a minority patient who just happened to be an officer of the law. *Here we go again...*

Dago Red stared holes of contempt into the flimsy confidence of a brand-new counselor. I heard it through his eyes: *No fuckin' way, coom.*

That cued my response. "James, I'm from Cleveland. When it was Murder Capital of America in the '70s, Collinwood was known as 'The Bomb City.' Kids were taught that police were the enemy. Collinwood was also a hotbed for racial strife. We hated blacks because of all the racial conflict at our school. But even during all that race hatred, cops became the common enemy for both sides."

They listened for me to unearth another landmine to either step on or defuse. "Change meant accepting things I wasn't ready to face. That's back when I still harshly judged people. I didn't notice that the enemy was us and our poison. Lots of us choking on lies and hatred drank ourselves into prisons and shallow graves. We despised heroes who kept our families safe from the likes of us. I thought I hated everybody except my immediate family and little circle of criminal, drug-abusing friends. But it wasn't really hate I felt for cops, blacks, straight society and whatever else was available for my wrath. All that raw emotion was garden-variety fear masked by aggression. When I'm high I'm not willing to be accountable. I was too scared to take a close look at me."

They seemed to hang on every word, "As it turned out, I married a woman of color. My own daughter is part African American, and I love her more than anything. My ex was a good woman, just flawed like us. While she was pregnant and temperamental I stayed out nights with other women because she lied to me before we got married. I refused to accompany her in the delivery room – too self-absorbed. Eaten up with resentments, she never forgave me. She just waited to better-deal me, using drugs and alcohol as an excuse. But once I sobered-up, my fears lost power. I realized we're all from families very much like our own, earning a living in a way we can, most of us just trying to get through life with the least amount of friction."

"I gotta be honest, bro, I hate cops too," Wilson admitted. "Cops and hacks are as low as child molesters to us cons. But fuck-it now, man, 'cause I ain't doin' shit wrong."

Russo blurted, "You a narc, man? This is a program of honesty, right? I read some stuff sayin' you gotta be honest to stay sober. So if you're a narc you gotta say it." Everyone, including me, nodded in agreement and waited for his response.

James elaborated through tears: "I drive a patrol car. I smoked pot in college and even snorted a little coke, but vodka is my drug of choice. I'm a blackout drinker. I've been known to nod-off with lit cigarettes, so I drop lit butts in my glass before I pass-out on the couch. Some days I wake up so sick I fish them and then finish that drink. Before I came here my wife and kids saw me do that and wept. I was raised by my mother. She put herself through school to become a nurse. My father left when I was a baby. The last time I saw him I was so small I had to stand on the sofa to look out a window, to watch him beat her in the front yard. He wanted money to get high with his girlfriend. He saw me watching but just kept yanking her hair and slapping her for money we didn't have."

Then he broke down into sobs: "Our oldest girl became very ill. She got thin and weak and kept getting sicker. We brought her to our doctor but he couldn't find anything wrong. Our beautiful 17-year old girl, so full of life, wouldn't eat and just stayed in bed. We brought her to a specialist who ran tests in a hospital. Agh . . . I need a minute. May I have a tissue? Okay, here goes. After they took a biopsy of her kidney we got the news. They said she was full of cancer with only a few months to live." He let out a wail that sent shivers through everyone in the room. "Oh God . . . Why her? She cursed us for giving her bad genes and cursed God for killing her. We prayed her test results were wrong. After awhile she became despondent, other than to make calls to the mortician and to the graveyard so we could have a family plot. She tried to save us the heartbreak from having to deal with those things. Every time I think about her voice I want to die so I can be with her. But I can't. I have two other kids and love them, too."

He dried his eyes with a tissue. "I like my job and used to be good at it. I'm an honest cop and a good father, and my wife is enough for me. But I'm an alcoholic who's about to lose my job, my wife *and* my mind. Don't go worrying yourselves about me being here. I need to get home. My wife wants a separation. I've tried AA meetings before and even outpatient one time, but still relapsed. She's fed up and doesn't trust me, and I don't blame her. She says she's not sure if she still loves me. I have to see her before she talks to a lawyer . . . before it's too late. But I won't drink this time."

I asked, "Would anyone like to share a similar experience with James?"

Old John smiled, "You're not alone here, brother. I'll be checking on you."

"Anybody can say anything, bro," Wilson encouraged. "Talk is just noise. Show her and your boss; show yourself. Do this for you, and your family wins. You know?"

Russo chimed in, "Don't bail, man. We can power through this shit together. It ain't nothin' but a thing, right? We'll just throw in and push through. Don't cur-out!"

The kid who had been asleep roused with a cone of foamy lather neatly piled on his shoulder and agreed, "We're a team, dude. Don't cut and run. We need you here, dawg. You're one of us now, bro. Hang tough with us, Jimmy. You'll be like me in a few days."

Dago Red gave the frightened cop a fist-bump, "Look at this part, man. It's tougher to get sober than to stay sober, but it's easier to stay sober than to stay high. Believe that. Trust Jack to help us to the other side of this craziness. I know I do."

I said: "Your daughter acquired that toughness from somewhere, and I'm guessing half of it came from you. We'll phone your wife to see if she's willing to visit this weekend. If she agrees, we can have a session in my office. Do we have a deal?"

Tears streamed again, "Thank you all for not judging me and for accepting me. I'm no quitter. If you guys are with me, I think I can make it. I'm a lot like old John over there and like Mr. Jack here. I don't like niggers, either. But the fact is: niggers come in all colors. Thank you, my brothers, and I do consider all of you brothers. Your secrets are safe with me, as I trust mine are with you. Okay, let's do this thing!"

Once the room cleared Dago Red said, "That Russo kid's a savage. I like him. Do we know his family, *coom*? Hey, and that Rican's a head-case too, ain't he? That old John dude seems like a nice enough guy. That fuckin' burn-out kid's tough to gauge. I hope I'm not like him in a few days or I'm really screwed. Even that cop seems okay – for a pig. They're just as fucked-up as me, just waitin' for that bounce. It looks like you got yours, Jackie. If you came back from hell so can I, right? Lots-a good times, *coom*, a bunch a crazy shit. Your dad's ol' double-barrel shined like spic-o-rican sweat behind the Uzi that spic had on me. Not to mention the other fuck that time . . . with the heroin. We got lots a history between us, *coom*, the kind of shit could still get us clipped. I trusted you then and still believe in you, okay? Show me what to do and I'll do it. I don't even get high off this shit anymore. I just do it so I ain't sick. Then every time I straighten-out and start feelin' human again, I go right back to it like I'm some fuckin' zombie."

I handed him a treatment plan: "Try writing about what haunts you the most, about those things that keep you awake at night and make you flinch when you're alone."

"You know what else, Jackie? You don't even seem crazy anymore. Okay, I'll give it a shot. What do I got to lose, right? But those other fucks don't need to see inside my head. This is between us." The next morning I found an envelope under my door:

> You're welcome to my nightmares. I'm not strong enough to carry this, anymore. I can't forgive myself. I want to climb on the roof and scream, God help me! Please save me! But why bother? I used to pray, but he can't do shit because he's nowhere. Fuck God for not looking out for me. And especially fuck me for being asleep at the wheel.
>
> I'm not even a person anymore. A monster clawed inside my back and chewed out what's left of my heart. I go through the motions but nothing changes. I try to hide but can't get away. I need rest, but I'm still breathing. There must be a way out. The dope covers my sickness for a quick minute. But I can't afford to stay high all the time.
>
> I'm awake now but these demons won't stop and the dope doesn't kill me. I was speed-balling like two motherless fucks, but that same, tired story just plays all over again. Can't focus. Can't trust. Can't love. I'm trapped in a cage with a killer. I hate myself. I hate life. I hate you.

For the next group, *Mad-Dog* and *Psycho-Loco* entered together. Russo puffed up: "Okay, I got somethin' to share. I'm here 'cause I got shook down by two pig-fucks in an unmarked car. They found a lock-blade knife and four Oxys. They said pills without a script bottle are a felony, even if they're mine and they're legal. They claimed they had pictures of me at a Wong Gongs party smokin' dope, and of me runnin' a crap game in my *WOP Uncle's* night-spot. Can you believe those cocksuckers actually said that to me? Then he hawked up a wad of phlegm and looked around for a place to spit. I passed him one of the handouts and nodded for him to continue.

"Motherless faggots," Wilson added for emphasis. "This is the kind a shit we deal with." It appeared as though he had already heard the story and anticipated the next twist.

Dago Red nodded in agreement, "Oh yeah. I seen this movie before."

"Swear to Buddha, it gets better," Russo said. "Watch this part. One of 'em has a stamp bag with a $20.00 piece in it and a little paper with a phone number. The other one says they're gonna give me that rock and the number or hand me a brand new case. My uncle taught me, 'nothin's free.' So I ask who I gotta kill. One pig says alls I gotta do is give the crack to a guy they're lookin' to violate. They called a name of a patch holder. He's second generation and a friend. His father is president. Anyways, they tell me hand him the bag, call from my cell, then alls I gotta do is hang up. Next came the threat. One of them pricks says if I don't I'm goin' away for a long time. It's the same old routine from those dickless pieces of shit. Dirty motherfuckers know they got me boxed-in. So how am I supposed to act behind all this?"

"No you didn't, bro," Dago Red blurted out. "I know you only two days and bet long money you don't touch that stank cheese."

"So I ride to this guy's place with some hot chick heatin' up the pussy pad on my scooter. We chill for a while, sippin' brews and talkin' shit. His bitch is there, too. I hand my friend the bag. Our girls liked the idea, so they smoked that measly pebble and then vanished. You know the way chicks always need an escort to take a fuckin' leak, right? We found 'em in the bathroom and had to pry 'em off each other. You know how chicks are, always gettin' all hot and horny at the wrong times? Anyways, I go ahead and make a call. Then we go on a beer run with our sweeties. It ain't five minutes till those same fuck-wads pull us over and call for backup. Pretty soon we're surrounded."

Dago Red pleaded, "Come on, man. Tell me you're only kiddin' here with this."

"But before we left I told him everything. My friend says, 'You know what, Roc? I don't even like this nigger dope but I'm tempted to smoke it on principle. Still, I ain't about to let those pigs win.' Well, I don't like speed neither, but I *was* tempted – just because. Instead, we let the girls burn that stone and then fired up our scooters. A few minutes later we got pulled over by those same two faggots. Guess what? They don't find shit. Then here's all these other cops standin' around with their thumbs up each other's asses, can't figure out why they're radioed in. So those two assholes had to cut us loose."

Dago Red asked, "Wait awhile, Roc. Why'd you make a call? What's that about?"

"Oh, I phoned my uncle and said we're gonna get pulled over by dicks that called his name. I couldn't phone mom on shit like this. You know how moms are, right?"

I grinned at my old friend, "This kid . . . Doesn't he remind you of Chilly?"

Dago Red furrowed his brow and asked, "Who?" Then he turned to Russo, "You look familiar, kid. I think I might know your family. We'll talk later, okay?"

Wow, he's more fucked-up than I thought. No way he can forget Chilly, especially after what we did for Benny. Ahhh . . . okay. I get it. Smart... The old memory loss routine, eh? Fucking Dago Red . . . solid as ever. Go on ahead, mad-dog coom-boom.

"Why didn't you alert someone?" asked James. "You know, like the authorities?"

"Yeah, right, whatever. I should'a called more cops, right? Or maybe I should'a prayed over it, huh? It's us and them. Besides Mom, my uncle's all I got. He's the only father I've ever known. You just don't get it, man, because you don't live in our world."

Wilson agreed, "Yeah, fuck 'em all, especially them pigs. No offense, Jim-bo. But remember what you said about the difference between *niggers* and blacks, bro? The same goes for *spics* and Latinos, *guineas* and Italians, or even pigs and cops, you know? My uncles taught us that all we need's each other. And fuck praying. What's their God done so far, eh *vatos*? We asked God to take the cravings away, then we pray for some money to score. God don't do shit one way or the other, you know? We don't feel that same God anymore. Right, Roc? Not the one they taught us about in church. Maybe there's a different God for kids. No disrespect, Mr. Jack, but me and Roc ain't sayin' the Lord's Prayer at these meetings. We like the Serenity Prayer so we'll say that one, okay?"

"Sounds okay to me." I said. "As far as I'm concerned, God can't get you high or keep you sober. Like it or not, it's up to you to make the next wise choice. I don't pretend to have the answer. But I do know this much: I'm smart enough to know that I'm not smart enough to know. Nobody knows for certain, and I'm definitely part of nobody."

Later I said to Dago Red, "Remember when I was on self-destruct mode with you guys? I was the odd-man-out – not addicted. Now, in rehab, I'm the third wheel again – not in the *program*. Sometimes *not* being a junkie can be the weird spot to be in. Some counselors teach, 'It's not your fault you relapsed. You had no choice. You're an addict. Relapse is a part of recovery.' Can you believe that? Junkies don't need an excuse to relapse. They need reasons not to. I'm a counselor not a prostitute. I'm not peddling that horseshit. But I'm learning. A useful thing I learned working here is to compromise."

"If I didn't know better, Jackie, I might think you're just another bullshit artist in denial. But I remember when you stepped away from the booze and the other hard shit. Lucky for you, you did. So how do you explain spirituality with you being an atheist?"

"I found out most addicts *need* to believe in something better than them. With things in their face, like nature and the group, it's not tough at all. I also learned they need to believe this is a disease, because it helps them deal with the guilt and shame and helps them know they're sick – not bad. So it's kind of like *Santa-Christ*. Sometimes I dish out an occasional *white lie* to help a soul save itself. No harm no foul, right?"

"I like when you said that being addicted is a fulltime job you pay to work, and that sobriety is making wise choices at the right times for unselfish reasons. That's the kind of truth we can relate to, Jackie."

"Some of my colleagues think I'm too vocal about non-traditional stuff."

"That's because you come from different planets, man. Most of them are total pussified liberals, limp-dick cowards cheating on their ol' ladies because they're crease-trained at home. To me, they're just as nauseating as those fuck conservatives with their aristocratic teabags dangling across their noses while they're suckin' off the big boys."

"You're right. And pathetic saps are campaigning for millionaire strangers and arguing against family for those bastards who couldn't care less about them. Are they too stupid to notice when they're getting ass-fucked?"

"These greedy motherfuckers are worse than junkies. They'll be dead by the time our country rots like a house of sticks. Their punk kids'll just move outta the country to where their grift is stashed. These other assholes pretend they're part of that *good ol' boy* crew. Don't they understand it affects their own families?"

"They want to pretend they belong to something powerful. But we're powerless, like with the drugs. I learned a lot in college and working here, but most of what I think I know came from experiencing life, and while on acid trips with bro-ham. You know; our unnamed accomplice? But no matter how many neck ties I wear, I'm not sorry for that night."

He shook his head and chuckled, "I guess you're still one sick individual, Jackie."

CH XX:
THE CLICK & THE "BOUNCE"

Before bro-ham left us in the 1970s to scramble like blind sperm in search of soulless ovum, I asked him during that last LSD trip, "If you had to describe the *Click* to somebody, what would you say? I mean, it's some pretty abstract shit. Maybe even a little crazy, right? We know it's out there. It's there to feel and taste, enough to keep us on our toes, yet almost out of reach. But we know it's there, just as sure as we recognize the wind or its temperature."

"If you've ever felt the *Click* you don't need an explanation. Those who haven't wouldn't understand mind-meld anyway. The way I see it, life is a dream of a dream that can be as bizarre as the strangest nightmares. You know, bro-ham, I used to believe dreams came true. I *used* for instant karma and maybe even sometimes because of all the lies. I used fast and hard till it used me up and almost broke me down. But thanks to the *Click* and the *bounce,* I've tasted the bottom of emptiness. I don't have to be afraid anymore."

"It's normal communication when you're tripping or stoned, or like when you're vibing-out with a cool ol' lady or sweetie, close relatives or a brother, or even with your dog – especially that. Some people choose to believe the *Click* is nothing more than schizo meltdown. Others make like it's the same as tealeaf readings or card tricks – just some bogus, crystal ball revelation invented after-the-fact to bait more suckers."

"Well, I'm fed-up with these dirty motherfuckers judging us in the middle of all this, just as much as I am of this whole drug scene. I hate it, bro-ham, all of it. We keep stumbling against other lost souls too blind to notice how fucked-up we are. They go through their little daily compulsions, fighting about nothing and being greedy about everything, pretending like any of this actually matters. How can anyone ever win this?"

"That's almost funny how people don't trust their own senses, yet they'll gobble up heaps of trash from strangers on instinct but argue the *Click* is *fugazi*. Okay, for example: these so-called big-shots in charge of our world go straight from crapping their diapers and bawling for momma's nipple to claiming they have the all the answers for everybody on everything. I mean, how's it possible so many idiots actually buy into that custom-made crock of shit? My ex, Butter, accused me of always wanting too much. Now she says I never wanted enough. I think she bumped her head."

"I guess that would account for balance . . . or off-balance. Anyway, then there's the *bounce*. It's fight, run or compromise. Most people pretend it's Divine Intervention because they don't want to deal with accountability and responsibility. If it's labeled *instinct*, that triggers worse fears. You know why, bro-ham? Because it reminds them we're mammals – animals just a little smarter and with enough dumb luck to evolve on land with limbs and to breathe air – luck of creatures before man . . . before God."

"Yeah, and it's pretty fucking obvious some of us are a little closer to being animals that others. But the *Click* and the *bounce* are just ordinary things for regular people, things like courage and appetite. Hey, speaking of that, I'm hungry. Are you?"

"Yeah, I'm about half-starved. Let's go eat. How's Chinese sound?"

"It sounds something like, *Hing, Ching, Ping, Pow*, or some shit like that."

"If I wasn't so goddamn hungry I might've laughed at that one."

We talked all night over take-out in paper cartons with chopsticks. Out of the loop and friends as gone as yesterday, a sense of meaning dwindled to abstract ideas about people and life, rather than making new bonds and growing as an individual. The more people I met, the less they seemed to matter. But years later, being a counselor helped me to stay engaged.

And engaged I was. My newest challenge in 2013 isolated and seemed as though he contemplated his newfound powerlessness. Body language and tough talk, gone at the moment, all served as barriers – yet he affected a courteous manner. He was the type of guy in treatment who men avoided like the law and women seemed to crave as much as drugs and drama.

Uninvited, I sat across from him. A cigarette burned in a large ashtray on his picnic table. From his chart I had learned he was about the same age as my Gina, youthful looking in his mid-30s, and also from Cleveland. *Maybe the ol' Neighborhood spiel might work with him*, I hoped.

"So what's up, Roc. How's it? You getting any visitors today?"

Without looking up he began: "Okay, Mr. Jack, I got a few things to say. You being a counselor means next to nothing. But so far you ain't preachin' for us to kneel and beg from some ghost that's been dead for a couple thousand years. You're not tellin' us to do the opposite of whatever we think, like some a these so-called *counselors* do. We accept things better when people talk *to* us, instead of *at* us. Your burnout friend says he trusts you, and he seems okay for an old dude. You're supposed to be some kind a professional, right? So maybe you can explain some stuff."

"Yeah, I'm supposed to be and maybe I can. If I don't know the answer I'll say."

"Guess what? You try to bullshit me and you won't have to say. Now I'm gonna tell you somethin' I told my mom. She says when I'm loaded I leave a dirty fingerprint on everything I touch. But I ain't too sure it's just the drugs. Sometimes I feel like my brain's broken, like there's no filter, like something needs reset in my head. I'll tell you why. Sometimes I hear things. But that started way before the drugs. I tried to fill my veins to make it stop, but it just got worse. Now that I'm sober this time the voices stopped and I'm not as likely to fly into a rage over some simple shit. Plus I'm sleepin' better, even though I still get these whacked-out dreams."

"We could talk about them, not that I'm any dream expert or anything."

"Maybe later. The thing is: my mom expects me to all the sudden lead a normal life. After I've lived like an animal for all these years, how the fuck do I just go out there and have a *normal* life? I've been trashed since I was a kid. Mom can't help. Don't get me wrong, she's an amazing person and everything, but she don't understand shit like this. How could she? I don't wanna cause her anymore pain. She insists I have to live a normal life, but I don't even know what that shit means. I know I can't be her."

"If you're looking for an exact definition of normalcy, my answer will be disappointing because I'm still working on that one myself. Normal might be less dysfunctional; trying to be a part of solutions instead of being the problem. Maybe it's not going out of my way for more abuse and being relatively satisfied with what I have. I suppose it's trying to remain open and teachable, and actually doing whatever it takes to get through the day as long as I don't hurt myself or anyone else. Does that make sense?"

He sat and smoked, stroking his beard. "I ain't done yet. The last thing is this one dream I get. I know you're gonna think I'm nuts, but fuck-it. I'll probably never see you again, anyways. Okay . . . here goes: Since I was a kid I have this same dream. In it I'm runnin' real slow and then trip over a rope. It's shaped like a noose that turns out to be a snake bitin' its own tail. *Say what?* Then I trip and fall into some water and try to kick away. But the more it swallows itself, the smaller and tighter that loop gets till it cinches-up and cuts through my leg bone till it reaches the back of its own head. *What the fuck is this about?* The pain's bad. I can't move . . . can't breathe. By then blood's squirtin' clots in the water till I can't see. I always wake up tryin' to catch my breath."

"That's very complex and interesting, Roc. *Shit…Now I can barely breathe.* So what do you think it all means? How does that struggle relate to your life?"

Finally he looked at me: "My mom says drugs are passive suicide and that I'm tryin' to take myself out. To me it just means my luck is pure fucking Kay shit-o."

"Whoa. Hold-up, now. What's that you just said to me?"

"Oh, sorry, Mr. Jack. That's Collinwood talk I picked up from my uncle. Anyways, it means life is pretty much shit and people are mostly bust-outs." He paused to light and drag off a fresh cigarette. He held in the smoke like it was weed. "Anyways, last night I had that same dream, but with a twist. I'm drownin' again and about to lose my foot. The pain feels real. But before the snake cuts through me it just disappears, 'cause it swallowed its own head . . . Pop! Just like that and it's gone. My foot's all fucked-up but the bloody water clears-up and I can see. So I crawl out chokin' and drag myself on shore. I woke up with my heart pounding like that crazy shit really happened!"

"Not to change the subject, but before we pursue this any further I have to ask you some questions. What's your uncle's name and exactly where is he from in Cleveland?"

"Why? Are you a cop, too? What's my uncle got to do with any of this?"

"No, I'm not a cop, but I'd like you to sign a release so I can speak with him. He can provide collateral information which might help coordinate your treatment. Okay?"

"Don't worry about it. He doesn't live in Cleveland anymore." Dark eyes, filled with betrayal and resentment, showed a new emotion when he said, "Well, alrighty then!"

CH XXI:
THE ARC COMPLETES ITS THRUST

I watched his chameleon eyes transform from cold stone to pools of translucent green as he turned to meet an approach from behind. Rocco met her radiant smile with a big grin and a gentle hug. I felt a rush when he asked, "Too bad I'm still alive, huh? Thanks for coming, Ma. I'm almost outta cigarettes. But that's not why I wanted to see you. Hey, you mad at me? I love you, Ma. I know. I see it. I've been a total fuck-up. But this is my first time here and it will be my last. I just couldn't get that opiate hook outta my back alone. But it's slipping out now, more each day. I feel it. And I'm really sorry, Ma. I hate to admit it, but my counselor here's been a big help. He reminds me of Uncle Pazzo."

Sometimes dreams come true, and not all are rooted in nightmarish fears. After years of no contact, I saw a mirage. An aging, yet stunning woman seemed not to recognize me with short, gray hair and neatly trimmed goatee, wearing a long-sleeved dress shirt, pressed khaki pants and cheap tie. Without looking at me she swept away blonde hair streaked with silver and said, "You've got to be kidding! I can barely believe this one. But it's really you, isn't it?" Then she turned and smiled heaven at me.

We embraced for longer than two friends from the old neighborhood. I sank into delicate arms and teared-up for the first time since childhood. Her rough-edged son looked stunned watching his mother's tears dampen his counselor's blue shirt collar.

"I see you've already met. Wow . . . You're a counselor, Jackie? Really? Oh boy, that's rich! How the hell did that ever happen? You were the worst one! Man-oh-man. Look at us, bro. If it weren't so sad, it would almost be laughable. You're some nerd with geeky clothes and glasses, and I'm an old spinster. Hey . . . I'm so sorry about Maggie. You know I loved her, too. What's happening, bro? Everyone around us is either dying or already dead. What's left for us? Wow . . . It's really good to see you're okay."

"What's left? Just a little more time, and then that's it. Death used to be car and bike accidents, shootings and bombings. But this old age, sickness and natural death stuff is way freakier. Just like my father always said till he died, 'The older we get the faster it comes, till death gets so close that before we're ready it's our turn to go.' He was right."

"Life really has been a crazy ride . . . and now this. I don't know about you, bro, but I'm not ready for this trip to end just yet. I almost wish I'd have known you'd be here. Maybe I wouldn't have come. But I can't stay. I just stopped by to bring my boy some money and cigarettes. Look at you! I haven't seen you in a tie since you were that little altar boy at Holy Redeemer. Wow . . . You're like some old ghost from the past."

"And you're still the same girl I fell in love with in kindergarten, the one I've wondered about for the past thirty-something years or so. Not one day passes where I don't think about you, Tessa. And yeah, I know Rocco. I'm your son's counselor. What are the odds of that? He's a good kid, just a little jagged around the edges, but he has great potential. Who's his father? I doubt it's a Neighborhood guy. You're way too smart for that."

He snapped: "Enough with the father bullshit! Mine's dead. Fuck him, anyways."

Just like the old days, her eyes did plenty of talking. Then she said, "Okay, son, easy does it. Sit down and listen. It's time we have a conversation, right bro?"

"Hmmm... Now I'm not so sure. But okay, I'm listening," I reluctantly complied.

"Are you really that burned-out and senile already, old man, or are you up to this? Ahhh . . . never mind. No, really, it's fine. Here, son, just take this. I need to go now."

"Whoa," I said. "Now let's just sit for a minute. Come on. You too, Roc."

Still etched in my mind was a slip of paper left on a bar after she had pressed innocence against fire. Those two words she wrote were the ones I held all night on my leather sofa, and then woke drenched in sweat with it still clenched in my fist. The dream of her seemed so real that upon waking I looked out the window for Doc's car. Her perfume graced a note that for years never left my wallet unless for me to reread it.

She whispered, "You doubt everything and everyone? I thought maybe we still spoke the same language. But you don't even trust your own instincts anymore, do you?"

Not willing to let her slip away again I held her hand and said, "I'm trying to."

Rocco backed up, "Holy shit! Ma, are you kidding me? You mean him? After all these years you're gonna tell me my father's alive?" He wiped moisture from his hardened face, "No fucking way! Shit! . . . *Sure*, why not? I should know better than to be surprised by anything, anymore. Alright, fuck-it . . . I guess we'd better just deal with it – or not. Whatever . . . I don't know what I mean. Man, this is really fucked-up!"

"Okay, son, here goes. That night you were conceived was the drunkest I've ever been and the last time I took a drink. When Grandpa realized I was pregnant he became a rabid dog in a cage. It was the only time he hit me – the only time I ever saw him cry. He suspected it might be a Neighborhood guy but couldn't prove who to kill. When I came clean with Grandma she went to auntie for advice. I begged them to lie for me just that once – to say I'd gotten pregnant by some stranger at a bar. She didn't understand my loyalty to a man who couldn't care less about me. But they knew Doc well. Fingers promised her, 'Don't worry, Auntie. Doc don't need to know. This is our secret. If she *loses* it, he'll just think it was a false alarm. Nobody's the wiser. Now go home and let me handle this.' He did exactly that. Then things got weird."

"If you're saying what I think, this is getting weirder by the second," I said.

She looked at me: "I'm not sure about you, bro, but I don't remember much after I took that lude and washed it down with more of Dad's wine. Once Doc knew I was pregnant, Uno and Benny were the only ones who could restrain him from going on a killing spree. Doc wanted to know why Fingers fell out with his best friend. Uno told him you'd turned into a degenerate, shooting dope and hanging out with junkies. He said they worried you'd end up working for the Feds and Fingers didn't want a dope fiend around his kids. Uncle Pazzo assured dad I'd never get mixed up with a loser like you. Doc really wanted to believe that. So that night at R-Bar, Uno slipped powder into your drink to make you manageable. And like a predictable drunk, you dove right into their plan."

"Wait awhile, Tessa . . . Hold up a minute. I gotta ask you one thing first before I say anything else. Let me get this part straight. So there really was a contract on me after all? I'll be double-dogged! Fucking Ansel was right! He warned me. This explains Benny's last phone call to me, and why Pazzo told me to just stay down. It all adds up."

"Fingers knew I got pregnant while you were still married to Butterscotch, who by then really was pregnant. I'd hear Neighborhood stories about what a mad-dog you'd become and that you were in over your head with the Wong Gongs."

"This is insane. I'm such an asshole. This is the worst thing I've ever done. I'm so sorry, Tessa. Somehow I'll make it up to both of you if you let me be a part of your life, yours and Rocco. Please find a way to forgive me."

"I remember when we toasted loyalty for a hundred years, even if I can't recall much afterwards. But it just wasn't up to me to tell you how to act after I found out. I don't blame you for anything. I was a big girl by then and made my own choices."

Rocco mumbled, "Man oh man, this whole thing is way too twisted. I can't even believe this shit is real. Wow . . . This whole scene is just way too bizarre for me to wrap my head around right now. Ma, I don't even know what to say here about any of this."

"Well, both of you boys better pay close attention, because I'm not about to repeat this. Doc made me go to California to stay at his sister's. He said I couldn't come back till I gave *it* up for adoption. Once I saw baby Rocco I knew I'd be out there till he died. You know how bullheaded he was. Because of me, Doc was a wild animal who found himself in a trap, about to chew off his own leg. Instead, he drank himself to death."

"Rocco. I swear I didn't know any of this till right now. But I'm sure your mom handled things the right way. She was always a lot smarter and better than me."

"Ma, you're tellin' me I had a father this whole time? Is this really for real? I need to try to digest this a minute," he said as he walked away shielding damp, red eyes.

"I wish I would've known. But at the time, I was on a collision course with the world," I assured her. "If I knew, the difference it made might have been even worse."

"Ahh. *difference*. Now there's an interesting word. Differences keep getting more extreme. I accidentally found meaning in a blackout. Maggie got lost in one forever."

"Yeah, I sure do miss ol' Maggie. She was amazing. Her heart filled up her whole chest. But she gave so much of it to friends she didn't have enough left for herself."

"Carly is really different now, Jackie. *Meaning* for her is inside a syringe. After Maggie died, she became a shell of that beautiful girl we knew. When I asked her about drugs Carly said, 'I'm feeling just well enough not to care enough.' I miss her."

"Yeah. Carly was solid before she sold her soul. Plus, I don't know . . . I guess I always figured she'd hook-up with someone cooler than flukey-doo. When Curtis got paroled they made a pretty big score so they could get lost in extremes, alienated and isolated together. Now she's a stranger even to herself."

"Speaking of mad-dogs, my cousin is way *different* than the person you remember. I really miss him. Fingers was my brother. You really changed, too. But I never lost faith in you, not even when you gave up on yourself. I figured you'd bounce back to your roots sooner or later, if you didn't die trying. It looks like you've done pretty okay for an old burnout."

"Ex-burnout. I haven't had a drink or abused any drugs for almost 30 years. I'm *so sorry*, Tessa. This is the worst thing I've ever done, even if I didn't do it on purpose or didn't know about it. But we're past all that. Still, I need you to know I never meant to hurt you or Rocco. I was too busy destroying my own life to even consider anyone else."

"Look, Jackie, you're not indebted to us for anything. We got along just fine without you. In the state you were in – with that lying bitch and you as drunk as my crazy father, you would've just complicated things even more. My family didn't need that. Doc drowned himself in the same barrel that caused this rift. I came back for his funeral. Mom didn't last long after that. You could say I killed her, too. The only thing that kept me from killing myself or going mad is with me right now. My son, our son, became my life.

"You know better than to spew all this *killing* talk around us. Besides, look what I did to poor Maggie. The truth is Doc killed himself *and* your mother with his constant stress. Is that what you want to do? Can you forget about your guilt and fear long enough to consider the future? What defines happiness for you, baby-girl? What are your goals?"

She stood looking at the ground for awhile, not blinking, gazing steadily, inside and through me. Then soft green eyes locked with mine: "Well, we do have some catching up to do. That's if you're interested. You don't seem all that crazy, anymore. But I'm giving you a heads-up. I don't have time to play games. I'll never be anybody's sweetie, Jackie-boy. You do remember that much, don't you? Stop me if I'm wrong."

"You're not even close to being wrong – not any wrongs I can see."

"Okay, tomorrow night then? I'll see if you cook as good as you talk."

I went home to reread hand-scrawled notes. From my earliest memories Tessa had possession of my soul. And every time she slipped away I turned more bitter. That night I fell deeply into the sleep of a safe child or drugged adult. I woke rested and worked in the yard bathing in sunshine as a delicate breeze excited aromas from my vegetable garden.

She didn't bother to knock but I heard her enter. When I looked, I found my watchdog seated on her feet with his head nuzzled against her legs. She continued as if there hadn't been a break in our conversation. "I've been thinking about what you said, and you're right. I shouldn't blame myself for Doc's death anymore than you should blame yourself for Maggie's. But there's a whole lot more. You have to be anywhere?"

"Yeah, right here, right now. How about you? You okay?"

"Yeah, I'm fine, thanks. Like I said, I heard stories that you turned into a mad-dog. Your buddy, Eggs, is a whole other story. Loony Lonnie told Dad that Eggs was the snitch when you went to court. He said Eggs whispered your name after some old-school, 1960s police brutality. The reason Yugo didn't get busted is because Eggs' wife was about to dump him. Eggs saved her brother so she wouldn't leave him."

"I didn't want to believe that for the longest time. But it's the obvious answer. After his ol' lady divorced him, he got all chummy with The Mick."

"Doc said Eggs was the one who set-up Loony Lonnie and O'Reilly while they monitored a jewel heist from their patrol car. Crazy stuff, huh? People really change."

"I'll say. We've all changed; some for the better. It depends on what you want."

"My father gave your *brothers* a good excuse to squeeze you out. Those guys just hung onto your coattails till they didn't need you anymore. Uncle Pazzo said you were in self-destruct mode and that Benny was a threat to everyone, so they cut their ties with both of you. He said it also had something to do with bringing those *schifoso* bikers into the Neighborhood and living with a black girl in Collinwood. But you lucked-out when Butterscotch walked in on the fight. Wow . . . I can't believe I just said all that out loud."

"Till my last breath, I have your back. I want a chance to be a part of Rocco's life. I owe both of you. But just as important, I need you in my life. I know for sure you're solid. You're the one link I have with that magic we shared as kids, back when people were real. Don't slip away again, Tessa. Give me a chance to remind you why I'm the person you trusted more than anyone else – please."

"Quit begging and stop whining or I might change my mind. Not everyone is out to hurt you. I don't have a college degree, Mr. Counselor, so I don't claim to have all the answers. But what I do know is you can trust this only if I can trust you 100%. So let's start the way we plan to continue," then she kissed me softly on my lips.

"Careful, baby. I've crashed through people's lives like a runaway train."

"No argument here. You messed-up big-time with Maggie. And I'm sure you've made countless other serious mistakes. So join the club. Get in line. Now try to get over yourself, bro. We're not all that special or powerful. The truth is my father and your Maggie both fixated on death and did exactly what they wanted to do – just like us."

"I loved Maggie. And even Carly too, the one before addiction. Friends addicted to gambling with their own lives avoided a middle ground like it was church. Speaking of that, after I got lost in that drug world I found out there really is a hell. It lives inside bad choices. But heaven is real, too. It's in making sweet memories for later."

"I'm sure you've had your share. What happened to the rest of your harem?"

"Butterscotch never forgave me for not forgiving her. Her husband worried she'd try to better-deal him too, so he split."

"There it is, Jackie. That's always the danger of leaving one person for another."

"Then Ahawi became so closed she pushed away everyone with her negativity. She hid behind resentments and fear, terrified she might get hurt behind her walls."

"I can guess, from personal experience, how that's working out for her. How about Gus, Jackie? Have you heard from him? Is he back inside or strung-out again?"

"Gus tried to fix the clocks to stay in that biker/hippie era long after the party ended. He finally got what he wanted – to be a patch-holder with the Wong Gongs."

"Ever since my cousin inherited Benny's spot he acts like he walks on blood."

"Yeah. Well from what I understand, he has and he does."

"Nino tried to go straight when he married that girl from Little Italy. But he's addicted to the lifestyle, just like her father. Now he's *consigliere* for Fingers. Nino wasn't ever as reckless as the rest of you."

"I suppose not. You hear about Yugo hanging himself in prison, Tessa? What a trip. And remember Shit-pants Joey? They say he's a doctor or something."

"Yugo was always weak. I'm not surprised. But Shit-pants Joey a doctor? Really? I can't even imagine him being an orderly. What ever happened to that buffoon, Slick?"

"Who knows? Fuck him. He probably drank himself to death."

"Then how about Inky? Did you find out what happened to him, Jackie?"

"That boy flipped-the-fuck-out. He thought everybody was after him, so he sat around shooting holes through the walls of his farmhouse. His wife wasn't allowed to leave. He said they'd use her to get to him. For awhile he had a brother go on store runs for him. But then he got to the point where he didn't even trust Webb."

"Sounds pretty rational to me. Would you trust Webb?"

"Anyways, out of cigarettes and beer, Inky decided to venture out one early morning with guns strapped all over him like a *bandolier*. His wife said he yelled at the top of his lungs to the woods surrounding them, 'Come and get it, you spineless fucking cowards. I'm right here. Come get ya some, son.' A car bomb ended his paranoia."

"I hate to say it, bro, but you were just as whacked-out as most of them."

"Talk about whacked. How about Curtis was in a stolen car while Astro strolled in that drugstore, bare-chested with chrome .45 automatics stuck in the waist of tie-dyed Levi's? When a bullhorn screeched, 'Put your hands in the air,' things got crazy – even for that nutty bastard. He strutted out, crossed his arms over his chest and shot himself with both guns. He must have figured he'd take himself out. Instead, he detoxed in a body cast with two shattered shoulders while in an institution for the criminally insane."

"Okay. Maybe you weren't as bad as the worst. That kid was *really* out there."

"One time Bee-Bee drove that space-cadet to my house, fresh out of the loony bin. He stretched out on my couch while fat-ass and I played eight-ball in my front-room. Then out of nowhere Astro said, 'Those faggots walk around with turds wrapped-up in toilet paper. They call 'em shit-babies and hold 'em against their nipples to breastfeed.' Then folded his arms across his chest like in a casket and didn't say another word. Because Astro shot speed instead of pool, he lost his mind instead of a game."

"Collinwood used to be a safe place. It turned into an asylum. Whatever happened to those sweet people, Jackie?"

"It was a combination of things, but drugs were a big piece. Regardless, our generation also changed things with kindness. Too bad it didn't last."

"Well, we went this far, bro. I guess I might as well trust you with this, too. You were right about wanting out of that Royal Flush. It really *was* them who set-up Benny, in a way, because they knew about it."

"No way. Somebody must've given you bad information on that one. I heard the order came from Uno."

"Benny associated with Ansel during those bombings. Word got back that Benny planned to double-deal both him and The Mick, and then take over everything."

"Interesting... Eggs was doing grunt work for Mick while feeding information to Uno. He must have cut class the day they taught loyalty at Collinwood, eh Tessa?"

"As Uncle Pazzo used to say, 'Sometimes loyalty wears many disguises'."

"When Uno hired Toby to kill Eamon Jr., Toby and I were sort of hanging out at the time. Mick found out who did it the same night it went down. Not long after, Dago Red told me he woke up on his front-room rug with wet pants. He thought he'd gotten too loaded and pissed himself till he found Toby's head next to him. When an ambulance got there he was curled-up in a ball holding Toby's head, crying next to his headless corpse."

"Doc said Doyle Kelly was the one who killed Toby. What happened, Jackie? Is anybody left who's not completely insane? Has the whole world gone mad?"

"My father was right. He said not to trust anyone other than family."

"I'm not so sure about family anymore, either. Although I do trust Uncle Pazzo. He finally retired from the railroad and moved to Florida. He's doing really well."

"There's another guy I miss. He was a like father and a brother to me. I'm glad he's enjoying retirement with that sweetheart wife of his. What about those whack-job cousins, Sal and Nicky? I ran into Sally-Boy not long ago."

"No kidding? I haven't seen those two knuckle-heads since Sally and Dad had their shoot-out behind the O.K. Inn. Nicky didn't come around after that. Doc said one time they got drunk and made a quick appearance at Mick's Shamrock Club. When they ordered drinks it was longneck beers in sealed bottles. They left with the beer. Supposedly, that was the same night Benny walked Paddy Kelly out at gunpoint."

"Good idea. I'm impressed. They say even chimps can learn simple tasks."

"He and Nicky moved to Pennsylvania to open a store. I heard Nicky dresses for work in his fruitcake, white uniform and Sal wears those garage coveralls with a "Vito" nametag on his shirt pocket. I'm not sure which one is crazier. I used to think you were paranoid, bro. But now I see nothing is the way it seems and nobody's who they say they are. Wow . . . I sound like you, Jackie. It must be as contagious as addiction."

"It is. The Neighborhood got infected by the disease. Greedy motherfuckers turned on one another for pussy and money. When Ansel wired-up Uncle Pazzo's car with Five Points money, the bomb *accidently* got triggered by a radio signal. Cops found a death-head belt buckle near a toasted bike stamped with his serial numbers. Whoever made the bomb packed enough C-4 in it to level a building. When bad-asses like Benny, The Mick, Black Bart and Ansel get wasted, everybody connected to them lays low for awhile."

"Ansel's not dead, Jackie. He's still president of the Wong Gongs. In fact, Doyle Kelly's sister, Maureen, lives with him."

"Wow . . . No shit? Just goes to show you how long I've been out of touch."

"After Uno figured out how to kill the Irishman and became boss of the Cleveland underworld, he got sent away on murder and racketeering charges. Doc said Doyle Kelly paid a skinhead to assassinate Uno in prison. The Wong Gongs were playing Uno and Mick against one another all along; you know, divide and conquer. Doc thought Fingers and Cagootz were in on it from the start. Mom told me everything."

"Fingers and Cagootz, huh? What a team... Those two deserve each other."

"Yeah, I'll say. One time Rocco ran into his Uncle Fingers at Ansel's when Rocco stopped there to see Ansel's son. Fingers warned him to never tell anyone he saw him there."

"That neighborhood turned into a circle-jerk for kamikaze pilots. Trapped in crossfire, I realized the most dangerous enemy was everyone. I'm glad I'm out. Now it's our time to cherish what we have, instead of worrying about what we've pissed away."

"I'm glad you're Rocco's counselor, and I'm glad I'm here. I'm even glad you're my son's father. Wow... I never thought I'd ever say this! Okay. Now maybe you can walk me to my car. Or do I need to go home alone again? Are you up to this, old man?"

"No . . . sorry . . . I can't watch you walk away from me again."

"Oh it's like this, is it? Well just remember, big-shot. This is a package deal. There's no turning back from this. I'm not strong enough to handle more disappointments alone, okay? My pain tolerance is about shot."

"Tell you what, Tessa. I'll share the pain with you 50/50. How's that?"

"How can you? Do you have Mr. Peabody and Sherman's WABAC machine stashed away?"

"Say what? I'm talkin' subtleties here. Now you're gettin' all literal on me. You're not exactly the sharpest needle in the kit, are you?"

"Look who's talking. You're pretty oblivious for a guy who gets paid to read people, aren't you? Hey, you do any couples counseling, or do you have to understand women to do that?"

"Not exactly. Okay, so how about this? You want true romance to last a lifetime? Then we're going for matching ink. You can get a tight Pit tat on that firm phat tit. Hey, I kind'a like the sound of that. I'm thinking about maybe putting that line in my book. What do you think?"

"I think you're pretty twisted. But seriously, I can't really get a *tattoo*. Can I?"

"I got a news flash for you, baby-girl. This is your life. You can do anything you want to do. Now how do you wanna act?"

"But a tattoo? Really? I mean, I'm too old for tattoos and romance. Right? Come-on...seriously. Tell me what you think."

"I think you're just over-tired. Maybe we should stay home and go to bed so I can study the canvas. You know, to make a better decision about this package deal. Then we'll sleep on it."

CH XXII:
THE FINAL CHAPTER

Dreams hadn't always been restful for Jackie and didn't only occur while asleep, but that's one of those things you learn about a person once you live together. He'd tell me, "Life is a dream of a dream, that slip of ecstasy between awake and asleep – a high that's pure magic." He stayed up late and wrote almost nonstop to meet a self-imposed timeline. "If I'm still awake at sunrise it's only because I'm waiting for an idea to stay alive long enough so I can capture its words before it slips away forever."

During the Year of the Snake, Jackie had three months vacation time built up by 2013. He used two of them for us to bond as one family.

While Rocco was still in treatment, Jackie bought four tickets for the Bahamas. I picked up Gina from her mother's house and drove her out to the hospital for a visit to meet Rocco. She and her brother clicked immediately, like they'd known each other their entire lives. When I had asked Jackie if we could afford a 5-day cruise he said, "Fuck-it. It's time for you to relax and enjoy life. Besides, our kids need to become real siblings. This trip will help jumpstart things for us. And who knows; maybe my manuscript will blow-up into something big-time for us and then money won't be an issue."

We left from Ft. Lauderdale the week our son got discharged from the hospital. But first we visited Jackie's mother, who by then was in a nursing home. He phoned but hadn't mentioned specifics other than to say I was coming along and that I had a son. By then Lucy had been diagnosed with beginning stages of dementia. We embraced and she claimed to remember me as a child. I thought she was being polite till she rattled off specifics about my parents and me when I was a little girl. Then she paused to squint at

Rocco. With trembling, gnarled hands she pulled him close with the handle of her cane.

"What a beautiful boy," Lucy sighed. "You look just like my husband when he was young. Don't you ever leave gramma again, honey. You hear me? I won't allow it. Your father is an idiot. You know that? Why he does these things to me I'll never understand. Your mother is too good for an imbecile like him. But I will say this much: you can learn a lot about mistakes from your father. He's an expert at making them."

Once onboard I was amazed at the vastness of the ocean. And near the islands the water is clear like a giant swimming pool. Those white beaches of fine, powdery sand cleansed against sudsy waves of crystal water, in year-round, summer temperatures offset by a caress of tropical breezes. It was even more beautiful than I had imagined. We got married in Atlantis by a Bahamian preacher, with Gina as my maid of honor and Rocco standing as Jackie's best man. Other than the birth of our son, that one day stands out as the most spiritual experience I've ever had. Our kids became best friends and ferocious allies, so that left him and me to be like kids again.

I learned a lot from our marriage. For example: I found out relationships aren't exactly the way you think they should be. But with something worth having, small adjustments are worth the trade-off. Never living with a man other than Doc, it didn't take too long for Rocco and me to settle in with Jackie's strength. Life got better with him at my side. It bothered me when we weren't together; yet I worried I might push him away by being too needy. Without him I felt like a schoolgirl. Because of that, I tried too hard to be perfect for him. Still, I harbored uneasy feelings about something.

Rocco reassured me, "You need to learn to relax, Ma. He ain't goin' anywhere. He's happy. Besides, Gina won't let him leave even if he tries. So just enjoy it."

With a month and a half of vacation remaining he walked in the house, and straight at me with a closed hand. Then he shoved his fist straight at me.

I said, "Go ahead. But if you hit me you'd better knock me out. Because if I get up, it curtains for you, boy."

"Nah, I wasn't planning on hitting you this early. Then I'd have to look at you in the daylight. It's not a pretty sight. Although I might hit *on* you. How'd that be?"

"That would be a shame. Because I'll have to say *no*, at least till you show me what's in your hand. Fair enough?"

"Fair enough, as long as you show me what's in your bra first."

"No way . . . Fuck that. I asked first. But if you play this just right..."

"Okay, what smells like skunk mixed with armpits and pineapple? One guess."

"You have weed? Let's smell it. Umm, yummy. It's been a long time, bro. And the brats aren't even here to bogart our stash. Where did you get this?"

"The same place I got this," and he produced a small one-hitter from his pocket.

"You're doing pretty good so far. Okay, now I want more info. Whose is it?"

"Wow, Tessa, I though you were able to track better. It's yours, dummy. I'll talk slower so you can follow along better. Let me know if I'm going to fast for you, okay?"

"Good one, Jackie. You're quite the kidder, all right. Now answer, please."

"It's from the infamous Horrible Hank himself. It's a combination Honeymoon/finish the book gift. It's a eighth of killer hydro. One dab'll do ya. Wanna try it, baby Tessa, the little coward?"

"First let me ask you one simple question. After all these years, why do you have to get high now? Go ahead. Take a shot. Say the right answer and win the magic prize."

"The thing is: this has nothing to do *have-to's*. But okay, I'll play along. The real answer is . . . because I feel like it. Why, what's the big deal? It's just weed."

"I can see that, genius. But isn't it just a little hypocritical, Mr. Counselor?"

"Hey, I'm off for two months. I'm just trying to get the juices flowing to finish this novel before we sail off into the sunset, so to speak. Besides, this is my honeymoon."

"This is *our* honeymoon, Mr. So-to-Speak. And I'm not a moron like your Indian princess. I totally get it, okay? The thing is I'm just worried about bad karma."

"I'm not saying I don't believe in karma. I'm just saying, fuck-it."

"Okay, fuck-it . . . no biggie. Just curious, that's all."

"If you tell me, I'll flush it right now and pitch this stem in the weeds Anyways, once we smoke this up I'll be done for another long while. And you know this."

"I believe you, Jackie. I trust you more than me, bro. But part of the problem is if I enjoy this sweet-smelling bud as much as I remember liking it, I just might go get the next sack. But don't worry. I won't try to corrupt your staunch value system."

"Now look who's the funny one. You got contact-buzz going on just by sniffing the shit. I can't imagine what a freak you'd be if you actually fired it up and inhaled."

"You won't have to, bro. Go get me the lighter. It's in the potholder drawer."

During that down-time I relearned why we all used to smoke pot in the '60s and '70s. Before bedtime, like a spiritual ritual, we would take one puff each and hold in that ganja like it was our last breath. On those vacation weekends we'd stay up till dawn, still like teenagers who couldn't get enough of one another, to reassure each other by sharing deep secrets as a show of trust while Billie Holiday, Norah Jones and Beth Hart lulled us till I collapsed in his arms. Other than one toke at bedtime, we choose to lead sober lives. After I crashed, his ritual resumed on the computer – doing his final rewrite till words began to swim across his monitor like fish in a tank. Then he'd lie next to me; wrap a firm arm across me and whisper sweet things as he gently stroked my hair and kissed my shoulders. I felt so safe with him beside me, the safest I've ever felt in my life.

On our last night together we played scrabble on our butcher-block dining room table. It was just the two of us . . . fortunately for him. I was in the process of winning the third game in a row. He made the mistake of taking his toke *before* we played. Towards the end of the last game, when it was obvious only the crummy letters were left, he couldn't make a word but was too stubborn to miss a turn and trade in those loser tiles.

"I'm tired. I quit. If you'd like to make-believe you won on default, you should do that. You know; to make yourself feel better about it. I mean, that's all you got, right?"

"No. I got plenty more. And because I got it, you're about to get it," he smirked.

"Oh, wow... I'm not sure if I should laugh, cry or puke on that lousy pun."

"Choose door number four," he said while exhaling an anisette-soaked Parodi, "Okay, here we go. First off I want to thank you. I almost went through life without knowing what this means. Remember how before we had kids there was no way for us to understand how strongly we'd feel about them, be willing to sacrifice anything for that little unknown person? What I mean is, I never actually believed in this type stuff – you know – romantic love. But I guess it really exists and is every bit as powerful."

"Wow . . . Check out Mr. Hard-ass. Getting all mushy now, are we?"

"Never mind, Contessa. Let's just go to bed. You said you're tired, right?"

"Bed? Really" I heard stories that you were some hard dude."

"Why, is *bed* some new concept to you? What are you, a fucking bat? I'll probably find you in the morning, hanging from those feet of yours, off barn rafters."

"Hold it right there. Let's review. First of all: my feet are perfect . . . to jab into that puss-gut of yours. Hey. When you mentioned sleep, did you mean like right now?"

"What are you, dizzy? What I mean is passionate sex now, followed by..."

The next morning he announced, "Okay, it's time I tell you something else."

"Oh? Hmm . . . Okay, let's see. It's not another woman; because you know I'll kill you in your sleep. Maybe you're finally going to get honest about how when I'm asleep you stroke my hair, gently kiss my back and whisper sweet things to me? Is that it?"

"Nope, I know when you're asleep by the way you breathe. But I gotta admit it; you're a pretty good fake sleeper. Nah, it's something more important than all this lovey-dovey bullshit. My manuscript is done! All it needs is a title – but not right now." Then he smiled, "We're going out to celebrate. No kids, though. Just you and me, baby-girl."

Just then the phone scared me right out of that serenity cocoon.

He sighed and picked up: "What's up, brother Hank? Tonight? Hmmm. Sorry, but I'll have to pass. We're on our way out the door in a few. Any other night is good, though. Okay . . . sure . . . so tell me right now. Hey man, are you okay? Alright, then it can wait, right? Easy does it, Horrible Hank. Everything's cool. Look . . . Tell you what. If it's that important, you and your ol' lady meet us at the Phish Pot in an hour. Jesus H. Christ, Henry! You're getting as bad as my mom. No, we're not waiting here for you. Come on, man. Well just say it then. Talk to me, friend... Okay, then fuck-it. Nope, no way.... I'm not taking *no* for an answer. Okay, I believe you. I'm sure it is important. All the more reason you should meet us. If youse aren't there I'm gonna feel bad. I'm hanging up now. Later, brother." *click*

When I asked Jackie what Henry wanted he said, "I don't know what's up with that guy. He was acting all spooky like some crack head. I wonder if he relapsed on that shit. You should hear how paranoid he is. I hope you're not disappointed that I invited them, but I'm a little worried about him. He was coming off all tense-like and shit. That's not like him. You know how laid-back he usually is."

When the phone rang again he said, "Don't answer it. I have a feeling it's bad news. I don't want anything to spoil our night. The answering machine'll catch it."

"Maybe it's the kids or your mom. Go check. Make sure everything's alright."

He checked the caller ID and said, "Nope, it was just Henry again. He knows where we'll be. If they want to meet us, they will. Now let's go fire-up that one-hitter for a quick taste and then get in the wind before we get trapped."

"No thanks; I'll pass. I don't want any right now, bro. You go ahead. Right now I'm distracted. Just call him back real quick to check so I don't have to worry."

"He's probably hassling with his ol' lady again. They need to get out. Let's us get the fuck out of here before something else happens. I'm starting to get that bad feeling."

"See? I have it, too? Why don't you just call and get it over with."

"Trust me. I sense it – just can't nail it down yet. But I'll get it."

"Alright, I'll have a puff with you. After all, this is a celebration!"

"Okay, now tap that out in the sink and let's boogie."

Jackie's eyes sparkled as we stood on our front porch to take in the stillness of dusk. He looked two decades younger than his 63 years. I remember thinking he had the same composed expression of that boy I met over a half century ago; before he had developed a mask to keep people at a safe distance. The sky was amazing. I felt like we were floating inside that magical moment when you're almost awake yet not quite asleep. He cocked his head to watch a lone cloud sprayed fiery orange by a glorious sunset as a woman in wrap-around sunglasses sped past in a Hummer as red as her windblown hair as he asked, "You feel it, too?"

"Wow, I feel dizzy . . . like I might faint." I was taken in by the power of the moment, as that shadow-blanket slowly crawled over us. I asked, "Whoa! Was that who I think it is, bro? What's that snake, Maureen, doing sliming around here?"

He dropped my hand to put an arm against me: "Wait here, alright?" he whispered as he moved toward our car. At the curb he squatted as if inspecting for splattered bugs and asked, "Is that a storm cloud? You do feel all this energy in the air, right?"

A chill ran beneath my skin on that warm evening as I asked, "What's wrong? Now I feel it, too. What is it? I shouldn't have smoked. Is this laced with something?"

He appeared to move in slow-motion. With a raised index finger he said, "Hold-up. Don't go too far. I need to do something real quick. You'd better go inside to check on the dog. While you're in there make sure everything's off, okay sweetie?" Once inside he gripped the steering wheel and blew our air: "I feel Chilly," then closed his eyes.

I'd known him all my life and felt sure that was the first time he'd ever deceived me. But sometimes my imagination worked overtime when it came to him, so I walked to our house like he asked. Little Sinbad began barking. I whined, "You've never called me *sweetie* before. What's with that crap? And how can you be chilly? Are you nuts? It's July. What's your problem? Are you hiding something from me?"

Then I saw the strangest thing. He smiled and pressed his radio buttons and then turned its knobs while the car and radio were still off. He pounded his fist on the dashboard and smirked, "Ain't this some shit? Just my luck, right? Go on ahead, Tessa. Do like I asked. Yeah, I know what time it is. Okay . . . just fucking bring it."

Our dog growled and bounced against the inside of our front door. I raised my voice, "What's with you two acting so crazy? Quiet, Sinbad! Do you want me to go inside, Jackie, or do you want me to bring something? Which one is it? It can't be both ways. Sinbad, NO! Are you angry now because I didn't rush inside to make sure *everything's off*? Is that what this is really about? Sinbad, quiet!"

When he shook his head with a disgusted look, a body rush of dread surged right through me. Eardrums roared; heart pounded. All I could hear was that non-stop barking and growling from our little Yankee Terrier who till that day had been worthless as a watchdog. "Sinbad, goddamnit, shut-up! What's going on here, Jackie? Talk to me."

Frozen in suffocating panic, throat constricted with terror, a wave of nausea overcame me. I begged, "No, Jackie! Please, baby. Don't do it," Legs numb, paralyzed with horror, I cried, "No! I won't let you do this! You promised you'd never leave me! You said you love me! I trusted you, Jackie. *Please!*"

He stretched out a hand, "You gotta be here when the kids get home, remember? No sweat, baby-girl, I ain't goin' no place." Then he mumbled, "Yeah, just fuck-it."

All the colors blurred to numbness when our car transformed into a smoking hunk of scrap. Sprawled on the ground, my last thoughts were: *This can't be real. I can't do this alone.* My last memory was a growl from a Harley as it grew softer and darker.

Back from the hospital, the first thing I did was turn down our sheets in hopes of finding his essence lingering on his pillow. When I held it to sniff it I found an envelope with the words "Trust This" scrawled across it. The very same words I had written in 1975, on a note above my phone number and his name even before I left my house. His letter read:

"I could say I'm sorry for ignoring you lately, or to tell you how I feel about you. But I don't have to, because you already know. I'm writing this to thank you for giving me your priceless gifts. I've been thinking a lot about time lately. I'm not sure how much I have left. I just know I don't have any more to waste. I believe we construct our own heavens and hells right here and now, but we don't control everything. For the most part, whatever happens, happens because of who we've chosen to be and what we're willing to settle for. At times, pain outweighs pleasure through no fault of our own, and that's just mileage. People are born in pain from pure ecstasy and then juggle extremes while pretending death won't really happen – like somehow we're special enough to beat the odds – anything so we don't have to accept the horrific inevitable. But life is the same for everyone. We learn to contrast opposing facts to synthesize newer truths, and then construct an evolving reality every bit as crazy as another's paradigm – right up until we realize it's all bullshit. Everything is temporary but nothing ever really changes all that much. Yet even though nothing lasts forever, nobody can ever take the time and truth we've shared. Thank you for always being there for me."

I collapsed on the bed, lost and so alone. Physically I was on the mend, but I wanted to die. The thought of going on without my friend was too much. I lost time curled-up in a fog of Xanax and vodka. In drug-dreams I'd run to Jackie; try to reach him in time – to stop him. But no matter how many times I replayed that scene nothing ever changed. I knew I'd always be alone except for what I carried of him inside me. I just couldn't handle anything. I quit my job before I lost my mind. But then I needed a diversion, so I recalled stories we shared in the dark while CDs whispered magic to us. Respite was temporary. I cried myself to sleep holding a plastic jewel case used to keep his novel safe. It was heartbreaking to see his life's work fit on one tiny computer disc.

Other than our two kids and a grizzled Yankee Terrier watching our door like an empty food bowl, Jackie left us with faith in spite of all the pain — or maybe even because of it. He also left me his story, the thing that gave me enough strength to continue. So I put away my pills and the vodka and picked up his obsession. At night, as I retired for the evening, I'd call Little Sinbad off his oval rug by the door to accompany me in the bedroom for my fixation with rereading Jackie's thoughts. I'd curl up on my husband's beat-up leather sofa from his earlier life, to rehash memories and to cry for him — anything to keep my Jackie alive a moment longer. I hoped his strength, even in absence, could somehow help me get through the worst time of my life. Eventually I added a final chapter, named the story for him, and then emailed segments of it to agents till I found the right fit.

It's kind of funny, in a pathetic way, but even after all that Neighborhood *paesano* bullshit Jackie admired so much, and all the friends he had accumulated over the years, only one felt the same way about breathing life back into Jackie's words. After Bee-Bee got ran over by that trucker in Alaska, Chilly returned to keep an eye on us. He knew Jackie even better than I did and remained as loyal as a good Pit-bull after all these years. Chilly was the only one I ever trusted besides my mom, Rocco and Jackie, and now Gina. In spite of all Jackie's recklessness and abuse of mind-altering substances, he was right about many important things.

Chilly said, "I'm not even going to try to tell you that he's in a better place, or that everything happens for a reason, or insult you by telling you God doesn't give us more than we can handle. You know what though, my friend? Jackie and I always thought we wanted more of everything. We figured we could do whatever, whenever. We had that terminal *fuck-it* attitude. But the older I get, the more I understand how there are a whole bunch of things I don't want more of, yet there's nothing I can do about it. For example: I don't want to get a day older, but at the same time I'm not quite ready to disappear."

I frowned and slowly shook my head as I told him, "I wish I could say the same and mean it. The only things keeping me alive are my children and this mission we're on. Maybe that's what gives me purpose for right now." Then I asked, "What about that *collective* Jackie talked so much about, the space he said you guys drifted around in so often? He claimed you first stumbled across it during psychedelic trips, but that now it's everywhere. I know I feel it, too. I always have. What's your version of that *Click?*"

"It's that electromagnetic field, my friend. The one you can feel but usually can't see. It's everywhere and nowhere. It's a pool of energy that creates, sustains and then reabsorbs all other energy. It's that one thing that always was and always will be. It's the same place where God was created and will finally disappear to when all the people are gone. But for now we're still very much alive and can elect to use it to our advantage. Yep, it's the *Click* and the *bounce*. Another way Jackie manifested living proof of that energy pool was through his creativity. Now it's up to us to make sure his ideas stay alive. We can do this, Tessa, so we will. And we'll be glad we did."

Born into an idealistic world, and then raised in a neighborhood full of drugs and violence, I still found Jackie to be the same torn child in adulthood that he was as a boy. That last day spent together, while bathed in a glorious dusk, he squeezed my hand and said, "I wish this moment could last forever. But you know me; I always want more. It's strange to think about, but sooner or later this little slice of heaven will have to suffice."

After I'd found that letter hidden on his pillow, I too became obsessed with *more*. I rummaged through dresser drawers and cupboards, pants and jacket pockets, above ceiling tiles and beneath heavy objects in the basement, and then rechecked everything. Totally spent, I passed out on that old sofa holding the plastic jewel case of his thoughts.

I woke in a panic. *Where is it?* I shook my afghan and felt my pillow. I tipped over the couch to search underneath. *Vanished.* I retraced my steps from the night before. *Nothing.* I needed a sign of his energy; proof that he really had been here with me. I looked in the bathroom, checked the kitchen. *Gone.* It was like that CD case never existed, like he had never been real. It was then I felt that I was losing my mind.

I sat on the floor with our dog nuzzled against me. The harder I wept, the closer Little Sinbad leaned on me, to watch me with tragic sadness in those deep brown eyes.

Hugging him I sobbed, "Fuck-it. Nothing means anything anymore. Everything is shit! How can I go on like this? Now what? I can't do this alone." Lucky for me I had that old dog. I trust him more any person I've known, other than our family. With my Jackie gone and Chilly almost ready to leave, I had our kids and a black & tan mongrel called a *Pit-bull*.

Eventually I attempted to reposition the small sofa and retrieve its leather cushions. Wedged in a groove where the back of the couch meets its base, in that place where socks, pens and change disappear, I found an empty Seconal bottle, a flattened joint all twisted, and a cheap drugstore lighter that still worked. *Did you plan this, too?*

The weed tickled my lungs. I held it in till I felt stress purge with the exhaled smoke. I decided to do something I hadn't done since my teens and burned the whole dube by myself in one sitting, using his empty prescription bottle as an ashtray. *There it is!* I spotted a corner of that plastic case, just barely revealing itself. But when I reached into that black hole to retrieve it I felt something else, something thick and paper. It was a large envelope. *Another letter!* The thick yellow envelope was still sealed. The words "Seed Money" scrawled across its face in handwriting I didn't recognize. Inside it I found more packets of $100 bills than I'd ever seen in one place since I saw my dad and Uno counting money on the kitchen table. I cried even harder but was out of tears.

The kids came home and found me on the floor in a shambles. Rocco asked, "What happened to you? Did somebody hurt you, Ma? Who was here?"

"Nobody, son, just Chilly. We had a nice chat about your dad. After he left I fell apart again. I don't know what we'd do without his friendship. He's been a true brother through all this, the only one to step-up after all these years."

"Don't, Rocco," Gina warned with a stern look.

Then her eyes softened when she looked over and assured me, "Yeah, Ma, you're right. Besides us, he's been right there for you and Daddy all along."

After they straightened out the room and helped me into bed I heard them from the front-room, like sensitive parents neither Jackie nor I ever had. Rocco protested in a hushed voice, "Wow! You, of all people, should know better."

"Who's she hurting?" Gina asked. "Nobody, that's who! Just let her alone."

"You don't need to scold me like I'm a little kid. How do you think I feel watching this?" he asked in a harsh whisper.

"I can guess. So then that means you know how I feel. And I'm sorry for yelling, okay? But as far as the little kid thing . . . I am two months older, Baby Rocco."

"Okay, alright," he conceded with a laugh. "And I'm sorry for being an asshole."

"That's okay. I'm almost getting used to my bro acting like a girl."

"HA! You're real fucking funny. I mean, besides the way you look."

"That's cool. I accept your apology. And you're not being an insensitive asshole right now. You're just being your usual dick-head self."

"If I wasn't such a nice guy I'd tell you to go fuck yourself."

"Whatever, Rocco. Just give her some space right now, okay?"

I yelled, "Okay in there! I heard every word that was just said. You two hear me? Every stinking word of it! And I want both of you to know how much I love you."

Looking back, I've learned a lot from loss and mistakes. I realized our people were wrong about a lot of things, but not everything. Our fathers' methods were harsh, but their lessons imprinted like a branding iron. Jackie saw at a tender age how painful it is to quit, even though at times he went out of his way to create even more pain.

He insisted, "Life's all about timing, about making brave choices at the correct moments." That's why he taught our children, "Live as if there's a monster sleeping inside you who feeds on the stench of things like betrayal, excuses and regrets. Remember: we never do anything we don't really want to do, even when it's something we'd rather not do."

Jackie saved my life – one I'm no longer sure I value. I almost missed the *Click* that saved my life, the same one that took my Jackie. Since then I've become intimate with a truth so dreadful…so permanent…no words could ever express the purity of my anguish. Now our kids show me reasons to bounce back from a dream-world of shadows I'd imprisoned myself in. So I'll keep trying. I won't ever quit. Not after all I witnessed that day. Instead, I'll keep Jackie's spirit alive with me. Then one day his soul will reabsorb mine. I really need to believe that – no matter how crazy that might sound – to trust in our own brand of faith without excuses or regrets.

As little kids, we were taught by calloused fathers that *any* hurt, no matter how painful, could be fought through and defeated. Our mothers argued that the worst of it simply gets washed away by persistent waves of time. So I listened. I fought as hard as I could and waited as patiently as I should. And I found out they were almost right. But they left out one very important piece. Because when the pain finally left, it took hostages.

"Nobody does this to one of us and skates. But no worries. It's all about timing. For now, I wait."

"Count me in, bro. This isn't over till we say."

Made in the USA
Charleston, SC
18 April 2013